LUNACY
AND
ACTS OF GOD

A NOVEL BY RUTH MAUS

Flint Hills Publishing

page 57 The Foundation did
Not control Topeka

Praise for *Lunacy & Acts of God*

"I invite you to come along as nine-year-old Melody Lark Freedrich stitches a story tapestry that is both universal and so intricately infused with time and place that it could have only happened in Topeka, Kansas, in the late 1950s. Through the innocent yet hard-lived eyes of a girl, this fine novel tells an American story, cast against a tumultuous time in America, featuring characters so broken and vulnerable and horrible and redeeming and real that you'd swear they can exist only in fiction—until you realize that you know them, only by different names, in real life, even now. Right now. That is the power and the humility of Ruth Maus' debut: It shows us our frailties and commonalities, our shared history, and our divergent lives, and it also serves as a reminder that we can move beyond that which binds us—as Melody surely does—even as the past comes swinging around, again and again.

—Craig Lancaster
Two-time High Plains Book Award winner;
author of *Northward Dreams* and *600 Hours of Edward*

"Ruth Maus's character, Melody Lark Freedrich, belongs in that august pantheon of American child characters founded by Mark Twain who are able to isolate and expound upon the madness of their times with a magnificent wit and wisdom so far beyond their years [that] you keep turning the pages to see them run circles around the oblivious adults. *Lunacy and Acts of God* is replete with fascinating collisions between science and religion, [as] she gives us an explosive period in psychiatric advancement and regressive cultism, both of which took place right in the center of the country: Topeka, Kansas. But at the end of the day, it's Melody's telling that propels us through and makes us wish there was always a Melody around to explain everything to us."

—Andrew Farkas
author of The Great Indoorsman: Essays and The Big Red Herring

"What a witty and wonderfully readable book Ruth Maus has given the world! Full of laugh-out-loud scenes, *Lunacy and Acts of God* will keep anyone who grew up in the 1950s or 60s up all night to find out what happens next. In addition to the wit, Maus has hidden so many cultural and societal icons amongst the pages for us to treasure. But the biggest contribution here is the way she confronts the genesis of all kinds of biases that we may not even recognize we possess. Through the eyes of the young protagonist, we allow ourselves a wry chuckle of recognition in the scenarios and characters that lead us through the rich plot. Even though this takes place in the middle of the 20th Century in Topeka, Kansas, the underlying message here is totally current.

—**Anne Spry**
author of *Finally Noticing: Photos and Poems Prompted by a Pandemic* and Kansas Authors Club President

"What can happen to a young girl in Kansas? Well, for Melody…[life brings] her and her family into contact with people she admires and fears. She tells her story…reminiscent of the young girl Scout in *To Kill A Mockingbird*. She listens and observes others as they describe their fellow Topekans in terms she doesn't understand and questions her relationship with God. Ruth Maus then weaves in an unsolved murder mystery in this page turning and engaging read. Maus's references to landmark locations…really personalizes her storytelling for this reader."

—**Michael Padilla**
Mayor and lifelong resident of Topeka, Kansas

"You can expect chuckles galore as you follow the misadventures of Ruth Maus's plucky nine-year-old heroine, Melody Lark [and] a barrel-load of insights as this winsome girl tries to make sense of the prejudices and loving loyalties of her quirky 1950s Kansas community, a community that may seem bygone yet eerily familiar, quaint yet relevant as today's headlines."

—**Tim Bascom**
Director of Kansas Book Festival,
author of *Chameleon Days* and *Climbing Lessons*

"Nine-year-old Melody Lark is certain that none of the things that happen in late 1950s Topeka, Kansas are her fault—not the terrifying cult leader that plagues her hometown, the murder, the arrival of the Mafia, rides in a police car and ambulance, not even the lightening that changes so much in her world. In her own words, Melody never could have guessed that her 'young life would bump up against a whole lot of history with such extreme consequences.' Still, it does, presenting Melody with the questions that are difficult to resolve, even for adults. Ruth Maus's *Lunacy and Acts of God* reminds us of how we are all part of history, revealing that some of the same societal challenges from Melody's time still face us, even decades later. A refreshing glimpse into history and human nature, Maus's novel is enjoyable even as it challenges us to consider our own places in the problems and solutions of our times.

—**Julie A. Sellers**
Author of the novel *Ann of Sunflower Lane* and
Kansas Authors Club Prose Writer of the Year (2020, 2022, 2023)

"A charming and fantastical coming of age story, set in 1950s Topeka, Kansas. A…young…girl's loss of innocence as she wrestles with the social ills of racism, prejudice against mental illness, the abuses of powerful patriarchal institutions and a fiercely loyal and strongly-rooted family facing the stormy conflicts around them. In the end, grown in wisdom and tolerance for life's many nuanced shades of gray, Topeka's history is embodied in this family's struggles to persevere."

—**Dr. Karen Bellows**
Former Menninger Clinic Faculty

Lee,
Happy reading!
Ruth Maus

Lunacy and Acts of God
© 2025 Ruth Maus
All rights reserved.

Cover art by Ruth Maus

Cover design by Amy Albright

Flint Hills Publishing

Topeka, Kansas
Tucson, Arizona
www.flinthillspublishing.com

Printed in the U.S.A.

Paperback Book ISBN: 978-1-966323-02-0
Electronic Book ISBN: 978-1-966323-03-7

Library of Congress Control Number: 2024924376

"From caring comes courage."
Lao Tzu

CONTENTS

CAST OF CHARACTERS

The Freedrich/Oots/Schiffelbein/Glenn family:

Melody Lark Freedrich - a nine-year-old Kansas girl

Harmony Freedrich - Melody's older sister, age thirteen

Mitchell Freedrich - Melody's younger brother, age eight

Alex and Louise Freedrich - Melody's parents

Richard Freedrich (deceased) **and Dale Freedrich Oots** - Melody's paternal grandparents

Dewey Oots - Dale's second husband

Rex Oliver Oots - Dewey's grown son from his first marriage

Rev. Gottfried Schiffelbein - Melody's great-uncle (Dale's brother)

Billy Glenn - Melody's uncle (Louise Freedrich's brother)

Little Poo and Black Mimi - the family housecats

Neighbors/Friends/Enemies/Community Characters:

Rev. Earl Wade - Dewey's former brother-in-law and head of Hosanna Baptist Church

Ava Wade Oots - Dewey's (deceased) first wife and Earl Wade' sister

Janie Bryant - the Freedrich family's neighbor across the street

Vivian Ostrander - local media magnate

Maynard and Virgil Shuckahoosee - father and son Native Americans from the nearby Potawatomi Reservation

Dr. Felix Kliban and Edith Kliban - president of the Meadowgreen Clinic and his wife

Brenda Messina - a Meadowgreen patient

Charlotte Fitch - Brenda's friend and a Meadowgreen patient

August "Big Augie" Messina - Brenda's father from Rhode Island

Tiny and Joey - Big Augie's associates

Cast of Characters Continued...

Salome Parsons - a detective hired by Big Augie
Miss Georgia Verne - Melody's piano teacher
Daphne Knott - Harmony's friend
Dr. Jerome Knott - psychiatrist at the Meadowgreen Clinic
and Daphne's father
Simon "Shep" Vargas - local band leader
Monroe Bates - Melody's Sunday school teacher
Duane Appelhans - Topeka Chief of Police
Orin "Cupcake" Drake - weekend manager of the Hotel
Jayhawk

Historical Figures:
John Brown (1800-1859) - violent Kansas abolitionist
Carrie Nation (1846-1911) - fierce temperance agitator in
Kansas
"Dr." John Brinkley (1885- 1942) - quack goat gland "doctor"
and twice unsuccessful Kansas gubernatorial candidate
General John "Blackjack" Pershing (1860-1948) - U.S.
Army commander in WWI
Dwight D. Eisenhower (1890-1969) - Kansas native and U.S.
President from 1953-1961
J. Edgar Hoover (1895-1972) - Director of the Federal Bureau
of Investigation from 1924-1972

Prologue

When I was nine years old, I discovered that Kansas had a surplus of weather and lunatics. That was the year the temperature dropped seventy degrees in one day, the year I got struck by lightning, and the year a blizzard killed twenty-three thousand cattle. That year I was terrorized by some certifiably crazy people—one of them liked to eat dirt—as a murder occurred so dramatically that even J. Edgar Hoover himself became personally involved. That year I got hauled off in a police car once, and put in the hospital twice, and Uncle Gott's wedding was interrupted by the Mafia (which was unusual for Kansas). That extraordinary year I almost lost my best friend. Oh, and that year Mother became an Avon Lady. Until then, I'd led a very quiet life.

Nowadays we're far kinder and don't use the term lunatics. And now I understand how in 1958 superior forces, institutions, and people converged to impact the innocence and ugliness of my small Midwestern hometown. So mostly none of this was my fault. How could I have known that my young life would bump up against a whole lot of history with such extreme consequences?

But then again, maybe some of it *was* my fault.

April 1959

The Psychiatric Capital of the World

My sister Harmony would later, in a rare moment of sympathy, try to console me. "You can't help the weather, Melody," she said. "Everybody knows that's acts of God. And you weren't responsible for the murder either. But mostly you couldn't help it because we live in the psychiatric capital of the world." She said this so matter-of-factly that I couldn't figure out if living in the psychiatric capital of the world was something good or bad. "Don't think about it too hard," she advised, "'cause I doubt if the Chamber of Commerce brags on this particular distinction.

"You know what Dad says," she continued. Our dad was an authority on lunatics, since he was around them every day at his Meadowgreen Clinic job. "He says that between the State Hospital, the V.A. Hospital, and Meadowgreen, every third person in this town is under psychiatric care and another third needs to be." That didn't include us, of course. Well, at least not in the beginning.

She explained that was what was wrong with all the people we saw walking around town conversing by themselves. That was the phrase she used too, "conversing by themselves." I believe what she said was, "Once they start conversing by themselves, Melody, sooner or later they're gonna end up in Topeka. Some get sent here against their will, but most of them are just drawn here, 'cause they fit right in."

It was true. We considered it part of the landscape.

"At least Meadowgreen mostly keeps their patients off the streets. But I think the State Hospital and the V.A. hold some kinda competition to issue the most day passes. Heck, those nuts are usually harmless. Though occasionally somebody really unhinged goes off the deep end and then it's too late. As *you* found out, Melody. Then you can't put the genie back in the bottle."

5

When I looked confused at this, Harmony reverted to her normal condescending tone. "It's a figure of speech, dummy. They're not real genies. They're disturbed, emotionally unbalanced human beings with frequent unacceptable social behaviors and occasional breaks with reality."

My sister talked funny like that because she herself suffered from "intellectual," a brain disease that affected a person's speech and behavior. It's hard to say where she picked it up and amazing we hadn't all caught it, but I heard Dewey tell Mother one time that Harmony sure was young to be so intellectual, so I knew she had it bad. It was a shame too, since here we were living in the psychiatric capital of the world and we couldn't even get Harmony's brain fixed. Harmony didn't walk around conversing by herself, so she wasn't crazy as far as we knew, just our weird older sister. The difference was important because I shared a room with her and had to be prepared in case she crossed the line. Mother told me not to worry about it too much, that there was a long way to go before the intellectual part became permanent. We had a lot of funny ideas about people back then.

My name is Melody Lark Freedrich, because Mother likes birds a lot. Especially meadowlarks, the beautiful state bird of Kansas. But since nobody names their daughter Meadowlark, they named me Melody Lark. Melody for short. Harmony said not only was I not melodic, but I was positively cacophonous. I didn't know what that meant until Janie Bryant across the street helped me look it up in the dictionary. It means an unpleasant sound.

Harmony liked to claim that my "experiences," the unsettling events that began in 1958 when I was nine, had their roots one hundred years earlier when crazy Kansas abolitionist John Brown went around murdering people because he thought God called him to free the slaves. There was a huge scary mural of him right across from the governor's office in the Kansas State Capitol, all wild-eyed and holding a Bible in one hand and a rifle in the other. Since there *had* been a murder in my experiences, maybe Harmony was right.

"Historically speaking," she insisted, "that was when Kansas accepted irrational violence as a means of settling social policy. Hence Carrie Nation, who enforced her temperance ideas with a hatchet, and the goat gland doctor who..."

"But that wasn't our family," interrupted Dad. He knew a lot about Kansas history and knew when Harmony needed interrupting. "It was when the boar ate Grandpa Richard that our family got changed. But—you know. Everything just hits Melody harder." He didn't mention the whole murder business at that point, or the fact that I was struggling, because we were a polite family.

"But on the bright side," Harmony switched perspectives, "the boar was also responsible for hauling Grandma Dale out of the dark ages. That's a lot of power for a barnyard animal with a ring in its snout." She always had to have the last word, part of her intellectual, I guess.

They were referring to one particular pig in 1954, the one who started all the strangeness. How, you ask? I will tell you.

(Five Years Earlier)
April 1954

The Pig

Since most of my relatives lived on farms we were all used to barnyard animals. But even in the large farming community surrounding Topeka there had been fascination, and a little suspicion, about the pig having eaten our grandfather.

Richard Freedrich, Dad's frugal father, had been a farmer since our ancestors came to Kansas from Germany in pioneer times. "He was so frugal," Dad would say, "that 'till the day he died he wouldn't get electricity or indoor plumbing for the farm, even though he'd socked a lot of money away." Great-Uncle Gott was in agreement. "Kids," Uncle Gott would say, "your grandfather was a good man and a righteous man. But he preferred dying with his money in the bank to living with a flush toilet in his house. Now that's frugal. No offense intended," he would add. Like I said, a polite family.

Grandma Dale, Dad's mother, was facing the prospect of hauling water from the well the rest of her life, when suddenly Grandpa Richard met with a tragic accident. He slipped and fell into the pig pen and was eaten by a rogue boar. There were no witnesses.

"What was the boar's name?" Mitchell, my little brother, had asked once. I guess he thought it had a name like "Killer" or "Widowmaker."

"I don't know," Dad replied. "We just always called him 'the boar.' He'd never eaten anyone before."

At ages four and five, Mitchell and I were deemed too young to go to Grandpa Richard's funeral at the Evangelical Methodist Church, but Harmony filled us in later, including how the casket had caused some problems. "It was so shiny it reflected my black patent leather shoes in darting shimmers all over the sanctuary." She paused to make darting shimmer movements with her hands, then resumed. "That, coupled with the overpowering floral arrangements, gave a sort of bumble-bee effect to the whole service. The fact that they had a casket at all was remarkable, given that there wasn't much of Grandpa left to bury."

Following the funeral, I tried to remember what he had been like in one piece. Mostly I remembered a gray-haired man in bib overalls who gave us sticks of spearmint gum, then our being prompted to shout "thank you" into his hearing aid. Once I woke up in the middle of the night wondering if Grandpa's hearing aid had been eaten too.

After Grandpa died, Grandma Dale made some changes from the dehydrated existence that had marked her entire life. She began by running electricity to the farm. Not just to the house either, but to the cow barn, the chicken houses, the garage, the tool shed, the implement sheds, and the granary. Then she ordered the hired hands Maynard and Virgil Shuckahoosee to bring the grain truck from the implement shed and drive her to town, where she bought an electric heating system for the house, an electric stove, an electric refrigerator, an electric Mixmaster, an electric washing machine, an electric sewing machine, an electric radio, an electric phonograph, an electric television, even an electric incubator for the henhouse. She bought electric lamps of all shapes, sizes, and colors and put them in every room. She bought several electric fans to use during the hot summer months and a salon-size electric hairdryer for her bedroom. She wouldn't pay to have anything delivered, though. She made Maynard and Virgil load everything in the back of the grain truck to bring home, then made them unload it all at the farm. The next day she returned to town and ordered a modern telephone, one without a crank and without a party line, installed in the dining room.

Finally, she hired workmen from town to regenerate her life with indoor plumbing, building her a sink and faucets in the kitchen, and an indoor bathroom complete with lavatory, toilet, bathtub, and a floor-to-ceiling mirror along one wall. She selected blue imported Italian tile to line the rest of the room. Every tenth tile had a blue fish on it. "I've never seen the ocean," she explained, "so I'm bringing the ocean to Kansas."

I'm only mentioning all this about the pig and the funeral and Grandma's new-found wealth so you will appreciate what happened next. Because just when we thought we'd seen the end of Grandma Dale's acquisitions, she picked out a new husband, because, she said, "I need somebody to help me share these pleasures and maybe give me a few new ones." Rumor was that Grandma and Dewey had met at a dance, but it seemed hard to picture a woman of that size dancing. Grandma Dale, after all, was a very round stout person who braced her legs when she walked, a condition left over from the polio epidemic of 1916 when she was young.

Dancing or not, that's how Dewey came into our lives. "Call me Dewey," he told us right off the bat, so we did. Dewey Oots was a big, raw-boned hillbilly from Arkansas. Not big because he was tall, but big because you couldn't take your eyes off him. He was not German, he was not a Methodist, and he wasn't particularly frugal the way Grandpa Richard had been. He was not even a farmer and did not wear bib overalls, instead preferring khakis at his blacksmith job for the Santa Fe Railroad shops in town. His wife had died, just as Grandma Dale's husband had, so I guess he was lonely too. He had a grown unmarried son, Dad's new stepbrother and our new step-uncle Rex Oliver Oots. Dewey and Rex Oliver and electricity and running water all arrived at my grandmother's farm simultaneously, all precipitated by that overwrought pig. That's when everything started changing.

May 1954 to July 1958

The Long Reach of The Supreme Court

One day when the crimson roses were blooming and robins and wrens had worked nests into perfect places, Mother and Dad took us for a drive to the west side of town, pointing out a sketchy new house under construction.

"It's going to be a wonderful house," Dad said. "We're all going to be very happy here." He and Mother were holding hands and smiling so we all felt very happy for the new house too.

But the next day Harmony explained this meant we had to leave our old house in Oakland on the northeast side of town, the only home we'd ever known. She said we would have to pack up all our clothes and toys, say goodbye to all our friends, and move away.

"No, we're not," I said. "Mother and Dad didn't say anything about us moving. I bet we're just gonna have two houses from now on." I didn't know anybody who had two houses, but it was the only explanation I could think of.

"No, dum-my," Harmony sing-songed. "Dum-my, dum-my, dum-my."

She motioned for Mitchell and me to follow her outside into the back yard where she climbed into the tire swing hanging from the elm tree. After a few token swings to prolong the suspense, she dug in her feet to stop. Harmony had on her good church shoes, because ever since Grandpa's funeral she had developed a fondness for black patent leather. So when she dug in her feet, the shoes and white anklets got filthy dirty. I just shrugged my shoulders at Mitchell. He shrugged his back at me because he always followed my lead.

"Look," Harmony said, "I'm going to impart to you two dummies some important knowledge about the real reason we're moving."

She was acting real superior in spite of her dirty shoes, so I knew her intellectual disease was flaring up. I shrugged my shoulders again. Mitchell shrugged his back at me again. We were used to this nonsense.

"Well, first of all," she began, "we're moving because Dad received a substantial inheritance from Grandpa Richard's death and he's using it to buy us a nice new house."

"I don't want a nice new house," I restated my position. "I like our nice old house."

"And second of all," Harmony ignored me, "we're moving because of the United States Supreme Court!"

"Huh?" blurted Mitchell.

"What's that?" I asked suspiciously. It sounded like something my little-miss-smarty-pants sister would make up.

"It's because of a lawsuit called *Brown versus the Board of Education of Topeka*. They've admitted Negroes to our schools," trilled Harmony. "It went all the way to the United States Supreme Court in Warshington, D.C." Like everyone in Kansas, she pronounced it *Warsh*ington. "That's why we're moving."

"What's the Supreme Court?" I asked again. "Why do we have to move? Are we going to live in Warshington, D.C. too?" I didn't understand this part either, but Harmony had deposited her nugget and was already gone.

But maybe Harmony had been right, because we did move and the Supreme Court seemed to be involved. Mother and Dad discussed it once with Great-Uncle Gott, Grandma Dale's bachelor brother who lived with her and Dewey and Rex Oliver on the farm. Uncle Gott stated that he loved American Negroes as much as their poor African brethren and came down hard on the side of something called "integration." We all had a lot of respect for Great-Uncle Gott. He was a man of the cloth, a retired Methodist minister who had spent twenty years in darkest Africa as a Methodist missionary following his vision from God. Even his name, Gott, which was short for Gottfried, meant God in German. It was a little scary having somebody named God for a relative, but in spite of Uncle Gott's opinion, Mother and Dad were uncertain if integration was a Biblical concept.

Harmony knew a lot about it, though, and for once explained it pretty clearly. "Integration, Melody, means that you and I will grow up to marry Negroes and have mixed children with kinky hair who like to play the drums a lot."

"How come I don't get integrated?" Mitchell complained.

"Because even Negroes won't integrate with a little reptile like you," she replied.

I'm ashamed to say that is how folks used to think back then.

Dewey was opposed to integration as well. He expressed this opinion at the first opportunity, our Sunday afternoon dinner at Grandma Dale's farm. We were used to Sunday dinners at Grandma Dale's after church, but we weren't used to having them cooked on an electric stove, or having an indoor bathroom, or watching Dewey and Rex Oliver eat. Watching someone eat can be a traumatic experience.

That first meal together Grandma sent us to wash our hands in the blue tiled bathroom which she now referred to as the Blue Grotto. "Go warsh up in the Blue Grotto," she told us children. We warshed. Then we all sat down at the big dining room table set with the Sunday tablecloth and dishes and for the first time I heard Dewey ask the blessing.

"Lord," he said, "we are very fortunate to have such a wonderful meal here before us." He paused. "It would be a shame to let it get cold. Thank you. Amen."

I could tell from his blessing that Dewey wasn't a Methodist. Methodists like to mention every reason we're supposed to be thankful for something and use words like fellowship and spirit and service which can take some time. But Dewey got right to the point. I guess that was his Baptist training. Mother always said early training was important.

In honor of the first dinner combining her old and new families, Grandma Dale had prepared a delicious pork roast, which she had resumed serving following a suitable period of mourning for Grandpa Richard. Heaping bowls of mashed potatoes, gravy, sweet potatoes, green beans, yellow beans, sauerkraut, garden lettuce with creamy bacon dressing, stewed tomatoes, and platters of pork and homemade heavy bread were passed around once and then again, while courtesy demanded we show our appreciation for Grandma's cooking by eating slowly, but with healthy appetites. All except Harmony, who sat and picked at her food, confirming her status as a foundling as far as I was concerned.

Grandma Dale was staring across the table at her new husband with a look I'd never seen her give Grandpa Richard, though I had seen it on some of the choir ladies during our last church tent revival. Dad frowned at his food to avoid this open display of emotion, but Mother just smiled.

I wondered what Dewey had that made him so interesting, so I started staring at him too. I noticed he didn't eat like a Methodist either. Methodists put a little of everything on their plates and take one bite of each serving, even if they don't like it, to be polite. But Dewey didn't touch the sauerkraut and took only pork roast, potatoes and gravy, and Grandma Dale's homemade heavy bread, which he ate loudly and with relish. Once he looked over and saw me watching him.

"You know, Melody," he paused, "your Grandma's cooking," pause, "is a won-der-ful thang." Pause. "I'm glad you're enjoying it too."

I didn't know what to say, so I looked at Mitchell. He and Harmony were both being unusually quiet for a Sunday dinner and Rex Oliver never said a word.

By the time we were through with dessert, a thick spice cake accompanied by home-canned plums, Grandma Dale could restrain herself no longer.

"I just love all of you and I love cooking for all of you," she proclaimed to everybody, but she was looking at Dewey. Her new husband nodded back to her. I figured he better be careful or he would be gaining a lot of weight from so much loving. "We're a whole new family now and I can cook and can for you on my new electric stove. I just love—electricity."

When she said the word electricity, she threw back her head and gave her hair such a tremendous shake I almost expected her to whinny. I don't remember her doing that with Grandpa Richard either. Dad coughed from the embarrassment of it all.

Uncle Gott, having finished his spice cake and coffee, asked to be excused, removed himself to the parlor, and there studied a crocheted doily on the end table. He didn't seem to be embarrassed by his sister's new personality, but that was because he had lived in Africa and was a man of the world. As Mitchell and I strolled into the parlor behind him, he launched into a sermon.

"*That* is progress," he said, referring to Grandma's last remark. "Electricity is progress, bringing light into the darkness." He leaned closer to the doily and extended his index finger to touch its delicate lace. "Now real wisdom," he continued, "is knowing when to get out of the way of progress."

Mitchell and I looked at the doily as well to see why it might require such advice. Without acknowledging that he had hooked an audience, Uncle Gott now rolled his eyes upward to the crack above the porch door. Mitchell and I followed his gaze like our heads were on a swivel.

"Real wisdom is God shedding His light on our darkness. Progress—" and here he paused dramatically, "is God's method of moving us out of the clutches of the forces of darkness."

Before we had a chance to speculate on what those clutches meant to our young lives, Dewey came in, sat down, and grabbed Uncle Gott's bait.

"Now, Reverend," he began. Dewey only had a third-grade education, but what he lacked in knowledge he made up for in style. Dewey bent over the side of the maroon overstuffed chair reserved just for him, pulled a brass cuspidor from behind it, and spat a black stream of chewing tobacco juice into the chamber. Beside me, Mitchell went limp with admiration. "Reverend," repeated Dewey, "the forces of darkness," pause, "are the ones who filed that Board of Education lawsuit to begin with."

Dewey had a slow, deliberate manner of talking which usually made his points easy to follow. That—coupled with his Arkansas twang, his ability to relay both sides of a dialog word for word, and the judicious tobacco punctuation—had given Dewey the ease of a natural orator. Now he was warming to his topic.

Mother had warned us of Dewey's dislike for Negroes. "It's because of his hillbilly background," she said. "His family was so poor and ignorant they couldn't find anyone worse off except the Negroes. Naturally it made them feel better to look down their noses at the coloreds. We know this is not good manners and not very Christian behavior, don't we children, especially from the son of a Bible-thumpin' Baptist." She said this because of Dewey's claim that his father had been a circuit-riding preacher in the Ozarks. He had also claimed kinship to the Dalton Gang.

"Now down at the Santa Fe," Dewey continued, "there's a Nee-gro name of Cletus." Pause. "Ole Cletus is as black as the ace of spades in a coal cellar at midnight." Pause. "I mean," pause, "he is *black*." Pause. "Fine credit to his race, Cletus is, but—" pause, "an exception to the rest of those—" pause, "well, you know." Dad frowned and looked at Mitchell and me, uncertain if he should comment.

"Now Dewey," Uncle Gott responded, "Christ died for all men, no matter how ignorant they are."

I didn't know if the ignorant part was referring to Negroes or to Dewey. Dewey wasn't sure either, but it was a fine discussion following a splendid meal on an agreeable Sunday afternoon. He wasn't about to spoil it by taking offense with his new brother-in-law.

I wanted them to get to the part where Harmony and I would grow up and marry Negroes, since I still hadn't met any. I wondered if Cletus had any sons my age, and if so, did they also resemble coal cellars. But before I could ask, Harmony came running in out of breath.

"Rex Oliver's shut himself in the cave," she huffed, "and he won't come out." She was referring to a subterranean storm cellar at the side of the house.

We all looked at Dewey, except for Uncle Gott who ignored everybody and bent forward to study the doily even closer. Dewey pulled out the cuspidor for a thoughtful spit.

"Well," he paused, "I expect the boy'll come out when it gets dark." Rex Oliver was thirty-three years old, the same age as Dad, but in everyone's mind he was still a boy.

Dad blocked the door to prevent us bolting for the cave. "Harmony, Melody, Mitchell, you kids leave Uncle Rex alone," he said. "I mean it." He could see there would be no peace until we'd ferreted Rex Oliver from his hiding place.

"How's Rex Oliver getting along nowadays?" Mother inquired as she nudged Dad aside, came in, and sat down, having finished helping Grandma Dale clean up in the kitchen. I think she was hoping to distract the men from the Negro issue, which she considered a puzzling and unpleasant topic.

Dewey reached into his pocket and pulled out a round tin of Skoal. He twisted the lid off, reached into the can for an ample-sized dip, and placed the tobacco in his mouth. His big jaw rolled slowly several times as he replaced the lid and eased the can back to its pocket. Nobody could hurry Dewey.

"As well as can be expected," he said presently. "He was a big help with the harvest," pause, "a big help. He's gonna miss those Indians come winter though." He nodded. He was referring to Maynard and Virgil Shuckahoosee, a father and son team of hired farm hands from the Potawatomi Indian Reservation north of town. There wasn't enough work for them on the farm during winter.

"We ask God to keep a special place in His heart for Rex Oliver," said Uncle Gott in his most comforting voice. Uncle Gott had made a career of preaching and comforting.

Seemed to me Rex Oliver was already in a special place. Rex Oliver, Mother had explained to us one day, was a little strange. Mitchell asked if he snuck out at night and ate squirrels. Mother said no, she didn't think so. We were allowed to play with Rex Oliver if we were at the farm, but mostly he preferred to be left alone. If he felt too crowded, he would go hide somewhere, frequently in the cave. He usually stayed long enough to come out smelling slightly of mold.

Mitchell had not given up on the cave. "Grandma Dale told us one time there could be snakes in the cave," he said. As if we'd be saving Rex Oliver from a terrible snake death if only allowed to go flush him out.

"I think Rex Oliver needs to be left alone right now, son," Dad explained. "I'm sure he'll be fine." Mitchell frowned hard and hung his head. We needed something better than food and doilies to entertain us at the farm and our new step-uncle was looking like a sure thing.

Dad resumed the discussion about our narrow escape from integration. "You know," he told Dewey, "you'd think Ike would have stopped it." Ike was what everybody called Dwight Eisenhower, a Kansan and a Republican who had become president of the whole country. Calling him Ike made him seem like one of our uncles, most of whom also had funny names, except that most of them never amounted to much. Dad liked Ike. "But even with that court decision," he continued, "it just so happens our new neighborhood doesn't have any Negroes. I guess they won't be able to go to our schools until they can afford to move to our side of town."

Dewey and Dad started talking about property values and at that point I lost interest because they weren't talking about Cletus and my potential husbands anymore.

By evening it hadn't gotten cold enough for Rex Oliver to emerge, so we all stood at the entrance of the cave and waved, yelling "Goodbye, Rex Oliver, goodbye," to him as we prepared to depart for our home in town. Dad pulled the blue DeSoto around to the driveway as the rest of us kissed Grandma Dale goodbye. Harmony rode in the front seat with Dad, while Mitchell and I curled up, sleepy, next to Mother in the back. The sunset was streaking red, purple, and gold on the flat horizon, a sight so beautiful it made me sad.

Dad was in a good mood though. "We're really lucky to live in a new house in a nice new neighborhood," he chuckled, then stated his new philosophy. "Things are looking up. I guess Ike's taking care of us." Dad really liked Ike.

I stopped looking out the window then and just listened as the engine hummed. It hummed and Dad was happy and Mother was soft and I was sleepy. I thought about Ike looking after us. Did he know our thoughts like God? Was he a distant relative? And just before we got back to our house in town, I wondered if Ike looked after Cletus and his sons, and after Rex Oliver in the cave, and if God was a Republican too.

August to
September
1958

The New Neighborhood,
the Avon Lady, and the Devil

Mother and Dad had moved us from the old Oakland part of town as quickly as the boar had departed Grandma's farm, leaving behind not just potential integration, but the flooding Kansas River, Billard Municipal Airport, the noisy Atchison, Topeka, and Santa Fe Railroad yards, and all the Mexicans who had moved there to work on the railroad and spoke a curious language called Spanish. I hadn't seen any sign of Negroes or any reason why we couldn't have stayed, but suddenly my familiar home and neighborhood were gone. I missed them terribly.

The new house on the opposite side of town looked just like all the other new houses in a modern development that had, until recently, been a cow pasture in the county. There were no trees, no grass or flowers, no fenced yards or paved driveways. Just naked little cracker box houses stuck in rows on naked brown dirt, with bare new concrete streets running back and forth. Once in a while a fire hydrant or a streetlight broke the monotony. Our house was white with a white roof and a concrete slab poured for the front porch. A TV antenna was stuck on the roof and a gravel driveway ran into the yard. The new neighborhood was so plain all I could do was sigh. At least there was a green park at the end of the block, with large cottonwood trees, a little creek, and meadowlarks among the other many songbirds who resided there.

Suddenly we were busy with music lessons, swimming lessons, Scouting, and Methodist youth fellowship and choir. I don't remember how we got there, but I don't think it was from our own choosing. Dad was always saying, "Isn't it great? Our lives are certainly looking up," but I wasn't so sure. Dad had a good job in the maintenance department of the Meadowgreen Psychiatric Clinic, something he enjoyed and was good at, but now, instead of working on old cars at home under a shade tree in his free time, he was planting seedlings that might, in twenty years, grow into shade trees. He seeded grass for our naked lawn, erected a clothesline, got us an old tractor tire to use as a sandbox, and found Mother a nice used car since there were no buses to the former cow pasture we now called home. Mother planted some red and yellow tulips, a lilac bush, and a large vegetable garden. Then she baked and canned and joined the PTA. She also found some neighbor ladies to talk to about Elvis Presley. "Elvis is always a good icebreaker," she claimed, "because everybody loves him." She decorated the inside of the house with some of our old furniture from Oakland and purchased a large new mirror for the living room. The mirror was plain on one half, but the other half displayed a picture of a large pink flamingo standing on one leg. Every time somebody passed through the living room, there was the pink flamingo.Worse than that, Harmony went right to work decorating our new shared bedroom in the excruciating shade of pink I associated with Pepto-Bismol. Then she put up big pink and yellow flower curtains on the windows and a shelf where her dolls, dressed in pink of course, sat staring at me like unblinking pink mountain lions, ready to pounce. I felt surrounded by a pink conspiracy. Mother let me hang a shelf on my side of the room for my collection of little horse figurines, which was as close as I could get to having a real horse of my own. Once in a while I would crochet little bridles for them so they wouldn't feel neglected. And so *I* wouldn't feel neglected.

Harmony and Mitchell seemed to have no problem with the new naked neighborhood, a new school, the Blue Grotto, Supreme Court decisions, hillbillies chewing tobacco, and a new step-uncle who smelled like mold. Mitchell wore his little Cub Scout uniform like he was born to it and Harmony even soloed with the junior choir in church a time or two. But like Dad said, I guess it all just hit me harder. Then Mother took up a new career that inadvertently delivered me to the devil.

"Hello, I'm Louise Freedrich and I wonder if I could have a few minutes of your time to show you these lovely Avon beauty products."

One Saturday, Mother called Harmony, Mitchell, and me into the living room. She looked different that day because she had on her new Avon face. Her lips had been artfully lined and glistened with a moist, red lipstick. Her complexion, which I'd never noticed before, today showed a delicate glaze of powder. There was a rosy tint high up on her cheeks and a subtle arch to her well-defined brows. Mother had fixed her blonde hair with bouncy curls and cemented them with hair spray, making Mother look, according to Harmony, just like Doris Day with glasses. Mother smelled nice too, and when she spoke, she would casually wave her hand through the air, accentuating her heavily lacquered fingernails. I had never noticed before how pretty Mother could be when she wasn't scrubbing floors or fixing meals. We were so impressed we would have bought anything she was selling.

What she was selling, it seemed, were these same strange beauty products. On the surface it seemed straightforward enough. Mitchell and I were old enough not to need her every minute and she needed something to get her out of the house more often. Or, as Harmony put it, Mother needed to expand her horizons. "Besides," Mother had said, "the way you little warts are growing, the extra money would be nice." She referred to us sometimes as "her little warts," a compliment, I was sure.

Now she wanted to turn one of the little warts into a little beauty. "I'm only going to be working part-time, but I need to practice on someone. So we're going to pretend that Harmony here," she patted Harmony on the shoulder, "is the lady of the house and that you," she pointed to Mitchell and me, "are the lady's children. Just watch and be quiet, okay? I'm going to be the neighborhood Avon Lady." I was going to ask why men didn't buy beauty products, but then Mitchell started making sounds like a doorbell going ding-dong and I got caught up in the whole play-acting thing and just followed instructions.

Mother addressed her adoring audience the way the Pope holds forth at the Vatican, with great serenity and self-assurance. "Why don't we sit here on the sofa so I can show you the latest in cosmetics and beauty care," Mother invited. We sat.

"Ding-dong," chimed Mitchell. He couldn't stand it that Harmony was getting all the attention from the beautiful neighborhood Avon Lady. Harmony kicked him without taking her eyes off Mother.

From out of a large black satchel we had never seen before, Mother produced a catalog, an order sheet, and trays of various cosmetic samples. Dozens of little lipstick samples the size of my thumb, each a different color of red, orange, pink, or beige beckoned, begging to be applied. Tiny vials of cologne, little pots of powder, colored eye pencils, tubes of eye shadow, skin softeners, bath oils, nail polish. Fluffy cotton balls and delicate facial tissues. Tiny glass jars and wispy makeup brushes. Different textures and colors and odors, assembled with containers and applicators of intriguing shapes and sizes. Mother was Merlin and the black satchel the source of her magic. We couldn't wait to get our hands on it. Even our cats, Black Mimi and Little Poo, had been pulled to the satchel by its newness and were busy sniffing around and trying to climb inside.

"Now, Mrs. Customer," Mother continued, "may I spray just a hint of our cologne on the inside of your wrist? I think you'll appreciate its subtle, yet stimulating, aroma." Harmony nodded as mother grasped Harmony's wrist, rolled it over, and applied the hint. "Now smell," Mother instructed. Harmony smelled the result, closed her eyes, and lifted her face as if to pray.

"Breath-tak-ing," she pronounced. I was dying to smell the sample too. So was Mitchell.

"Can I smell?" he asked.

"You dummies go outside and play," yelled Mrs. Customer. I think she wanted the sample for herself. "Besides, you already smell." Harmony also thought she was funny.

The Avon Lady frowned, ignored the exchange, and held up a small gilt-framed mirror to the potential customer. "Why don't you pick out a favorite lipstick from these samples and try it on," she suggested.

"Oh, I would love to," Harmony replied sweetly.

My sister was new to lipstick, so of course she selected the brightest, most glaring red she could find. Holding the mirror in one hand, she searched for a secure grip on the tiny sample, hesitated, then gave it two quick swipes across her mouth as we had all watched Mother do many times. She pressed so hard the sample broke off and stuck to her lower lip, an effect Harmony pretended was her contribution to the world of beauty.

"How do I look?" she asked.

"Ding-dong," tolled Mitchell.

Harmony whirled and glared at him, but considering her exaggerated lips, couldn't decide whether to chase him or burst into tears. Mother sighed, gave up the sales pitch, and began to gather all the little samples back into the tray.

"Well, I hope my real customers behave themselves better than you kids do," was all she said.

"Don't feel bad," I said. "You're an Avon Lady and everybody knows how beautiful they are."

"Yeah," added Mitchell. "Too bad you can't improve Har-mon-y in that department." This time Harmony lunged for him, but Mitchell had taken a precautionary headstart and was already flying out the door. Black Mimi and Little Poo exploded in a scramble for cover, just as Mother tried to shield the sample tray from the commotion. Black Mimi and the tray collided, Mother shrieked, Black Mimi yowled, and a dusting powder sample fell and broke open on the floor. A strong dusty floral odor filled the room. Gardenia, I think. Little Poo padded to the spill, sniffed it, then flopped on her back and rolled in what was left of the dusting powder before racing away in a frenzy of powdery cat tracks.

And that's how Mother's career began.

Out in the front yard the would-be customer, with what looked like a huge gash of crimson where her mouth used to be, was sitting on Mitchell who was screaming "Ding-dong, ding-dong, ding-dong," at the top of his lungs. Mitchell was practically impervious to pain, so it did no good to pound on him. But he was terrible ticklish.

"Take it back," yelled Harmony as Mitchell tried unsuccessfully to get away.

"Okay, okay. I take it back," Mitchell screamed, but I could tell he was lying.

Dad had been in the side yard measuring where to put the new garage he had just decided he could build with Mother's extra income. When he heard the yelling, he came out to the front yard in time to spot Harmony letting Mitchell up. So did Janie Bryant, the neighbor lady across the street. Although Janie was a young single woman and not a bad looker, Dad referred to her as Janie Bryant the Giant Killer because she thought there was a Communist under every bed. He said Janie made it her business to know everyone else's business in case they had subversive tendencies and in case any of them were eligible bachelors. Either way, he said, she reduced grown men to idiots.

Janie took a look around, saw that the fuss had subsided, and was about to go back in her house when she spotted Harmony's mouth. She circled in for a closer inspection.

"Lord, child. What happened to your face?" she demanded. That sent Mitchell into spasms, but he stayed out of Harmony's range.

"Uh, it's just lipstick, Janie," I volunteered. "Harmony's not real good at it yet." My sister's face had turned the color of the new cosmetic. I almost felt sorry for her.

"Alex, that girl's only thirteen years old," Janie Bryant said to Dad. "Don't you think that's too young to be wearing lipstick?" Janie knew everybody's age. She also knew what age a person had to be to do certain things.

"Well, Janie, we'll, uh, we'll certainly discuss it," replied Dad. "Say, how's those congressional hearings going?" Dad had told us before, he could always get Janie wound up by asking about the congressional hearings. He said it was a safe bet somebody somewhere in Congress was holding a hearing about something and that Janie knew all about it. In fact, he said, her regular job as a secretary paled in comparison to the hours she spent scrutinizing the federal government for Communists. Sure enough, Janie launched into a replay of the House Un-American Activities Committee. Dad nodded and made polite responses, while Harmony slipped into the house where I hoped she would scrub the lipstick off her mouth. Mitchell and I left Janie for Dad to deal with while we strolled to the back yard.

It was at that point that I decided Mitchell and I should examine Mother's black satchel, or at least get a hold of some of its contents.

"Hey, Mitchell," I said, "let's make a plan to get some stuff from the Avon satchel. But we can't tell anybody. Okay?"

"Okay," Mitchell replied.

That's how easy it was. Mitchell and I spent a lot of time making plans about things, then executing them. This time I didn't know exactly what we were going to do with the black satchel once we had it, but I knew it was impossible to leave alone.

"Maybe," I explained to Mitchell, "we could get some of those little Avon samples to give to Miss Georgia." My piano teacher, Miss Georgia Verne, was someone Dad had once described as hanging on to middle age for dear life. We just knew she was plumpish and obviously in need of some beauty products. Mitchell shuddered at the thought. His experiences with Miss Georgia and piano lessons had caused him to take up the trombone instead. Using Miss Georgia as justification seemed to me a good excuse for going after the satchel. We decided to wait until Monday evening to assess Mother's first day on the job. If things had gone well, she'd be happy and in a generous mood to grant our request for samples. If the Avon experience had not gone well, Mother might give us the whole satchel out of despair. Either way, the samples in that satchel would soon be ours.

When we got home from school Monday afternoon it was obvious Mother wasn't there. There was no greeting, no afternoon snack, and nobody to complain to about school. Unfortunately, we'd received Mother's instructions earlier—music practice and homework. It was no use trying to avoid this, as Mother had recruited Janie Bryant as her willing spy.

Janie and Mother had made an arrangement for my daily torture, practice on the old piano in Janie's basement, because we didn't have a piano of our own. Although Janie didn't play the piano herself, she had purchased it at an auction after being told it once belonged to J. Edgar Hoover's neighbor's niece. Mitchell and I had watched six healthy-looking men carry it off a truck and down the stairs to Janie's basement where they dropped it with a heavy thud against the east wall. They said they hoped that piano was going to stay in one spot for a while. I had a terrible feeling it would. Then Janie offered the piano's use to Mother on my account so I had a convenient spot to practice my music lessons. It also gave Janie the satisfaction of a captive audience for her lectures.

Today she was determined to tell me why Harmony was too young to wear lipstick.

"I've been awake all night thinking of poor Harmony," Janie shared.

"Yeah, poor Harmony," I agreed. As far as I was concerned, my sister had been pathetic long before she'd ever heard of lipstick. But I didn't feel like listening to Janie today because I wanted to finish practicing and see how Mother's job had gone. And how close I might be to getting some Avon samples. I figured I'd profited from Harmony's bad example and would be able to apply lipstick to me and Mitchell in any color, and not break it either. "Janie," I began, "I'd really like to discuss Harmony's ruin, honest. But 'Barcarolle' from *The Tales of Hoffmann* needs a lot of work, so would you please excuse me? I really have to practice."

It was true. Every day it was a toss-up whether to subject myself to Janie's ramblings in order to postpone the dreaded piano practice, or to subject myself to Miss Georgia's wrath if I hadn't practiced. Miss Georgia never actually struck me, but one time when I didn't know my pieces, she locked me in the den of her house with her ancient crone of a mother who had a deep voice and a chin down to her waist. I practiced.

After endless attempts at "Barcarolle," I gave Offenbach a break and went home. I figured it was about time for supper anyway. To my surprise, Mother still hadn't returned from her first day at work. Harmony was in the kitchen wearing Mother's apron and showing off by trying to cook salmon patties. Dad loved salmon patties. Mitchell was in the living room giving Little Poo astronaut training in a small shoebox. He was spinning the shoebox on the carpet because he said Little Poo needed to learn about centrifugal force. I don't think Little Poo liked astronaut training very much because she vomited right after that.

Dad and the blue DeSoto arrived home from work, but Mother still hadn't appeared. We were setting the table when a very frazzled-looking Mother finally walked in the back door. She sat down at the kitchen table and buried her head in her hands.

"Honey, what's wrong?" Dad asked her.

Mother looked up slowly. "Looks like dinner's ready," she said. "Let's sit down and eat. I've got to get some food in my stomach." Whatever Mother had experienced her first day on the job, it hadn't affected her appetite. She ate two salmon patties, some carrots and peas, green Jello, a glass of milk, and a roll. Her beautiful Avon face was starting to return.

She put down her fork and began. "I wore my best dress today, for good luck." We all murmured at the navy and white polka-dot dress she was wearing. "Then I said a little prayer, shouldered my black satchel, and set off to sell Avon. I started by going to Janie's house and then up the street to some of the girls I knew from the PTA so I wouldn't feel so nervous. Sure enough, I sold four lipsticks, a bubble bath, and a face powder, and two ladies wanted order blanks so they could buy some things next payday. It made me feel like a real

Avon Lady.

"Then I came to a street a few blocks over where I didn't know anybody. There was a big green house at the end of the block and the mailbox said 'Reverend Earl Wade.' I figured a minister's wife would be friendly to me, so I decided to try there. Well, I saw about seven or eight little frizzy-haired kids playing in the yard, and bless their hearts, they were awfully plain looking. I went up to the closest one and asked if I could please speak to her mother. The little girl just turned and ran into the house without saying anything. I thought maybe I hadn't been understood, so I walked up the sidewalk, climbed the porch steps, and rang the doorbell. I was feeling really uncomfortable because of all the other little children watching me.

"Then the door opened a crack," Mother continued, "and there was this woman, who turned out to be Mrs. Wade and who was also very plain. I introduced myself and explained about the Avon. Mrs. Wade said she wasn't interested. Well, the Avon district manager had told me not to give up too easily, so I tried another approach. 'I see from your mailbox that your husband is a minister, Mrs. Wade. Perhaps you know my husband's uncle, he's a minister too—Reverend Gottfried Schiffelbein?'

"'He a Baptist?' the woman asked. 'We're free-will Baptists.'

"'Well, no,' I said. 'Actually, he's a Methodist.' Then I remembered Dewey said he was raised a Baptist, so I asked Mrs. Wade if she knew my stepfather-in-law, Dewey Oots. I thought maybe the Baptists all knew each other." Mother paused, and here her voice started to tremble. "And when I asked her about Dewey, Mrs. Wade's face just got real hard. She finally says yes, she did know Dewey, and for me to wait right there. And pretty soon, she comes back with this tall, frizzy-haired man who looks a little familiar to me and she says, 'Earl, this woman is Dewey's daughter-in-law.' I started to say 'How do you do,' but Reverend Wade just looked at me and I sort of froze. It was his eyes. He had these cold gray eyes that looked right through a person. I was paralyzed. I was hypnotized, just like a snake hypnotizes a little bird. Only he was the snake. And when I tried to speak, Reverend Wade leaned his face and his snake eyes real close and spoke. The funny thing was," Mother wrinkled her brow, "he didn't have a hissing voice like you would expect. He had a high-pitched squeaky voice, almost like a girl's, except it was real loud.

"He squeaked at me 'So, you're related to that ignorant Dewey Oots and his murderous lunatic son,' which made no sense to me. But I saw out of the corner of my eye that all the little Wade children in the yard had frozen too. They were paralyzed too. 'Don't you know the unclean spirits have possessed that boy?' he kept squeaking, getting louder and louder like he was preaching to a whole tent full of sinners. 'He's fill-ll-lled with the Devil.' He drew out the word filled," Mother said, "as if he meant not just a little filled but a whole lot filled. Then he came up right in my face, almost touching me and squeaked real loud, 'Do you want salvation, woman?' Well, I backed up so fast I almost fell off the porch. Reverend Wade kept coming forward, squeaking and pointing at me. 'Let Je-sus cast out the Devil from your family. Let Je-sus warsh the murderous blood of the son of Satan from your soul.'

"And then," Mother said, "he began to giggle. A high-pitched 'Hee, hee, hee, hee, hee.' It just sent chills down my spine. I turned and ran down the steps as fast as I could. I ran past all the frozen little Wade children and kept going until I was out of breath at least a block away." Mother held a hand to her chest and took a deep breath, unconsciously reliving the exertion of her escape. "Then," she paused, shook her head and took another deep breath, "then I noticed I didn't have my black satchel anymore. I must have left it on the Wade's front porch." Her beautiful Avon face drew up in a wail and two tears spilled over onto her cheeks. I don't remember Mother ever crying before.

Dad jumped up from the kitchen table like a scalded dog. "Tell me where their house is, Louise. *I'll* get your satchel back." Now it was my turn to freeze. The tone in Dad's voice was reserved for truly terrible situations, frequently resulting in somebody inflicting punishment on somebody else.

"Alex, wait," Mother, sniffling, held out her arm in restraint. She knew that tone too. "I think we'd better talk to Dewey first and see what this is about. I don't even know who this Reverend Wade is or what Dewey and Rex Oliver have to do with him. Please, Alex."

Dad wavered. He gulped a couple of deep breaths and looked toward the door. Finally, he pounded his fist against the door frame, gave one enormous sigh and said, "All right. Let's call Dewey." I didn't relax until Dad walked into the living room for the phone.

Since Dad wasn't going to kill Reverend Wade outright, we at least wanted to listen to his conversation with Dewey. This was the most exciting thing that had happened in a long time, and nothing was required of Mitchell and me but to enjoy it. But Mother was afraid we were too young, as she put it, "for any strange information." Just in case, she stayed with us in the kitchen as we washed and dried the dishes, which we hated anyway.

I couldn't hear Dad speak over the running water, so I thought about a plan for retrieving the black satchel. After midnight, Mitchell and I could sneak out and find the Wade's big green house at the end of some nearby block. We could check the porch, but if it wasn't there, chances were the Wades had discovered it and burned it as some kind of devil's artifact. The thought of the pretty samples burning made me sad. I was sadder at the loss of the samples than at the insult to Mother, because I knew that between Dad and Dewey, Reverend Wade would decide to apologize. Dad had that strict German Methodist idea of right and wrong, and what had been done to his wife that day was wrong. And Dewey, being related to the Dalton Gang, was not to be fooled with. I wondered about the plain little Wade children and how they were going to feel when my dad punched their dad's lights out.

Harmony was excused from doing dishes since she had cooked supper, so she sat at the kitchen table and told us how Vivian Ostrander, Uncle Gott's girlfriend, had a bumper sticker on her Cadillac that said, "Warning: In case of Rapture this car will be unmanned." Vivian was a Pentecostal who believed in big flashy cars, big stiff hairdos, and big dramatic events. Mitchell, ever the astronaut fan, said you needed a rocket to get up high enough for that Rapture stuff.

Dad returned. "Dewey said it's a long story and one he needs to tell us in person. I told him we'd be right out."

Mother tried unsuccessfully for fifteen minutes to find a babysitter to keep an eye on us. I think she suspected my plan to go after the black satchel if left alone. Finally she agreed we'd all have to go to Dewey and Grandma Dale's.

Dad was still angry, so he drove the DeSoto really fast all the way to the farm, upsetting Mother all over again. "Slow down, Alex," she said. "I've already tangled with one crazy man today. I don't need you to go berserk and get us all in a wreck on top of everything else." Even though Dad slowed down some, we still got to the farm a lot sooner than usual that evening.

Dewey and Grandma Dale met us at the back door. There was no sign of Rex Oliver or Uncle Gott, which was probably a good thing. Uncle Gott might have felt obligated to defend another reverend and we weren't in any mood to coddle Rex Oliver. We just wanted to hear Dewey's explanation. After a brief consultation between Dewey and Dad, Dewey looked our way. "Come on in here everybody. You kids might as well hear all this, 'cause you'll eventually hear people talking about it anyway."

We pulled up chairs in the parlor. Dewey took his large overstuffed maroon chair under the fake velvet tapestry of *The Last Supper*. Harmony sat with Mother on the settee while Mitchell and I sat on either side of Grandma Dale. Dad stood and paced the room. Grandma Dale had made some lemonade, as if whatever was to be served up in conversation would go better with something to drink.

"First of all, I'm sorry, Louise," began Dewey, "that you had a run-in with the Wades on my account. I had hoped we'd never have to deal with them again. But..." his voice trailed off. "Dale here, already knows what I'm about to say. I told her the whole story before we were married. She said it wasn't going to stop her from becoming my wife." He half-smiled at Dale, then continued.

"Alex, Louise, you both know that I was married once before, to

41

Rex Oliver's mother. That woman, my wife of twenty-three years, was Ava Wade, Earl Wade's only sister."

Mother's jaw dropped open.

Dad stopped pacing the floor and shot a strange look at Dewey.

"And now I'm going to tell you how she died."

Dewey stopped and put a fresh dip of Skoal in his mouth. Even in an important moment like this you could never hurry Dewey.

Mental Cases

As he sat below *The Last Supper,* Dewey viewed his audience with a practiced eye. I wondered if he knew how much he looked like a king on a throne, sitting in the maroon overstuffed chair on the far side of the parlor. Right now, he looked like a weary king considering something unpleasant that had to be done.

"When I married Ava, my first wife, over thirty-five years ago, I knew her family was odd." Dewey began slowly, emphasizing every word. He would pause often between sentences. Now he paused after the word odd to let the impact sink in. "Ava told me herself how odd they were and that that's why she left home and got a job elsewheres. We met when we were both staying at the same boarding house here in town. I'd come up here from the Ozarks looking for work on the Santa Fe and Ava'd moved away from her crazy family in Beloit.

"She was a handsome woman, yes sir, a handsome woman. So we courted for a while," Dewey paused to lean over his chair and spit into the cuspidor, "and then we married. Well sir, pretty soon, Rex Oliver come along. I was working at the Santa Fe making a little money, so we got us a house over in Oakland where most of the Santa Fe workers lived. Everything was going along pretty good for a couple of years. Then one day, I come home from work and there's a man sitting in the front room.

"'Dewey,' says Ava, 'I'd like you to meet my brother, Earl Wade.'

"'Earl, howdy do.'

"Course I'd of known him for some relation of Ava's anywhere, 'cause of the resemblance.

"'Earl's a soap salesman, Dewey. He's here to…'"

"Wait a minute. He's a soap salesman?" interrupted Dad. "I thought he was a reverend."

"Well, in those days he weren't no reverend," said Dewey. "He was a soap salesman. So I had a salesman for a brother-in-law. I thought that was really something, me with not much education having a dressed up big-time salesman for a brother-in-law. I was even a little proud of him. After that, he starts dropping by more regular, especially at supper time. He wasn't married then and he didn't have no money. But I noticed that when Ava said her family was odd, she wasn't lying. When Earl was around—well, it's nothing I could quite put my finger on, but I've been around horses like that and no matter how tame they act you can never trust 'em. Because some day, they'll hurt you. That's the feeling I had around Earl."

Grandma Dale said Dewey had more natural instincts about horses than six people could learn in a lifetime. I had seen this ability myself.

"Before long, Earl began to get a few regular soap customers. Even had a few other salesmen reporting to him. Everybody said he had a way of just hypnotizing folks until they'd agree to buy some of his soap. But there was always something strange about his work. He was always having difficulties getting the money he collected sent back to his company. When his company complained, he'd just get 'em real tied up in paperwork until sometimes they'd give him extra time to pay, because he did sell a lot of soap. We even bought some ourselves, just to help him out. It was called Colossal Soap because you could do a great big warsh with it. It wasn't too bad, as far as soaps go. So he was successful in that way and got to be known all over town as the big Colossal Soap salesperson. Oh, there was a customer or two who tried to return their soap for some reason, but Earl seemed like he took satisfaction in making them wish they hadn't. I think it was a game to him. Well I don't mind telling you, I was a little afraid of that man myself.

"About that time, I noticed how Rex Oliver, he must've been about ten years old, would get real quiet whenever Earl was around. That boy was afraid of him too, I could tell.

"'He ever hurt you son?' I asked him. "'No, Pa,' was all he'd say. But something was going on there. Rex Oliver just got real quiet after that. Real quiet. Folks say he's strange, I know, but he's not strange like Earl.

"And then Ava started having problems with her nerves. She'd been real sensitive all her life and we'd seen little spells of hers before. But she'd always gotten over them. Not this time. She started going off into a corner by herself a lot. Couldn't do even the simplest thing. Just sat there, staring off into space. Then sometimes she'd get these crying spells. She'd cry and cry and cry. I couldn't get her to stop crying. The doctor finally give her some shots and she'd sleep for a few days, but then she'd wake up and cry some more. It's what people call a nervous breakdown. Life was just too hard for her to deal with, I guess."

Dewey took a spit break. Mother had told us once that spitting was Dewey's way of showing emotion.

"One day the doctor said we'd have to put her in the State Hospital. Said she was real sick in her mind. Oh, that *hurt*, yes sir, that hurt. I didn't want to, of course, but I didn't know what to do. She just wouldn't stop crying. This was back during the middle of the Depression and we didn't have no money for anything better. Even Earl said there wasn't anything else to do. He said their mother'd had the same sickness with her nerves, only she took to her bed and cried for ten years until she finally cried herself to death. So that's what we did. Took the poor woman to the State Hospital." Dewey sighed and spat again.

"That must have been horrible for you, Dewey," murmured Mother.

"Yes, ma'am, it was," Dewey replied. "She stayed there for twelve years. That's a long time to be without a real wife, or a real mother for Rex Oliver. We missed her, but there was nothing we could do about it, so—we just got along as best we could. Rex grew up and I could tell he was sensitive like his mother. He got drafted during the war, but they wouldn't take him. Said he was real smart, but something about his personality wasn't right. I expect it's something that runs in that Wade family line. Rex had a little trouble keeping a job or two, but he never hurt nobody or did anything bad. Finally he just stayed home and raised a big garden for us and had a few newspaper routes for some spending money.

"Then about 1947, I get a letter from the State Hospital that says Ava can come home. Well sir, after all those years... Rex Oliver and I fixed up a room for her at home. We thought she might like some privacy. Then we went out to the State Hospital and brought her back."

Dad had once driven us through the sprawling grounds of the Topeka State Hospital to show us the contrast with the beautiful Meadowgreen campus. I recalled some ancient and ominous looking buildings with bars on the windows. Some of the lunatics got locked up there for the rest of their lives, Dad said, much different than at the Meadowgreen Clinic. He even showed us a cemetery on the grounds for the patients who had lived there so long nobody claimed them when they died. At least Ava had somebody to go home to, somebody who claimed her.

"We brought Ava home and tried to make her comfortable. Rex Oliver would even bring her flowers from his garden, but I never saw the woman smile again. Wasn't long after that, that one day, while I was at work," Dewey paused for a very long time, "Ava picked up a butcher knife and cut her wrists open." Dewey looked down at his own wrists as if picturing how a person could do such a thing. Harmony immediately put both her hands behind her back. "She bled to death in the little room we'd fixed up for her. I guess she just had a hard time facing everyday life."

Dewey's thoughts were far away for a moment. Nobody spoke or even moved until he continued, but I heard Mother swallow real hard.

"When I got home, Rex Oliver was setting beside her on the floor. There was blood all over him too, where he'd tried to stop the bleeding. They were just together there, one propped up in the chair and one setting on the floor rocking back and forth, back and forth. The police came and they asked Rex Oliver a lot of questions, but he couldn't talk to them very much. They finally just came out and asked him if he did it, if he killed her. I expect they had to ask in a case like that. But he said 'no' and I believed him. So did the police. They believed him.

"But Earl now, Earl didn't want to believe that his sister would kill herself. So he made up a story and convinced himself that Rex Oliver had killed her. He said Rex Oliver was crazy. Then you know what he did? He tried to get us put in jail! He ranted and raved to the District Attorney trying to get him to bring charges against Rex Oliver for murder. His own nephew! His own flesh and blood!" Dewey shook his head as if he still couldn't believe it. Then for extra emphasis, he pounded his fists together hard and spat.

"There was an inquest, and even though there was no evidence against Rex Oliver—well the strain—it just affected him real bad. Finally it seemed best, and the doctor suggested, that maybe Rex Oliver would feel better if—if *he* went and got some help at the State Hospital too. I wasn't too convinced they could help him, seeing as how they didn't much help Ava. But there was no place else for him to go."

Mother not very discreetly opened her purse to get a hanky. "You poor man," she whispered.

"I was feeling pretty bad about that time all right," Dewey agreed. "And I was particularly mad at Earl Wade. I'd had to mortgage the house to pay for Ava's care all those years and now I had to put my boy in the hospital too, on account of Earl's accusations. Since Earl didn't want to take me on, he got back at me by writing Rex Oliver hateful letters in the hospital, calling him a murdering lunatic. Terrible, just terrible things he said to that boy.

"One evening after work, I waited by the sidewalk outside Earl's office. He didn't see me when he came out because it was winter and already dark by then. I walked up behind him.

"'Earl,' I said. 'I ain't never killed nobody before.'"

Dewey's voice had gotten very quiet. I leaned forward to hear better.

"'But I could kill you right now on this sidewalk and I will if you don't leave Rex Oliver alone.' Course he's such a coward he started to holler, but I just eased a little bit of cold steel I had in my coat pocket against his ribs and he shut right up. I said, 'Do we understand each other, Earl?'

"'Yes sir.'

"I let the man go. Next day, the police came after me. Said Earl said I threatened him with a gun. I said no sir, I never did that. I didn't tell them I had a piece of metal pipe in my pocket that possibly did feel like the barrel of a gun. Heck, they couldn't prove anything so they let me go. So Earl stops pestering Rex Oliver, and after a couple of years, why, my boy gets to come home. I guess that was a few years before I married your mother."

He looked at Dad. Then at Mother. "So that's why Earl Wade hates me so much."

Everyone was silent, thinking about what we had just heard. I wondered if Rex Oliver had electric wires hooked on his head when he was in the State Hospital. Miss Georgia said her cousin got electricity shot into her head when she had to go there because she was setting fires all over North Topeka.

Harmony piped up just then and asked, "So how did Earl become a minister?" I guess she'd been thinking about Earl and wondering how anybody that mean could call himself a man of God.

Dewey snorted. "We didn't hear much about him for a while, a couple of years. Pretty soon I heard round about that Earl was back in town, married, and was calling himself Reverend Earl Wade. Now I don't know if he's a real reverend or if it's just another one of his tricks. But he claims to operate a church and he's even convinced a few people to support him and his religious ideas."

"That sounds scary to me," said Grandma Dale.

"I hope he burns in hell," came a voice just outside the parlor doorway. We all turned to see Rex Oliver standing in the shadows. Again, everyone was silent.

"So do I," said Mitchell. He spoke directly to Rex Oliver, as if the two of them were having a private conversation. "I hope he burns in hell too. Don't you, Melody?" He looked at me. "And then we can get

Mother's Avon satchel back and Dad can build his garage and everything will be okay."

Rex Oliver walked slowly into the room and over to Mitchell. He squatted down next to where we were on the sofa and very slowly raised his arm and placed his hand on Mitchell's shoulder.

"Thank you," he told Mitchell, and looked at me, nodded his head, and repeated, "Thank you." He rose to his feet, turned, and slowly walked out of the room. A very slight odor of mold lingered in the air.

"Now I know why Reverend Wade, I mean Earl, looked familiar to me," said Mother. "He looks like an older version of Rex Oliver."

"There's Wade blood in the boy, all right," said Dewey. "But there's Oots blood in him too."

"So, what are we going to do about my Avon satchel?" Mother asked. Mitchell had reminded her of the lost satchel and the new career she had tried to begin only this morning.

"Louise, it's not my nature to walk away from a fight. So if you say the word, Alex and I..." He glanced at the doorway to see if Rex Oliver was still listening and saw that he was not. "Alex and I will go to Earl's and get your satchel *back*." From the tone of his voice, we knew with a certainty that Dewey would accomplish his mission. I just wanted to be there to see it happen.

"But," he paused, "for Rex Oliver's sake, I'd just as soon not get Earl stirred up again. Why don't you let me buy you a new one instead and just let this whole matter drop. Maybe we can all put this man behind us and go on."

Mother hesitated. I could tell she wanted her satchel, her original satchel, pretty badly. And she was tempted at the idea of sending two grown men to redeem her honor. But Mother was practical too. "I suppose it would be safer for everyone to just get a new one," she sighed. "I just want to be a good Avon Lady."

I was disappointed and I think Dad was too, because now he had even more reason to enjoy beating up Earl. Dad was strong enough to do it too. He'd grown up doing heavy farm work and had lots of muscles.

"Well I've no intention of letting this Wade fellow spoil any more of our lives," Grandma Dale huffed. "I'm glad Gottfried's not here to hear me say this, but I hope the man burns in hell too. Now, how about some more lemonade?" In Grandma Dale's experience, food was the answer to many a tight situation.

"No thanks," Dad said. "We'd better be going because the kids have school tomorrow. You know how they get if we keep them up too late on a school night." I looked at him in amazement. How could we possibly face school when these exciting events were going on all around us? I knew I'd be awake all night just thinking about it.

We said our goodbyes and took our spots in the car for the ride back to town. Mother and Dad discussed why all of this had never made the news when it had happened, but decided that even if it had, Dewey wasn't related to us then so they wouldn't have paid any attention.

Dad was much calmer on the drive home, which was a good thing because the night had become very foggy. The farther we went, the denser the fog became, and the slower we drove. We didn't see any other traffic on the road.

By the time we made it home, it was way past our bedtime. Mother whisked us off to bed immediately, but I lay awake, hoping to wait until midnight and go recover Mother's satchel. I knew I'd have to find it without Mitchell, because he had already fallen asleep in the car during the ride home. I wondered if Uncle Gott had predicted the fog and realized it would now be harder to spot the green house at the end of some block. Then I thought what if the fog were so thick that I'd get lost and wander around all night trying to find my way? I wondered if I would spot any landmarks to help guide me. I remembered the little cemetery at the State Hospital, and I thought what if I got lost in the fog and wandered all the way to that little cemetery and Ava Wade was there with bloody wrists, walking toward me holding the black satchel? And what if I heard her calling my name, Mel-o-dy, Mel-o-dy, Mel-o-dy...

"Melody, it's time to wake up, sweetie," Mother said as she pulled back the curtains. The fog had given way to sunshine. It was morning and time to get ready for school.

Reverend Weatherman and
His Middle-Age Romance

If you thought Dewey and Rex Oliver's history with Earl Wade was strange, wait 'till I tell you about the unlikely romance developing between two important people in this story.

Great-Uncle Gott was not at the farm that evening hearing Dewey's explanation because he was in town having an argument with his lady friend Vivian Ostrander. That's what Janie Byrant told me the next day when I went over to practice "A Little Polish Mazurka" after school. She'd overheard Vivian and Uncle-Gott talking in front of Antoinette's Pearl of Beauty, the beauty salon she and Vivian had frequented for many years. Janie said Uncle Gott had been trying not to argue, but Vivian was being difficult.

Vivian Ostrander was a middle-aged widow who owned ninety percent of the communications industry in Topeka, meaning the only morning and evening daily newspapers, the only television station, and the major radio station in the capital city of the state of Kansas. "That woman," Dad once told Mother, "has had every elected official and business tycoon in the state courting her public and private favors. And I mean courting hard! With her influence and money, she could have picked anybody she wanted. So why is she sweet on Uncle Gott?"

None of us knew Vivian personally, so her attraction to Uncle Gott was a mystery to us and likely to Uncle Gott himself. "Actually," said Harmony, "I think it was divine guidance." Once again, she may have been right, because they had met through one of Uncle Gott's supernatural visions.

Following his retirement and return from Africa around the time of Grandpa Richard's death, Uncle Gott had settled into life on the farm with his sister Dale, her new husband Dewey, and Rex Oliver. He wanted God to call him to his next job, he said. "The Bible says to wait upon the Lord," he explained. "So that's what I'm going to do. Wait. And pray. God will tell me in His own time what it is He wants me to do." He prayed and meditated and waited for about three months, but nothing happened.

Then one day he was helping Rex Oliver and the Indian hired hands Maynard and Virgil castrate and vaccinate some of the big calves in the squeeze chute in the cattle pens. He liked to help out with the farm work when he wasn't praying and meditating, and that day the boys really needed his help. Rex Oliver controlled the stanchion in the front of the chute, Virgil had the syringe with the vaccines, and Maynard got to do the castrating once the calf was secure in the chute, providing, of course, it was a bull calf. It was Uncle Gott's job to herd the calf into the chute, then grab its tail, twisting it up tight over the calf's back. As any farmer knows, this will keep the calf immobile.

"I had a Hereford calf, a really big one, by the tail in the chute," Uncle Gott recounted later, "when all at once, a wind began to blow. It was just out of nowhere. And it blew harder and harder. It began to pick up dust and blow it around everywhere. It wasn't just dust that got picked up, either." Uncle Gott was referring to the main ingredient of any cattle pen, particles of dried and semi-dried manure. "I was trying to hold on to the calf's tail, when this great big, dried cow plop blew across the pen and landed on my ear, my right ear. Well, without thinking, I guess I let go of the tail to wipe the manure away."

Everyone gasped at that point in the story. When you've got a big calf with its head locked in a stanchion chute and its testicles being squeezed with a giant clamp, the last thing you want to do is release its tail.

"That calf hauled off," said Uncle Gott, "and kicked backwards with both hind legs, catching me in the teeth so hard it lifted me clear off the ground. Blood and teeth and calf testicles were everywhere. It was then I saw stars and a vision from God about my next job."

"I know. I know," said Mitchell jumping up and down and waving his hand like he was in school. "You saw stars, so that meant you should become an astronaut." Mitchell got excited over the chance to mention his favorite theme. It didn't take much.

"No, stupid," injected Harmony. "He got his front teeth kicked out, so that meant God wanted him to become a dentist. Didn't He, Uncle Gott?"

"Those are good choices, all right," said Uncle Gott who was unfailingly polite. "But my vision from God was that I become a TV weatherman. You see, God told me that a real weatherman would have predicted that wind that stirred up the cow plop."

"Oh-h," we all nodded and agreed since there was no arguing with a vision from God.

During the time it took for Uncle Gott's mouth to heal and for him to become comfortable with his false teeth, he studied everything he could about weather forecasting. When he felt ready, he found out who owned the city's only TV station, marched into Vivian's office, and announced that he, Reverend Gottfried Schiffelbein, was offering his services as a weatherman. Vivian admitted later she was so taken aback by this approach that she decided to give him a try as a weekend weatherman. Being a sharp businesswoman, Vivian billed her new employee's slot as "getting the weather straight from Gott's mouth."

Uncle Gott's broadcasts soon became very popular. Mitchell and I even watched him sometimes on our new television set when the weather came on, right after *The Adventures of Superman*. For one thing, he was humble when he said, "This is Reverend Gott with your weather," at the start of every show. And of course, the reverend thing didn't hurt because sometimes he'd slip and say, "I know we've all been praying for rain—oops! I'm not supposed to say that," and everybody except a few atheists loved it.

People started calling and writing, requesting that he be used more often. So Vivian bowed to the demand and gave him the weekday evening weather. Then she ran a whole series of promotions showing Uncle Gott with his hand up, pointing his index finger to the sky while a bolt of lightning flashed in the background. In big yellow letters were the words, "Gott only knows the weather." She ran these ads in her newspapers, as a spot on her radio, and of course many promotions on her TV station. She also bought billboards and bus panels all over town. I thought it was a little unnerving seeing Uncle Gott's face everywhere I looked.

Uncle Gott became the new—and one could say the only—media celebrity in Topeka. Being an ordained minister, he carried the authority of the pulpit, which pleased the conservative members of Topeka's viewing audience. At the same time, he took on a sort of cult status among the city's professionals for his precise scientific explanations of the weather. He became so popular that it was not unusual for total strangers to solicit him for their weddings and family funerals, especially if he could guarantee a beautiful day.

Uncle Gott's fans weren't the only ones taking an interest in him. Vivian, who had been watching the parallel between Uncle Gott's rise in popularity and her TV station's rise in viewers, decided to become better acquainted with her protégé.

It had started innocently enough. "How would you like to go as my guest to the Rotary luncheon next Tuesday?" Vivian asked him. Uncle Gott knew the Rotarians as a fine God-fearing group, so he accepted. Next it was as her escort to a series of business lunches, then dinners, then a few of Vivian's country club functions.

"I'm flattered," Uncle Gott told us. "But I feel somewhat reserved. After all, she is my boss."

"Just be yourself, Gott," Grandma Dale had advised. "You can't go wrong being yourself."

As always, he was polite with Vivian because we were a polite family. Vivian, who was used to dealing with slimy politicians, took this as encouragement. Perhaps because he was the only man in town who didn't care about her wealth and influence, or perhaps because Uncle Gott had a sort of ecclesiastical charm, or maybe just because she enjoyed his weather broadcasts, Vivian fell in love with Uncle Gott.

"Vivian's starting to flirt," Janie had informed us. "And she can flirt with the best of them."

"What does that mean?" Mitchell had asked. "What's flirting with the best of them?"

"That means Vivian has stopped wearing underwear and started swinging her behind when she walks," Janie replied. "This must be difficult for Vivian, since she has the reputation of being married to her work and is testy and Pentecostal. Although," Janie conceded, "she's never met a man before whose visions from God coincide so nicely with her business interests."

"Curiouser and curiouser," I remarked at that bit of news. I had been reading *Alice Through the Looking Glass* about that time.

Now my great-uncle and Vivian had apparently been arguing about clothing. "Gottfried," Vivian had said. She only called him Gott when she was marketing his business services. "You know how the public loves you. You were practically born for occasions like this."

"The public can love me just as well in a plain dark suit," Uncle Gott had replied. "The tribal natives in Africa didn't care what I wore, or if I wore anything at all. Although of course, I always did."

"Well, those Africans may not have cared anything for clothing, but you're in America now, and in this country, we care, Gottfried. We care!"

We had already noticed some changes in Uncle Gott's wardrobe. This was a wise move on his part, since Mitchell and I thought he dressed like a woolly caterpillar with nubby threads hanging from everywhere. Although some of his fans obviously liked his old look, Uncle Gott was slowly modernizing with white shirts, bow ties, and a crew cut. Grandma Dale said she'd never seen her brother act like a young colt before, even when he was young.

"Gottfried, I'd like to ask you to give this matter serious and prayerful thought," Vivian had requested outside the beauty shop where he was dropping her off for her weekly appointment. "I'm sure you won't be sorry. After all, God called you to speak to the masses. And besides, you're just so handsome."

"That last sentence," Janie relayed, "was accompanied by her brushing up against him. You know how she is."

Since Vivian had never brushed up against me, I had to admit, I didn't. "No," I said, "how is she?"

"Well, she's old enough to know better," said Janie. "I know that for a fact. Since we share the same hairdresser, sooner or later I know most of what goes on in her life. And let me tell you, when it comes to your great-uncle, that woman is shameless. I approached her one day at the beauty shop and asked her if Uncle Gott had picked up any hidden talents while he was in Africa. Vivian just looked at me and said, 'Yes, but since it involves honey and an anteater with a twelve-inch tongue I wouldn't want to get you over-stimulated by describing it.' I'd call that shameless, wouldn't you?

"Never mind," she interjected before I had a chance to figure out what tongues and anteaters had to do with anything. She sounded a lot like Harmony when she used that tone. "Well anyway, since your Uncle Gott is more or less helpless against those tactics, he told Vivian he'd think about her suggestion."

"I still don't know what the suggestion was," I said. "What were they arguing about?"

"About the Meadowgreen Ball, Melody. Vivian wants your uncle to give a speech about the weather at the Meadowgreen Halloween Ball in two weeks. That part, the speech part, I think he's willing to go along with. But she insists he has to wear a tuxedo. That's where your uncle said he draws the line."

I had to admit, I'd never seen Uncle Gott, or any other member of my family, in a tuxedo. Tuxedoes were for rich people and movie stars, not farmers, mechanics, and a weatherman like our family.

"Why does she want him to wear a tuxedo?" I wondered out loud. "Is that supposed to be his Halloween costume?" Mitchell and I loved Halloween.

Janie gave a hollow laugh. "In his case, probably. But actually, I think it's to impress all Vivian's hoity-toity friends at the Meadowgreen Clinic Halloween Ball."

Now I have to explain why that was such a big deal. You see, Meadowgreen, very discreetly, controlled Topeka.

October 1958

The only connection
with Nixon and the foundation
was his health reform

The Meadowgreen Psychiatric Clinic

D ad referred to the Meadowgreen Clinic as a private, very
exclusive mental health treatment center, one of the best in the
world. He said it that way because that's where he worked and he
couldn't say it was a loony bin for rich people, which is what we called
it when Dad wasn't listening. Meadowgreen was so exclusive that Dad
said many movie stars and foreign royalty passed through those doors.
But Meadowgreen usually kept a low profile in town and guarded its
patients' anonymity with an awesome power. Billy Glenn, Mother's
brother on the fire department, said he personally once saw Edith
Kliban, the wife of Meadowgreen president Dr. Felix Kliban, pick up
the phone and call Vice President Richard Nixon. She wanted him to
order the Mayor to order the fire department to drive a bus of visiting
dignitaries on a Meadowgreen retreat. An organization with that kind
of clout can pretty much call its own shots in a town like ours.

Their annual attempt at community outreach was the
Meadowgreen Halloween Benefit Ball, a chance for the good citizens
of Topeka to rub elbows with the most important psychiatric teachers
and doctors in the world. For a price, of course. But in order to receive
an invitation to the Ball, an ordinary citizen needed the right
connections. My piano teacher Miss Georgia, whose connections as
far as I was concerned were pretty dubious, showed up every year in
the same off-the-shoulder gown calling it her diva costume. She said
she wouldn't miss it for the world. I asked her once what did the
Benefit Ball benefit, and she said it benefited her circulation.

But Vivian Ostrander did have outstanding connections. Not only
was she the town's media mogul, but she was on a first name basis
with Edith Kliban. Vivian and Edith worked the city's Junior League
and country club circuit, where Vivian was introduced to some of the
clinic's important doctors and their wives. Once Edith invited Vivian
to fly to New York with her in the Meadowgreen plane for a week of

shopping and Broadway shows. In return, Vivian made sure the Meadowgreen name was never sullied in the press. "It's just another instance where money talks," Dad said.

Now Vivian wanted to make a big splash at the Halloween Ball by getting Uncle Gott to give a speech about the weather while wearing a tuxedo.

I thought about this some more and figured it was going to be tough. Uncle Gott was just getting used to his white shirts and bow ties. I doubted he felt prepared to leap into any more fashion statements.

"She's testing him," said Janie, evidently thinking the same thing. "She's pushing him to find his limits."

I didn't think I knew what Uncle Gott's limits were either. Even when he got his teeth kicked out, he had never complained.

"I think Vivian was going to be late for her hairdresser's appointment, so she got Uncle Gott to promise her he would think it over. That's more than I thought he would agree to. It must be the swinging backside..." Janie's voice trailed off thoughtfully. Janie herself had never been married. She was pretty picky when it came to men.

"Actually," Janie lowered her voice to share with me a really important bit of gossip, "there's more. Now you have to promise you won't tell. Do you promise?"

"Okay," I said.

"Vivian plans to use the Meadowgreen Ball to announce her engagement. Her wedding engagement. To your great-uncle. She's using the idea of Uncle Gott giving a speech as a pretext for getting him into a tuxedo. Since he's agreed to think about it, she has two weeks to persuade him. And of course, to get him to propose. Although right now things don't look so good." Janie rushed through her secret so fast her cheeks were flushed. "Now promise you won't say a word."

"I promise," I repeated. I couldn't wait to tell Mitchell.

I knew Uncle Gott had been a determined bachelor all his fifty-five years. Some of the Sunday school women had tried, but nobody had convinced him marriage was better than single life with his sister and her family on the farm. But now he'd met Vivian. Grandma Dale once told us that her younger brother was basically a shy person. She said on the farm where they had grown up, Gottfried had been so shy he would only talk when spoken to. Then when he was fifteen, he had a vision from God that told him to become a preacher. So the boy with the country-school education worked his way through seminary. He got good at speaking, she said, when he had to give sermons, which was why most everything he said came out sounding like church. And it was part of the reason he went out with Vivian. Because as everybody knows, a Pentecostal will always try to dominate a conversation and Gottfried wouldn't have to speak so much. Plus, Vivian had proven herself to be a kind and honest person, despite her money, business acumen, and sophistication.

In many ways it was an almost perfect relationship. Uncle Gott just didn't know it yet.

Jews, The Messiah, and
Preparing for the Halloween Ball

As soon as Mother got her replacement satchel and resumed selling Avon, our lives went on pretty much as before. There was no sign or mention of the Wades and even riding my bike as far away as I dared, I could never spot their house. I did see some plain, frizzy-haired children in school, but none of them were in my grade or Mitchell's grade, so we never found out if they were Wades. Harmony and Mitchell and I questioned our possible relationship to the Wades. Since the Wade children were Rex Oliver's cousins, and since Rex Oliver was our step-uncle, then would we be step-cousins to the Wades? I said yes, but Harmony said she wouldn't claim them even if they were. She said she'd never even met the plain little Wade children, but she already knew they were despicable. Mitchell asked if despicable meant ugly and Harmony said it meant ugly clear to the bone.

Harmony surprised us by bringing home a friend one day from school. The two of them would sit in her room, which of course was also my room, and read poetry out loud to each other. It was disgusting hearing people talk like that. I always left when the friend came over. But I was grateful that Harmony had made a friend, because now she didn't pester Mitchell and me as much with her intellectual stuff.

The friend's name was Daphne Knott, which easily translated into Daffy Knothead as soon as Mitchell and I got hold of it. Daffy talked in poetic phrases just like Harmony, but she sounded funny the rest of the time too. Even so, we tried to be nice to her.

"Where you from?" Mitchell asked her one afternoon. It was the neighborly thing to find out where someone was from.

"New Yawk," said Daffy.

"That out in western Kansas somewhere?" Mitchell wanted to know. Western Kansas was a very big place.

He was answered by a chorus of laughter from Harmony and Daffy, a very un-neighborly reply to his question. Mitchell looked at them awhile, took a few steps closer to the door, and casually changed the subject. "Say—I heard on Uncle Gott's news," he paused, a technique I felt sure he'd picked up from listening to Dewey, "that Kansas farmers are looking all over the state," pause, "for the new Kansas Pork Queen." Harmony shot him a suspicious glance. Mitchell stepped closer to the door. His final sentence was quick, clean, and straight to the point.

"I'm callin' to tell 'em not to look so hard," he yelled, "cause Porky and Daffy are right here." He was running as he said it.

Incidents like that drove Harmony to spend more time at Daffy's house, a bigger, nicer house in the exclusive Westboro section of town. She bragged how Daffy's father was a psychiatrist at Meadowgreen.

"That's too bad," Mitchell and I told her. Psychiatrists fell into the "not entirely trustworthy" category since they were either Jewish or foreign or both. Psychiatrists talked with heavy accents so they could confuse people easily and run up high bills because crazy people couldn't comprehend money. Worst of all, the psychiatrists at Meadowgreen hated being in Topeka, because as Janie Bryant once pointed out, they didn't consider beer, bowling, and country music to be cultural pursuits. On the other hand, Mother remarked she couldn't understand why the Meadowgreen folks insisted on something called lox and bagels for Sunday brunch instead of good old bacon and eggs for Sunday breakfast. The only thing everybody agreed on was that the Meadowgreen patients benefited from being stuck in the middle of nowhere with these guys, since life was simpler here, their privacy was protected, and the only way they were getting out of this town was to die or show improvement.

Now Harmony was getting to know one of the outsiders. One week in early October, she put down her fork during dinner and asked, "Dad, how come Jews are different?"

"What do you mean?" Dad asked.

"Well, Daphne and her family are Jewish. What does that mean?"

Dad looked at Mother and rolled his eyes. "Well," he began. Then he stopped. I could tell he didn't quite know what to say. "Well, the Jews in the Bible, uh, didn't believe in Jesus."

"Are they atheists?" asked Mitchell.

"No, son. They believe in God just the same as we do. Only they call him a different name and they use a different language, and they can't eat certain foods. Sometimes they grow long, long beards and wear black clothes and big, tall hats. And sometimes they wear little round skull caps. The men, that is. And they drive really hard bargains…"

"Worse than gypsies," interrupted Mother.

"Only it's not polite to point that out even if it's true. And also, they don't believe in Christmas."

"Wow," said Harmony.

"And there are some other differences that you kids don't need to know about just yet." He exchanged a knowing look with Mother, who nodded her approval.

"Like what?" said Mitchell.

"Oh, never mind," said Mother.

"Are they crazy?" asked Mitchell. He was serious. Dewey's stories about mental illness had left an impression on everyone.

"No, no, no, no," Dad shook his head. "They're not crazy. Just different."

"Why don't they celebrate Christmas?" asked Harmony. She was enamored with what she called "the sanctity of the ambiance of Christmas," one of her intellectual phrases that even Mother said was a bit much.

"Well, because Christmas is a celebration of Jesus's birth and they don't believe he was the Messiah, like we do."

"Who do they think *is* the Messiah?" I questioned.

"What's Messiah?" asked Mitchell.

"Do they believe in Halloween?" asked Harmony.

"Look kids, why don't you look it up in the encyclopedia," said Mother. Mother believed that reading was good for us and had persuaded Dad to purchase a set of new encyclopedias to enlighten our young minds. Harmony was the only one who read them.

"Okay," said Harmony.

"What's Messiah?" persisted Mitchell. He did not discourage easily.

"Go-look-it-up, young man," Mother responded in her firmest voice.

"Messiah is the king of Heaven and of the angels and everything and He saves people, only He's not quite as good as God, dummy," Harmony volunteered. Why did we need encyclopedias when we had Harmony?

That question satisfied, Mitchell turned to Dad and asked, "Dad, do only Jews live in New Yak?"

"New Yak? Where's New Yak?" Dad looked puzzled.

"New Yak. That's where Daffy said she was from."

"I think she meant to say New *York*, honey. You know, the place where the Statue of Liberty is." Dad smiled. "People in different parts of the country talk a little differently sometimes. They don't always have good schools, like we do, to teach 'em how to talk right."

Mitchell put his elbows on the table and held his head up between his hands. He was thinking hard.

"So, are the Jews related to the Negroes, or the Mexicans, or the Indians? Which one? Daffy doesn't talk like any of them and she looks like us, only she doesn't talk like us. So what is she?"

"Mitchell, sometimes it may seem on the outside that people are different. Our skin may be a different color, or our religion is different, or we have different languages and customs. But on the inside, we're all God's children." The Methodists preached that stuff a lot. About all of us being God's children.

Mother added, "Just like each of you three children is different and special, but Dad and I still love all of you the same. Just like God loves His children the same." I wondered if God referred to His children as His "little warts" too. I hadn't seen it mentioned anywhere in the Bible, although He did call them sheep.

"Even the atheists?" I asked. "Does God love the atheists too?" Janie Bryant had given Mitchell and me several lectures how the atheists were all a bunch of Communists trying to overthrow the Constitution. An atheist was as low as a person could get.

"Yes, Melody. Even the atheists." Mother smiled at us. "So, you two be nice to Daphne from now on. She's Harmony's friend."

I almost said that was enough to make her questionable right there, let alone the Jewish part, but thought better of it.

"Alex, do you know this Dr. Knott?" Mother asked.

"Well," Dad said, "I've heard the name at work, but never connected it to Daphne. I think he works with some kind of, you know, female stuff. A lot of strange looking women in that office. I'll check to be sure next time I'm in that building."

Before we could ask what "female stuff" was, Mother jumped in. "Well, I'm sure Dr. Knott is a very nice man, because Daphne seems to be a very well brought up young lady, which is more than I can say about you little warts sometimes." She was smiling though.

We sure didn't know much about other people back then, with our preconceived and mostly erroneous ideas about Jews, Blacks, Mexicans, Native Americans, gypsies, hillbillies, Pentecostals, Communists, atheists, and the mentally ill, and some others I'll be telling you about soon. Not to mention the role of women. Maybe we still don't. Are we really all God's children?

We soon forgot about Jews being different because the next week was spent deciding on our costumes for the Meadowgreen Halloween Benefit Ball. Meadowgreen employees and their families got free admission, so Mother thought we were all old enough to attend this year. This would be the first Halloween Ball for Mitchell and me. But we had to promise not to pick or scratch any places we shouldn't be picking or scratching, not to swear or hit anybody, and not to turn and run if we saw Miss Georgia dressed like a diva. We promised.

Mitchell decided right away he was going as an astronaut, which

I said was about as original as a litter of kittens. Harmony and Daffy were going as Charlotte and Emily Bronte, two old sisters I'd never heard of. After much thought, I decided to go as an animal faith healer. Everybody, including Mother and Dad and Dewey and Dale, asked me what that was. I said animal faith healers did the same thing to animals that Uncle Gott used to do to people before he became a weatherman. Only since animals are generally smarter than people, their faith is stronger and they get well quicker. "Ask Dewey," I said. "He'll tell you."

"Well-ll," said Dewey. "I expect she's right. Animals are very smart." Dewey understood everything about animals.

"So what kind of a costume does an animal faith healer wear?" Mother wanted to know.

"Bib overalls," I said after some thought. "Only I'm going to get a stick and paste a construction paper gold star on the end to carry as my magic wand. Then when I spy any sick animals, I'll lay my magic wand on them and ask them in the name of Jesus to be healed."

Dewey nodded his head again, "Seems reasonable."

"Would your magic wand help Miss Georgia?" Mitchell wanted to know.

"Mitchell," Mother said, "be nice."

Mitchell thought he was being nice the following weekend when we all went to the farm. While the grown-ups were in the house, he and I were in the enormous garden watching Rex Oliver play with some pumpkins. Rex Oliver didn't know we were watching him, or I don't think he would have given them names like Trixie, Darla, and Jane. I wasn't sure what kind of game he would be playing with three pumpkins, but before I could find out Mitchell popped off and invited Rex Oliver to the Ball.

"Hi, Uncle Rex," he started. "You wanna dress up in a costume and come to a Halloween party with us? You get to be anything you want. Only there's no trick-or-treating and you're not allowed to toilet paper anything and there's a dance for the grown-ups. But I guess you can dance if you want to. Do you wanna go?"

Rex Oliver said, "Just a minute, Darla," to the closest pumpkin, lifted it into the crook of his arm, and looked at Mitchell. "What costume are you wearing?"

"Astronaut," Mitchell said proudly.

"And you, Melody?"

"I'm going to be an animal faith healer," I told him.

Uncle Rex wrinkled his brow a bit, but otherwise accepted this pronouncement.

"What would I go as?" Uncle Rex asked. "Do you think I should go as a pumpkin?" With that he turned his gaze back to Darla and ran his hand down her rough orange side, then sat her back on the ground with the others.

"I don't know," said Mitchell. "It's got to be something really good."

The three of us sat down together on some hay bales at the edge of the garden to discuss Rex Oliver's choices.

"You could go as an Indian," I suggested. "Maynard and Virgil would probably let you borrow some of their war paint and bows and arrows."

"Nah," said Mitchell before Uncle Rex could respond. "Only little kids dress up like Indians."

"Guess that leaves out ghosts and clowns," I mused. The pumpkins rested quietly on the ground between Rex Oliver's feet as we considered and rejected Superman, the headless horseman, and Davey Crockett.

"I know, I know, I know, I know," yelled Mitchell. "You can go as the Messiah. It's sorta like the king of Heaven and I bet nobody else would have a messiah costume."

Uncle Rex shot his eyes sideways and the corners of his mouth began to twitch. He wouldn't look at Mitchell or me, but he appeared to be trying to smile, only it just came out like a lot of twitching. Finally he reached down and patted Darla two or three times, the way one would pat a good dog. Mitchell and I looked at each other, since we didn't know if he was being funny or just being strange.

"You know what?" Uncle Rex said when his mouth finally stopped twitching. "That's a good idea, me going as the Messiah. That would just be all right. I haven't been to a Halloween party for..." He paused to remember, "for a very long time."

"Do you know how to dress like the Messiah?" Mitchell kept asking him. "I don't even know what messiahs look like. Do they have halos or wings or what?"

"I know," Uncle Rex answered. "I know just how to be a messiah. Especially on Halloween."

Then he picked Darla up off the ground, tucked her under his arm again, stood, and walked away. He left Trixie and Jane and Mitchell and me sitting in the garden without so much as a goodbye.

The adults weren't quite as excited about Rex Oliver's social commitment as we were. There was talk about if he could handle it, but finally Dad settled the issue with the kind of question that causes guilt to override sense.

"When was the last time the boy's been out and had some fun, Dewey?" Dad asked.

"It's been a while," Dewey admitted.

"Well now, everybody needs to get out and have some fun from time to time. Louise, that's okay, isn't it? You and the kids can keep an eye on him all right, don't you think?"

"I guess so," Mother said. "I hope he won't be any trouble."

Dad would be with us at the start of the ball, but he would be working during most of it, so Mother would be on her own with us. This time he wouldn't be working as a mechanic for Meadowgreen, which was his full-time job. He'd be playing guitar in the weekend country-western band called Shep and The Big Dogs. He played partly for the extra money, but partly because we were a musical family and he enjoyed it.

This year Shep and the Big Dogs had been hired to give the ball a more rustic theme, a departure from its usual chic sophistication. Dad said the band members were all pretty excited about playing at a big society event like this. They had decided that since it was Halloween they would forego the western boots, pearl-button shirts, and cowboy hats they usually wore and instead dress up like different kinds of dogs in keeping with the band's name. Dad thought that he, being German, would go as a German Shepherd. But Simon Vargas, a Mexican who lived in Oakland and was the leader of the band, said that he should get to be the German Shepherd since his stage name was Shep. Then the drummer said Simon ought to go as a Chihuahua since Simon was Mexican. Dad said Simon got mad and said what the hell was the damn Polack drummer going as—a weenie dog? So to keep the peace, Dad had conceded the German Shepherd spot to Simon. Dad was now a St. Bernard.

It had taken God and a little hair spray to get Uncle Gott to change his mind about the tuxedo. That was the latest report from Janie Bryant the Giant Killer. Janie was at our house early the next Saturday morning to borrow some coffee. Usually, she didn't get up that early unless she had something real juicy she was dying to tell Mother. Mitchell and I pretended to draw in our connect-the-dots books, but we really hung around the kitchen so we could listen to Janie.

We all knew Vivian and Janie scheduled their weekly hair appointments together with Antoinette, a seventy-year-old beautician who specialized in high stiff hairdos. Janie herself wasn't Pentecostal, but she envied the Pentecostal look.

"Well," said Janie to Mother, "Vivian and I had been discussing Uncle Gott's resistance to the tuxedo. Antoinette was spraying a third layer of hair spray on Vivian to make sure the 'do' would set up nice and firm. 'You know, Vivian,' I told her, 'it's gonna take another vision from God to get that man into a tux.' Vivian leaped up like she'd been goosed, rubbed her eye, threw her hands up in the air and shouted, 'Glory' the way those holy rollers do. Then she turned and hugged me and hugged Antoinette and said, 'Thank you, Janie, and God bless you too Toni.' She ripped the beautician's smock off her neck with one hand, jumped in her black Cadillac, and shot over to the studio. Her hair hadn't even finished setting up yet. What happened next was like something out of a very religious Rock Hudson movie. Vivian cornered Uncle Gott right after the six o'clock weather. She said it was very important that she talk to him right then because she'd had a vision from God and he was in it. Well, that got Uncle Gott's attention all right. He asked what the vision was about.

"'It's about us getting married,' said Vivian.

"'Huh?' Uncle Gott finally replied. 'What, uh, happened exactly in this vision?' Vivian told me he started fumbling with his bow tie. Apparently, it was a clip-on and he kept clipping it on, then off.

"So Vivian told him that several months ago she had a feeling they should get married. She asked God to send her a sign if He really did mean for her and Gottfried to be together as husband and wife. Vivian said she'd been waiting for a sign all these months, when suddenly today, at the beauty shop, Antoinette was spraying her hair and accidentally got some of the sticky hair spray square in her eyeball. Now Antoinette's been spraying hair for fifty years and this was the first time she'd ever gotten spray in Vivian's eye. And it glued it shut. Tighter than a…" Janie stopped to think of a comparison, but evidently couldn't come up with anything. "Oh, you know," she said waving a sign of dismissal with her hand. "Real tight.

"'I just know it was a sign from God,' Vivian told your uncle, 'because things like that just don't happen unless there's divine providence at work.'

"'Oh?' Uncle Gott inquired. 'But… How… Hair spray…?' Vivian had him stammering.

"'You see,' Vivian told him, 'There I was with only one good eye. But the Lord's meant for us to see the world with two eyes. Because it takes two eyes, Gottfried, working together, to get the whole perspective. Just like it takes two people, being together, to get the full picture of life. So don't you see, darling? It's a sign. God wants us to get married.'

"Now here's where it gets real interesting," said Janie to Mother. "You see, Vivian was so excited she almost fainted, causing Uncle Gott to throw out his arms to steady her. Vivian took that as an embrace from her intended, revived in a hurry, and launched herself hard into Uncle Gott's outstretched arms.

"Uncle Gott's bow tie flew off and his glasses slipped half-way down his nose. But then," Janie continued, "Vivian became aware that Uncle Gott was, shall we say, 'extremely interested' in her warm female body with no underwear pressed up against his. So interested, if you know what I mean, that he was struggling for words and his face went blank and his eyes rolled up to the ceiling."

Mother shot a look at where Mitchell and I were connecting the dots, but before she could say a word Janie plunged ahead with her story.

"'That's all right, darling,' Vivian told him. 'It's a sign that you love me. Praise the Lord.'

"And Vivian, vixen that she is," added Janie, "probably just wiggled a little harder."

"Janie…" tried Mother, but Janie could not be stopped.

"Vivian, still in Uncle Gott's arms, figured out they could announce their engagement at the Halloween Ball and get married sometime the following June. That would give them time to select china and cutlery patterns, for Vivian to shop for a trousseau, and for them to move Uncle Gott's things into Vivian's house.

"By this point, Vivian had also decided she needed an engagement ring. 'Darling,' she told him, 'it doesn't have to be too big. The ring, I mean. Maybe I could give you a raise and we could go pick one out. Don't you think that would be nice?'

"Uncle Gott," Janie said, even though he wasn't Janie's uncle, "was acting just like Rock Hudson in those romantic movies. He was so overwhelmed that he just nodded, disengaged his arms, pushed his glasses back up his nose, picked up his bow tie and said, 'Excuse me.' You know how polite he is. Then he went to the men's room and didn't come out for ten minutes. Vivian told me she didn't know if he was praying, throwing up, or twittering the ole' turtl…"

"JANIE!" Mother yelled this time. "Kids are here!"

We looked up hopefully at Janie to get her to say whatever it was she'd started to say. But Mother didn't want her to say it.

"Skip that part," Mother told her. "What happened next?"

"Well," said Janie, "Vivian told me Uncle Gott looked pretty shaken up when he came out of the bathroom. But he walked over to Vivian, nodded his head, and said, 'okay.'"

"Okay?" asked Mother. "That's all he said? That's not very romantic." Mother liked romance the way Harmony liked poetry.

"Then Vivian made him promise not to tell anybody so it would be a surprise when it was announced at the Halloween Ball. She said she would make him a good wife and that he was a good, godly man, and that they would be very happy together. Uncle Gott just nodded his head some more. Vivian asked him if he felt all right and Uncle Gott said he thought so, but he could use a drink of water. Vivian said one of the cameramen had some hooch in a locker that she could get so they could toast this special moment.

"'Okay,' Uncle Gott said again."

"I didn't know Uncle Gott touched hard liquor," said Mother, frowning.

"Oh there's probably a lot of things he's never done before that Vivian's going to teach him," Janie replied.

"Hmm-m," said Mother.

Then she turned to Mitchell and me. "Now listen, kids. I don't want you to repeat one single word of what you heard us talking about this morning. Not one word. Not to anybody. Do you hear me?"

"Is it a secret?" I asked her.

"Even from Dad?" asked Mitchell.

"Well, I guess we can tell Dad," Mother decided. "But nobody else."

"Not even Harmony?" Mitchell said. We both wanted something we could hold over Harmony.

"Oh—I don't know. Why don't we wait and discuss this when

we're all together tonight at dinner."

Janie left to go tell all the other girls she was friends with, Mother said.

"So why can't we tell anybody?" I asked.

Mother stopped, looked us straight in the eye, and said, "We have no control over Janie's inability to keep a secret, but that doesn't mean *we* can't keep one. Because it's real important to Vivian that this news comes out when she can get the maximum amount of attention. Not before. That's why she's so good at the communications business."

"Do you think Uncle Gott will stop being a weatherman now?" Mitchell asked.

"Well, Honey, I don't know," said Mother. "We'll just have to wait and see."

One week before the Meadowgreen Ball, Janie was back at our house with additional information. It seemed a letter had arrived addressed to the editor of *The Topeka Daily Capital*. The letter said it had been revealed to the author that Satan and all his demons were inhabiting Topeka through the bodies of the mentally ill. "GOD HATES LUNATICS!" the letter said. "He will rain down His wrath on the ungodly." The letter was signed: "The Reverend Earl Wade, Hosanna Baptist Church."

The editor, who received strange letters on a regular basis, showed the letter to Vivian. She couldn't figure it out either, but since it talked about the mentally ill, she showed it to her friend Edith Kliban. Edith, the wife of the president of the most prestigious psychiatric clinic in the world, said the guy sounded like a nut to her, and threw the letter away.

westboro
Baptist?

76

Murder At the Halloween Ball

The week of the Meadowgreen Halloween Benefit Ball it began to rain, just as Uncle Gott had predicted it would. Any leaves still remaining on trees were whipped off, leaving the streets and yards burdened with soggy masses of decay.

By the time Saturday afternoon rolled around it had rained steadily for five out of seven days and I had picked up a cold. Mother threatened to keep me home from the Ball, but I pitched a fit and told her truthfully that I felt fine, only my nose was stopped up and sometimes I sneezed. She took my temperature and I had no fever, so she reluctantly said I could go. I was so excited I could hardly keep from tickling Mitchell, just for fun.

Simon and the band members had come over early and picked up Dad so they could go to the fairgrounds and set up their band instruments. It was Mother's job to get us kids and herself in costume, drive to the farm and pick up Rex Oliver, then pick up Dad's St. Bernard costume from the rental store close to the fairgrounds. She would have plenty of time to deliver it to Dad before the Ball started. Harmony was going with the Knotts and would meet us there.

Since it was still early and I didn't have much to do for my costume, I stood at the door and passed out Tootsie Rolls and bubblegum to the trick-or-treaters, trying not to sneeze on them. Our neighborhood, being new, had many young families with small children, all of whom darted around that evening clutching a bag and begging homeowners for sweets. I missed being able to go with them because I really loved Halloween and I loved candy, which we didn't get very often. But Mother said I would have been tempting fate walking around in the rain with a cold, and besides, just like Cinderella, I was going to the Ball.

I could hear Mother giggling from the other room as she got ready. Whatever she was wearing, she was keeping it a secret.

Mitchell came out in his astronaut costume for my inspection. His idea of an astronaut was to wrap aluminum foil around a cardboard box, then punch some holes in the box for his arms and head. He couldn't figure out how to get aluminum foil to stay on his legs, so he wore an old pair of Dad's long white underwear, cut off short enough for Mitchell's height. Since he didn't have any astronaut shoes, he wore Harmony's white boots from her baton twirling outfit. That left only his helmet. He had wanted to wear a large goldfish bowl on his head, but Mother said it was dangerous. He tried it anyway, but soon found he couldn't breathe inside and besides, it kept fogging up. Finally, he settled on another foil-covered box with punched-out holes.

"You don't look like any astronaut I've ever seen," I told him. "You look more like a robot."

"Well *you* look like a damn Polack," Mitchell replied. He wasn't sure what a damn Polack was, but ever since he'd heard Dad's story about Simon Vargas and the drummer he knew a damn Polak was something despicable. He knew enough not to say it in front of the folks, though.

I had made a magic wand out of a fly swatter, to which I had taped a construction paper gold star. That and my bib overalls, a shirt, and cowboy boots was all I needed. Mother said it wasn't much of a costume, but I just said, "Oh ye of little faith," since I was an animal faith healer. Mother rolled her eyes and said that as long as I was happy with it, she was.

When Mother emerged from the bedroom, she really surprised us. She was dressed in a long black skirt, a black sweater, a black velvet cape, and a tall black pointy hat. She also carried the kitchen broomstick. She had used her Avon samples to make her face dark, with great big eyebrows and a large brown mole by her upper lip. She wasn't exactly scary looking, because Mother was incapable of looking scary. But if you didn't know her you might think she had at least boiled a few toads. "You look great," Mitchell and I both said.

"Thank you, kids," she said. "Halloween's supposed to be fun." She giggled again. I liked it when Mom giggled.

Mom drove us in the blue DeSoto out to the farm through a cold, steady drizzle. Night was beginning to fall by the time we arrived.

I hadn't given any more thought to Rex Oliver's costume since we'd convinced him to come with us two weeks ago. Now I wondered if Grandma Dale, Dewey, and Mother would be as excited as Mitchell and I were about this religious side of Uncle Rex. I rushed into the house to find out.

"Where's Uncle Rex?" I wanted to know. He wasn't anywhere around.

"He's in his room," answered Grandma Dale. "He won't let anyone see his costume, but he'll probably come out now that you're here. Have some cookies before you go running off." Grandma Dale indicated a plate of warm Halloween cookies in the shape of black cats and jack-'o-lanterns with candy corn for the eyes. We each stuffed cookies in our mouths and ran to find Rex Oliver.

When Uncle Rex heard us, he opened the door to his room and slowly stepped into the hallway. The effect of his costume was even better than I'd imagined. He had obviously spent some time on it because he looked just like the picture of Jesus that hung on the wall of our Sunday School class. He had on a long, sparkling white robe that he'd evidently sewn himself. It had long flowing sleeves and a rope tied around the waist as a belt. He wore sandals on his feet, and he had let his beard and red hair grow shaggy. In one hand he carried a large metal crucifix and in the other a willow branch. That was the only part I didn't understand. Even so, if Harmony would have been here, she would have said Uncle Rex looked "stunning."

"What's that branch for, Uncle Rex?" I asked him.

"It's supposed to be an olive branch, only a willow branch is about as close as we got in Kansas."

"Oh, yeah," I said. "I see."

"You look real good, Uncle Rex," Mitchell added. "Did you make your costume yourself?"

"Yes," he replied. "It took me all week because it was a secret until tonight. You look good too," he said to Mitchell. "And Melody, what are you again?" he asked me.

"An animal faith healer," I reminded him.

"Yes," he said. "Well. Very interesting."

"Thank you," I said.

"You're welcome," he answered.

We took Uncle Rex into the living room to show everybody his costume. "Look at Uncle Rex, everybody," I said. "Can you guess what he is?"

"Isn't it great?" asked Mitchell.

Grandma Dale inhaled sharply and put her hand over her mouth. Dewey's brow wrinkled, then he frowned hard and reached for the Skoal. Mother just studied Rex Oliver without a sound. Finally she walked over to him and walked all the way around him, looking over the effect from top to bottom. Then she looked at Mitchell and me, shook her head and sighed.

"What, uh, big imaginations you children have," she said to us. Then she turned and smiled at Rex Oliver. "You look very original, Rex Oliver. Are you—Jesus?"

"He's the Messiah!" yelled Mitchell before Uncle Rex could answer. Mitchell had been about to explode with the secret all week. The only reason he'd kept it this long was from my threat of unmerciful tickling if he told anyone.

Uncle Rex did his twitchy attempt at a smile back at Mother. "Thank you," he replied.

While Mitchell and I got Uncle Rex some cookies, there appeared to be a brief conference of the adults in the hallway. I couldn't hear much of what they were saying, but I did hear Dewey ask Mother to, "keep a close eye on him." Mother said she would.

I noticed it was dark and reminded Mother we needed to get going to pick up Dad's costume. I didn't want to be late for my first big Halloween party. As we drove back to town, I saw Mother roll down her window just a bit, saying she needed some air. Uncle Rex didn't seem to notice. He and Mitchell were in the back seat trading stories about how each had assembled his Halloween costume.

By the time we arrived at the rental shop, Mitchell and Uncle Rex and I were getting excited about the Ball. We didn't know exactly what we'd do there, but we'd heard so much about it for so long that it just had to be fun.

Mother left us in the car while she went inside to get the St. Bernard costume Dad had reserved weeks earlier. She was gone a long time. When she came back, she looked unhappy, which gave her witch's costume a more realistic appearance. She got in the car holding a large clothes hanger with something furry on it.

"They didn't have the St. Bernard costume," she said. "They didn't even have any dog costumes left. So they gave me this—this chipmunk costume. It's supposed to be Alvin."

"Wow!" said Mitchell. "That's even better. Alvin and the Chipmunks have a bunch of hit records and Shep and the Big Dogs don't even have one."

"Well, I don't know..." muttered Mother. "Your Dad's not going to like it. Just when he'd made his peace about being a St. Bernard too."

The fairgrounds' entrance was full of cars dropping off costumed characters. Mother parked the DeSoto, then we ran through the drizzle, showing our complimentary employee tickets at the door. The Meadowgreen Halloween Benefit Ball occupied the entire Agriculture Hall at the fairgrounds, a site chosen to suit this year's theme: "Hold on to Your Hat." This supposedly referred to farmers' straw hats, which we could see were being used everywhere as decorations, along with orange and black crepe paper. Mother's brother, Billy Glenn, had said since it was Meadowgreen giving this shindig it should have been called "Hold on to Your Sanity," or at the very least, "Hold on to Your Money," since Meadowgreen was known to be very expensive.

Before we could investigate the Ball, we had to go find Dad and deliver his substitute costume. It was hard trying to stay together because there were so many people between us and the stage. Mother pushed her way through the crowd, using her broomstick to give a little nudge to people sometimes so they'd step aside. She always said, "Excuse me," which was funny coming from a witch. Mitchell followed her, then Rex Oliver, then me. We hadn't found Harmony and the Knotts yet. I was so excited and so busy looking at everybody's costume that I almost got left behind. I wanted to see if there were any people dressed as sick animals that needed healing. Harmony had told me earlier what a stupid idea that was, but I said she didn't have any faith either. Faith was real important in our family.

When we came to the stage, a German Shepherd was adjusting one of the microphones.

"Simon," Mother said, "is that you?"

The German Shepherd looked up to see a witch, an astronaut, a girl in bib overalls, and a red-headed Jesus.

"Hi, Louise," he said. "Do you have Alex's costume? We're almost ready to start."

"Well, uh, there was a mix-up at the rental store and, uh, I'm afraid they didn't have any dog costumes left at all. Not even a cocker spaniel. So they gave us, uh, this costume." She held up the clothes hanger to the German Shepherd. He took it.

"What is it?" he said.

"Well, it's Alvin. Alvin the Chipmunk."

"Alvin the Chipmunk? Are you kidding me, Louise? Is this a joke?"

Just then, Dad walked on stage carrying some equipment. The German Shepherd called him over. "Hey. Alex," he said. "Guess what *you* get to wear?"

As Mother went through the story again, I saw Mitchell and Rex Oliver eyeing a table of what looked like refreshments. There were lots more real straw hats and crepe paper decorations and pumpkins and jack-o'-lanterns, and in the middle of the table sat a great big yellowish cake in the shape of a straw hat. Across the brim of the hat was the word Meadowgreen in brown frosting. There was also a brown frosting hatband. The whole thing looked nice and sweet and was making my mouth water.

"Hey, Uncle Rex," I said, "let's go get some cake." I figured since Uncle Rex was an adult, Mother wouldn't care if we went with him. Mitchell came too.

There were lots of people at the table so we had to wait our turn. Just when we got to the front of the line, Mitchell asked a question. "Uncle Rex, is the Messiah allowed to eat?"

"I don't know," said Uncle Rex. His hand was frozen midair over a plate with a piece of cake on it. "I never really thought about it before." He was staring at the cake.

"I betcha he can eat manna from Heaven," I said to Mitchell. "That's in the Bible. Loaves and fishes too. I'm not real sure about cake though."

We were holding up the line and a Little Bo Peep behind us was trying to reach around Mitchell to the punch bowl. I wondered if she had any sick sheep that I could heal, but mostly I wanted something to eat. It wasn't polite to eat in front of Uncle Rex, though, if he couldn't.

"Let's go find Uncle Gott and ask him," Mitchell said. "He knows everything about the Bible."

We told Mother we were going to go look for Uncle Gott. Mother was busy talking to Miss Georgia and said fine.

We walked around for about ten minutes looking for Uncle Gott among the clowns, Raggedy Anns, ghosts, and Lone Rangers. But we'd forgotten to ask if Uncle Gott was wearing a costume over his tuxedo, so we had to stop and ask almost everybody who they were. Usually, they'd answer they were a clown or a ghost, so I'd explain, no, I meant what was their real name because we were looking for Reverend Gottfried Schiffelbein. And then people would say, "Oh, is he here?" because he was such a celebrity from his TV weatherman shows and we'd say, "Yes, sir" or "Yes, ma'am, thank you anyway." Sometimes people would look at the three of us and ask us who we were, so we'd tell them what our costumes were. They'd usually go, "O-o-oh," and nod their heads like they understood perfectly, but sometimes they looked at us strange too.

That made me wonder if any of the Meadowgreen patients were here. Dad had said there probably would be some of the outpatients attending. I didn't know how we were going to tell the nut cases from the normal people, since everybody looked pretty silly right now.

The crowd was thickest in the middle of the room, so we tried to work our way to the edges, studying everyone's costumes for a resemblance to Uncle Gott. Blocking our way at the moment were two women dressed as potted plants having an angry conversation. They had on round brown imitation flowerpots around their mid-section, their arms and hands looked like green branches with leaves pasted on, and their heads had flower petals in a circle around their face. Only they didn't look like lovely flowers right now because their faces, one a rose and the other a dandelion, had turned hateful. Just as we tried to pass them the rose exploded in rage.

"Take THAT, you awful ugly weed!" the rose shouted at the dandelion as she flung a handful of dirt from the pot around her midsection. I hoped it didn't contain any wet fertilizer.

"Oh yeah? Well, take THAT! And don't try to tell me my business!" screamed the dandelion, throwing wet dirt from her pot as fast as she could right back.

The dirt was flying and some of it splattered and flew all over Rex Oliver's sparkling white messiah robe. He didn't look near as godly with wet dirt all down his front. I think it scared him a little bit too.

The rose, the one who started throwing first, grabbed Uncle Rex by the arm. "Oh. Hey, I'm sorry. I was aiming at…"

But Uncle Rex jerked back before she could finish. "Don't touch me!"

"Look, I'm really sorry. I didn't mean to get you dirty," the rose insisted. She kept trying to take Rex Oliver's arm and apologize and he kept backing away from her.

"Don't touch me. Don't touch me," he kept saying, while trying to brush the wet dirt off his robe.

The dandelion came over and stood behind Uncle Rex so he

84

couldn't back up. "Say, buddy," she said. "Didn't you hear my friend? She's trying to apologize to you."

It startled Uncle Rex and he whirled around in surprise, accidentally catching the dandelion with his willow branch. The dandelion reached into her pot, retrieved a handful of wet dirt and deliberately threw it on Uncle Rex. Then the rose threw dirt at the dandelion, only Uncle Rex was in the way, and it hit him instead. "DON'T HIT ME!" he screamed. I could tell he was getting frightened. He tried to shield his face with his arms, but the potted plants just kept throwing more and more dirt at each other and it kept hitting him. Finally, he lashed out with his arms, swinging the crucifix and willow branch around in big wide circles to keep the potted plants away from him.

Mitchell and I were always taught that two against one is never fun, so I started hitting one of the potted plants with my magic wand. "Let's get 'em, Mitchell," I yelled to Mitchell. I knew he'd help me. People were screaming and Uncle Rex was yelling and dirt was getting all over everybody.

A bunch of Meadowgreen security guards rushed over. A couple of them grabbed the rose and her friend and two of them grabbed Uncle Rex to stop his swinging. He screamed again not to touch him, and I ran up beside him.

"You'd better not touch him," I yelled at the security guards, "'cause he's the Messiah and he's real sensitive."

"Oh, he is, is he?" one of them said. He was being sarcastic, and I didn't like it. "Well, Mr. Messiah, why don't you just come with us this way," and they started to take him out of the ballroom.

"Just a minute," said a voice. "This man is my nephew. Please let me talk to him." It was Uncle Gott.

The security guards let Rex Oliver go, but not before Mitchell kicked one of them in the shins. We both started talking to Uncle Gott about how the potted plants started it and it wasn't our fault and we were just defending ourselves and helping Uncle Rex. Uncle Gott wasn't listening to us. He was talking softly to Rex Oliver, only I noticed he didn't touch him.

"You know, Rex Oliver, that's certainly an interesting costume you're wearing. Did you design it yourself? That's very creative. I can't remember when I've seen a more creative costume. We're all very proud to have such a creative person in the family. Would you like to come with me to find a private bathroom so you can clean up a little? I think I know where one is. You'll be looking good as new in no time. And have you had any refreshments yet? Why don't we clean up first and then go get us something to eat."

It was one of the only times Uncle Gott didn't sound like church. Rex Oliver's eyes slowly started to focus on Uncle Gott, but he was very silent.

"Hey Uncle Rex, I kicked one of those security guards for ya," said Mitchell. "I wasn't gonna let him hurt you. I would have kicked the other one too, real hard, if Uncle Gott hadn't come along."

Before anyone could say another word, the band broke into "Home on the Range," the Kansas state song.

Oh give me a home, where the buffalo roam,
Where the deer, and the antelope play...

We tried to talk above the noise, but people started singing with the band because everybody liked "Home on The Range." Uncle Gott motioned for us to follow him. I saw Mitchell reach up and take Rex Oliver's hand and lead him after Uncle Gott. I guess it was okay if Mitchell touched him.

We went through some closed doors, down a hallway, and turned the corner into a different hallway. "Home on The Range" grew dimmer the farther we went. We stopped in front of a door marked *Toilet*.

"Who wants to go first?" asked Uncle Gott. But before we could answer he looked at me and said, "Melody, why don't you go clean up a little bit. You've got mud on your face and on your overalls." I hadn't noticed how dirty I had become in all the commotion.

I took my time in the bathroom, even washing my gold star where it got muddy beating on the potted plant. When I came out, Uncle Gott said, "Okay, Mitchell, it's your turn. Hey Rex, he's pretty little. Why don't you go in and help him..."

"I am not..." Mitchell started to say, but Uncle Gott grabbed his shoulder and squeezed hard while he said, "And then maybe Mitchell can give you a hand getting the mud off your robe. What do you say, fellahs? Mitchell? Rex?" Uncle Gott gestured with his arm to the open bathroom door.

"Okay," said Mitchell, looking at Uncle Gott. Then he turned to Rex Oliver. "Come on, Uncle Rex." They walked together into the bathroom.

I could hear, *where seldom is heard, a discouraging word,* being sung from the ballroom.

"Is he gonna be all right, Uncle Gott?" I asked. Before he could answer, I noticed something different about Uncle Gott.

"Hey!" I said. "You're wearing a tuxedo. Are you and Vivian gonna get..." And then I remembered it was supposed to be a surprise, so I said, "Are you and Vivian gonna make any speeches or anything, you know, about the party?" Uncle Gott just sighed and said yes. Then he reached into his pocket for his handkerchief and mopped his head.

"Well, you look real nice," I told him.

"Thank you, Melody," he replied.

"You're welcome," I said.

After that, nobody talked for a while. We could hear the water running inside the bathroom and we could faintly hear "Your Cheatin' Heart" from the band. It sounded lively out in the ballroom. I wondered if we were going to be able to stay and enjoy it.

"Gottfried, oh Gottfried. There you are. I've been looking all over for you. There's a disturbance outside. Please come quickly." It was Vivian. I had to look hard to be sure, because she was covered with sequins. She looked like a real Cinderella would look if she were covered with sequins. I wondered if she'd parked a pumpkin coach out in the parking lot.

Vivian ran up to Uncle Gott, grabbed his arm and said, "Come quickly. There's a group of people saying hateful things outside the entrance."

"Do they look like plants?" I ventured.

Vivian looked down and saw me for the first time. "Uh, no, Melody. Plants? No, dear, they're people with horrible hateful signs. Oh, Gottfried, please come quickly."

Uncle Gott looked at the closed bathroom door and then at Vivian who was pulling him up the hallway by his arm.

"Melody," he yelled, "keep an eye on them. I'll be right back."

I waited for a long time, but nobody came out. So I knocked on the bathroom door. "Hey, you guys," I told them. "You taking up homesteading in there? Come on out. We're missing all the fun."

Pretty soon the water shut off and the door opened. Mitchell and Uncle Rex looked pretty soggy, but most of the mud was gone.

"We're missing the fun," I repeated. "There's some people being hateful outside on the sidewalk. Let's go watch."

The band was cranking out something real twangy that I didn't recognize, but nobody was listening. Everybody was pushing and shoving, trying to look into the driveway. I was pushing too and wasn't getting very far, but then I smelled some of that wet mold smell from Uncle Rex and I started sneezing. I get attacks of the sneezes sometimes and I just sneeze and sneeze. I guess that was what happened. I was sneezing so much I couldn't see where I was going, but I think I sneezed my way through the crowd. Pretty soon I wasn't pushing against anybody anymore.

When I looked up, I was outside in the drizzle. There on the sidewalk were a dozen people marching back and forth carrying signs. There was a tall man, a woman, and about seven or eight children. All had frizzy hair. There were also several other adults with regular hair.

I looked at the people and then at the signs. They each said something different. "Crazy Isn't Christian." "Meadowgreen Possessed by The Devil." "House of Unclean Spirits." "God Hates

Lunatics." "Satan Loves Insanity." And there were drawings of the devil with horns and pitchfork. This didn't seem like Halloween stuff, though.

When I stopped looking at the signs, I saw a girl about my age coming my way on her march around the sidewalk. Her sign said: "Nuts Forfeit Salvation. Nuts Equals Damnation." I just watched as she got closer and closer. I could see she didn't have any kind of costume on for Halloween, but her face had on the same look as Mother's. I looked again and saw she had on lipstick, and eye shadow, and nail polish on her fingernails. And I looked at the grown-up woman and at all the other little girls and saw they were all made up like that. They all looked like Avon faces.

"Hey!" I said to the girl coming toward me. "You're one of those despicable Wades. You better give my mother's Avon satchel back or I'll…" I never got to finish the sentence because I sneezed. The drizzle wasn't doing me any good.

I looked up and saw the tall frizzy-haired man carrying the "God Hates Lunatics" sign marching toward me.

"What seed of the devil are you?" he squeaked. I saw the gray eyes, the bottomless gray snake eyes my Mother had mentioned, and I felt paralyzed by them too. I felt like he was a frizzy-haired cobra, and I was just a little bird, a little bird in the drizzle with the sneezes. I sneezed. I sneezed all over him. I couldn't help it.

"No!" a voice screamed from the crowd. "Leave her alone, Uncle Earl. Let her be." It was Rex Oliver who was pushing his way to the front of the crowd with Mitchell.

Earl Wade lowered his sign from over his head. I think he'd been about to strike me with it. He turned at the sound of his grown nephew's voice. "Lunatic," he squeaked at Rex Oliver with a shout. "Crazy murdering lunatic. Be cast into the fires of damnation!"

"Look at the crazy lunatic," he told the crowd, pointing to Rex Oliver. "Purge this madness from your soul. Wipe out the evil from among you. Deliver us from this INSANITY!" He began to giggle, "Hee, hee, hee, hee, hee."

Then he turned back to Rex Oliver and started to walk up to him. I saw Rex Oliver tremble, but he held his ground. Mitchell was trembling too.

"You murdered her, didn't you?" said Earl.

Uncle Rex was shaking his head, no, no, no.

"You took a knife, and you murdered my sister because you're just plain crazy, aren't you boy? Confess! Confess in the name of Jesus! Beware of the devil within you! The devil has filled you with unclean spirits and stolen your soul unto hell! BE GONE, DEVIL! BE GONE!" He squeaked at the top of his voice.

Uncle Rex was paralyzed by those snake eyes too, but he kept shaking his head no, no, no. Just when Earl was almost up to him, Rex Oliver gave a hideous sound, a sound that wasn't even human, and ran down the sidewalk and around the corner of the building.

"Uncle Rex, wait," I screamed and started after him. Suddenly, I was grabbed by the back of my overalls and a familiar figure in black pushed me behind her. It was Mother.

"Look what you've done," she shouted to Earl Wade. "How dare you pick on a child with your nasty hateful attitude. You should be ashamed of yourself." That was about as harsh as Mother could get, even when she was worked up.

"Mother, they took your satchel," I piped up, feeling braver now that Mother was shielding me. "Look at them wearing your Avon." I sneezed a few more times. I couldn't help it.

Mother looked. Sure enough, just then the older lady came around again, and Mother saw she wasn't plain Mrs. Wade anymore, she had on the Avon face. Mother looked even more horrified, then angry, then she whirled and whacked Mrs. Wade on the bottom with her broom.

Then all the Wades, big and little, ran over and started to hit at Mother with their picket signs. Of course she had to hit back with her broom. So I started hitting anybody I could with my magic wand and kicking and screaming. I think some people from the crowd and some security guards might have been part of the whole thing too. I hit somebody so hard my gold star popped off and bounced into the street.

There were sirens wailing louder and louder. Mitchell came running over and the next thing I knew, Mother, Mitchell, and I were being escorted to a police car. I could see Uncle Gott in his tuxedo, Dad in his Alvin the Chipmunk suit, and Vivian in her sequined Cinderella costume talking to a group of police and pointing to us, then to another police car with the adult Wades inside. Edith Kliban, dressed as Annie Oakley, stood next to Vivian. There were lots of police cars there with lights flashing and it looked like everybody who had gone to the Ball was standing on the sidewalk in the drizzle watching the live entertainment we had provided. I couldn't hear the band playing anymore. I wondered if they were out here watching us too.

Mother was cuddling Mitchell and me on either side of her in the back seat of the police car. Mitchell's astronaut box was really soggy and didn't fit very well in the back seat, so he finally took it off. It crowded us a lot though. The policeman had put Mother's broom in the front seat where we couldn't get it. We sat there waiting and I wondered where my gold star was now.

"Are we gonna get handcuffed, like in *Dragnet*?" Mitchell inquired. He looked worried. We were real *Dragnet* fans at our house and loved all the television police shows.

"I doubt it," Mother sighed. "But if anybody gets handcuffed it'll be me, not you kids."

"I hope we come here next year too," I told Mitchell. "This Ball business is a lot more exciting than trick-or-treating. I haven't been in two fights in one day for a long time."

I don't think Mother heard me for a while. But then she looked at me and said, "*Two* fights? You mean you were in another one?"

So, Mitchell and I explained about the potted plants throwing dirt and getting it on us and Uncle Gott saving us from the security guards.

"Oh no," Mother said. "I hope your dad doesn't get fired over this. Who were those people? Do you know? The potted plants, I mean."

"I don't know," I said. "It was just two women dressed up as potted plants."

We waited and waited and then a policeman came running up to the main group of police and pointed around the side of the building where Uncle Rex had run. We heard somebody say call an ambulance and the first policeman say it's too late. All of a sudden, I got real worried for Uncle Rex. I hadn't seen him for a long time.

Finally, a policeman opened the car door and told us that Dr. Kliban said to let us go, even though the Reverend Earl Wade wanted to press charges against Mother for assault with a deadly weapon. The policeman chuckled and said, "I told him, 'Sir, a broom used as part of a Halloween costume is probably not gonna be considered a deadly weapon by most any court in Kansas.' But just in case, lady," he looked at Mother, "stay off that broom."

Mother thanked him and looked around for Dad and Uncle Gott. In spite of the excitement, or maybe because of it, Mitchell and I were getting pretty tired. We were ready to go home. I knew we had to find Uncle Rex first, though.

Dad came up and put his arm around Mother and tousled our hair one at a time. I wondered if Harmony had seen any of the evening's events. We still hadn't seen her. Dad told us Shep had let the band members go because the Ball had come to a screeching halt. "Let's go home," he said.

"Just a minute, Alex." Uncle Gott came striding over from where he'd been talking to a group of policemen. "I think you'd better call Dewey and get him down here right away. There's been an accident. A woman dressed as a plant was found with her skull bashed in behind the building over there. I'm afraid she's dead. Rex Oliver's crucifix was what did the bashing."

"What?" said Dad.

"Oh my God," exclaimed Mother. "Where's Rex Oliver now?"

"That's just it, Louise. We can't find him. You know how he likes to hide when he gets scared. I thought maybe Dewey could help look for him. The police are looking mighty hard for him too. Why don't you and the kids go on home. We'll let you know if anything happens."

Mitchell started crying when we heard about the dead plant lady and Uncle Rex being missing. It takes a lot to make Mitchell cry, but now I noticed he looked really scared.

"Let's go home, kids," said Mother. She looked worried too. All at once I got real scared. Scared for me, and scared for Mitchell, but mostly scared for Uncle Rex Oliver. He was real sensitive, after all, and having the police after him must have been terrifying. For the first time in my life, the blood in Halloween was real.

November to December 1958

The Hunt For Rex Oliver

For once, Vivian was not able to completely squelch the newspaper story about the disastrous Meadowgreen Ball. Too many prominent citizens had been present and had seen the whole thing. The next day, the Sunday edition of *The Topeka Daily Capital* ran a small article on the fact that a woman, whose name was not released, had been found dead on fairground property at the same time as the Meadowgreen Ball. Police were investigating, was all it said. At least it didn't mention Rex Oliver.

Dad came home about noon. He took off the Alvin costume and said that he, Dewey, Uncle Gott, and the Police Department had searched high and low all over the fairgrounds in all the buildings and barns, all the closets and back rooms, and even the adjoining neighborhood. But there was no sign of Rex Oliver. "You'd think it wouldn't be too hard to spot a red-headed guy dressed up as the Messiah, would you," he said. "I was just hoping Dewey and I would find him before the police do."

"I know how to find him," said Mitchell, who was eating a peanut butter and jelly sandwich. Mother hadn't felt like cooking a Sunday dinner with all the activity and we certainly hadn't gone to church.

"How?" asked Dad. It hadn't occurred to him to ask a small boy how to find a somewhat larger boy in a grownup's body.

He had to wait for his answer until Mitchell worked the peanut butter off the roof of his mouth. "Let Maynard and Virgil find him," said Mitchell. "They know him better than anybody and they can track anything that moves."

Dad was silent a moment while he rolled this idea over in his mind. Then he started nodding his head and finally he said, "Well, son, you may be right. I guess it's worth a shot."

He called Dewey at the farm and told him Mitchell's idea, then reported back to us.

"Dewey said since Maynard and Virgil don't have a phone he'll drive up to the reservation and ask them to help," Dad relayed. "Although he said he's never needed them this late in the year before and doesn't know if they even stay around Kansas over the winter. I told him I doubted they'd saved enough for a tropical vacation on the wages he pays them." Dad had been up all night.

Right away, Mitchell and I were determined to go too. We'd never been to the Shuckahoosee's, although Dad had driven us around the Potawatomi Reservation once for fun. Dad and Mother said no, we couldn't go, especially since my cold was not getting any better after being out on the rainy sidewalk last night.

"But Mitchell understands Rex Oliver in a special way," I said. "And Mitchell won't go unless I get to go too." At least that's what I was hoping. Mitchell nodded at me, and we both looked hopefully at Dad.

"Oh, all right," said Dad. I think he was too tired to argue. So we decided we'd pick up Dewey and all go to the reservation together while Mother stayed with Grandma Dale. Harmony was still at the Knotts and would miss her big chance to see where Virgil and Maynard lived.

The Potawatomi Indian Reservation was about twenty miles north of Topeka. It was easy to tell when we got there because the roads suddenly turned to gravel, or in some cases just plain dirt. Dad said the Indians did their own road work and the state and federal government couldn't tell them how to run their land.

We drove past a few farmhouses, mostly very old looking buildings or occasionally a trailer house. There were miles and miles of unbroken land in between and nothing else. Much of the land didn't even look like it was farmed. It just looked neglected and sad. Of course, it was almost winter and everything in Kansas was soggy right now from so much rain.

Dewey knew where the Shuckahoosees lived so he gave Dad

directions. Once we almost got the DeSoto stuck in the mud, but Dad managed to get us going again.

As it turned out, Maynard and Virgil lived side by side in a rather dilapidated house and a more reasonable looking mobile home. Virgil, the son, lived by himself in the trailer. When we got there, we didn't pull off the road and into the yard for two reasons—the driveway was nothing but deep muddy ruts, and several large barking dogs made it clear what kind of welcome we could expect if we left the car. That was nothing unusual for the country though, so Dad honked the horn to see who was home.

Pretty soon Virgil opened the door of the trailer. He saw who it was, called the dogs off, and picked his way through the mud over to our car.

"Hello, Mr. Freedrich, Mr. Oots," he said, acting not the least bit surprised to find a blue DeSoto full of white people in the middle of a muddy Indian reservation. "Hi, kids. Please come on in." Virgil was always polite too. I was ready to go in. I wanted to see their bows and arrows and eagle feathers. But the invitation made Dewey uncomfortable.

"Actually, Virgil, this ain't a social visit. I came because I need your help. My boy's in trouble."

I felt real bad for Dewey then. He'd been up all night too and had a lot on his mind.

"What's the matter, Mr. Oots?" asked Virgil.

About that time, the door to the main house opened and out came Maynard. He looked like he hadn't been out of the house for several weeks and smelled like maybe some of the dogs had been in there with him. Maynard was a large man anyway, but now he looked like he'd put on a few pounds.

"Hello, Maynard," we all said. Maynard nodded hello. He was going to let Virgil do the talking, as he usually did, but he seemed curious about our visit.

"Boys," began Dewey. He always called the Indians "boys." "Last night Rex Oliver was at the fairgrounds at a Halloween party.

And a woman got murdered and the police think maybe Rex Oliver did it. Now, we don't know that and nobody saw anything. But we can't find him. We've been looking all night and we wondered, that is, I hate to bother you fellas, but since you and your dad are friends with Rex Oliver, I'd be much obliged if you could lend us a hand."

"I told 'em what good trackers you are," added Mitchell.

Virgil looked at Mitchell. Then he looked at the sky. "It's been raining all night," he said. Then he looked at Maynard, who nodded. Virgil looked back at Dewey. "Mr. Oots, we will do what we can. But, we'll need a ride into town. Our car's been stuck in the driveway for a week."

"That's no problem," said Dad.

We waited for the Indians to get their things. Mitchell and I now had to share the back seat with them on the ride back to town. I wondered if we'd have to keep the windows down all the way to Topeka because of Maynard's hygiene, which with the rain and Dewey spitting tobacco out his driver's side front window, could be a problem. But when Maynard came back a few minutes later he had cleaned up considerably.

On the drive back, Dad and Dewey explained the circumstances. Mitchell and I got to explain the part about the potted plant fight because we were there when it happened. Then we explained about Earl Wade scaring Uncle Rex and him running off and about Mother and her broom and the police just like *Dragnet*.

"Sounds like quite an evening," Virgil said.

When we got to the fairgrounds, we found it still taken over by the police. Dad knew quite a few of the policemen and motioned for one of the captains to come over.

"Larry," Dad called him by name, "having any luck?"

Captain Larry looked in the car, saw Dad, Dewey, two kids, and two Indians and just shook his head. "Not a bit," he replied. "The suspect seems to have covered his tracks pretty well." That made me shudder. I never for a moment considered Rex Oliver to be "a suspect," which was what the bad guys on police shows were, so to hear him referred to that way was horrifying.

"Well, that's why I'm here, Larry," Dad continued. "This here is Maynard and Virgil Shuckahoosee," he indicated toward the back seat. "They're hired hands for my family and you'll never find a pair of better trackers. How 'bout giving them a chance to find our runaway?" He didn't have to say they were Indians. Anybody could tell that by looking at them. And he didn't call Rex Oliver "a suspect."

Captain Larry rubbed his chin while he thought about it. Evidently, he had been up all night too and was thinking slowly. He turned and looked at all the police cars spread out around the fairgrounds, then finally frowned and shrugged his shoulders.

"Heck, why not," he said. "At this point we could use some fresh men. You fellas understand what we're looking for?" he said to Maynard and Virgil as they got out of the car.

"Yes, officer," said Virgil carefully. "Mr. Freedrich explained it to us very well."

"Well, you let me know if you come across the suspect. Don't try to apprehend him yourself, you hear?"

"Yes, sir," answered Virgil. He continued very respectfully, "Uh—Mr. Freedrich, we would appreciate it if Mitchell and Melody could come with us to walk us through again everything that happened last night."

"Well, okay," Dad said. "Dewey and I need some rest anyway. We'll get a cup of coffee and wait for you back in the car."

Virgil asked us to tell him everything about that night, starting from when we picked up Rex Oliver at the farm. Virgil asked about Rex Oliver's costume and even asked if he smelled like mold. I said I had noticed just a whiff, and that Mother had rolled her car window down on the ride to town. Mother had the best nose in the county, Dad always said. I also remembered how the moldy smell had made me sneeze.

We told Virgil about the mix-up with the St. Bernard costume and the refreshments and the fight with the two potted plants. Virgil would ask us some questions from time to time, but otherwise let us continue.

He wanted us to show him where the fight was, then the bathroom where we washed up, then where the Wades scared off Uncle Rex. So we did. After that we didn't know any more.

"Okay kids," said Virgil when we were all talked out. "Thanks a lot."

"Can we come with you?" Mitchell asked. After all, it was his idea to bring Maynard and Virgil here.

"I appreciate the offer," said Virgil, "but we work best alone."

I saw Maynard looking up at the sky and testing the wind, then he held his head at an angle like he was listening real hard for something. He listened and listened until I started listening too, but I couldn't hear anything except the traffic noises from the street. Then Maynard started walking around the corner of the building where we'd last seen Rex Oliver. He hadn't said a word the whole time.

Mitchell and I walked back to the car. Dewey and Dad were both asleep, Dad in front and Dewey in back.

"Hey, Mitchell," I whispered, "why don't we go look for Uncle Rex on our own?"

"You think we'd get in trouble?" Mitchell wondered.

"The police already let us go last night, dummy, because we're not criminals."

"I'm not worried about the police, dummy," Mitchell said, but I couldn't think of any other reason for him to be so reluctant.

"Well, since you're too afraid, I'll go by myself," I said, using the tone I'd frequently heard Harmony use. Of course then Mitchell had to come.

We wanted to stay out of the policemen's way, so we decided to skip the Agriculture Hall, the Grandstand, and the Midway, and go to the Livestock Barns at the far side of the compound. I figured it would remind Uncle Rex of the farm, plus I always liked the feeling I got there. It reminded me of the farm too and of all the animals that had been well cared for and brought to the fair healthy and clean and shiny, proudly shown to the judges and the other farmers. Since we'd lived in town our whole lives we'd never belonged to the 4-H, but we always came to watch the judging during the fair.

Now as Mitchell and I walked through the sheep barn we decided to make a plan for finding Uncle Rex.

"After we find Uncle Rex," I said, "we'll hide him somewhere so the police won't get him and we'll bring him food every day."

"I don't know," said Mitchell. "We'd have to get a lot of food out of the house. I bet Janie Bryant would see and tell on us. She sees everything."

"Yeah," I agreed. "Well, what if we buy Uncle Rex a ticket to Mexico? On TV, people running from the cops are always trying to make it to Mexico. If both of us cashed in our savings bonds booklets, we'd have almost $20, enough to get Uncle Rex to the border. Then he'd have to swim for it."

We were just discussing if Uncle Rex knew how to speak Mexican when I felt something tap me on the shoulder. I turned around but there was nothing there. When I turned back around, I saw something on the ground, half hidden in the hay. It was the gold star from my magic wand. I didn't know which direction it had come from, but I knew it came from Rex Oliver. In a way, this really was a sign from God, or at least from the Messiah.

"Uncle Rex," we whispered. "Uncle Rex, where are you? We're alone. It's safe to come out. Uncle Rex? Please come out Uncle Rex."

We sat down in the barn on some straw, right in the middle of the aisle and waited. Even with my cold I could still smell those lingering barnyard odors. I loved those smells because I loved the animals that made them. But sometimes they made me SNEEZE! I got overcome all at once by another attack of the sneezes. Mitchell started slapping me on the back real hard, which made me want to tickle him unmercifully, except I was sneezing too hard to grab him.

After about fifty-two sneezes and nearly that many slaps, I looked up and there stood Uncle Rex. He was very dirty, wet, and cold, and his terrified eyes darted back and forth, scanning the barn. But he had come out.

"Uncle Rex," Mitchell threw his arms around him, which came to about Rex Oliver's waist, and began to bawl. I got one whiff of Uncle Rex and started sneezing again. Between Mitchell's crying and my sneezing, we were barely paying attention to Uncle Rex. I think that's what began to calm him down. We were the only ones who didn't want something from him. We just wanted him to be okay.

"I didn't do anything wrong," Uncle Rex finally said, heavily. "But I sure am hungry."

We didn't have any food on us, so before we searched for some, we all sat down and told Uncle Rex our plan for getting him to Mexico. "Can you speak Mexican, Uncle Rex?" Mitchell asked.

"Just a few words in Oakland."

I was starting to get hungry too about then. It was almost supper time.

From somewhere in the shadows, I saw Virgil and Maynard stand up very gently. I don't know how long they had been watching us.

"Rex Oliver," called Virgil softly. "It's okay, my friend. I brought you some food."

Virgil and Maynard slowly walked up to where we were sitting. Maynard reached under his extra-large shirt and pulled out a knitted bag of some kind with food in it. I wondered if he kept food under his shirt most of the time.

The Indians sat and shared with us Maynard's food, which turned out to be cold chili dogs. I wondered if the smell of all those chili dogs under Maynard's shirt was what we'd noticed earlier at the reservation. I didn't want to think about that too hard. As soon as someone would finish one chili dog Maynard would hand them another one. We all ate a lot of chili dogs. Uncle Rex began to look a little better, but Mitchell looked like he felt queasy. Finally, Virgil looked at the ground and said, "How can I help you, my friend?" to Rex Oliver.

"Uncle Earl thinks I'm crazy," said Rex Oliver. "He wants everyone else to think I'm crazy too, but I'm not. I'm not a murderer either. I didn't kill Momma. I swear I didn't kill her."

"I know you didn't," said Virgil. "And I know you're not crazy.

Why don't we go tell the police that. I'll stay with you, I promise. Maynard too." Maynard nodded his agreement. It occurred to me I had never heard Maynard speak.

"The police know I didn't kill Momma. They already know. Have they changed their minds?"

Virgil was quiet for a while. Then he asked, still looking at the ground, "Why did you run away last night, Rex Oliver? Did anything happen that made you want to run away?"

"My Uncle Earl, he says I'm the devil. But I'm afraid of *him*. I'm afraid when he looks at me and when he comes near me, because I think he's—he's gonna hurt me bad."

"We won't let him hurt you, Rex Oliver," Virgil said. "You have lots of friends and people who love you and we'll never let Earl Wade hurt you. Do you believe me?" Virgil did a lot of talking for an Indian.

"Sometimes I believe you," said Rex Oliver. "But sometimes I get afraid."

"I know," said Virgil. "It's okay to be afraid. Only a stupid man is never afraid and you're far from stupid. So—why did you run away last night?"

"I got afraid, and I ran, and after that I don't remember," said Rex Oliver.

"Do you remember what happened to your crucifix?" asked Virgil.

"Crucifix?" Uncle Rex stared down at his hands and looked puzzled. "I don't know. I guess I must have lost it. Do you know where it is?"

"I believe the police have it," said Virgil. "They want to ask you some questions about it."

"They do?" Rex Oliver thought a long time about that and finally said, "Do they think I did something bad, Virgil?"

"They're not sure, Rex. A woman died last night, a woman you and the kids here had an argument with. The police just want to ask you some questions."

"How did she die?" Rex Oliver whispered. He had turned almost as white as his messiah robe.

"She was struck on the head with your crucifix," said Virgil.

Rex Oliver almost relaxed. "But she didn't cut her wrists?" he asked.

"No," said Virgil, understanding. "No, she didn't cut her wrists."

"I didn't kill nobody," said Uncle Rex. "And I'm not crazy. Say..." He had a new thought. "Do they want to put me in the State Hospital again?"

"Nobody's said anything about that," said Virgil. "I don't think that's gonna happen."

"She didn't cut her wrists," repeated Rex Oliver. "Well. Thank you for the chili dogs. Will you come with me, Virgil, and you too, Maynard, and Mitchell and Melody? I'm not crazy, you know."

"We know," said Virgil. "We'll all come with you."

Mitchell, who had kept still during the whole conversation, made a strange noise, tried to rise, then threw up. The cold chili dogs on top of peanut butter and jelly had been too much for him, I guess. I should have known, because Mitchell always did have a delicate stomach.

Well, I figured, the police can probably find us now by smell alone. All they have to do is hunt for a moldy messiah, a chili dog Indian, and a little kid with vomit all over him. It was enough to make me queasy too.

I guess Virgil had the same thought, because he stood up quickly and told Mitchell to come with him to find a bathroom. Maynard and I and Uncle Rex moved away from the scene of Mitchell's accident but didn't speak.

"Yuck," I finally said.

When Rex Oliver surrendered to the police he was questioned at length about his activities the night of the murder. He said he couldn't remember anything, but that he never killed nobody.

Dewey and Dad, Virgil and Maynard, and Mitchell and I had followed the police and Rex Oliver downtown to the police station. Once inside, there was a lot of paperwork that had to be filled out, though the police hadn't yet decided whether to charge Rex Oliver with murder. We all stayed as close to him as we could, until finally the police had to take him away. Then we waved goodbye again, just like we always did when he was holed up in the cave on the farm. This time he wouldn't get to come out on his own. I felt really bad for him and I know Mitchell did too.

Behind me I heard Virgil discreetly clear his throat. "Excuse me, Mr. Oots," he addressed Dewey. "Have you given any thought to retaining counsel for Rex Oliver?" I didn't know what he meant. Virgil usually talked like an Indian and didn't say too much or use big words.

"Huh?" said Dewey.

"I mean, do you have a lawyer in mind you'd like to hire to help Rex Oliver through all this?" said Virgil.

"Well—no," said Dewey. "I haven't given it any thought."

"Then perhaps I could offer my services as legal counsel, at no charge of course, to my friend Rex Oliver."

"Huh?" said Dewey again. "Hell, Virgil, you ain't no lawyer." It wasn't like Dewey to swear. He was really rattled.

"Actually Mr. Oots, I am," replied Virgil.

This time we all said "Huh?" Virgil and his dad had worked as field hands for Grandma Dale eight months of every year for the last twelve years. If either of them had a life outside of that it was news to us.

"As I'm sure you're aware, Warshburn University has an excellent law school," said Virgil. Washburn was Topeka's local university, though I doubt Dewey, like the rest of us, paid it much attention. Certainly not the law school.

"It's worked out well, because my job on the farm has allowed me to go part-time evenings and full-time winter classes now for several years. I passed my bar examination in July. That means I can practice law anywhere in Kansas."

None of us knew what to say. Finally, Virgil spoke what was on everybody's mind.

"I guess you're surprised to see an Indian go to college, let alone graduate from law school. I can understand. But the tribal council voted to send me to law school. I'll be working for them on some legal affairs part-time and, who knows, maybe I'll run for a tribal office someday."

"Does that mean you'll be chief?" asked Mitchell. He was the only one who had recovered from what Virgil had just told us.

"Sorta like that," Virgil replied.

"Well, uh, congratulations, Virgil," Dewey said and shot Maynard a dirty look for keeping this secret. "I guess everybody is just real proud of you."

"Yeah, Virgil," agreed Dad.

"So anyway, Mr. Oots," Virgil continued, "if you have no objections, I'd like to serve as Rex Oliver's lawyer."

"Well, uh, I don't know, Virgil. I..." Dewey was stuttering around. He looked up again and saw Maynard looking at him. Maynard nodded a very slow nod.

"All right, Virgil. You got the job." Dewey was worried, I could tell, but he was a man of his word.

"Thank you, sir," said Virgil. "You won't be sorry."

The Lesbian Thespian
Margarine Heiress

The dead woman's name was Brenda Messina. We heard the scoop on her later that same day from another second-hand source, our Uncle Billy Glenn. Most people thought Glenn was his middle name, like Billy Bob or Billy Joe. But it was really his last name. Everybody just got in the habit of calling him Billy Glenn and it stuck. He was Mother's only brother, a tall, skinny fireman with many friends on the police force, which was how he'd gotten the information he was now sharing. He was also Catholic, given to smoking, drinking, cussing, card playing, and buying a new Thunderbird every year, things good Methodists never did. Instead of taking Mitchell and me to places like the zoo, he had once driven us in his new car out past Forbes Air Force Base, where he pointed out every tavern, palm reader, and strip joint along Topeka Boulevard. We didn't get to go in any of them, though.

"Brenda was a twenty-eight-year-old socialite and margarine heiress from Newport, Rhode Island," Uncle Billy Glenn began after he'd settled into an easy chair and got Mother to bring him a cold drink. "She was also an outpatient at Meadowgreen. What a surprise." He said this sarcastically. Dad coughed. After all, he did work at Meadowgreen and felt he should be loyal.

"Brenda came to Topeka and Meadowgreen six months ago for treatment of some confidential condition that even the police aren't privy to. Eventually she got a little better, to the point where they let her out of lockup and let her rent an apartment. Well," he continued, "she took up with Topeka's theater crowd and began 'entertaining,' if you know what I mean, a lot of the women. Guess that makes her sort of a 'lesbian thespian.'"

"What's a les…?" Mitchell started to ask.

"BILLY GLENN!" Mother screamed and jumped up. I thought for a minute she was going to get violent, which would have been a first for Mother. "Don't you EVER use that word in this house again! Look what you've done." Mother indicated how Mitchell and I were eagerly following the exchange.

I looked at Mitchell and we exchanged a look that meant we'd find out from Harmony later about that word. It was obvious the adults were telling secrets again.

"Billy Glenn, you've got to promise you'll watch your language," Mother said. "We're very careful about what the children might pick up."

"Maybe you kids should go in the other room," Dad said to us.

"NO," we said in unison. "We want to hear about the dead woman," I complained.

"Yeah," agreed Mitchell.

"I don't think so," said Mother. "This is getting a little too graphic. Go play in the other room."

Mitchell and I fussed and groaned, but it was no use. We got sent to Mitchell's room. What Mother and Dad didn't know, was that we'd discovered some time ago that we could put our ear to the heating vent and hear everything that went on in the living room if people there talked in a normal voice, but only when the furnace wasn't blowing. When the furnace came on, we couldn't hear a thing, plus your ear got too hot to get close.

Mitchell and I crowded around the heat vent and sure enough, we could hear Uncle Billy Glenn real clear. He felt he could talk freely now that we were gone.

"Brenda's artistic tendencies and choice of friends apparently made her a little hard to get along with," he was saying. "Also, she liked to eat dirt."

"Huh?" whispered Mitchell to me. He only ate dirt when I made mud pies, but I hadn't done that for several years.

"That's why she was dressed as a plant," I whispered. "She brought her own food."

"Oh," said Mitchell, nodding in agreement.

"I don't know what that has to do with anything," Billy Glenn continued unaware of the commentary in the next room, "except the police interviewed some of her neighbors and discovered this interesting side of Brenda's personality. I'll bet she was real happy in Kansas," he reflected, "'cause we got some of the best dirt in the country.

"But what has the police really worried," he said, "are Brenda's heavyweight relatives."

"What do you mean?" Dad asked, which of course was what Billy Glenn had been waiting on.

"It seems that Brenda's mother is some big mafia princess from Providence who married this margarine king from Newport. Little Brenda darling was their only child, which might explain a few things. Anyway, rumor has it that some pretty tough characters are coming to Topeka to seek a little justice of their own."

"What's mafia?" Mitchell whispered to me. "Is that a country like France? Is her mother a princess from France?"

"No," I whispered back. "Well, I don't know." Sometimes Mitchell asked too many questions. "We'll check with Harmony later."

"Say, Louise," Uncle Billy Glenn started again, "doesn't your friend across the street know J. Edgar Hoover?"

"You mean Janie?" Mother said. "Well, 'know' might be too strong a word for it, but J. Edgar ought to be aware of Janie by now, as many letters as she's written him."

"Maybe she ought to write him about this situation," said Uncle Billy Glenn.

"Why did Brenda Messina get hit on the head?" Mother was sure there was more to this topic.

"Well, I don't know," said Billy Glenn. "That's what the police are trying to find out."

"Was she the woman dressed as a rose or as the dandelion?" Dad asked. I'd wondered about that too. I wasn't sure if she was the one who tried to apologize to Uncle Rex or the other one who started throwing dirt on him.

"Well now, I don't know that either," Uncle Billy Glenn said. He never liked questions he didn't know the answers to.

"Are the police sure it's Rex Oliver's crucifix they found?" Dad asked.

I hadn't thought of that. Maybe there had been more than one crucifix at the ball that night, although I didn't remember seeing any others. It wasn't like crucifixes were normal accessories for people's Halloween costumes.

"Yeah, Alex, the police already checked that one out. It's Rex's all right." He was happy with Dad for asking something he knew the answer to. "The P.D. thinks Rex Oliver could have murdered Brenda with the crucifix, or somebody could have found it in the bathroom where Rex and the kids went to warsh up. Maybe this person picked it up to give it back to Rex, or maybe they knew it was his and wanted to frame him for the murder."

"Frame him?" asked Mother. "Why would anybody want to do that?"

"Maybe because of his history of, uh, problems," Billy Glenn replied. "Who knows? The police are looking at all the angles. They'll schedule a formal inquest to see if they can get to the bottom of it all. It's not like a trial, of course. It's to determine all the facts surrounding Brenda's suspicious death. But depending on those results, it could lead to a trial. Boy, I'll bet there are some nervous officials over at Meadowgreen." He laughed at the thought.

Since that was all he knew on that subject, he switched to another, telling Mother and Dad a story about how at the fire station they'd blown one of their buddies right off the toilet as they were trying to flush some fish heads down the kitchen drain using the big fire hose.

Later when we asked Harmony what mafia was, she said it was Italian crooks that were real mean and talked funny and wore striped suits like on *The Untouchables,* another of our favorite police shows on TV.

"So, the dead lady's mother is a princess from Italy instead of France," Mitchell concluded. "I guess I just had the wrong country."

The lesbian thespian definition was another matter. Harmony was embarrassed to admit it, but she didn't know what it meant. She said she'd look it up in the encyclopedia and come and tell us, but I guess she forgot.

Stella Mae Dixon
In 1938 was list
on J. Edger's list
Known as her mother
Princess from Italy
Mafia

The Engagement and Secret Lives

Throughout all of Rex Oliver's troubles during and after the Halloween Ball, we'd forgotten all about Uncle Gott and Vivian's surprise engagement announcement. But it was very much on Janie's mind.

She was already in our kitchen when Mitchell, Dad, and I returned from delivering Rex Oliver to the police and the Indians back to the reservation, complaining to Mother about Meadowgreen. "That's why I didn't go to their old Halloween Ball," she said. "There are just too many leftist Hollywood liberals there trying to straighten themselves out. I've written J. Edgar Hoover about it." She left out the part that she hadn't received an invitation.

"Too bad Vivian's big night fell through," Janie continued. "She had planned to make the engagement announcement around the middle of the Halloween Ball to give everybody a chance to loosen up first, including Uncle Gott. Also, Vivian wanted her dear friend Edith Kliban to feel like Meadowgreen got their money's worth from the party before Vivian's announcement upstaged her." Janie dramatically emphasized the words "dear friend" a little too much, showing what she thought of Mrs. Kliban. "Of course, Vivian hadn't informed Edith about this whole announcement plan. It would have been a big surprise to her." Janie had just come from Vivian's and learned her side of the previous evening's events. Now she would tell us.

I had to quickly think of an excuse to stay in the room so I could hear this bit of news. I started opening the cupboards one at a time like I was looking for something, hoping they wouldn't notice me. But Mitchell followed me in and started looking over my shoulder into the cupboards. I knew he was going to ask me what I was doing, so before he could say anything I motioned for him to be quiet so we could hear Janie. Then I crouched down by one of the floor cabinets, stared into the inside, and stayed low. So did Mitchell. He was feeling much better now.

"Vivian complained to me that because of Earl Wade, the fight, and the murder last night, she didn't get to announce her engagement to Gottfried. You know she spent a veritable fortune on that sequined thing she wore, don't you?" Janie commented to Mother. "And she sat through a special appointment at Antoinette's to get her hair puffed out extra high. All for nothing.

"*Now* Vivian's worried that there's not going to be another big shindig like this soon. She may be right." Janie reflected. "After the events of last night, Meadowgreen may never hold another public function. On top of all that, how will she ever get Gottfried to wear a tuxedo again?"

"Was he wearing a tux?" Mother asked. "I don't remember seeing..."

"I did," I said, before I remembered I was trying to go unnoticed. "He looked real nice." To look real nice was a high compliment.

"Well at least Gottfried managed to produce a ring," Janie went right on. "I've seen it. It's the ring a man picks out if he's trying to be modern—the latest in diamond settings, very 50s, and a li-i-i-tle too much platinum for my taste. But Vivian loves it," Janie said. "That's all that matters. She told me it wasn't the biggest ring and it wasn't the flashiest ring, but that everything Gottfried gives, he gives from the heart. Including his delivery of the weather. Vivian still considers him her *numero uno* weatherman." Janie arched one eyebrow to Mother when she said *numero uno.*

Mother nodded in response.

"What's *numero uno*? Is that German?" Mitchell asked Mother. We weren't doing a very good job of keeping still.

"It means he's the best," said Janie. "It's Mexican, not German."

The ease with which she replied meant it wasn't anything secretive, like when Dad spoke German with Grandma Dale or Uncle Gott so we kids couldn't understand. Maybe Mexican wasn't used for telling secret things. Maybe Janie just arched her eyebrows to be dramatic, like Harmony did when she was being intellectual.

"Apparently it was your sister Harmony who first identified the picketers as Earl Wade and family," Janie turned to Mitchell and me. "She and the Knotts were late arriving at the Ball because for some reason Dr. Knott said he didn't want to go. But apparently they convinced him, because just as they got there they ran into these picketers all over the sidewalks. At first they thought it was part of a Halloween prank, but Harmony told the Knotts it was the despicable Wades. She ran inside to find you, Louise, only she ran into Vivian first. Vivian was hard to miss in her sequins, don't you know." Apparently Janie didn't approve of Vivian's costume either. She turned back to Mother and went on with the story.

"Vivian told me that when Harmony mentioned the name Earl Wade, she remembered how her newspaper had gotten a weird letter from the Hosanna Baptist Church a few weeks earlier. Of course, Edith remembered it too and remembered how she'd thrown it away. So Edith decided to call the security guards and her husband, Dr. Felix Kliban.

"But apparently the security guards were occupied separating you kids and Rex Oliver from a fight with some potted plant ladies. It was one of them they think he killed, wasn't it?" Janie didn't wait for an answer. "So Edith runs outside to see for herself what Harmony's referring to. Well there's the Wades and their hateful signs marching bold as you please around the entrance to her big party. When she figured out what those signs meant—and Vivian told me what they said—my goodness! She must have had coronary arrest."

Janie stopped and nodded her head at the thought.

"It just goes to show," she said, "that Meadowgreen can't control everything in Topeka. I betcha when Meadowgreen planned a community outreach event they never expected the community to reach back like *that*."

"You can say that again," Mitchell said.

"I mean, let's face it," Janie turned again and started talking to Mitchell as if he were an expert on The Meadowgreen Clinic's community relations. "Edith's got no experience with people showing disrespect for Meadowgreen. Here she was with these upstarts saying nasty, vile things and they weren't even invited. Edith was so outraged she called President Eisenhower..."

"Calling the President? Again?" Mother interrupted. "They *do* have friends in high places, don't they?" She didn't know whether to be respectful or not. Sometimes Meadowgreen's exclusiveness got a little tiring.

"However a very nice person at the White House told her the President was at a Halloween party at Camp David and couldn't be reached. Same for Vice President Nixon, who was Edith's second choice."

"I wonder what their costumes were," speculated Mitchell.

"Edith couldn't call out the National Guard without higher authority, so she developed a migraine headache. Maybe she needs to go to Meadowgreen to get her head fixed." Janie laughed at her own joke.

"Daphne's dad, Dr. Knott, helped Edith to a chair back inside the ballroom. It was Dr. Kliban, the real brains in the family, who decided to call the police. Vivian ran off to find Gottfried. Harmony and Daphne went to look for you, Louise.

"Dr. Kliban intercepted Uncle Gott just as Vivian was pulling him to the front door to see the picketers. He wanted Gottfried, as the local celebrity, to appeal to Earl Wade's civic responsibility and persuade him to leave. Your Uncle Gott wasn't sure that was such a good idea because he was already nervous about announcing the engagement and this made him even more nervous. That's about the time you got outside with the picketers, wasn't it, Melody?" Janie asked.

"I don't know," I replied truthfully. "I only saw the picketers and I was sneezing a lot. I didn't see Uncle Gott or Dr. Kliban."

"Well, it was," Janie said. She wasn't even there, but she was going to tell the story her way. "All those things happened before the police got there and before Louise took revenge on the Wades for stealing her satchel. Good for you, Louise." She smiled at Mother. Mother smiled weakly back.

"After you gave the Wades a trouncing, Edith Kliban demanded that Earl Wade and his bunch be arrested for causing the disturbance. But Reverend Wade said he was practicing his First Amendment rights on a place of public access. Or some such legal double talk. No one in his group was breaking the law, he said. To arrest any of them was gonna be a violation of their rights of free speech and free assembly and would be grounds to sue the police, Meadowgreen, and any other person involved.

"He's nothing but a *Communist*," Janie hissed, "throwing all those legal ideas around to prevent the police from doing their job. He ought to go back to Russia where he belongs."

I hadn't known the Wades were Russians. Maybe that was why the craziness ran in their family. That made Uncle Rex part Russian, but he was part American too.

"Evidently the police did back off and went to look for the District Attorney. He was at the Ball dressed as Zorro. And he said that as much as he hated it, the Wades were acting within the law, which sent Edith's headache straight into orbit.

"So instead of getting upstaged by her friend Vivian, Edith got upstaged by a group of religious nuts.

"Anyway," Janie continued, "Edith begged Vivian to keep this whole 'scandal,' as she called it, out of the news. Vivian looked around and saw a dead body, most of the city's police force, and all the town's prominent citizens. She told Edith that was gonna be tough.

"By the way, kids. What are you doing?" Janie asked. Mother looked at us too. Mitchell and I were still crouched down by the bottom cupboards.

I reached in the cupboard and moved some dishes around. "I thought maybe I saw a mouse run in here, so I was just checking to see if I needed to go get the cats," I said. Our cats were too lazy to be mousers, but it was all I could think of.

"Uh-huh," said Mother. I don't think she believed me.

Many times, the hard winter in Kansas holds off until January. Not that year. Uncle Gott correctly predicted the first snowfall would occur the week after the Halloween Ball. It was a big snow, cold and with enough wind to send people digging for mittens and mufflers and hats.

Uncle Gott had graduated to a gentleman's topcoat as his winter protection, a big step up from the plaid hunter's jacket he had always worn before. Vivian was slowly but surely influencing every aspect of his life.

The little matter of their exact wedding date had never been resolved. Everyone was concerned with Rex Oliver and forgot to ask about Vivian's ring. Uncle Gott didn't know if he should bring up the topic of the wedding or wait until Vivian did. After a week of worrying about it, he asked his sister's advice. Grandma Dale said good advice on a cold day was always preceded by good hot chocolate, which she was also happy to supply.

"Gottfried, I'm surprised Vivian's waited this long to mention it," said Dale, who told us about the conversation later. "Has she been acting strange lately? I mean stranger than usual?"

"Well—I think, maybe—yes. I have been thankful for God's generosity in bringing me together with Vivian, only..."

"Only what, Gottfried?"

"Only Vivian is a very strong-minded woman."

"That she is," responded Grandma Dale. "Is that a problem?"

"I pray that our Lord will show me the way to soften Vivian's heart, just a little, and let us begin our new life together soon." Grandma Dale told us that the way his eyes glazed over when he said the word "soon," you could tell Vivian's swinging backside had had its effect.

"What's the matter, Gottfried? Do you want to talk about it?" asked Dale. Grandma Dale was the kind of person people came to with a problem. Dad said Grandma Dale was made of love and common sense, and everyone who knew her respected that.

"Dale, does Vivian recognize that another person might not always agree with her? And that it's okay for us to hold different opinions?" Gottfried was serious.

Dale thought about that a moment. "I know she really loves you Gottfried. I can tell by the way she acts like a woman with you and not like a boss. That's a healthy sign you know. And I know Vivian loves God. Her heart is as big and as kind as they come.

"Gottfried, remember when the African colonies nationalized, and the new leaders asked you to leave? Their opinion was different than yours. You thought God wanted you to stay and save the natives. But the natives, when they took control, wanted their own race to do their preaching and not any more white people telling them what to do."

"Yes, I remember," said Gottfried.

"Well, I think Vivian's a lot like those Africans. She had folks telling her what to do for so long when she was young, that when she gained her independence, she decided not to listen to nobody. And to her credit, she's got good judgment when it comes to running her business and her life. But I think Vivian is ready now, even if she doesn't know it, to meet another human being halfway. That's why God brought you two together."

Gottfried sighed.

"Being married isn't always easy. And I'm sure you and Vivian will have your share of problems. That's life. But I also have a sense that you will be very happy together."

Grandma Dale had the sixth sense the way Gottfried had visions from God. She didn't always have it when she wanted to have it, she said, but many times during her life she had knowledge come to her in ways nobody could explain. Her knowledge always turned out to be right. I knew what she meant because once or twice the same thing had happened to me.

Uncle Gott said he felt the wisdom in his sister's words. He finished his hot chocolate, got in his car, and drove straight to the studio and Vivian's office.

The next part of the story was filled in by Janie Bryant later, who as always got it straight from Vivian. It seems Uncle Gott marched into Vivian's office unannounced, just as he had done the day he asked for a job as a TV weatherman. This time Vivian was on the phone to her newspaper editor downtown.

"Hang up the phone," said Gottfried to Vivian.

Vivian was stunned because he didn't even say please and usually Gottfried was so polite. Vivian said I'll call you back to her editor and hung up the phone.

"Woman," said Uncle Gott, "you are like the natives in Africa."

"I beg your pardon?" said Vivian. She thought Uncle Gott had been out in the cold too long.

"When you gained your independence, you thought you would answer to no one. But now God has brought us together and there will be times, not often, but occasionally, when..." Uncle Gott was searching for words, "when we will compromise on our wishes. Do you understand me?"

"Not exactly," said Vivian.

This was getting harder for Uncle Gott. "There will be times when I don't get my way and you don't get your way. But we each have to give in a little bit."

The light was starting to dawn on Vivian. "What is it you want me to give in on, Gottfried, you big loveable hunk, ummm?" Vivian was very good at this.

"Well," now Uncle Gott was almost floundering. "Well, I don't want to wait until June. To get married." There. It was out.

"O-o-oh," said Vivian, a little relieved. "And when would you like to get married, sweetikins?" She came closer to Uncle Gott.

"Sooner. Much, much sooner," said Gottfried.

And Vivian snuggled up to him and said that was fine with her.

"So anyway," Janie relayed the story, "now the wedding has been moved up to Valentine's Day and those two are acting like a couple of lovesick teenagers.

"That part about Vivian gaining her independence," Janie paused and asked Mother, "what's that about?"

"Oh," said Mother. "I'm surprised she hasn't told you. Well—you see—Vivian comes from an unusual background. When she was just a baby, she was abandoned at a traveling circus in Ohio and raised by the owner and his wife. I guess they made her sell tickets and work the carnival booths from the day she was old enough to walk. She never had a day off or a kind word, but she learned a lot about hustling for a dollar. That's why she's such a good businesswoman. Judging from the way she swings her backside, she learned a lot of other things too."

"No," said Janie in disbelief. "Then what happened?"

"When she was fifteen, the circus came to Topeka. Vivian wandered over to a Pentecostal tent revival set up in a vacant lot next to the circus, and at the service she found Jesus or He found her or they found each other. So did this older gentleman standing next to Vivian at the altar. Well afterwards they got to talking, and pretty soon one thing led to another, and anyway, they decided to get married that night, just like that."

"Just like that? They didn't even know each other. And if she was only fifteen how…?"

"Well, it turns out this guy was Earnest Ostrander, the owner of half of Topeka and a lonely widower. He was also eighty years old at the time."

"Eighty years old? Wait a minute, Louise. Are you kidding me?" said Janie.

"Honest to God, Janie." Mother held up her right hand as if to say I swear. "So they went to see Vivian's parents, the circus owners, for permission since Vivian was underage. Of course the circus owner smelled money the moment he looked at Earnest and says how it's gonna be a real financial hardship without his beloved daughter to work there, blah, blah, blah. So some money changed hands. Vivian never would tell me how much, but she called it the price of her emancipation. And Earnest and Vivian ran off to Oklahoma where there's no waiting period and got married that night. About five years after that Earnest died and left her a bundle."

"Wow," said Janie, deep in thought. "That's quite a story."

"And one I doubt she wants repeated all over town, if you don't mind. Please, Janie, I think Vivian would appreciate it if you keep this to yourself."

"All those times we sat together under the hair dryers at Antoinette's and she never told me," said Janie. "You just never know what secret lives some people have."

"So what's yours?" Mitchell asked her.

I already knew the answer to that one. Uncle Billie Glenn said his police friends had once caught the lady across the street, meaning Janie, during a raid at an illegal nudist colony south of Topeka. Dad said you'd never suspect her as the type. Mitchell had asked what a nudist colony was and Dad said it was a bunch of people who prayed for warm weather.

Janie wasn't about to fess up to Mitchell anyway.

"Now Mitchell, it's not nice to ask people about their private lives," said Janie. "You're old enough to know better too." Then to Mother, "Louise, you need to teach that boy some manners."

"He's usually more polite than that," sighed Mother.

I thought about what Janie had said about everybody's secret life. During the last six weeks I'd learned that Vivian had worked in a circus, Janie was a nudist, Dewey's first wife was crazy, Virgil was a lawyer, Brenda Messina ate dirt, Maynard stored food under his shirt, and Uncle Gott liked swinging backsides. I thought about other people I knew, and for the first time considered what kind of life they had besides the one I saw. I wondered about Simon Vargas, and Miss Georgia, and Dr. Jerome Knott. Even Edith Kliban, did she have a secret life? Even President Eisenhower and J. Edgar Hoover. Did they all have secret lives?

And what about Grandma Dale, and Mother and Dad, and Uncle Billy Glenn, and Uncle Rex Oliver? What secrets did our very own family have? It made me a little confused and even worried. What if our parents were really somebody else and not our parents at all? What if Grandma Dale pushed Grandpa Richard into the pigpen with the rogue boar so she could get electricity? What if Uncle Rex really did kill his mother?

And what about the real murderer? That person was keeping a *big* secret!

I started thinking and thinking and I wanted to talk to somebody about all of this. But then I thought, no matter who I talk to, that person will have a secret life too, so they won't want to talk about it. I started to feel real bad and went into my room and pretended to read an encyclopedia. I was just flipping through looking at the pictures in volume L-O. I found some real good pictures of lemmings, muskrats, and opossums, but mostly I was still thinking about Janie's comment.

Harmony came in and asked me why was I reading the encyclopedia. Did I have a fever? I looked up at her and said, "Harmony, I want to talk about our secret lives."

Harmony rolled her eyes, so I said it again. "Come on, Harmony. Just between you and me. Do you have a boyfriend? Do you have a training bra? Do you have iron-poor blood?" That was from a TV commercial. I wasn't exactly sure what iron-poor blood was, but it would be nice to know if Harmony had it and if it was contagious.

"Go away," said Harmony. This time she didn't even bother being poetic.

"I don't have to go away. This is my room too," I said.

"Then grow up," said Harmony and walked out.

I started to throw the encyclopedia at her, but I didn't want to tear the animal pictures in it so I didn't.

All at once a strange thought came into my head. The thought was that Earl Wade had a secret life too. It wasn't just the thought either, it was the knowledge, like the sixth sense, that Earl Wade had a secret life and that he didn't want it revealed. But as with all such knowledge that occasionally came unbidden to my mind, it was only information. It did not come with instructions on how or if to use it. So I decided to just store it away for now.

The Religious Picketers

E arl Wade's public life, however, was becoming known all over town. Ever since Vivian had received Earl's first letter at the newspaper, Earl and his Hosanna Baptist Church group had made it their mission to proclaim the evil in mental illness. When he found out the police were holding Uncle Rex, he and his followers—Mitchell called them his "gang"—went down and picketed the police station. They carried the same signs as on Halloween, only they'd added one that said: "Crazy Murderer."

Of course the police were not at all happy to be the recipients of this attention. Chief Duane Appelhans even went out and tried to talk Earl out of it. Earl Wade told him he had better get used to it, that the Hosanna Baptist Church was doing the Lord's work and no force on earth could stop them.

Their preferred method of sharing this message was by picketing the mental health hospitals and activities in town, or often just picketing well-frequented public places. Nobody knew why they selected only mental illness as their target, or why they thought picketing would stop it. But soon it was a common sight to see the group carrying signs and marching on the sidewalks around Topeka. Dewey said it was because the Wades were afraid of the craziness in themselves. Earl Wade claimed it was God that made them picket. "The legions of Satan are taking over Topeka," said Earl, "and the voice of God has called me to stop them." He told a *Topeka Daily Capital* reporter he was on a mission from God to save the city from its own iniquity, and that the Hosanna Baptist Church wouldn't rest until every last lunatic was converted by the blood of Jesus. He quoted Bible verses about "unclean spirits," because he believed unclean spirits were the devil making people crazy. Dewey said in Earl's case that was probably true.

The church group developed a regular picketing schedule to

accommodate the vast number of lunatics in town. On Mondays at noon they picketed the V.A. Hospital which had a large group of what Mother called "troubled souls." Tuesdays the Wades set up their signs outside the State Hospital, where Ava Wade Oots and Rex Oliver had been treated. Wednesday was Meadowgreen's day to be picketed. Thursday and Friday the group stood with their signs next to prominent city intersections where thousands of drivers would spot them. Saturday evenings they picketed a west side restaurant owned by a former Meadowgreen patient.

Sundays were reserved for picketing several churches. That's because some of the churches preached that what Earl Wade was doing in the name of God was wrong. These churches believed that God was love, not hate. They said that God didn't hate lunatics and that to carry signs to persecute the mentally ill was not godly. So the Wades picketed those churches. It became a real religious war, Dad said. He said he wondered, with so much picketing, when the Hosanna Baptist Church had time to conduct their own church services.

I hadn't seen the Wades since the disastrous Halloween Ball, which was fine with me. But one Sunday they were picketing in front of the sanctuary entrance of our church. "It's the despicable Wades," Harmony yelled, as if we wouldn't know them anywhere.

"Hide your eyes," I told Mitchell. "Don't look in Earl's eyes or he'll paralyze you like a cobra." I was a veteran here and had to save Mitchell.

"That's right, kids," Mother said. "Don't even look at him or his nasty signs. What does he think being Christian is all about anyway, preaching such hatred?"

Dad was ready to stop and exchange words with Earl, but Mother and some of the other church men pulled Dad back, which was too bad. We all went peacefully inside and tried to pretend we were thinking about Sunday School.

It didn't take long before people got tired of having to run the blockade of Earl and his obnoxious picketers everywhere they went. Every day, letters to the editor of *The Topeka Daily Capital* demanded that the police and District Attorney do something to stop Earl's obnoxious behavior. There was more mail about Earl, Vivian told us, then any other subject she could remember since she'd owned the paper. The police got so many complaints about the Hosanna Baptist Church that the mayor threatened to fire the police chief if somebody didn't arrest Earl for something. But no matter how many times the police tried to arrest Earl, he would quote them his rights of free speech and free assembly and he would be right. "Earl's sly that way," Dewey told us. "He'll always stay just within the law because it's all a game with him."

So people began organizing against Earl on their own. Billy Glenn told Dad that "Eat Me Earl" graffiti began cropping up at the State Hospital and soon spread all over town. "Nobody's sure if it's patients or staff responsible," he said. "But it's spreadin' like hotcakes." Mother said Billy Glenn liked to talk in what she called clichés a lot.

"It's a funny thing," he continued. "People from mental health agencies are gettin' together and puttin' on educational speeches about mental health for the community. Patients from the V.A. and a bunch of staff from the State Hospital and their families held a dance last week to benefit the mentally ill. All kinds of church groups and health groups and them Jewish psychiatrists and Christian clergy are comin' together with lost souls and tormented bums and law enforcement officials. The P.D. says there's every color, every religion, and every economic status represented, and all they got in common is their dislike of Earl Wade."

"Hmmm," mused Dad. "Sounds like Earl, in his own ugly way, is doing more to unite Topeka than the Chamber of Commerce."

"You can say that again," said Billy Glenn.

Dewey felt differently. "My former brother-in-law," he said, "is crazy."

That wasn't news to anyone. "Now wait a minute," Dewey said, "I don't mean just regular crazy, I mean a real special kind of crazy. He reminds me of John Brown."

Everybody in Topeka and half of Kansas had seen *Tragic Prelude,* the famous John Steuart Curry mural of John Brown on the wall in the State Capitol. It was huge and colorful and scary. John Brown had a long gray beard, and his arms spread open wide holding a rifle in one hand and a Bible in the other. In the mural he was standing outside on the prairie with a strong wind blowing and the wind whipping up his beard and his clothes and blowing things around his head. But the scariest part were his eyes. Even in the mural his eyes burned right through a person. A hundred years ago John Brown had massacred five men in the middle of the night in cold blood, right up the road at Potawatomi. Then there was the whole Harper's Ferry thing, which helped touch off the Civil War.

His kind of crazy had been dangerous and mean and that's what Dewey meant. I was glad Mother hadn't gone inside the green house that day she met the Wades. I also wondered what the plain little Wade children felt like, living with a madman as a father. Since they all picketed, were they all crazy too or did he force them to do it?

"Do you know any of Earl Wade's children?" I asked Dewey.

"No," he said.

"Well, are all Baptists like that?" I knew Dewey himself was a Baptist, so I was treading on dangerous ground.

"Course not," he replied. "In this country everybody's got freedom of religion, which is good as long as we don't break the law or nothin'. But sometimes crazy people like Earl use the idea of religion to hide behind, 'cause it gives them a sense of power they wouldn't get no other way. I believe Earl likes having the whole town afraid of him. He likes all the attention and having everybody talk about him. Heck, he probably considers himself some kinda martyr for God, which makes him extra dangerous."

I remembered how I felt like a little bird paralyzed by a cobra when Earl looked at me with his icy gray eyes. Well, I thought, I'd just have to close my eyes whenever he was around. Maybe we should all just close our eyes. I remembered John Brown's wild eyes in the mural and wondered if fanatics' power came from their wild eyes, like

Samson's power came from his hair. Then I thought, hey, what if Earl Wade wore dark glasses so the rest of us couldn't see his eyes? Maybe Mitchell and I could think up a plan to get him to wear dark glasses. But it was winter, and nobody wore dark glasses in winter in Kansas. I decided to think about that for a while.

Eyetalians in a Snowstorm

Brenda Messina's father August Messina, the margarine king, picked the wrong day and the wrong way to come to Topeka. "Big Augie," as he was known, decided to charter a plane from Rhode Island and fly directly into the Municipal Airport in the Oakland section of Topeka. According to Uncle Billy Glenn, after finally landing through the season's first snowstorm, "the wop figured out there weren't gonna be no spaghetti joints in Oakland."

I'm ashamed to say that's how some people, including our own uncle, talked back then.

"Watch your language, please," Mother instructed her brother. Uncle Billy Glenn had dropped by for a free meal and to inform us of the latest happenings in the Brenda Messina case. "I got one word to say," he said. "Mafia." Then he went on to say a lot more. He said that normally Topeka was too small potatoes to have any Mafia problems, because with our agricultural roots nobody, but nobody, was Italian. He pronounced it Eye-talian. "How many Eye-talian farmers you seen?" he asked Dad. "Kansas City, now, they got Mafia problems. Somebody's always blowing somebody up down in some warehouse by the river in Kansas City. That's life in the big city for you," he said.

"Now you take this Brenda Messina murder," he went on. "Not much about it in the news, right?"

We all nodded. There had been only a few brief details, which it said police were investigating.

"'Cause that's the way Meadowgreen wants it and that's what they get. But Big Augie, now he's got other ideas. According to my police friends," he paused to make certain we appreciated the authority of what he was about to tell us, "Big Augie has demanded that the killer of his only daughter be tried and executed as quickly and as publicly as possible."

Mitchell gasped, gave a little whimper, and put his hand over his mouth. We knew Kansas got to hang people sometimes for what Dad called "capital crimes," which he never completely explained, but it did include murder. We didn't want to see Rex Oliver hang, like the bad guys did on *Gunsmoke*.

"Big Augie doesn't run the criminal justice system in Topeka," Dad said, because he could see that Mitchell was going to start crying. "Don't worry, kids. Even if Rex Oliver did it, which I doubt, and the jury convicts him, which I doubt even more, he'll never hang because of his history of mental illness."

That made me feel a little better, but Mitchell was still welling up.

"What else did you hear?" Dad asked Billy Glenn.

"Well," said Uncle Billy Glenn, "Big Augie brought a couple 'a friends with him, two guys named Tiny and Joey who the police are watching closely. Tiny and Joey talk funny, 'cause instead of saying 'the,' they say 'da,' like in 'da' town of Topeka. Isn't that funny? But nobody laughs at them to their faces.

"Big Augie's rented a suite of rooms at the Hotel Jayhawk for him and his boys. He's been holding meetings with Police Chief Appelhans, with some of Meadowgreen's top people, and with Vivian because..."

"Vivian?" said Mother. "Why Vivian?"

"Well, because of the publicity thing," said Uncle Billy Glenn. "Big Augie wants to offer a big reward and get everybody in town to help him find the murderer."

"Wait a minute," said Dad. "Does that mean he thinks Rex Oliver didn't do it?"

"Apparently, he said his daughter had 'a strange and turbulent history,' whatever that means, and he wants to look into several possibilities. But one thing's for sure," said Uncle Billy Glenn. "Between trying to watch Big Augie and his gang, and trying to keep an eye on the Hosanna Baptist Church and their gang, the police are going friggin' nuts."

"Billy Glenn," Mother said again, "please watch your language."

"Just a second," said Dad. "I want to go back to these meetings that Big Augie's holding. Tell me again about the reward."

"Okay," said Uncle Billy Glenn. "The reward is $10,000 for information that leads to the conviction of Brenda's killer. But in order to get the word out about the reward it has to get in the news, so everybody knows about it, right? Only here's the thing, Meadowgreen don't want no publicity about this murder 'cause it looks real bad for them when their big society patients get bumped off. So you got Meadowgreen putting pressure on Vivian on one side to stop the story, and Big Augie and the boys putting pressure on her on the other side to print it. But this Augie guy's pretty smart. He don't threaten nobody, see, but he tells Vivian he wants to pay big money to buy advertising in her newspaper and TV commercials. Now Vivian has the right not to take his advertising, he tells her, but if she don't, he'll go to a private print shop, print a couple hundred thousand announcements, and hire fifty guys to pass them out at every intersection in Topeka for a week.

"Well obviously Meadowgreen can't stop that. So Vivian figured she'd rather have the money than let Big Augie spend it somewheres else. Starting tomorrow *The Topeka Daily Capital* and *The Topeka State Journal* are gonna have some big ads about this reward. That oughta make things *real* interesting."

"Hmmm," said Dad. "I'm gonna call Dewey and tell him about this."

"How tiny is Tiny?" asked Mitchell.

"About as tiny as a freight train," said Uncle Billy Glenn.

"Have you seen him yourself?" said Mitchell.

Uncle Billy Glenn stopped, looked at Mitchell and frowned. Then he said, "Excuse me just a minute I gotta get some more coffee," and left the room. When he returned, he asked Mother, "Say, do you think the woman across the street would go out with me?"

"You mean Janie? Janie Bryant—the Giant Killer?" Mother said.

Uncle Billy Glenn nodded.

"Well—are you a Communist?"

"No."

"Do you believe in J. Edgar Hoover?"

"Do I believe in J. Edgar Hoover? What do you mean do I believe in J. Edgar Hoover? That he really exists or what?" asked Uncle Billy Glenn.

"That he's right up there with God and Ike and Mickey Mantle," said Mother. "That's what Janie thinks. And by the way, she's not a Catholic."

"So what," said Billy Glenn. "Alex ain't no Catholic either, but you married him and that ain't turned out so bad."

Mother looked at Harmony. Then she smiled and said, "No, it hasn't turned out so bad at all."

"So you think it's okay for me to ask Janie out? You know, I was thinkin' maybe you should invite her over for supper some night and I could come too. You know, nothing obvious. That way we could meet and see how things go."

"Are you a nudist?" I asked him.

"What! What did you say?" yelled Uncle Billy Glenn.

"Remember when you told us about the police raid on the nudist colony? Are you a nudist too?"

"Oh good Lord, Louise. Why are your kids asking such questions?" shouted Uncle Billy Glenn jumping up from his chair. I wondered how he and Janie Bryant would get along, since she loved to ask questions and he hated answering them. Still, this romance business was hard to predict.

"Well, I'll see what I can arrange with Janie," Mother said.

Billy Glenn changed the subject then and started telling Dad more fire station stories, which I'd mostly heard before, so I went to look for Harmony. Harmony had been acting very strange lately, carrying around a small notepad and stopping to write furiously on it every couple of minutes. She wouldn't tell anybody except Daffy what she was doing, not even Mother or Dad. I figured it was probably some more poetry stuff, but I wanted to see for myself.

Harmony was holed up in our room all right, writing. She was half-laying on the bed with Little Poo, and when I came in she turned her back to me, but otherwise didn't acknowledge my presence or stop writing.

"How much is that doggie in the window?" I started to sing.

I was a pretty good singer from all that church choir stuff, so I didn't hold back. I was about to go for the second verse when Harmony rolled over and yelled, "Can't you shut up, you little twerp? I'm trying to write."

"I can sing in here if I want to," I said sweetly. "Maybe if I knew what you were writing I would be quiet."

"Get lost," said Harmony.

"How much is that doggie…" I began again. But Harmony, with a yell, grabbed her pillow and socked me with it as hard as she could. So I grabbed mine and let her have it back. Little Poo went diving for cover while Harmony and I screamed and hit each other and jumped up and down on the beds and hit each other some more. Mother heard the noise and saw Little Poo bolt out of our room. She came to investigate.

"Stop it! Stop it! Stop it! Stop it!" Mother raised her voice to be heard above our racket. "You're both going to be in big trouble if you don't learn to get along with people."

"She started it," Harmony said.

"I did not," I replied.

"Yes, you did. You were singing real loud just to annoy me."

"It doesn't matter who started it," said Mother. "I want you both to settle down. Melody, quit singing when you know Harmony's trying to write."

"But she writes all the time," I protested. "When am I gonna be able to sing?" Singing had suddenly become my fondest desire.

"You two will have to work it out," Mother said. "Now I don't want to hear any more fighting." Mother left and closed the door.

I waited a few minutes until I was sure she was gone, then started humming "In The Garden" real softly. "In The Garden" was my favorite hymn from church, only I sing alto, so I was humming the alto part.

"MOM!!!" Harmony jumped up from the bed, threw open the

door, and screamed again. "MOM!!! SHE'S *HUMMING*!!"

"I was just practicing for church," I said. "What's wrong with that?"

Mother came back in and said, "Okay. That's it. You're both grounded for a week. I've just about had it with you two fighting all the time. You have to share a room so you'll just have to learn to get along. Harmony, try talking a little more with your sister instead of ignoring her. And Melody, be more understanding of Harmony's need for privacy. You'll be feeling just like her in a couple of years. Now I'm going to leave this door open and I don't want any more fighting!"

Mother was trying to be firm. She left and I stuck out my tongue at Harmony. Mother was wrong, I was never going to be like Harmony.

*The p*olice held Rex Oliver for several days, considering him the prime suspect in the murder of Brenda Messina. Virgil had explained to him that the only reason the police thought he did it was because of the crucifix and the dirt throwing fight. He said that was circumstantial evidence and definitely not premeditated murder, so there was no danger of the death penalty. He told Rex Oliver not to worry, that he, Virgil, believed he didn't do it and would clear his name.

Then Virgil went before a judge to request that Rex Oliver be turned loose on bail. Dad explained to us what that was and how Virgil had convinced Judge Maxwell to set a reasonable bail because Rex Oliver had lived his whole life in Topeka and wasn't gonna run any farther than the cave. Dad said Grandma Dale had put up the money, even though Vivian had offered to do it. Vivian was getting ready to marry into the family and was kissing up, Dad said. Never mind, he told Mitchell, who was about to ask what that was.

Dewey and Grandma Dale and Virgil and Maynard picked up Rex Oliver and took him back to the farm during the heavy snowstorm, the same one Big Augie flew into when he came to town. Maynard had become a sort of silent partner in Virgil's legal services, said Grandma Dale, although nobody was exactly sure what he did. But his presence seemed to calm Rex Oliver.

They'd only driven two blocks from the police station when they came across a big Lincoln from a rental agency skidding sideways all over the road.

"That guy oughta learn how to drive in the snow," said Dewey. Knowing how to drive in the snow was as natural as breathing if you lived in Kansas over a winter.

Grandma Dale told us the Lincoln fishtailed its way up to Sixth and Kansas Avenue, then had to stop for a red light. "When it tried to start again it just spun its wheels in the snow, blocking everybody behind it," she said. "This great big guy in a nice suit gets out, but he didn't have on a coat or gloves or hat or galoshes, or any kind of protection from the weather, and he starts trying to push the car. By this time the snow's up over his shoes and every time the wheels spin they throw snow on the guy. Pretty soon he was just covered.

"We all felt sorry for him, so Virgil and Maynard got out to help." We nodded in agreement. It was the neighborly thing to do.

"But whoever was driving just kept gunning the engine like a dummy, making the wheels spin. Virgil goes around and knocks on the window to ask the driver to use the engine to rock the car. He can see one guy driving and somebody else sitting in the back. He said none of 'em were dressed for winter, so he figured they was from out of town.

"The driver doesn't understand about rocking the car, so Virgil offered to get in and rock it for them. I guess this driver fella looked him up and down and saw an Indian dressed in old farm clothes offering to get in his nice, rented Lincoln. They probably thought he was gonna steal it."

"No. Huh, uh. He wouldn't do that," we all said at the same time. Everybody knew Virgil was an honest Injun.

"Well of course, not," said Grandma Dale. "The guy in the back seat leaned forward and said he would be very appreciative of Virgil's help. So the driver gets out and just stands there, doesn't even offer to push, and Virgil gets in and starts rocking the car, and Maynard and the big guy push the car out.

"Before Virgil can even pull over to the curb, he feels a hand on his shoulder. He looks at the back seat and there's a $5 bill in the guy's hand and the guy's saying thank you.

"Virgil said he put the car in park, then turned around so he could look the man full in the face. 'We don't take money for helping people here, mister,' he said. 'It's just the neighborly thing to do.'

"Then Virgil asks the driver, 'Where you fellahs headed?' so we could follow 'em there to make sure they didn't get stuck again. The driver's mouth dropped open and he said he'd have to check with the boss, only he said 'da' boss. You could tell they weren't used to people being helpful. Wouldn't you hate to live in a place like where they're from?" she asked. We all nodded again. We knew we were lucky to live in Kansas where people helped each other.

"So the driver checks and says da boss says da Hotel Jayhawk, which was just a few blocks away. We followed the Lincoln over to the Hotel and that was that.

"Then we drove home. Never did learn their names. We didn't have any problems getting home in the snow, but if we'd waited too much longer the driveway would have been drifted shut." We knew what she meant. The driveway at the farm was always a problem when it snowed due to heavy wind and drifting from the north.

Grandma Dale had fixed a big welcome home dinner for Rex Oliver. Since Virgil was going to be working as Rex Oliver's lawyer and Maynard as Virgil's assistant, there was no point in their going back to the reservation every day, especially since their car would likely get stuck in the snow and frozen muddy ruts. Rocking the car was of no use in deep muddy ruts. It had been decided that Virgil and Maynard could sleep in a little room over the garage. The room had a small kerosene heater and was suitable for temporary quarters. When the weather got better, they'd go home for a few days. Virgil made arrangements for somebody to watch their place on the reservation and feed the dogs.

When Rex Oliver got home he bolted out the door and headed straight for the cave. It wasn't hard to know that because you could see his tracks through the snow by looking out the kitchen window. There were no tracks coming out of the cave either. Grandma Dale, Dewey, and the Indians were hungry, so they ate the welcome home dinner without him.

By evening the temperature dropped enough that Rex Oliver, half-frozen, hungry, and reeking of mold, came out of the cave and into the house, quickly ate dinner, and went to bed. What he didn't know was that Virgil and Maynard took turns watching outside his door all night.

Bad Dreams, Music and Sin,
and the Piano Recital

Mitchell was having problems sleeping. Always before he'd slept like a log, *the sleep of the innocent*, Mother called it. But now he began waking up at night crying softly. Sometimes this would wake Mother, and she'd go talk to him until he felt safe and sleepy again. When this continued for several weeks, she and Dad started to get worried.

I was also puzzled by Mitchell's bad dreams. We'd always done everything together and now I couldn't understand what was making him unhappy. I asked him what it was. He just looked at me and hung his head.

Dad decided to spend some time in the evenings paying special attention to Mitchell. But it was winter and now too dark and cold after supper for outdoor stuff and anyway Dad wasn't the type for sports. So he reached out to his son his own way.

Dad asked Mitchell to play the trombone on some songs while he accompanied him on the guitar. I kept hanging around out of curiosity and was invited to play the piano. Then we asked Harmony to play the flute and she said yes. We kept trying to play "The Thunderer," a John Philip Sousa march with a big trombone part, but the piano part was real hard with lots of octave chords and stuff, which were hard for me to reach. Sometimes Mother came in and tried to sing, only there were no words to "The Thunderer" so she just sang "la, la, la," to everything. Mother didn't have a real pretty singing voice because she always tried to sing too many high notes. But she had a lot of enthusiasm. We played and played and even if our music didn't get much better it seemed to reassure Mitchell somehow. Dad said something to Mother about music soothing the savage. I guess he was talking about Indian chants.

Dad was still playing with Shep and the band most every Saturday night. The weekend before Thanksgiving he arranged for Mother to bring us all out to The Driftwood Bar and Grill to hear him. Dad thought it might inspire us kids to practice our music lessons more and give Mitchell an idea of how other people appreciated what musicians do.

I started gagging right away because the place was full of smoke and the music was real loud and hurt my ears. But it was fun to watch Dad in his cowboy clothes with the pearl snap buttons as he sang country songs. People were dancing too, which was something I didn't see much except on *Lawrence Welk* and the square dances we learned in Girl Scouts. Not that kind of dancing, though. This was cowboy dancing. Shep said this was the kind of dancing where you and your partner give each other's belt buckles that high gloss buff. I never saw that on *Lawrence Welk*. People were drinking beer too as they smoked. The louder the music got the more beer they drank and the more they smoked. Nobody in our family smoked or drank hard liquor, but all of Mother's Catholic relatives did, including Uncle Billy Glenn. Dad sometimes had a beer when he was watching TV in the living room, which seemed to me to be living dangerously. Our branch of Methodists didn't believe in dancing, drinking, or smoking, but Dad thought what the preacher didn't know wouldn't hurt him.

I wondered if Dad started drinking beer when he learned to play the guitar. Then I wondered if practicing the piano would lead me to drink beer and take up smoking and hard liquor. I wondered if I should warn Mitchell about his trombone. Then I got confused because I remembered they played the organ and we sang hymns in church. If music led to sin, why did we sing hymns in church? Or was it only the guitar that was responsible? I noticed they never played the guitar in church. I wasn't sure who I should ask about that.

The Driftwood visit didn't do much to inspire me. That was too bad because my troubles were also related to music, only I wasn't sinning. Miss Georgia and the adults had informed me I was in a piano recital the first week of December, which had totally ruined my Thanksgiving. I hated piano recitals. Because no matter how well I knew a song, the minute I had to play by memory in front of people my mind went completely blank. This had happened at my two previous piano recitals where I forgot "Minuet in G" and "Fur Elise." This year's disgrace was to be "Habanera" from *Carmen*. I kept playing it over and over on Janie's piano, but that was in the basement by myself. On stage I expected another disaster.

It wasn't just my playing that was awful. Mother had given Harmony and me home permanents so our fine hair would have body and curl. She thought we were cute that way, but it reminded me of how Harmony's stupid dolls looked. "Cuteness is a disease," I reminded her, "and sometimes people never recover." I could see that if my hair looked like Harmony's, I should go hide under a rock. I told Harmony *she* should.

I felt so bad the night before the recital that I prayed for a huge blizzard. I tried not to ask God for favors very often because it wasn't good to be beholden to anybody. But when it came to piano recitals I was desperate. I didn't just ask for a regular blizzard either, but one that would shut down the whole city. I didn't know what to promise God in return, but I finally decided I wouldn't tickle Mitchell for a month. God heard me too, because during the night it snowed a little. But I guess He thought Mitchell needed tickling more than I needed rescuing from public humiliation, because the snow didn't shut down anything.

The day of the recital I told Mother I thought I had a fever. "Oh, you do, do you?" she said. I don't think she was fooled since it was common knowledge that many of Miss Georgia's piano students came down with fevers on recital day. "Not only that," I continued, "but I feel real irregular." I'd seen that on TV. Maybe Mother would buy it. I knew I was gonna have to produce some terrible illness to convince her.

"Do you even know what irregular means?" she asked.

"Yup," I said, "I know. If people who are irregular take that medicine they sell on TV they're lucky to make it to the bathroom the next morning without crap in their pants. That's what Uncle Billy

Glenn told Mitchell and me."

"Billy Glenn's gonna get you two in trouble," Mother said. "And if anyone knows about trouble, he does. Don't use that word again. And don't change the subject."

I shook my head. I was hoping Mother would talk about her wayward brother and forget about the recital.

"So sick as you are, you're going to your recital anyway. It doesn't matter, honey, if you do good or not, although I hope all those lessons have counted for something. The important thing is for you to keep trying. Now go get dressed."

Mother was not dissuaded. I was starting to get that trapped feeling and thought maybe I really would be irregular, but it takes a lot to get me sick. So I went to my room and started getting ready. I put on some heavy winter underwear, my favorite dark green wool turtleneck sweater, and a plaid red and dark green wool skirt. Then because it was cold, I put on some heavy knee socks and a pair of big black boots.

"What kind of outfit is that?" Mother asked when I came out to the living room. "I wanted you to wear your print dress with the lace on it and your patent leather shoes. It's so pretty."

I hated that frilly stuff and besides, it wouldn't keep me warm. "It's too cold," I told Mother. "I'll be freezing and I can't remember any of the notes when I'm freezing."

"That's not the point, young lady," Mother said. "You need to look dressed up for the occasion."

"It's not gonna do any good," I replied. "My hair looks so awful it doesn't matter what I wear, so I might as well be warm. It's cold and snowy outside." I tried to appeal to her sympathy.

"Well, she's right on that point," Dad agreed. "About it being cold outside. Why can't she go the way she is?" Dad always dressed for the cold too, so he understood.

The question of style versus comfort was a subject of endless debate between Mother and Dad and Mother and me. As far as I could tell nobody ever persuaded the other one, but nobody gave up trying.

This time Mother surprised me by her response. "All right," she said. "If you're warm maybe you will remember the notes better."

Being warm was better than nothing, but I still had to go to the recital. It was depressing. When I looked in the mirror, I saw a gangly skinny kid dressed for an arctic expedition, with masses of fine curly hair going off in all directions. "Don't worry, Melody," said Mitchell trying to help me feel better. "Some people are never destined for life in the public eye." Harmony's speech was rubbing off on him.

Miss Georgia, on the other hand, would be holding forth in the American Legion Hall as if she really were a diva. Ten of her students would be playing that evening and Miss Georgia treated us as if we were the Kansas City Symphony instead of a bunch of awkward, perspiring youngsters.

When we got there, I saw that Miss Georgia had on a cocktail dress which Dad said was designed to draw attention away from her face. All I could see was that her chest was going to get cold. She also had pinned to her dress a large, showy orchid. It was bright pink and white. Mother said it was unusual to see an orchid this time of year. Dad said who was looking at the orchid? Mother said for him to be nice.

Miss Georgia also had on a pair of the largest earrings I had ever seen. They were metallic and orange, with shiny lumps all over them, and they dangled and made clanky noises when she moved. Miss Georgia was what Janie Bryant called a suicide blonde, which she had explained meant dyed by her own hand. The range of colors from her orange earrings to her pink orchid to her dyed blonde hair was like a neon sign to Mitchell, who couldn't take his eyes off her. I hoped he wasn't going to suddenly run screaming from the room.

Worse yet, I hoped Miss Georgia didn't wiggle around and cause one of her earrings to drop down the front of her dress. I was afraid it would get stuck there and look like Miss Georgia had an orange lumpy deformity in the middle of her chest.

The lights were dimmed and we started to take our seats. Miss Georgia was standing at the front of the room ready to introduce the program when a young couple walked by holding a baby. The baby focused on the sound and spectacle of the clanking, shiny earrings as its parents kept on walking. The baby, who was otherwise less coordinated than your average turnip, suddenly and with perfect timing, reached out an arm and snatched the lumpy earring off Miss Georgia's left ear. Miss Georgia spun around and grabbed her ear. The baby had already slobbered all over the earring and was working the whole thing into its mouth.

All at once it made a hideous face, shook its head, pulled the earring out of its mouth with about a pint of slobber, and screamed. Not just a regular scream, but the kind of ear-piercing total-lung scream that babies do so well. Everyone in the room winced. Then the baby drew back its arm and hurled the orange ornament through the air. The earring bounced off the back of a chair and plopped into the exposed strings of the baby grand piano at the front of the room. THUNK, it sounded. It was in the middle register of the piano strings. Twang-ng-ng-ng it echoed.

Miss Georgia rushed up to the piano and reached into the open strings. She braced herself and pulled, but the large earring was wedged between E flat and D. She braced herself again and pulled harder. Then harder. But the earring wouldn't budge. She finally gave one last jerk at the offender, which caused her other earring to gently roll off down her shoulder, and into the upper register of strings. THUNK. Twang-ng-ng-ng.

Several people walked over to help Miss Georgia, including Dad, but nobody could get the earrings unstuck without either busting the piano or busting the earrings. It was an awkward situation, made worse by the baby screaming.

At last Miss Georgia turned to the audience and announced over the screaming that due to "technical difficulties" the recital would be postponed until after the holidays.

"Thank you, God," I whispered. Now I didn't know if I had to not tickle Mitchell for a month or if that deal only counted if God had brought the big blizzard, which He hadn't. I decided to compromise at two weeks, just in case God was keeping track.

As most people put on their coats and filed out, I noticed it was starting to get cold in the room. I was glad I had worn my warm clothes, especially now that I didn't have to be singled out for attention.

Just when I was ready to leave, I heard a soft noise next to the piano. I turned and saw Miss Georgia leaning on the piano with one hand and covering her eyes with the other. She was crying. *Poor Miss Georgia*, I thought. Her evening of glory has been ruined by earrings and a baby tantrum. So I went over to see what I could do. I guess all those years of watching Uncle Gott comfort people had rubbed off on me. Funny how years of watching the grown-ups had an influence.

"Miss Georgia," I began, "it's okay. We'll have other recitals someday." I hoped it was some day in the very distant future. "Don't cry now." I handed her my hankie. Mother always made us carry a clean hankie everywhere.

Miss Georgia must not have had very many people hand her hankies in her life because she started telling me a story of her lost love, which I hadn't really planned on hearing and which had nothing to do with the recital.

"It was Blackjack Pershing, the World War I hero, who gave me those earrings," she began. "Well, he didn't exactly give me the earrings. He, uh, left his uniform jacket with me one evening, which I'm not going to go into, and never returned for it. So I took the brass buttons and had them melted down into earrings."

I'd once heard Dewey say something about meeting General Pershing, whoever he was. It had something to do with a bunch of sheep and a Mexican bandit named Pancho Villa. I wondered if Miss Georgia knew Pancho Villa too. I decided to ask Dewey the next time I saw him to tell me that story again. It was hard to picture Miss Georgia in her diva dress with a bunch of sheep and Mexican bandits.

I was getting cold and Miss Georgia was talking about the meaning of love, which was really boring. I gave a parting look into the piano guts and thanked my lucky stars for General Pershing's brass buttons. Then I remembered I needed to ask Miss Georgia a question.

"Miss Georgia," I said, "do you smoke or drink or dance?"

"Why?" she wanted to know. "What does that have to do with anything?"

"Well, I just wondered." I figured it was too much trouble right now to explain the connection between music and sin.

"Actually, it's not polite to ask those kinds of personal questions, Melody. But—Jack and I once danced a very, shall-we-say, exotic tango in Havana."

"Uh-huh," I said. I was afraid of that. "You can keep the hanky." On the way home I thought about music and people sinning. There seemed to be music all around me, especially this time of year with Christmas carols and holiday music. But the carolers in the stores and church weren't smoking and drinking. I started to wonder if people just went to special places like The Driftwood when they wanted to sin, and the rest of the time they were normal. I couldn't figure out how they knew when it was time to go and be sinful and if it was just instinct like birds knowing when to fly south for the winter. Only those taverns seemed to have people sinning every night. I guess their instincts all had different schedules.

It seemed to me to be like church, only in different buildings. Being holy was in a special holy building. Different groups of people went to church on different days and got holy, then the rest of the time they were normal. But if it was because of instinct, why did some people have sinful instincts and some holy instincts? Apparently, people could work real hard and change their instincts from sinful to holy. That's why we always had to repent and why Uncle Gott saved people from their sins.

That finally made sense to me. Sin had to do with what building you were in and your natural instinct and not with music. In a way I was glad, because I didn't want Dad, who after all spent some weekends in taverns with the band, to be sinful just because he was a musician. But in another way, this meant I had no excuse to give up piano lessons.

146

By the time we got home, we realized why the American Legion Hall had gotten so cold. Our house was freezing too and the cats were curled up into tight little balls just to keep warm.

"I wonder what's the matter," Mother said. "The furnace is turned up, but it won't come on. I'm calling Janie to see if she knows anything about this."

Sure enough, she came back with a worried look. "Alex, we're in trouble," she told Dad. "Janie says a major gas line's ruptured east of town. Everybody like us who uses natural gas for their furnace will be without heat for at least the next two days. Not only that, but Uncle Gott's been on TV warning there's a winter storm moving in and the temperature's gonna drop below zero with strong northerly winds."

"Oh-oh," said Dad. "This is gonna be fun." He was being sarcastic. "I guess we're all gonna learn how to be Eskimos real fast."

Blizzard

Vivian was still at the TV station when the news came in about the ruptured gas main. She told us later the first thing she did was to send a reporter out to cover the story. The second thing she did was to call Uncle Gott in his office. He had finished the six o'clock weather but decided to stay in the studio to keep an eye on the upcoming winter storm.

"I want your expert assessment of what the next twenty-four hours will bring, weather-wise," she instructed him.

"All right," said Uncle Gott. "We've both lived in Kansas long enough to know how our lives revolve around the weather. Well, Vivian, this is one of those times Heaven will demand that acknowledgment. There's going to be bitterly cold temperatures combined with *very* strong northerly winds. Possibly eighteen, twenty inches of snow. Maybe more. Maybe over several days. This is a full-blown blizzard, Vivian, and it's going to hit us square in northeastern Kansas." He said it the way Moses pronounced the plagues upon Egypt, but with a lot more concern for the recipients.

Vivian, who was always at her best during an emergency, told him to put on all the warm clothes he could find and stay at the studio all night. Then she ran off to find the studio engineer. She had to make sure the TV and radio could still stay on the air without heat, and maybe, if the storm got bad enough to knock out power lines, without electricity too. She called the newspaper and told them to do the same thing. Then she sent an employee out to stock up on food and get one of those little camping stoves to heat it on, so at least the crew wouldn't starve. She let everybody go home that wasn't essential and asked those employees who were and who lived close by to go home and put on their warm clothes, make sure their families would be okay, and get back to the station as soon as they could.

"I take my responsibility to keep the public informed very

seriously," she told the chief engineer. "Especially when a storm like this is coming. In times like this, we *are* the weather!"

Uncle Gott had called Grandma Dale and told her why he wouldn't be coming home that night. Dale and Dewey weren't worried about the ruptured city gas main for themselves, because like most farmers, they had their own supply of heating fuel from a propane tank in the back yard. But if the electricity went out, then they'd have to rely on the wood stove in the parlor and two kerosene stoves leftover from Grandpa Richard's frugal days. Either way, the farm would still have some heat.

Like most farmers, what they were more worried about was the livestock. The extreme cold meant the animals needed extra feed and water. If they were in a barn and healthy to start with they could last out the storm, because their own body heat would keep the temperature reasonable. But in the open pasture, even with some sort of wind block like a grove of trees or a low hill, the cold would freeze the ponds and water tanks and blowing snow would drift over any hay. During a blizzard there would be no way for humans to get to them, so a prolonged winter storm meant many animals would die from starvation and exposure. Grandma Dale told her brother she hoped the storm would hold off till the next day so they'd have a chance to collect the cattle, because it was already too dark to find them tonight. They had to be herded in closer to the barn to have any chance for survival.

"I believe the storm will hit before morning," Uncle Gott replied. "But the matter is in God's hands."

Dewey and Uncle Rex Oliver and the Indians went outside and hauled a big stack of firewood from the woodshed onto the back porch, just in case. They also cleaned and filled the kerosene lanterns and stoves. Then they went back to the horse barn and gave the horses extra hay and the barn cats extra food. The animals' behavior had told Dewey a storm was coming several hours ago, so he wasn't surprised at all. He patted the horses and told them everything would be all right. They always responded to Dewey.

Grandma Dale finally reached us after the botched piano recital and said we'd better come and stay at the farm with them where we'd at least have heat. "But don't dawdle," she cautioned Mother, "or you'll get caught in the elements."

"We're on our way," said Mother. She'd been raised on a farm too and knew all about respecting the weather.

Dad's sense of duty compelled him to go to Meadowgreen and help them switch over to emergency fuel in the main buildings, and to shut off the water in all the remaining buildings so the pipes wouldn't freeze and break when the power went out. He would probably be tied up there through most of the next day. Mother would take us kids and the pets to Grandma Dale's immediately.

I was excited about the storm and felt good for the first time in weeks. My Dad was being a hero to go help Meadowgreen, Mother was a hero to drive us kids to safety, and Uncle Gott was a hero to warn people about the storm. Not only that, but I had been delivered from my recital and it was looking like they'd have to cancel school. I wondered why God had been one day late in sending the big blizzard I had prayed for. Maybe God was really so busy trying to answer everybody's prayers that He got his dates mixed up. Only that wasn't supposed to happen with God.

We gathered up our snow clothes and boots and packed some things. At least the car heater was working. The hard part was getting the two cats convinced it was in their best interest to get stuffed in a car and hauled off to a strange place. They were meowing like crazy.

"Hold on to those cats, kids," Mother told us. "Otherwise, they'll get down under the car seat and not come out." That had happened to us once before when we tried to take Black Mimi for a ride. This time we held on to the cats so they couldn't get away. I just hoped they didn't get car sick.

By the time we got to the farm the night had grown very cold and still. Not only could you see your breath, but you could almost see your breath freeze. I put Little Poo under my coat so she wouldn't catch cold on the way into the house, but I couldn't help but stop, just for a moment, and admire for the thousandth time the beauty of the brilliant nighttime sky from out in the country. I loved to look at the stars. The more I looked the more it seemed like Uncle Gott was wrong about the storm because there wasn't a cloud in the sky. But Dewey said the animals had told him a storm was coming. He said the more you were around them the more you got to understand their language. Not through words, of course, but through their behavior and the way they would suddenly do unusual things. He said then you could be sure it was going to storm.

Little Poo was struggling to get out from under my coat so I had to hurry into the house. I wondered if Little Poo would ever tell us if a storm was coming. She wasn't the smartest cat we'd ever had, in fact she was almost retarded, so maybe she didn't know herself.

Grandma Dale welcomed us while Dewey helped Mother unload the car. We shut our cats in the pantry so they wouldn't fight with the farm cats. Of course, they were terribly offended—Harmony called them ungrateful little beasts— and kept meowing. Rex Oliver came up to the pantry door and stared and stared at it for a long time, but I guess he thought better than to get into a meowing contest with the cats on the other side. Finally, he said, "They'll get used to it," and walked off.

I suppose Maynard and Virgil had already gone to bed above the garage because I didn't see them, but it was late.

Mother and Harmony were given Uncle Gott's room since he wouldn't be home, and Mitchell and I got the spare upstairs bedroom. We'd slept there before during our summer visits, but wintertime was different. Grandma Dale was afraid the storm would come up in the night and cut off the power, so she piled her homemade quilts on the bed until we could barely turn over from the weight. She also left us a flashlight. That was a mistake because Mitchell and I took turns putting the flashlight in our mouths and turning it on and off just for the effect.

Sometime during the night I woke up. I wasn't sure for a second where I was, but then I remembered why my whole body was weighted down, only not from the cats lying on me like at home. I listened carefully and could hear a low wind outside. I listened some more, but that was all I heard.

Usually at the farm, the roosters make an infernal racket at daybreak and nobody with normal hearing can sleep through it. But the next morning all we could hear was snow being driven against the windows. I poked my head outside the covers and recognized that the furnace was still on, so I got dressed and went downstairs. Mitchell woke up too. We didn't want to miss the big storm.

Mother and Grandma Dale were in the kitchen baking cinnamon rolls and Harmony was hanging around trying to be helpful. Of course we had to eat a real breakfast first before we were allowed a warm roll, but that was not a problem. They had the radio on and it was giving announcements of all the school closings and meeting cancellations because of the storm.

"What's the storm gonna do?" I asked Grandma Dale. I could tell she'd been up for a long time.

"Gott called early this morning to say there's a huge moisture system from the southwest going to collide right over Kansas with bitterly cold air from the north. You know how he talks that weatherman talk." she said. We all nodded. "Temperatures are going to be dropping all day and be well below zero soon, with forty mile-an-hour winds making it feel even colder. On top of that he's expecting two foot of snow. That means we'll have no visibility and drifts—big drifts—everywhere. Now that's frostbite conditions," she said. "You kids are gonna stay in the house."

"No," we all pleaded at once. We wanted to go play in the snow. We could see snow coming down everywhere and the wind pushing it into drifts in some places and sweeping it clean in others.

"Listen, you three," said Grandma Dale. She wiped her hands on her apron, pulled up a chair and sat down at the table with us. "I don't think any of you have been through a real blizzard before. Big snows, yes. But this is different. In just a little while the wind and snow will get so strong that out here in the country it's possible we'll get a 'white out.' Then you won't be able to see anything because the snow is so heavy. You won't even be able to see the house from the barn and you could lose your way and freeze to death in just a little while. Dewey and Rex Oliver and the Indians are out there right now..." She raised up her head and gave an anxious look out the kitchen window, "...trying to find where the cattle have sought shelter in the pasture so they can drive them into the cow lot if there's still time. But the worse it gets, the more danger to humans and animals.

"So please, you three, *please* don't fuss about going outside right now. After the storm stops you can go out and play as much as you want, I'm sure. Just enjoy your cinnamon rolls and try and read or play checkers or watch for Uncle Gott on television until the menfolk come in. They'll tell you how awful it is outside."

I was real disappointed we couldn't go outside and play. After all, when it snowed was the only time we could build snow forts and go sledding and sliding and make snowballs and snow forts and play fox and geese. What was the use of getting out of school if we had to stay in the house all day?

I was fussy, I guess, and almost went and tickled Mitchell just for orneriness. But then I remembered my compromise with God and my two-week ban for tickling Mitchell. That made me even fussier. Why did God have to bring a storm that would kill the cattle and cause people to freeze to death? I hadn't asked for that. I hoped everybody wasn't gonna blame me for the storm, even though I'd prayed for it. This praying business was really touchy. I guessed next time I decided to pray for something I would have to be very specific about all the details so God wouldn't misunderstand.

So then I thought, if praying had got me into this mess maybe praying could get me out. I went into the Blue Grotto and locked the door and prayed to God to not let the storm hurt any people or animals and for it to be just a gentle little snow so we could go out and play in it but for school to still be canceled all week. Then I had to think of something to do back for God in return. I couldn't think of anything except not tickling Mitchell for the other two weeks of the month. But I told God He'd have to be punctual this time or the deal was off. Then I said "Amen" and stood up and flushed the toilet to avoid suspicion. I felt better having addressed this important subject.

The wind had increased outside to the point where tree limbs were banging against the house. Mother and Grandma Dale kept cooking things and looking out the window all the time. They tried not to show it, but they were worried. I started to get worried too because the wind was howling so hard, but then I remembered my prayer and felt sure God would handle everything. To pass the time I started up a discussion with Mitchell. It was a topic that had puzzled me for a long time.

"Mitchell," I said, "did you ever think about what if people had tails?"

"Nope," he said.

"Would people be born with different style tails, or would they choose their style? For instance, would you choose a hairy bushy fluffy tail or a sleek little rat tail? And would you dye it and tease it and spray it and curl it, or would you let it go natural?"

"Ummm," said Mitchell.

"Would you wear clothing, like a scarf or a sleeve or something, on your tail? Would Methodists have different tails than Catholics, and would some tails be considered sinful? What about tail jewelry? What about shaving your tail? You ever think about that Mitchell?"

"Nope," he repeated.

"Well, how would people's furniture and cars be different so we could sit down with tails?" I had wondered a lot about our shape as people and the shapes animals had and why some things were the same and some different. I wished I'd been born with retractable fingernails, for instance, because it would have made climbing trees much easier.

But try as I might, Mitchell wasn't in the mood to talk about tails. He kept looking out the window for Uncle Rex Oliver and the other men. I sighed and turned on the television.

There was Uncle Gott with a Special Weather Bulletin. He looked tired and like a woolly caterpillar again, but also concerned. He repeated everything Grandma Dale had told us earlier about the weather and then said for God's sake to seek shelter, avoid travel, and stay warm. "This storm is life-threatening," he said, "and should be taken seriously." Then he read the list of emergency shelters again.

After the Special Bulletin ended, I turned the TV off. I tried to see if Harmony wanted to play carom, but she was writing in her notebook and said she didn't want to be disturbed. "You're already disturbed," I told her, and walked back to the kitchen.

Something was the matter with Grandma Dale. She looked like she'd just collapsed in the kitchen chair and her face was as white as the snow falling outside. Mother had rushed to her side and so did I.

"Dale. What's the matter?" Mother cried.

"Alex," she said. "Alex is in trouble. I just saw it in my mind, clear as you're standing here."

"Oh my God," said Mother. She rushed to the phone. "Please God, please let the phone still be working," she whispered almost to herself. It was. Fumbling and frantic she dialed Meadowgreen's number for the maintenance department. "It's ringing," Mother said. She stood there holding the phone waiting for someone to answer.

Grandma Dale was still sitting, staring straight off into space like she was looking at something far away. I had knelt by her chair and had my hand on the side of the chair. Her face was still pale and she was breathing in short gasps when she remembered to breathe at all. I had never seen a person like this before.

All at once she took a quick deep breath and then let it out very slowly. Her eyes seemed to look around the room like she had just returned from somewhere else and that's when she saw me kneeling next to her.

Very gently she put her arms around me. "Oh, Melody," she said softly. "Your daddy's been in an accident. But I feel sure that...there was an intervention...I saw it...and..." Her eyes looked far away again, "...and he's going to stay with us."

Then she looked at Mother who was still holding the phone. "It's okay, Louise," she said. "Alex has been injured, but he's okay." Mother was crying, still waiting for someone to answer on the other end of the phone. Grandma Dale gave me a quick squeeze, then stood up and put her arms around Mother. "There, there, Louise. It's okay. It's okay. He's going to be okay."

Harmony and Mitchell had heard Mother crying and came into the kitchen. "What's the matter, Mom?" Harmony asked. Lately she'd started calling our mother Mom instead of Mother.

"I think your father may have been in an accident," Mother told her. "But Grandma Dale says he's okay now."

"What kind of an accident? How do you know? Did somebody call you? I didn't hear the phone ring."

Harmony was puzzled and impatient, her way of hiding the sudden fear I could tell she felt and would rather die than show.

I was trying to figure out why everybody was fussing so much. Mitchell got in accidents all the time and he was always fine. I was sure Dad would be fine too. Nothing bad would happen to us, because we were a good family.

"My sixth sense showed me a picture all of a sudden of your daddy in danger, Honey." Grandma Dale got right to the point. "It was a feeling like I had only once before when he was in the war and the ships on either side of his were bombed and sank. I knew then and I knew today that his li...that he was in danger. And both times I felt another force or presence too. I think—well I guess I'd call it his guardian angel. It just sort of wrapped itself around your daddy..." She made an embracing movement with her arms, "and, and saved him. Thank you, God." She lifted her eyes to the heavens and silently thanked whatever forces she was in touch with for saving her only child's life once again.

There. I was right. Dad's guardian angel protected him from anything bad happening.

"Is Dad in the hospital?" asked Mitchell. "Are you trying to call the hospital?"

Mother didn't answer him. She was thinking. "Maybe the

hospital's trying to call us. Maybe I should free up the line. Only—it's just so hard not knowing. Maybe Meadowgreen's phones are dead from the storm. Well I'm going to hang up and hope we hear something soon." Mother hung up.

I had a lot of questions I wanted to ask Grandma Dale about her sixth sense. I'd tried to ask my Sunday School teacher Monroe Bates about it once and he said it was from the devil, that normal God-fearing people didn't need to know what went on in the spirit world. That really confused me, because I knew the Bible had prophets who could tell the future. I wondered if that could be the same thing as the sixth sense. So I finally asked Mr. Bates again if wasn't it the same as the prophets and he said absolutely not, that the prophets received their visions from God and this sixth sense business was from "the other place." I asked him how a person could tell the difference and he said, "By their fruits ye shall know them." Well in that case, I said, I think my grandma could have a book of the Bible written after her. The Book of Dale, it would be called. Maybe I could get Harmony to write it someday since she liked to write. Mr. Bates said, "Don't be a smart aleck, Melody," and changed the subject.

Just as I was going to talk to Grandma Dale, the back porch screen door whipped open with a violent bang that made us all jump. Mitchell ran to the kitchen door and opened it. A violent gust of wind and snow and bitter cold almost knocked him over. He took a step backward, but held on to the door. We all rushed up behind him, mostly to close the door, but also to help Dewey and Uncle Rex and the Indians and Rex Oliver's dog Sophocles. They had all made it back, but were so stiff and frozen we had to help them off with their coats and boots.

We got everybody into the kitchen where it was warm, closed all the doors, and Mother and Harmony got everybody some hot cocoa and a warm cinnamon roll. Dewey said first he had to dry off Spot, which was his name for Sophocles. Mother said no, Melody would do that, that Dewey needed to get warm. So Mitchell and I took some old rags and towels and rubbed the ice out from between Sophocles' toes and rubbed him dry real good. Of course he stood up and shook all the snow off all over us once, but we gave him some warm water to drink and part of Mitchell's cinnamon roll. There was snow all over the kitchen floor anyway from everybody's wet boots, so a little more from the dog didn't make much difference.

"That Spot saved our lives," Dewey finally said when he warmed up enough to talk. "We couldn't see nothin' so we tied ourselves together and told Spot to take us home and he did. That's one hell of a good dog." Nobody even told him to watch his language.

Grandma Dale made sure everybody was dried off and warming up before she asked about the livestock.

"We never got that far," said Dewey. "We were only about a quarter mile from the barn when the wind picked up so bad you couldn't see nothing. Right then we dismounted and roped all the horses together so we wouldn't get separated and tried to retrace our tracks. But the wind was covering 'em as fast as we was making 'em, so we had no way of knowing which way was home. We decided to see if the animals would show us the way, and they did. They knew. The horses, too, was all wantin' to go in the same direction. It's like I always said, take good care of your animals and they'll take good care of you."

"Did you get the horses put up okay?" Grandma Dale asked. And then answered her own question. "I expect you did. I've never known you not to take care of your animals first." There was love and pride in her voice, mixed with a great deal of relief.

"They're all fine and dry in the barn," said Dewey. "We almost stayed there too, but then decided we could be there for days in this storm. Anyway," he paused, "we figured you was cookin' something good and Mitchell here would have it all eaten if we didn't get in here soon." He smiled at Mitchell who smiled back.

"Harmony, think we could have another cup of cocoa?" Harmony rushed to comply.

The men looked chapped, cold, and exhausted from just a short time out in the storm. Now I felt really bad about what was happening to the cattle and just kept hoping God would stop this storm soon.

Grandma Dale was filling the men in about Dad when the phone rang. Mother rushed for it and nearly fell down on the wet floor. She said "yes" then "speaking" then just listened for a minute then said, "Oh thank you, thank you, thank you!" and hung up. She placed both hands over her heart and gave a big sigh.

"Alex almost got electrocuted," she said. "But he's okay. They wanted to take him to the hospital just to be sure, but the roads and visibility are so bad they couldn't risk it and anyway they have real doctors already there at Meadowgreen." I knew the doctors she was talking about were all shrinks, but I supposed they were better than nothing.

"So one of them looked Alex over," Mother continued, "and uh—he's got some mild burns on his hand and he got knocked unconscious and hit his head a little bit when he fell down. But other than that, they said he's okay and he'll be fine. They said they're gonna put him in one of the patient rooms for observation, but if I know Alex he'll be up and back to work before evening."

"Did they say how it happened?" asked Grandma Dale.

"No, they didn't," Mother replied. "I guess we'll have to wait for him to tell us."

Wait was what we all did for the next two days. Twice a day the men would feel along a rope they had tied between the house and the horse barn so they could find their way to feed and water the animals. Sometimes they couldn't get the porch door open because of drifting snow, so they had to work hard just to get out of the house and into the barn.

By the end of the first day the wind had snapped the power and phone lines. We fired up the wood stove and put on our long underwear and warm clothes. We used the kerosene lanterns after dark and it made Mitchell and me feel like real pioneers. At night, lying under the heavy quilts, we could hear the wind blowing and howling outside and there was absolutely nothing we could do except go to sleep and hope the next day would bring an end to it.

Finally after three days, the storm stopped. God had been too late again.

Guardian Angels,
Unanswered Prayers, and "Varmits"

Even after the storm stopped and we dug ourselves out of the house, we were still isolated. To put some of our pent-up energy to good use Grandma Dale said to go outside and haul some firewood and shovel a better path to the barn and clear off the sidewalks. But the snow was so deep we couldn't get very far. Dewey and Uncle Rex and the Indians got the tractor dug out and started clearing a path to the main cow pasture. They got one stretch open, so they hauled a load of hay up there and chopped a hole in the ice on the pond so any cattle still alive could get to water. Dewey wouldn't let us go with them because he was afraid they were going to find dead cattle everywhere.

I felt really guilty and angry at God for not listening to my second prayer and getting the first one wrong. I didn't know why I even bothered with God, but then I remembered that Dad's guardian angel had saved his life two different times and that was in spite of Dad's occasional beer drinking. I couldn't figure out what I had done wrong that God wasn't paying any attention to me.

I had worked myself up into a good case of mad and had caught Harmony behind the ear with a snowball. After three days of being cooped up in the house I was spoiling for a fight with somebody. Harmony would do just fine.

She jumped on me and knocked me over backward in the snow, then held me down and started pushing armfuls of snow across my face. I tried to get up, but Harmony was too heavy, I had on too many clothes, and the snow restricted my movement. I was yelling and struggling and calling Harmony names and she just kept throwing snow in my face. Mitchell came over and watched but didn't say anything. Finally, he threw a snowball at Harmony, only she ducked, and it missed. So he threw another and got her in the arm. She jumped off me and started chasing him. I think she was enjoying herself.

The men came back from the pasture and said about half the cattle were dead, but their bodies had blocked the wind and kept the other half alive. Dewey said it would be a while before the "dead wagon" could get through to pick up the bodies, but he guessed it would give the coyotes something to feed off of in the meantime.

"You won't be the only folks taking a loss on this one," Virgil told him. Maynard never said a word.

We still didn't have power, so without the radio or telephone we couldn't find out if power and gas had been restored in town. "Won't matter if they have been," said Dewey. "You can't drive home till the roads get plowed open anyhow." I hadn't thought of that.

I was still disgusted and went and hid high up in the hay loft of the big cow barn. I wanted some time to think and be by myself after being cooped up with everybody for so long. I laid back on the hay and stared up at the cupola where the wild pigeons lived. It looked like they'd made it through the storm okay.

I thought about why people were so helpless. We went to school and learned stuff to make us smart, but then a storm came along and we just let it. Why couldn't we be smarter than some old storm? Or if God brought the storm, why did He want to hurt people and animals? Weren't we part of His creation? Didn't He love us anymore?

I felt bad and confused and started crying. I cried for quite a while, but then I guess I fell asleep in the hay. Sometime after that, I guess it must have been getting dark, I woke up and saw Rex Oliver lying back in the hay a little ways away. It was probably warmer than the cave. He was staring at the cupola too. I didn't feel like talking and I guess he didn't either, so we both watched the pigeons come in and go to roost. I was still real sad. Now I knew how Uncle Rex felt when he needed to go off by himself and be melancholy. Mother had told us what that word meant and now I understood. I didn't like being melancholy.

The next morning the snowplow came through. We were eating breakfast and heard it on the road. "That's good," said Dewey. "That means the line repairmen can get back here now and get us some power and a phone."

"Hey, Dewey," I said, "can you tell us that story again about General Pershing and Pancho Villa and the sheep?"

Dewey looked at me sorta funny. "Why do you want to hear that, Melody?"

I was gonna tell him about Miss Georgia, but then everybody else was listening and I didn't know if she wanted everybody to know about her lost love. So I said, "Oh, I just heard General Pershing's name mentioned around town." Mother laughed but didn't question me.

"Well," said Dewey, who didn't need much coaxing to tell a story, "when I was just a young man, the age you kids would call a teenager, I left the Ozarks to go to New Mexico and help one of our old neighbors. This neighbor had moved to New Mexico and got himself a sheep ranch there because the Ozarks was too civilized for him. But the ornery sheep kept running off all over the desert, so I would get sent to round them up.

"One day, I was out on horseback chasing sheep when I hear a group of men ride up behind me. They're soldiers. General Blackjack Pershing and his boys."

"Did he have his uniform jacket on?" I asked Dewey.

"Let me think," Dewey said. "Yes, I believe he did, but it was pretty dirty from so many days in the saddle. Anyway, ole Blackjack told me to get back to my friend's ranch right quick and forget about the sheep, because Pancho Villa had raided inside the U.S. border and was gonna kill anybody in his way. Well, I had no desire to become the next in-ter-na-tion-al in-ci-dent, so I turned around and went back to the ranch. The sheep business never did amount to much, but ever since then I haven't had much use for Mexicans." Dewey would have spit, but he was at the breakfast table and Grandma Dale didn't allow any spitting at the table.

"Did you see any women with them?" I asked.

"Women? With the Cavalry? No sir, I didn't," said Dewey.

I was busy turning over in my mind if Miss Georgia and Dewey's paths might have crossed somehow out in the desert. I had never been to the desert, but it didn't sound like a very friendly place. Of course, right now, neither was Kansas.

Harmony, who ate like a bird, finished her breakfast and asked to be excused. Pretty soon she came running back to the kitchen all excited. "Come quick, everybody," she said. "There's people marching at the end of the driveway."

We all got up and looked out the window and I'll-be-darned, there was the despicable Wades in their winter coats carrying hateful picket signs around and around where the driveway met the road. Their signs were all saying mean things about Rex Oliver being crazy and a murderer. One called him a "Lunatic Devil," one said "Murder Is a Sin," and one just said "An Eye for an Eye."

"Doesn't that son of a buck have anything better to do?" yelled Dewey to nobody in particular. Rex Oliver had turned slightly pale and was getting ready, I think, to make a run for the cave. Dewey started cussing to himself, looked up and said, "Excuse me," to all of us.

"You boys come with me," he told Virgil and Maynard. "We're gonna get to the bottom of this."

Grandma Dale almost said something to him but thought better of it. Uncle Rex did grab his coat and bolt out the back door then. Mitchell and I wanted to go with the men. I was sure there was going to be a fight and didn't want to miss it. But Mother wouldn't let us, so we glued ourselves to the window instead. We watched while Dewey and the Indians walked down the long drive and saw Dewey stop Earl Wade. It looked like they were having some pretty strong words because there was a lot of arm waving and pointing back up toward the house, but all the other picketers were getting in the way of our view.

All at once the roar of a gun blasted through the winter air. We all jumped a mile. So did everybody on the road. Then we saw Grandma Dale with her coat and boots on, limping down the driveway with the shotgun smoking in her hand. About halfway down she stopped, took aim at the group, and fired again. Dewey and the Indians and most of the Wades either dove to the ground or ran for safety before the second shot got off. But they could see, and so could we from the window, that Dale was reloading and limping farther down the driveway. The Wades all ran back to their truck, jumped in and sped off, but not before Grandma Dale got off one final blast over their heads.

I was speechless. Grandma Dale was the sweetest person I had ever met. I'd never seen her do a hurtful thing in my life, except maybe kill a snake in the henhouse once. The thought of her shooting somebody, even somebody as despicable as Earl Wade, was more than I could comprehend. Mother was speechless too.

By the time Grandma Dale limped back up the driveway the men had caught up with her and helped her into the house. We got in on the tail end of their discussion.

"...don't wanna hear no cussin' and complainin' around this house about varmits. There's only one way to handle varmits and that's to show 'em real plain they're not welcome and never will be."

I guess I'd never classified Earl and his gang in the same category as rats, skunks, and chicken hawks, even if he did have snake eyes. But evidently Grandma Dale did. Looking at it from that angle, she was just defending her brood.

"I'm not saying you're wrong, Dale. In fact, I'm real glad you got rid of those, uh..."

"Don't say it," said Grandma Dale.

"Yeah," said Dewey. "But now you wait. The sheriff's gonna be out here shortly and what are we gonna tell him?"

"I'm tellin' him the truth, of course," replied Grandma Dale. "That I saw a pack of the blackest-hearted buzzards that ever smelled a carcass circlin' up at the end of the driveway and they was after one of my chicks. One of my wounded chicks. Don't nothing come after my chicks. It's not illegal to shoot at buzzards that's after your chicks, now is it?" Grandma Dale had fire in her eyes.

"Right," agreed Mitchell loudly. "I saw buzzards too, Grandma. Circling just like you said. I'm gonna tell the sheriff that too."

"Thank you, honey," said Grandma Dale. She looked around at all of us to see if anyone else felt like challenging her. Maynard was making a big deal about brushing snow off where he'd had to throw himself on the ground real fast or get shot, but otherwise nobody did anything.

"Well now," said Dale, "do you expect those varmits will have the nerve to come back here again? I don't." She turned and walked off with the shotgun. Dewey was still trying to figure out what had just happened with his normally peaceful wife. I could tell he was thinking back through the morning's events.

"Boys," he said to Virgil and Maynard, "did you happen to notice how Earl reacted when he heard that first shot? He tensed up all right, but the way he turned his head and tried to find out where the shot was coming from, and the way his wife rushed over and hollered at him to get down, well—it was almost as if—maybe his eyes weren't working real good. Did you notice that too?"

"Now that you mention it, I did," said Virgil. Maynard was still brushing off snow, but he looked up and nodded.

"Dewey," I said. "I been thinking about Earl's snake eyes too. You know how they look right through a person and make you feel paralyzed? I was thinking how we should wear dark glasses so we wouldn't have to look at his eyes. And now you think maybe he's got eye trouble. Well, maybe he's blind, Dewey! Maybe Earl has to have all his family and followers around him because he can't see by himself. Maybe that's his secret life!"

I felt certain this was what my sixth sense had told me that day when I was thinking about Earl's secret life. That Earl was blind. I was so excited at making this connection that I started jumping up and down. Maynard stopped brushing off snow and looked at me and sat down.

"Well, even if he is, what difference would it make?" asked

Harmony. "He's still despicable and causes trouble for everybody all over town. Being blind hasn't seemed to stop him any."

Harmony always made me mad when she said stuff against what I had just said. Especially when she was right. I couldn't think what difference it would make either, but it seemed like it should be important.

"Well in some ways you have to feel sorry for the man," said Mother. "It would just be horrible to be blind."

Not only did no one else express sympathy for Earl, but Dewey found his cuspidor and gave a very deliberate spit. "Them Wades all got something wrong with 'em," he finally said.

We eventually learned that the storm had hit hardest in western Kansas with winds of sixty miles per hour and drifts ten to thirty feet deep. Twenty-three thousand cattle and ten people had lost their lives across the state. Uncle Gott and Grandma Dale had been right about the storm's danger.

It took ten days for things to get back to normal. So many power and phone lines were down, not to mention the gas main, that repair crews were called in from all over the Midwest to help. The snow got plowed and streets and stores and schools opened again. The dead wagon hauled off all the dead livestock. Eventually people forgot that Mother Nature could hold us all captive any time she chose.

With everything else going on, it took some time before the sheriff came out to talk to Dale and Dewey about the shooting incident. By then he said that although he had lived in Kansas all his life and felt sure that buzzards flew south in the winter, that if Dale said she saw 'em after her chicks at the end of her driveway that was good enough for him. He didn't like Earl Wade either.

Dad was fully recovered from his near electrocution. The accident had happened when he had asked Meadowgreen's main electrician, Geezer Roy, to lock out a 110-volt electric line so Dad could rewire it to the auxiliary power system. Geezer, a man with thirty years' experience, had told Dad the line was locked out. Just when Dad went to reach for it, "a little cloud of doubt," he said, came across his mind and told him that perhaps he should check the lock-out himself. But his hand was already too close to the line and his boots had snow on them and the electricity jumped over to his hand, burning it and knocking him unconscious. He said he was really lucky with the snow and everything that he hadn't been killed. It seems Geezer had accidentally locked out the wrong line. Geezer just felt terrible and didn't know how this could have happened and just kept apologizing over and over, Dad said. The poor guy had already sent Dad a huge fruit basket when the stores opened and said he could expect a real nice Christmas gift too. Dad got all embarrassed and told him to please stop it, that accidents happen, and it had all turned out okay.

Vivian and Uncle Gott only had enough backup power to continue their radio broadcasting when the power went out, so the TV station had gone off the air. Vivian had gotten hold of the police and the Red Cross early in the storm and found out about emergency shelters and other survival information. She had the announcers repeat that as often as possible. Fortunately, the power company always considered Vivian's stations a public safety priority, so the power to the radio and television station got back on real fast after the storm was over. Then the reporters had to really scramble to find out current information and get it to the public. Now they were all exhausted and in need of a hot bath, but also happy that they had undoubtedly saved lives in northeast Kansas by staying calm and staying on the air.

Uncle Billy Glenn had worked four days around the clock. First the firemen had helped with the ruptured gas main, then by dealing with frozen and busted water lines, and finally they just helped any way the mayor asked them to. He said dealing with emergencies was what his job was all about. I think he felt too tired to brag, but undoubtedly we would hear more about these exploits when he recuperated.

Janie Bryant had gone over to her sister's home where there was a fireplace. Other than the fact that her brother-in-law belonged to the

ACLU, which was second cousin to a Communist, she had gotten along okay.

Uncle Billy Glenn said the police had lost track of Big Augie and his boys and Earl Wade and his gang because there was too many other things going on with the storm. Well, said Billy Glenn, turns out old Augie and friends tried to charter a plane out of town back to Rhode Island, but couldn't find a pilot stupid enough to brave that storm no matter how much money he flashed around. So then they tried to drive east, but it was snowing so hard they ran off the road in East Topeka and would have froze to death in their Lincoln if a colored man and his family hadn't found them and took them over to a church basement, which was an emergency shelter. "I bet that was quite a sight," said Uncle Billy Glenn, "them wops from back east stuck in with all them coloreds for three days."

"Watch your language," said Mother.

"So where are they now?" asked Dad.

"Well, it so happens after that they flew back to Rhode Island for Christmas, but they booked rooms at the Hotel Jayhawk for right after New Year's. So I guess we'll have the honor of their presence again shortly," Uncle Billy Glenn had answered.

It did seem like God gave us a break from all our problems then. For the next two weeks Topeka was filled with the Christmas spirit. The Salvation Army bell ringers reported a large increase in their donations. Church groups adopted needy families and gave presents to patients at the V.A. and State Hospital who had no one to remember them. The National Guard collected broken toys, repaired them, and gave them to underprivileged children. Carolers treated their neighbors with songs and everybody put up decorations.

In school we sang carols too and made Christmas ornaments, while my Girl Scout troop made long, felt Christmas stockings. In church we had a special Christmas program and Mitchell got to be one of the shepherds in the nativity scene. I sang alto in the junior choir pageant. The Christmas music was really pretty, I had to admit.

Two other strange happenings occurred during that time. Earl Wade and his followers suddenly stopped picketing. Dewey said they were probably still picking the buckshot out of their butts. And the Mount Calvary Temple church in East Topeka, the one used as an emergency shelter during the blizzard, received a donation of a beautiful stained-glass window from Mr. and Mrs. August Messina in memory of their daughter Brenda. The window was the large circular design known as a "rose" window.

January 1959

Existential Crisis at Age Nine

The day of New Year's Eve Janie Bryant received a personal letter from J. Edgar Hoover. The first we knew about it was when we suddenly heard loud screams and whoops coming from the direction of Janie's house and increasing in volume as she raced across the street toward ours. The noise was so loud that Mother met her at the front door.

"What's wrong, Janie?" Mother screamed herself. We thought maybe the Communists had finally launched a missile attack on Kansas.

Janie was panting so hard from the exertion of screaming and running across the street that she couldn't talk. As she stood inside our front door gasping for air Mother was getting more and more anxious that maybe we needed to take cover from the missiles. "For God's sake Janie—are we under attack?"

Janie managed to shake her head no and finally thrust the letter in Mother's face.

"What's this about?" asked Mother. Then she proceeded to read it out loud.

    Dear Miss Bryant,

        Thank you for your kind and
    constant words of encouragement and the
    patriotism you exhibit against the evil
    forces that would tear asunder our
    beloved democracy.
        You will be pleased to know that
    under the leadership of your fellow
    Kansan, President Dwight D. Eisenhower,
    our country is becoming stronger every
    day. He has authorized the Federal

Bureau of Investigation to continue our
efforts to root out Communism wherever
it may occur and to prosecute to the
fullest extent of the law those
individuals involved.
  I plan to speak to a group of
Kansas City business leaders on this
topic January 30 and wonder if you
would care to attend as my guest. I
would be delighted to hold a ticket for
you should that be convenient. Please
contact the address below for details.

  With warmest regards,
  J. Edgar Hoover

"So we're not under attack?" Mother asked. "This is what you were so excited about?" Janie nodded her head yes. "That is exciting, Janie! J. Edgar Hoover writing you himself! What are you gonna wear?" She didn't bother to ask if Janie would attend.

I lost interest when they started talking about clothes, except I wondered if Janie could get J. Edgar to sign my Junior G-Man membership card. It was somewhere in my room. I went to look for it, but after digging around in my treasure drawer, which is what I called the drawer with all my good stuff in it, I still couldn't find it. I wondered if Harmony had seen it, but she had gone over to Daffy's so I couldn't ask her.

When I went back in the living room, Mother and Janie were giggling together about Uncle Billy Glenn. Mother had separately asked Janie and Billy Glenn to drop by that evening for some Parcheesi and snacks to usher in the New Year. I suddenly had a sickening feeling that by this time next year we could be calling Janie "Auntie." This wasn't my sixth sense, this was just thinking ahead.

The more I thought about it the stranger it seemed. If Janie did become part of the family, then both she and Vivian would be working women in a family where the women had always been homemakers. I didn't count Mother's Avon as a real job since it was just part-time and she herself said it was just for pin money. All around me I saw that women, because of their nature I guess, didn't have the strength and boldness of men to handle the exciting and dangerous stuff of life. That's why their opinions weren't as valuable as men's. Women didn't get to be president or even mayor, because they just weren't supposed to handle that kind of work. Instead, women baked pies and had babies and wore girdles and white gloves.

I hated that stuff. I wanted to be a boy and get to do real work and talk with the men about the important things of life, instead of discuss recipes and diapers and petunias with the women. I wanted to wear comfortable clothes and build great monuments that would last as long as the Empire State Building, instead of cook a tuna fish casserole that would be gone by six-thirty. I wanted to be Tarzan in our games and not Jane. I mean, let's face it, even God was a boy.

But I was not. I knew there would come a day when I would no longer be allowed to continue my tomboy ways and the strange behavior of womanhood would be demanded of me. I dreaded even thinking about it.

Harmony, on the other hand, was born a little lady. She loved to give tea parties for her dolls. Her side of the closet was full of ruffles and lace and big stiff petticoats. Harmony loved to cook, and she loved babies, and she loved the color pink. Harmony was from another planet.

Now the possibility existed we would get two career women as relatives. I wasn't sure why this made me uneasy, but it did. If the pioneer women who had settled Kansas had been strong, and I saw that Grandma Dale was strong, then why couldn't other women be strong too? Even though I loved Mother dearly, I saw her role in life as less interesting than Dad's. But I also saw that when Vivian and Janie had tried to make careers for themselves they had a harder time. I gave up trying to figure this out. Life was just too complicated sometimes.

I didn't get any answers from the adults that night either. Janie was acting dumber than usual about stuff I knew she knew, just to impress Uncle Billy Glenn. He was bragging more than ever about his dangerous job and the heroic rescues he'd made and the citation from the mayor he got once. It was like being around two strangers, when these were people I'd known all my life. Was this what love did to people? Changed their personalities? Did they stay changed, I wondered, or did the change wear off and they went back to their normal selves. Boy, was their partner gonna be surprised if that happened. I hoped I'd never fall in love if I had to pretend I was somebody else.

We were allowed to stay up late since it was New Year's Eve, but I didn't last that long. I just hoped 1959 would be better than this year had been. What with the Halloween murder and Uncle Rex Oliver's problems with the police and the blizzard and Dad's brush with death and the despicable Wades after us and God ignoring me, I felt I was due for an improvement.

I guess the Parcheesi must have gone real good because after New Year's Eve we saw Uncle Billy Glenn's Thunderbird in Janie's driveway a lot. In fact, once it was there real early in the morning, which Mother explained meant he probably had mechanical trouble and had to leave it in her driveway overnight. "Well, that kind of mechanical trouble," Dad said, "can get a man fouled up *real* fast if he isn't careful." Mother just sighed. "It's their lives," was all she would say. Mitchell said he was never gonna buy a Thunderbird when he grew up if they were that dangerous. Dad turned to Mitchell and said, "Son, you have no idea."

After New Year's, the Wades resumed their daily picketing rotation and Vivian and Janie met weekly at Antoinette's to get their hair done and discuss romantic entanglements. Janie said at least now she had a romantic life to entangle. Uncle Billy Glenn reported that Big Augie and his boys had returned to Topeka and hired a private detective named Salome Parsons, a woman with a dubious reputation, to help find Brenda's killer. Billy Glenn had undergone the same drastic change in his wardrobe that Uncle Gott had when he fell in love. That is, he looked totally unnatural. Mother was still selling Avon part-time, and Dad finally finished off the huge block of sharp cheddar cheese that Geezer Roy had given him for Christmas. Harmony started playing her flute a lot more. Then she'd write in her notebook, then play some more. It drove me crazy.

"If you're trying to write a symphony," I advised her, "it would be better off like Schubert's— unfinished."

She gave me a hateful look. "You're gonna be so sorry you made fun of me when I'm famous."

"Famous what—a famous dogcatcher?" I asked. She wouldn't talk to me for a week after that.

A few days later she announced during dinner that she, "had composed an exquisite ballad of love and tender yearning."

"Oh yeah?" I said. "If it's that stuff you've been playing on the flute it sounds like Little Poo caught in the screen door."

Harmony ignored me. "Following dinner," she said to Mother and Dad, "Daphne will be here so that we may perform the piece for those respectable individuals accustomed to quality."

Mother smiled. "That will be lovely, dear."

And Dad said, "Oh, a new composer."

"Do you consider yourself respectable?" I asked Mitchell.

"I guess so," he replied with a shrug.

After the dishes were done, we hung around to hear Harmony's song. Daffy came over in a peach-colored dress which was real showy, but much too light-weight for Kansas in January. Harmony had also changed into what she called her aqua frock. Together they looked like two Little Miss Muffets.

While Daffy sang the words to the new song, Harmony played her flute for accompaniment. The song reminded me of something Dad would sing at The Driftwood. It was slow and talked about, "you loved me as a meal ticket, but I was the gravy in your miserable life."

Or something like that. Mother and Dad applauded politely when it was done and I asked if they could do "One-Eyed, One-Horned, Flying Purple People Eater." Harmony ignored me again and bowed to Mother and Dad.

"Please excuse us," she told them. "We're leaving to give an encore performance at Daphne's house." Then they left.

Mother turned to Dad. "Well, at least one of my children isn't afraid of music."

"Yeah," said Mitchell. "Too bad it's the one with no talent." Then we both ran giggling out of the room.

Harmony's song—she called it "Meal Ticket"—was just one of many she and Daffy were writing. They had put their poetic interests to music, Mother said, which showed some ambition and industry. Harmony wasn't content to just write the songs either. She knew she and Daphne would have to finish school before they could become big stars, so she pushed those songs off on everybody else willing to perform them.

First, she asked if Vivian needed any love songs for the wedding. Vivian said well yes, but not anything country western or sappy. So Harmony said maybe they could write a song just for her and what kind would she like. Vivian hemmed and hawed around and finally said for Harmony to write something about waiting your whole life to find true love, only not to sound like Johnny Cash. Harmony came up with a song she called "Locket" about a woman who keeps the picture space in her locket empty until her true love comes along. The words were actually pretty good, but the tune was awful and everybody told her so. She asked Dad to help her, and Dad said why didn't they get Simon Vargas to help.

So then Simon started putting music to Harmony and Daphne's songs, only they were country western kinds of melodies. Simon started playing them whenever Shep and the Big Dogs got a gig, but Vivian didn't like what they'd done to "Locket," so she told Harmony she was gonna pass on it for the wedding, thanks anyway.

"Hey, Harmony," I said. "I know who could write you some

music for 'Locket,' but you're gonna have to be real nice to me if I tell you."

"How nice?" she wanted to know.

"Warsh dishes for me for a week."

Harmony actually thought about it, which surprised me. "How about three days?" she countered.

That was more than I had hoped. "Deal," I said and told Harmony about Miss Georgia Verne and her lost love General Pershing. "I bet Miss Georgia would love your song and would write some music for it for free if you told her it was for a wedding. She's sentimental like that, you know." I felt since she still had my hankie, I could make that claim.

Harmony said okay and did the dishes like she promised for three days, then called up Miss Georgia to discuss the song. I think Daffy's parents must have driven the girls over to Miss Georgia's, because Harmony wanted this to be a surprise for Vivian. I felt sure it would be.

Vivian was trying to pin down all the details for her Valentine's Day wedding. Since theirs was a marriage of two different religions they had a problem right off the bat deciding on which church and which preacher. Harmony explained that even people who never go to church get real picky when it comes to getting married or buried in somebody else's church. Why this was a problem I didn't understand, but Harmony didn't elaborate. Only Uncle Billy Glenn commented that God was gonna strike those Pentecostals dead for setting foot in the Methodist church, since that was the punishment He sent to Catholics for going anywhere else. I guess a person was just supposed to stick with his own kind, especially on important occasions like these.

After much discussion, Vivian and Uncle Gott decided to get married in the Methodist church since, after all, Uncle Gott was an ordained Methodist minister. But they would have pastors from both denominations perform the ceremony. No one had ever heard of this happening before and some people even used the word sacrilege behind Vivian's back. It didn't bother Vivian any.

Since the wedding was on Valentine's Day she had picked out red and white as her colors. "I hope that means everything isn't gonna be decorated in cupids and hearts," Uncle Gott expressed. "However, I suppose I can live with red and white for a few hours. It will be a small ceremony, won't it?"

"Well, Gottfried," Vivian had replied, "there are all those business associates I need to invite. And since I eloped for my first wedding, I really want this one to be a big production. A real extravaganza. Besides," she told him, "you're the celebrity in town. All your fans will want to come and wish you well. We can get a lot of publicity out of this if we do it right. And still have it tasteful and meaningful, of course."

"Okay," said Uncle Gott. I was beginning to understand this was his favorite method of dealing with Vivian when she overwhelmed him. He just said okay and that was that.

Vivian had asked Mother and Grandma Dale and Edith Kliban to be bridesmaids and had surprised everyone by asking Janie Bryant to be her maid of honor. Janie had been so overcome by emotion—"I bet she almost wet her pants," Mitchell interjected—but she said sure. The next week Vivian took everybody to Kansas City to select very expensive bridal wear. Mother said the bridesmaids' dresses were lovely, "But Vivian's wedding dress is gonna take your breath away."

As for Uncle Gott, he asked Dad to be his best man and Dewey and Rex Oliver and one of his fellow weathermen, Ed somebody-or-other, to be groomsmen.

"Well now," replied Dewey, "I'm happy and honored to oblige. But," he paused, "there could be a problem getting Rex Oliver into a tux." Pause. "He hasn't been out since Halloween and, well," pause, "you know." Pause. "Anyway, with his inquest coming up soon," pause, "nobody knows exactly if Rex Oliver will be in or out of jail."

"I understand," said Uncle Gott, "but Rex Oliver is important to this family and I would like to include him."

"Good enough," said Dewey.

"What about Virgil and Maynard?" I asked him. "Shouldn't they be included too?"

"Well, Melody, they're not family."

"Neither is Ed what's-his-name, the weatherman," I said.

"Uh, yes, that's true," said Uncle Gott. "But Melody, Virgil and Maynard are Indians, so they're not interested in this kind of thing. And anyway they'll be invited to attend the wedding as guests. So don't worry about them. They'll understand."

But I wasn't sure I did. We kids were gonna help take presents and stuff at the wedding, but mostly we would be on our own which was fine with me since this wedding business had everybody acting differently. Mother started sewing cute little Valentine's Day dresses for Harmony and me to wear, but I said they had better be real warm because in the middle of February I didn't wanna catch pneumonia on account of no stupid wedding.

"I'm making red velvet dresses for you and your sister, Melody. And you can wear white tights to keep your legs warm and pettipants over those as long as they don't show under your dress. That ought to keep you plenty warm enough."

"I guess that sounds reasonable," I said, "as long as I can wear shoes that'll hold up to a good snow."

"Just pray for good weather," Mother said.

"When it comes to praying about weather, count me out!" I told her.

While we were preparing for a wedding and Janie was fussing over her upcoming meeting with J. Edgar Hoover, Topeka made the international news in a big way. A plane that had been based at Forbes Air Force Base was shot down while on a reconnaissance mission near the Soviet Union. The commander was killed, three crewmen were missing and presumed dead, and the pilot and navigator were taken prisoner. President Eisenhower denied the plane was in Soviet air space and demanded the release of the prisoners, but so far nothing had happened. The daughter of one of the missing airmen went to my school, so I felt real bad.

We saw big planes fly over Topeka all the time from Forbes, but we never knew they were going over to Russia to take pictures and spy. Now Russia was accusing us and we were accusing them and some Americans who had been part of Topeka were dead. I didn't think I would ever understand the world of adults with their wars and their killing.

But in a way, I figured it was no different than the war we had going on with the Wades. Of course, the Wades were crazy in the head, but they were still pesky and dangerous. That was the problem. You couldn't just lock them up because they were always quoting their constitutional rights. You couldn't just shoot them like you could a varmint, although Grandma Dale was less convinced about that. And they seemed impossible to convert. So we just went back and forth in our war.

I asked Virgil about the subject one time. "Why do people have wars, Virgil?" We were in the hay loft at the farm throwing down fresh hay for the horses.

"I'm the wrong one to ask, being an Indian and all," Virgil said. "Indians always seem to be on the wrong side of wars." But then he told me his opinion anyway.

"Everybody's raised with different values, Melody, only some people try to force their values on others and then there's war."

"So how can you stop people from thinking their values are better?" I asked him. "And anyway, if Earl Wade is crazy and we're not, doesn't that automatically mean our values are better?"

"Melody," he said, "be careful when you use the word crazy. Many people throughout history have been called crazy who were not, because society didn't understand their ideas."

"Yeah," I said, "but what if they really *are* crazy?"

Virgil sighed. "Tell me, Melody. What is crazy to you?"

"Well, hurting yourself or hurting other people. Like how John

Brown went around killing people because he said God told him too."

"I was wondering when you were gonna bring God into this," said Virgil. "I think if you study history, more killing has been done in the name of God— no matter what name He's called—than for any other reason. And I agree with you, anybody who does that *is* a little crazy.

"As for Earl Wade," he added, "he's indirectly doing this community a big favor by making us examine an issue most people would rather not discuss. Remember when all the different religions and doctors got together with the V.A. folks and the State Hospital folks and the Meadowgreen folks and everybody talked about mental illness?"

I nodded.

"Do you think that would have happened if it hadn't been for Earl being so persistent?" He didn't wait for my answer. "Probably not. So in that sense, he is making this a better place to live, which may not be so crazy after all. The fact that his tactics make us uncomfortable means we need to listen harder to what he's saying. Maybe a tiny little part of what he says is true. Maybe not. Think about it."

It seemed like all I did anymore was think about things. Mitchell and I didn't seem to play the way we used to and I really missed him. School was almost always a drag and Girl Scouts was only fun if we went camping or made crafts. I was really upset with church and God now too. I couldn't figure out why life had to be so complicated when I was only nine years old.

Other Suspects, The Detective, and Meeting J. Edgar Hoover

W e hadn't been seeing as much of Billy Glenn since he now spent his free time at Janie's. But today was Saturday and Janie had gone shopping for a new outfit to wear to meet J. Edgar Hoover. I think Billy Glenn was feeling neglected, so he'd stopped at our house with his latest information.

"Salome Parsons was originally from Amherst, Massachusetts, so she and Big Augie both talk funny, like they all do back there. Salome followed a fly boy to Forbes ten years ago, but then caught him running around and dumped him like a hot potato. She didn't have nothing to go back to Massachusetts for, so she stayed in Topeka and took odd jobs, some of them odder than others."

That was the story on the female detective Big Augie had hired, according to Uncle Billy Glenn via his police sources.

"She's about thirty-five," he said, referring to the lady detective, "licensed to carry a concealed weapon, and would be attractive except the broad looks like she got rode hard and put away wet a few too many times."

"Billy Glenn, I wish you'd—oh darn it! Kids would you both go in the other room, please." Mother knew she was fighting a losing battle when it came to her brother.

Mitchell and I expressed some token complaints to divert suspicion. But we went into Mitchell's room anyway, closed the door, and glued ourselves to the heat vent in time to hear Mother saying something about "...your language around the kids."

Our uncle was on a roll. "The word on the street is that Big Augie wants Salome to find out about his late daughter's uh—what shall I call them, uh, her 'lady friends'—which is why he's hired a woman. There's some places those East Coast mob boys can't go, and a Kansas lesbian bar is one of them. Ha. Ha. Ha. Ha." He laughed a lot at that, only I didn't understand what was so funny. "So the cops is watching Salome too, 'cause they don't want no catfights with dykes and pistol-packin'…"

"BILLY GLENN," shouted Mother interrupting him and quite upset, "I told you to watch your language in this house and I mean it!"

"Hm-m-m," he said, and continued. "The gal dressed as a dandelion at the Halloween Ball, the one Brenda Messina was throwing dirt at, was a Meadowgreen patient too. Her name's Charlotte Fitch and Meadowgreen won't give out no information on her. None. The police can't even question her because she's back to an in-patient status, which they think is a deliberate ruse to avoid us. I mean avoid them." Billy Glenn had so many police friends he sometimes thought he was a policeman too.

"But sometimes she gets a weekend pass and shows up at a certain women's bar in town. All the lesbos in town know each other, so they can spot an undercover cop a mile away. But ole Salome is so, uh, seedy herself that she fits right in and can find out the dirt on Charlotte. At least that's what Big Augie hopes. Boy, would I like to be a fly on the wall there."

"That's disgusting," Mother said.

The furnace kicked on just then and we couldn't hear any more. I decided I had to find out what lesbian meant. It was obvious it was something having to do with lunatics, only from the way Billy Glenn talked it was only the women lunatics. I wondered if Miss Georgia's cousin that was in the State Hospital was a lesbian. Then I wondered if Ava Wade had been a lesbian. I wondered if that's why she killed herself.

I'm ashamed to say that's how a lot of folks talked and thought back then.

The next day I asked my teacher at school, Miss Swanson, what a lesbian was. But instead of answering me she had the principal call Mother, which really soured me on fourth grade for the rest of the year. Mother called me into her bedroom that evening and said I should never ever use that word. She said it was something awful and that I was too young to understand. I figured it must be something even worse than atheist if Mother wouldn't tell me. I didn't know who I could confide in that would tell me, but I really wanted to know.

Then I decided to look it up in the dictionary. But all it said was something about a group of women associated with the Greek poet Sappho on the island of Lesbos. It didn't say anything about being crazy. *Well,* I thought, *Harmony is a female poet only she's American, not Greek. I wonder if that makes her a shirttail lesbian.* Of course, her friend Daffy was a poet too, so maybe they were lesbians together. They just seemed like regular snot-nosed thirteen-year-old girls to me.

Virgil and Maynard had moved back to the reservation for a week after helping Dewey clean up from the blizzard. The court had set Rex Oliver's inquest for the end of February, so at least Uncle Gott's wedding would be out of the way by then. We were all frightened about it and wanted him to be found innocent, but he wouldn't talk and spent most daylight hours in the cave. Dewey asked me once, "Melody, how would you like to spend your whole life running from your feelings and smelling like mold?"

"Well, it would be a real waste," I answered.

"Yup," said Dewey. "It is a waste."

One Sunday when we were at the farm, Mitchell went into the cave to visit Rex Oliver. He was in there about twenty minutes, but he wouldn't tell me what they'd talked about and he never went in again. I felt very left out of whatever was going on between them.

Toward the end of January, Vivian and Uncle Gott came out to the farm for Sunday dinner. After Rex Oliver had gobbled some food, warmed up a little, and ran back to an afternoon of cave dwelling, Harmony cleared her throat and asked, "I was wondering, do you think the despicable Wades will try to picket the wedding?" Harmony was taking this whole wedding thing very seriously.

"We've been wondering that too," said Dewey.

"What can we do?" asked Mother, as if the Wades were too

powerful for any force on Earth to stop.

"Maybe I should just stand on the sidewalk in front of the church holding my shotgun," said Grandma Dale. "They listened to what Ole Betsy had to say last time."

"So would that be a 'shotgun wedding?'" Dad joked, and everybody laughed. I hoped Grandma Dale wasn't serious. I didn't want another of my relatives going on trial for criminal activities.

"Why don't we ask Virgil if there's any legal stuff that can stop those Wades," said Harmony.

"You know," said Vivian, "she's right. I remember Representative Gillis told me he'd introduce a bill to stop the Wades when the legislature convened. Well, it just convened ten days ago. I'm gonna call the ole' boy up and make sure his bill includes picketing churches and that it becomes effective immediately. And if they can't do that, I'm going to call in all my chips with the City Council and get them to pass an anti-picketing ordinance before the wedding. I expect Earl will go to court to block it, but if we time it just right, we'll already be married."

"Harmony," she said turning to her, "that was a wonderful idea you had. Thank you."

"You're welcome, Vivian." We were always a polite family.

So Vivian collected her political friends together and started the process in motion. She told Janie later she felt a little guilty doing this for such a selfish reason, but she didn't want her entire wedding party wearing "Eat Me Earl" buttons. The buttons were a take-off of the popular graffiti and had become a sort of cottage industry in town. She said the City Council seemed pretty receptive to the anti-picketing ordinance, but the hard part was going to be timing the proposal and passage of it just right for Valentine's Day.

Uncle Gott was trying to stay very busy so he wouldn't have to think about the fact that he was getting married in less than three weeks. He had decided to work with Vivian's advertising specialist to come up with a new campaign for his weather program. He said he was tired of seeing those billboards of himself with the lightning bolt all over town and after the horrible blizzard he wanted a more positive image of the weather.

Gloria Bates, Vivian's advertising executive and also the wife of my Sunday School teacher Monroe Bates, came up with the slogan "Dear Gott, what's the weather doing now?" a slogan which Vivian approved. She thought they should design a new billboard using a non-denominational stained-glass window as the background and Uncle Gott in a clerical collar in the foreground. Uncle Gott told her he never wore those collars and he certainly wasn't going to wear them on television, but the rest of the idea was okay with him. Gloria did some research and found out about the new stained-glass window that had just been installed at the Mount Calvary Temple church in East Topeka. She thought they should use it for the photo shoot and said it also wouldn't hurt relations with Topeka's Negro community. So that's what they did.

I wasn't that fond of the new slogan, mostly because I thought the whole Bates family, which included Monroe, Gloria, and their son Harold Bates who was Harmony's age, was nothing but a bunch of tight-lipped whiners. Mr. Bates was always telling me I was a smart aleck in Sunday School and said I had a bad attitude. Harmony said nobody liked Harold in school either. She said the girls called him Harry Bates and the boys called him Master Bates. I didn't get it, but Harmony seemed to think it was funny.

Vivian and everybody else liked the new slogan, so the new billboards with the stained-glass window in the background got put up all over town. *The Topeka Daily Capital* in its Saturday religion section ran a picture of the new TV promotion and a story of Uncle Gott's ministering weather career. That was Vivian's idea, using her newspaper to market her new TV weather campaign. The reporter who wrote the piece interviewed the Mount Calvary Temple folks about the origins of the beautiful window. He cited by name the window's donor, Mr. August Messina, and wrote a few lines about Augie's dead daughter Brenda, omitting Meadowgreen and the murder, of course. He never realized that *The Topeka Daily Capital's* owner, his employer, would soon be related by marriage to the person accused of killing Brenda.

He found out real fast when Earl Wade picketed the Mount Calvary Temple church on Sunday and Vivian's TV station on Monday. Earl and company had made some new signs saying things like "Lunatic Blasphemes God's House," "Unclean Spirits in Window," and "Stained Souls Soil Stained Glass."

In one way the publicity over this flap helped Uncle Gott's weather campaign, because nobody liked Earl Wade. But it did raise the whole issue of the murder again and caused Dewey and Dale to hide the newspapers and unplug the TV at the farm for a week so Uncle Rex Oliver wouldn't feel criticized.

But Big Augie felt criticized. "Big Augie don't appreciate having his dead daughter called a lunatic by a fruitcake like Earl Wade," was how Uncle Billy Glenn put it. "When Chief Appelhans heard Earl picketed the church, he hopped on over to the Hotel Jayhawk and paid a personal visit to Big Augie. 'Listen Augie,' he says. 'I agree with you that Earl Wade's an ignorant son-of-a-bitch who needs to be taught a lesson.'"

"Billy Glenn," warned Mother.

"Sure, Louise," said our uncle, "but you and your boys are gonna have to leave Earl alone,' he says to Augie. He said the police would handle Earl according to the law, and if anything unpleasant happened, Big Augie and his bunch would be arrested so fast it would give new meaning to the word instantly. But then, to leave things on a lighter note, since after all, he's up against the Mafia, the Chief told Augie he thought the stained-glass window was real nice.

"Big Augie thanked him for that," continued Billy Glenn, "but said that Duane had better keep Earl away from him or he wouldn't be responsible for what might happen.

"So the police are really watching this whole thing pretty closely. They've even sent an officer to watch the Mount Calvary Temple church for a few days, in case some other crazy nut reads about this whole thing and tries to break the window. Some days are like that, you know?

"Heck, a lot of these problems could be avoided if Meadowgreen would just allow the police to question Charlotte Fitch."

"What do you mean?" asked Dad.

"Well," said Billy Glenn, "basically Rex Oliver and Charlotte Fitch are the only other possible murder suspects, at least with the evidence that's turned up so far. But Rex Oliver's also suspect because we know he ran from the murder scene around the time of the murder, and we know it was his crucifix that bashed Brenda's head in." Uncle Billy Glenn was back to talking as if he was part of the police force.

"Also, Rex was seen arguing with Brenda earlier during the dirt throwing incident. Now it's true Charlotte was quarreling with Brenda too. But unless the police can talk to Charlotte and get her to confess, or unless they have a witness who saw her commit the murder, she's probably not gonna get charged. Just because Rex Oliver's the main suspect though, don't mean there's enough evidence to convict him."

"But how would the police's talking to Charlotte have prevented this mess with Earl Wade and the window and Big Augie?" Mother asked. Mother was sewing our dresses for the wedding and listening to her brother at the same time.

"Because," said Billy Glenn, "if Charlotte and Brenda had a—you know—lover's quarrel and Charlotte murdered Brenda, then it's not a mental health thing anymore and Earl Wade should leave it alone. His big gripe is because they were both crazy, which he considers, you know, ungodly."

"I don't follow you," said Dad. "Even if it is a lover's quarrel, why isn't it still a mental health issue? Charlotte and Brenda were both Meadowgreen patients."

"True," said Billy Glenn. "But a lover's quarrel means this happened because they were les…" He looked at us kids and changed what he was about to say, "Because they were you-know-what, and that's different from being crazy."

"Is it?" asked Dad. "I thought that was probably why they were out there at Meadowgreen, to get themselves straightened out and back to their rightful persuasion."

"Nobody can find out why those two were there, 'cause Meadowgreen won't release nothing to nobody," said Uncle Billy Glenn. "Maybe it's because they were you-know-what, but maybe it's for some other reason.

"And another thing," he added, "I think Earl Wade might back off if Rex Oliver didn't remind him of his own sister being crazy and killing herself and of his unfinished business with Dewey."

"That's a possibility," said Dad.

"So how do we get Charlotte out or get the police into Meadowgreen?" Dad said. "I wonder..." his voice trailed off. "Maybe I can talk to Dr. Knott, Daffy's, I mean Daphne's, father. I don't really know him, but I know he treats patients having trouble with their, uh, persuasions. You know what I'm talking about?" He gave a meaningful look to Billy Glenn. Billy Glenn gave him a wink.

"Maybe there's something he can tell us," Dad continued. "He probably knows both those gals. Maybe they're even his patients." And then before anybody could answer, he continued, "I'll do that. In the meantime, well, maybe Salome Parsons can find something out through her, uh, channels. Maybe Big Augie is going about this the right way after all."

Janie, as maid of honor for Vivian's wedding, was throwing a bridal shower for Vivian at the Pentecostal church. She had invited all the ladies she could think of who knew Vivian, including Edith Kliban and Antoinette. Harmony and I even got invited. I made Vivian some potholders that I wove with colored yarn. Harmony embroidered some pillowcases for her. Mother bought her some beautiful towels and Janie said she was gonna give her a see-through nightie, not that she needed it, she said.

Vivian was exhibiting nerves of steel about this whole wedding business. I figured it was her circus training. Janie, on the other hand, was a nervous wreck. The day of the shower she started hyperventilating and we had to stick her head in a paper bag. Eventually she was okay, but we had to open most of the shower presents without her, which was too bad since she was the hostess. We saved her a piece of cake, though.

She reminded us that her "date" with J. Edgar Hoover was only two days away, something we'd forgotten about with everything else going on. Well, *she* hadn't forgotten, Janie said. A Kansas Highway Patrol car was picking her up and driving her to Kansas City for the event. I still hadn't found my Junior G-Man membership card to send with her and guessed Little Poo must have eaten it. She did that sometimes.

We all wished Janie the best. "We want to hear all the details when you get back, Janie," Mother told her.

"Don't worry," Mitchell said to Mother. "We will."

Sure enough, we were the first ones Janie told about her big day, but that was only because Uncle Billy Glenn had to work that evening. Janie came gliding over at a pretty good clip, which was her way of running in high heels. She hadn't even bothered to change clothes and still had on her hat and white gloves and a great deal of costume jewelry. In a way she reminded me of a younger version of Miss Georgia.

We were in the middle of dinner, but Mother invited Janie to pull up a chair and tell us all the details. She also offered Janie some food, but by that point all we had left was some mixed vegetables that none of us kids would eat and some bread and butter.

"My, my, my," said Janie, "you're all such delicate eaters." She hadn't seen what we'd already put away.

She then proceeded to tell us how J. Edgar, as she now called him, had held a reception for her and all the other Kansas City area business and civic leaders who were friends of the F.B.I.

"I don't understand why little-old-me was invited, because everybody else there was such a big shot," Janie began. "I guess it's because of all the letters I've written him over the years, don't you expect? J. Edgar came by and shook my hand, and when he found out my name said, 'Oh-h, it's you.' Now isn't that exciting?" Janie asked. "That he knew me from all those folks? Then he had a photographer take an individual picture of him with each guest. Wasn't that just so thoughtful?"

She produced a photo of herself and J. Edgar. In the photo Janie looked about ready to hyperventilate again.

"Did you hyperventilate, Janie?" I asked.

"Almost, but no, I didn't."

I wondered if J. Edgar knew Janie was a nudist. I bet he did. I bet the F.B.I. knew everything about everybody.

Suddenly I remembered what Uncle Billy Glenn had said about not having any information about Charlotte Fitch. I bet the F.B.I. knew.

The idea hit me so hard I choked and the milk I'd been drinking came out my nose.

"Yuck," said Harmony.

"Janie! Janie!" I yelled. I wiped my mouth and nose on my napkin and told her about Charlotte Fitch and seeing if J. Edgar could get the information. Dad and Mother turned and stared at me in amazement. I thought maybe I still had milk on my face or something, so I wiped it again.

"That's really good," said Dad to me. "That's a really good idea."

He turned to Janie and said, "Janie, do you think your friend J. Edgar could get us that information?"

"Oh, I'm sure he could," said Janie. "All I have to do is ask him."

My Nocturnal Misadventure

Uncle Billy Glenn reminded us he had suggested some months ago that Janie contact the F.B.I. about Brenda's murder. Of course, that was before he had actually met Janie. We had all thought he was just being forward.

Since it had been his idea originally, he insisted on helping Janie write the letter to J. Edgar asking about Charlotte Fitch. He let Janie add some personal greetings, but they signed only her name at the bottom because of her close personal friendship and all. I thought I should get some of the credit too, but now everybody was ignoring me again.

Probably as a reaction, this next part actually was my fault.

Outside the weather had gone crazy as well, this time with warm temperatures, which was almost as bad as the blizzard. Everybody knew warm temperatures weren't good for farmers, who needed a snow cover to protect the crops during the rest of the winter. Uncle Billy Glenn said the farmers had been taking it in the shorts this year with the weather. "That goes with the territory," Grandma Dale said, and she was right. Farmers expect their life's calling to include some bountiful years, but also, inevitably, some lean years.

Right then it had gotten so warm that Mother wondered if our wedding costumes would still be suitable. It was evening and she had made Harmony and me try on our red velvet dresses for some adjustments. They were almost finished.

Mitchell observed us parading around in our matching outfits until he could stand it no longer.

"I bet that red velvet won't look so good with big sweat stains under the armpits," he said.

"Oh yeah? Well, I bet you won't be so mouthy either, after I get done tickling you," I replied.

"Melody, stop it," Mother yelled at me. "Take that dress off

194

before you start roughhousing. I mean it."

"It's okay," I told her. "I can catch Mitchell with my dress on just fine."

I had started down the hall after him when Little Poo walked out of the kitchen. I guess the sight of me in a dress must have been pretty scary, because she tried to run and hide under the record cabinet at the edge of the hallway. She got her head and one shoulder under the cabinet and assumed that the rest of her must be hidden too, so she held real still, just like a big fat ostrich with her head in the sand. She had done this a number of times before because she was so dumb.

I had to jerk myself to a stop real suddenly so I wouldn't run over Little Poo, but that put an un-wedding-like strain on the red velvet. I felt a pressure, then a sudden give accompanied by an ugly ripping sound. The darn dress had ripped up the side, leaving a big hole where the seam had been. Now I knew I was really gonna catch the dickens from Mother.

I reached down and pulled Little Poo out from under the record cabinet so she wouldn't trip anybody else. That may have helped her but it didn't help me, because I got enough white cat fur on the red velvet to make a small sweater. But then I figured, what the heck. The official wedding colors were red and white, and now I was wearing them both.

I knew the only way to keep from getting horribly punished was to turn the incident around somehow. Mother always said I had a vivid imagination. Now seemed like a good time to use it.

"Mother, Mother," I ran screaming into the living room. "I just saved Little Poo."

"What?" said Mother looking up from pinning Harmony's dress. "What happened to Little Poo?"

"She was stuck," I said. "She had her head stuck under the record cabinet and she couldn't move, and I had to get her out real fast to save her." And then in a regretful voice I continued, "But when I pulled her out, I had sort of an accident." I held up my arm so Mother could see the rip and then said real fast, "But I had to save Little Poo because she's too dumb to save herself."

Mother grabbed my shoulder and spun me around to examine the rip.

"Oh Melody," she wailed. She was really upset trying to see if the rip could be fixed. "Didn't I tell you to take off your dress before you started playing? Now what are you going to do for the wedding? And look at all this cat fur. All this work for nothing." Mother was on a roll, and it was best just to let her get it out.

"But Little Poo..." I began.

"Never mind Little Poo," said Mother. "Your new dress is *ruined*, Melody. There's no way I can repair this rip."

She was very upset. But so far, she hadn't mentioned anything about punishment. I was almost home free.

"So young lady," Mother's voice took on a different tone all of a sudden, "just exactly how are you going to your Uncle Gott's wedding? Do you want to pay for another dress out of your allowance? Because you don't have any other good dresses for a wedding. I try to get you nice clothes, but you always have to act like a tomboy and..."

She went on like that until I was almost ready to cry. All over a stupid dress. No wonder I hated dresses.

Mother's solution to my wedding outfit—and a horrible punishment—was for me to wear one of Harmony's old hand-me-downs. It was a ruffly, crinkly red dress with white polka dots on it that made me look like Little Orphan Annie on a bad day.

"I don't think I can wear that dress and keep food down," I told Mother.

"Well, isn't that just too bad. Because that's all there is for you to wear."

I felt real bad then and went into my room, shut the door, and started to cry. Only then Harmony came in and yelled out the door, "Mom, she's cry-in'." I could have smacked her.

Mother came in and sat down on the edge of the bed. She was still mad at the dress being ruined, but she didn't want me to cry either.

"Oh, Melody," she sighed and patted me on the shoulder. "You're just my little tomboy, aren't you." I don't think Mother quite knew what to do with a little tomboy.

I felt that although she'd never say it, I was something of a disappointment to her. What she really wanted was another daughter like Harmony, another "sugar and spice and everything nice" kind of daughter. I sobbed into my pillow because I was such a failure.

"Honey, what's the matter?" Mother said.

I didn't know how to tell her why I felt so bad. God ignored me, my parents expected me to be another kind of person, my Sunday School teacher thought I had a bad attitude, my fourth-grade teacher turned me in to the principal for asking a normal question, Harmony barely spoke to me, Janie spied on me, Miss Georgia shouted at me if I wouldn't practice my piano lesson, and Uncle Billy Glenn thought children were only good for income tax deductions. Of all the people in my world, Mitchell was the only one who loved me no matter what. But Mitchell had been acting strange lately. Anyway, he didn't understand why I felt alone sometimes, because everybody loved *him*.

I thought Grandma Dale loved me no matter what too. But I didn't get to see her every day. Dewey and Virgil and Maynard were always nice to me too and I suppose so was Rex Oliver. But I couldn't talk to them much about my problems. And Uncle Gott and Vivian were real nice, but they were in love right now and therefore practically worthless for anything else.

At that moment I felt like nobody in the whole world understood me. How could they love me if they wouldn't let me be myself? Wasn't I a good person? I obeyed the Ten Commandments most of the time. I tried to be nice to Mitchell and little animals. I tried to help old people whenever I could. And I used to say prayers asking for good things to happen to people.

But even God had given up on me. I must have been even worse than an atheist or a Communist or a lesbian for God to have done that.

If a nine-year old can have a dark night of the soul, that was mine.

I cried so long without talking to Mother that she eventually covered me with a blanket and left me alone. Harmony came in and went to bed and one by one I saw the lights go out in the house. But I couldn't sleep.

I had never been afraid of the dark, so after a while I got up real quietly. I still had on the ripped red velvet dress covered with cat fur, only now it was all wrinkled. I went out in the living room and thought about why nobody loved me anymore and I still couldn't come up with a reason. I wondered if I should run away and find new parents who would love me, but I knew I would miss Mitchell and the cats and Grandma Dale too much.

So I decided to make a plan to get everybody to love me again. It had to be something really unusual so they would be impressed and not forget me again right away. I thought about school and church and our entire lives, and the only thing I could think of that would be real impressive would be if I could get Earl Wade to stop picketing. Then the whole town would love me.

I wasn't sure how I was gonna accomplish that, but I figured I had to try. And I figured I had just as soon start now looking for his house while it was warm, as the temperature would most likely get cold again. So I very quietly got my coat and boots and tiptoed to the back door. I would have preferred to have changed out of the red velvet dress, but I knew Harmony would wake up if I started fishing around through my dresser for my everyday clothes. I was careful not to make a sound as I left. I'd never done this before, sneak out like this, but it would be okay since I was gonna be a hero.

The night wasn't particularly dark, so I was lucky. I knew I needed to look for a green house on the end of a block that had the name Reverend Earl Wade on the mailbox. I didn't know which way to even start, so I just kept walking and walking and if I felt like turning a corner, I did. I didn't know if my sixth sense would lead me to Earl's house or not. I really didn't know anything except that I had to say something to Earl to get him to quit.

I was thinking so hard that I didn't see a big hole in the pavement and I tripped and fell down hard. Both my knees were skinned and bleeding and they hurt. I think I also skinned my arm because it hurt too, and my coat was ripped on the sleeve. But I couldn't sit down because the ground was too muddy. So I just kept walking.

Once I looked up and there was Uncle Gott's face on a billboard above me. "Dear Gott, what's the weather doing now?" was what it said. I saw the stained-glass window in the background and wondered what it would be like to be Brenda Messina at a Halloween party one minute and be dead the next. I couldn't imagine what she had done to deserve getting murdered. Even if she was a lesbian and crazy. I didn't recall anything in the Bible about lesbians, so I couldn't figure out why they were so bad. After all, King David, who wrote the Psalms, was a poet, only he wasn't crazy or a woman, and he wasn't bad. It didn't make sense. So much of my world didn't make sense.

I think I must have walked around with my knees bleeding for a long time. I saw a bus stop bench on a corner and I was starting to get tired, so I decided to sit down for a little rest. I guess I must have gone to sleep for a while.

When I woke up it was starting to get light. I still hadn't found Earl's house and by now I was cold and I had to get home and get ready for school. But I didn't know where I was.

I started walking again and then I started running because I needed to get home before anybody knew I was gone. Just about that time, a kid on a bicycle delivering newspapers came by. He stopped when he saw me running and looked at my bloody knees. I think he was worried.

"You okay?" he asked me.

"Yeah," I answered, "but I don't know where I am."

"Well, where do you want to go?" the paperboy said. He was in a hurry to get his papers delivered.

I suddenly wondered if maybe he knew where Earl Wade lived, because maybe Earl took the newspaper.

"To Earl Wade's house," I said. "You know where that is?"

"Oh sure," the kid said. "Everybody knows where Earl lives. Right there."

He pointed to a green house that I hadn't seen before. Sure

enough, the mailbox said Reverend Earl Wade.

I walked up slowly to the edge of the sidewalk and stopped. Earl himself was sitting, all alone, on a chair on the porch. He was staring off into space just like he had been waiting for me all night. The idea that he knew I was coming made him seem even more evil and suddenly I got real scared. Then I remembered he couldn't see and so I felt a little braver.

Very quietly I walked up the sidewalk to the bottom of the porch steps. Even though I thought Earl was blind, it still seemed like he was watching me. Before I could think of how to open a conversation at dawn with a blind man after sneaking up on him on his own front porch, he squeaked, "Why have you come?" I nearly jumped out of my boots. "Why have you come?" he squeaked again, this time a little louder.

"Mr. Wade, I mean Reverend Wade," I began, "I want to ask you, to please, please stop picketing everybody."

"Who are you?" Earl squeaked. "Do I know you?"

I thought about telling him we were almost stepcousins but then I thought maybe that would get him thinking about his crazy sister, so I didn't.

"I'm Melody," I said. "And nobody sent me. I'm here all by myself." I felt like Dorothy in *The Wizard of Oz* when she first gets to Oz and is trembling in fear before the great and powerful wizard. I was trembling too, partly in fear and partly because I was cold and I had to pee real bad. I didn't think I wanted to ask to use Earl's bathroom, because I was afraid if I went inside, I'd never be seen alive again.

"Well Melody-all-by-yourself, go HOME!" He jumped up so fast from his chair and pointed down the street that I thought he was coming after me. My legs couldn't work fast enough to obey the signal my brain was sending to run and my bladder totally lost control from the shock. I think I fell down and re-opened the scabs that had started to form on my bloody knees. I was gasping for air and trying to get away all at the same time.

Just then a big hand reached out and grabbed me from behind and I think my heart stopped dead. I don't remember anything after that.

Hospital

I heard a noise finally. It was way off in the distance and it sounded like voices. Gradually the voices sounded closer and then it seemed like they were next to me. I opened my eyes, but all I could see was a red light going around and around in the sky. Somebody was trying to talk to me and I think I saw the newspaper kid pointing at me. I was wet and somebody had wrapped me in a blanket. Then I could see a little better and the person trying to talk to me was a policeman. "How are you feeling, honey?" he kept asking. Then he would say, "Everything is gonna be okay. Don't worry." Before I could answer I heard a noise like a siren way off in the distance and it got louder and louder and got so loud it hurt my ears. Then it came real close and stopped. I wanted to sit up then to see what was going on. I wondered if there was a fire and maybe Uncle Billy Glenn was there on a fire truck. But the policeman kept saying to just lie still for a minute, so I did.

"Is there a fire?" I asked once.

"No," he answered. Then he motioned for somebody to come over. Two men in white coats came and lifted me on a stretcher and started carrying me toward an ambulance.

"Hey, stop that," I told them.

"It's okay, honey," the youngest man said. For some reason, everybody wanted to call me *honey* all of the sudden. "You'll feel a lot better at the hospital."

He stayed with me after they loaded me in the back of the ambulance and was listening to my heart and stuff with his instruments. I heard the policeman tell the other ambulance guy something about assault, but I didn't know what he meant. I was hoping the ambulance guys weren't gonna notice that I'd wet my pants, but it was pretty hard to miss. If Mitchell had been there, he would have said that pee and blood on red velvet didn't look so hot.

All at once I missed Mitchell and I knew I was gonna be in big trouble because now, not only had I not convinced Earl to stop picketing, but I'd left home at night without permission, missed school, got skinned up, cost my parents the price of my ride in the ambulance, and shamed the family by peeing my pants.

I started crying and the policeman and the other ambulance guy came over. "Poor little thing," said the policeman. Then he repeated, "Everything's going to be all right. I'm going to call your parents and they'll meet you at the hospital. Who are your parents, honey? And what's your name?"

I wanted to tell him I was just passing through from California with a wagonload of gypsies, so Mother and Dad wouldn't find out about this. But I figured if I lied to the police, they would take me away in handcuffs in the ambulance. So I told him the truth and then started crying again.

The ambulance guys closed the doors and turned on the lights and siren, so I stopped crying then because it was interesting. Only I was real tired and cold.

We got to the hospital fast and the ambulance guys grabbed the stretcher and took me in the door that said "Emergency." They sure were making a big deal out of a couple of skinned knees. The nurses put me in a little place and pulled some curtains around me and the ambulance guys left. By this time, I was really cold and wanted breakfast.

"Do you think I could get some food?" I asked the nurse. But she stuck a thermometer in my mouth instead. Some doctor came in and started looking at me and had the nurse take off all my clothes and put a hospital gown on me which was cold too, only at least it wasn't wet.

Just then Mother and Dad came running in. Mother was crying and hugging me so hard I almost bit the thermometer off. Dad hugged me too. "I'm gonna kill that son-of-a-bitch," he told Mother.

"Alex, let the police handle this," Mother said. I didn't know what they were talking about. I hoped it had nothing to do with me.

By the time the nurse took out the thermometer the doctor came back. He told mother and Dad he was going to give me a complete examination to look for any evidence. I still didn't know what this was all about, but nobody stopped to ask me what I thought. Mother and Dad said they would wait right outside, then they stepped outside the curtains.

The doctor gave me a funny kind of exam because my regular doctor never did all the stuff he did. I didn't like some of it either. I kept telling him I was cold and hungry and I even started shivering. Finally, the nurse put a blanket around me, which helped, and the doctor put down his instruments and said, "Melody, tell me what happened."

So I said, "I don't think I can until I get some food." I realized it was my chance to find out what was going on, but I was so hungry and tired and cold I was really too cranky to care.

The doctor sent the nurse off for whatever food she could find. "Melody, can you talk to me while the food is on the way?"

"I'm gonna be late for school," I said. It was all I could think of as tired as I was.

"It's okay to miss school today, Melody. I'll write you a note for the teacher so you'll be excused."

"Okay," I said. "What do you want to know?"

Then he asked me a whole bunch of questions about Earl and did Earl touch me or hit me or do anything to hurt me. Well, I didn't want to say that I was so scared of Earl that I wet my pants, so I just shrugged my shoulders. I didn't want to be rude, but I was really hungry.

"Melody," the doctor tried one more time, "it's real important for you to tell me what happened."

"Why?" He was a nice enough doctor and all, but I still hadn't seen any food.

The doctor had that look on his face that Monroe Bates got just before he would tell me I had a bad attitude. So I pulled the blanket up around me real tight and stopped talking. The doctor frowned, wrote something on his chart, and left. I heard him talking with Mother and Dad about multiple abrasions, torn clothing, wet undergarments, and running some tests. *Well, that's it,* I thought. Now that Mother and Dad knew, I was in so much trouble I wouldn't be able to sit down for a month.

All because of a stupid dress.

Grandma Dale and Dewey got there just as the nurse brought a donut and some hot chocolate. It wasn't as good as Grandma Dale's hot chocolate, but it was hot. Everybody was fussing over me, but I was trying to avoid looking at Mother and Dad and just concentrate on the donut. Dewey came over and put his hand on my cheek and just stood there shaking his head, not saying a word. Then he turned and looked at Dad and said very softly, "Has he been arrested?" Dad nodded. "What have the police got to say?"

Dad motioned for him to come outside of the curtains. I could hear them talking and Dewey getting louder. It sounded like he was mad. I guess Dad told him about how bad I had been.

Well, I thought, *maybe I should just stay in the hospital for a little while so I won't have to go home and face the music.* I was too tired to think of another plan just then. I called for the nurse and when she came, I asked if I could please have a couple more donuts and another cup of that hot chocolate.

After I'd eaten some more donuts I started to feel better. I think I wasn't so cold anymore and the food had given me energy. I started to try and concentrate on a new plan to keep me from getting about the worse punishment of my entire life.

Dad and Dewey came back in just then and everybody was standing around my bed and staring at me in my stupid hospital gown like I was an exhibit at the zoo. I remembered how everybody had ignored me before. Now that I was bad, they at least paid attention to me. Only it was the kind of attention that made me really uncomfortable.

"Sweetie," Dad said to me, "I want you to tell me exactly what happened last night. It's real important that we find out because the police think that maybe Earl hurt you and they've arrested him and taken him to jail. Did Earl hurt you, honey?"

I looked up at him and then at all the faces watching me. Why were they so worried about Earl when I was the one that was gonna get punished? "I don't want to get punished," I mumbled. I was very uncomfortable with this conversation.

"Nobody's going to punish you, sweetie. But we need to know the truth. Can you tell us what happened?"

"Maybe Melody would rather talk to us women about this—uh—delicate matter. Why don't you men go get a cup of coffee and let us visit with Melody for a while." Grandma Dale had sensed I was not at ease talking to Dad and Dewey about this. She was right.

After the men left, Grandma Dale and Mother started plumping my pillows and tucking in my blanket and did everything except ask me if I wanted a teddy bear. Finally I was getting the kind of attention I wanted.

"Melody Lark," Mother began. She hardly ever used my middle name, so this was serious. "Now tell me the truth. Did Earl Wade hurt you?"

"I don't know," I replied truthfully. "I got scared and tried to run away and somebody grabbed me and—and—I don't know after that." I still didn't want to tell anybody about wetting my pants, not even Mother.

"*Who* grabbed you, Melody. Did you see?" Grandma Dale asked.

"I don't know," I said again. "I was trying to turn around and Earl was on the porch and a hand grabbed me from behind. Only—I don't know how Earl could have done it because I moved real fast and he was still on the porch, I think. I don't know."

"From what you do know, did Earl touch you at all, honey?"

"No."

"Not even a little bit?"

"No. I was on the sidewalk and he was on the porch the whole time that I remember."

"Then how—? Honey, when the police found you, you were all cut up and bleeding and—and your panties were wet. Honey, it's okay to tell me. You won't get in trouble, I promise. How did that happen?"

I hung my head because I was ashamed. Mother put her hand under my chin and lifted my face up so she could look me in the eyes. I was gonna have to tell her.

"I fell down in the street in a big hole and I scraped my knees and my arm and they were bleeding." I moved to show her my wounds, now cleaned and bandaged by the nurses.

"And how did your panties get wet, honey?"

I sighed. "Well, I think, when I got so scared at Earl's house I—just—couldn't—help it. I had to go real bad. I'm sorry." I hung my head in embarrassment.

But instead of a scolding, Mother threw her arms around me and gave me a big hug. "It's okay, honey," she said. And Grandma Dale added, "Sometimes we all get scared and do things we'd rather not admit. But it's okay. I'm glad nothing bad happened to you."

"But I wonder who grabbed you..." Mother continued, puzzled. The policeman said there was nobody else there but you on the sidewalk and Earl on the porch."

"Did you send the police after me to put me in jail?" I asked.

"Oh no, sweetie. We were just waking up when the police called to tell us you were going to the hospital. We didn't know you weren't home asleep."

"Well how did the police know where to find me?" I asked.

"The paperboy called them, they said. He saw you all bloody running down the street with torn clothing saying something about Earl Wade, so he found a phone booth and called the police. And when the police got there, they found you unconscious on the sidewalk. I guess everybody thought Earl had hurt you."

But I had another thought. I turned to Grandma Dale. "Maybe it was my guardian angel that grabbed me." Grandma looked at me and said, "Hm-m. Do you think so?" But I thought guardian angels saved a person's life, and this one, if that's who it had been, had frightened me almost to death. I couldn't figure it out.

Mitchell made me tell him three times the story of how I had snuck out at night and scared Earl Wade into stopping his picketing. He especially liked the part about me getting to ride in an ambulance with the siren and red lights and how traffic just pulled over to let us by. Even though he was real impressed, he said I shouldn't get to acting like the Queen of Sheba because I was still gonna have to wear Harmony's old dress to the wedding.

Mother said my experience with Earl was almost a miracle and Dad said it was almost a disaster. He said he and Dewey had been real tempted to go ahead and press charges against Earl for assault on a minor. They said they probably would have got him sent to Leavenworth for a couple of years, or at least to jail for a while. But they got to talking about it and there wasn't any real evidence that he had hurt me. Anyway they were Christians and wouldn't feel in their hearts that it was the right thing to do. Grandma Dale said she didn't think the Christian part would have stopped Dewey if he could have found a way to get back at Earl.

The policeman who had found me filed a report stating there was no one else present at the scene when he arrived except Earl and me. He questioned the neighbors and the paperboy and all the rest of the Wades, but nobody would admit to having grabbed me.

Then Dad said maybe Earl would sue us because of getting him arrested and all. But Dewey said we didn't call the cops, it was the paperboy that done it and if Earl wanted to sue a paperboy for his pocket change, he would get tarred and feathered and run out of town for sure.

Grandma Dale had called Vivian right away to make sure the whole thing didn't get into the news. But of course, Earl's neighbors had seen the police and ambulance that morning and seen Earl escorted into the back of a police car. So people started speculating how Earl had hurt me, because the paperboy told a couple of the neighbors about my torn dress and bloody knees. Earl's neighbors couldn't understand why Earl wasn't sent to the slammer or even, some said, hanged. In fact, by the time Earl was released, somebody had hung him in effigy in his own front yard with a sign that said, "Eat THIS, Earl!" The neighbors didn't know Earl couldn't see it because of his blindness.

Earl had been staying out of sight and everybody hoped he had finally stopped his picketing for good. Vivian's friends on the City Council went ahead and drafted a no-picketing ordinance, but they didn't vote on it because there now appeared to be no need.

Fred Phelps
was probably
metaphorical blind —
hatred/lack of empathy

February 1959

Wedding Rehearsal

About a week before the wedding, a Negro social worker named Mrs. Washington came to the house and gave Mother some official papers accusing Mother and Dad of being unfit parents. If found guilty, the State would send me to a foster home as a delinquent child. It was Earl's doing all right. He had filed a complaint with the State Department of Social Welfare.

"We all know Reverend Wade is doing this out of meanness," Mrs. Washington told Mother, "because everybody knows how that man operates. Even so, the State of Kansas is obligated to investigate all complaints, regardless of the source."

Mother got real upset and called Dad at work. "Don't worry, Louise," Dad said. "Everybody in the neighborhood and church and school will vouch for us as good parents. As for Melody being delinquent, I'm personally gonna chain that child to the bedpost every night from now on unless she promises to cut out her nocturnal adventures."

I knew he was only kidding about the chaining part, but I promised anyway. But I did point out that my nocturnal adventure, as he called it, had apparently stopped Earl's picketing even if it wasn't exactly how I had planned. "You were very lucky," Dad said. "But don't push it."

When Mrs. Washington came back in a few days she said she had interviewed my teacher Miss Swanson and our preacher at church and even Janie Bryant, as well as some of Dad's Meadowgreen buddies. She said she saw no basis for any of the charges and would recommend that the complaint be dismissed. Mother and Dad thanked her profusely and called me to come out and say, "Thank you" to her too. I was playing Three Stooges with Mitchell and was in the middle of imitating Curly, so I came out in the living room and did a few "Yuck, yuck, yucks" and knuckle-poppings for her so she could see I was not delinquent. Then I thought, *Hey, what if Negroes don't like the Three Stooges?* This was the first Negro I'd ever talked to, what's more, the first one that had ever been in our home. Even though she seemed nice, I knew I had to be careful, because this lady had the power to put me in a foster home.

"Do you like the Three Stooges as well as Amos 'N Andy?" I asked her. Mother made a funny noise and tried to grab my arm, but I was too far away.

"I like them both," Mrs. Washington said with a smile.

"Good," I said. "Because I can't do Amos 'N Andy." Just to show her I meant to be friendly, I knuckle-popped again. This time Mother grabbed me.

"She's a very imaginative child," Mother told Mrs. Washington.

Two days before the wedding I got a huge boil on my face. It was right on the side of my nose where everybody could see it. I had gotten boils before, and they were awful. The last one had been while I was camping at Girl Scout camp and I had gotten one in my ear which was really painful. Mother had taken me to the doctor then and he said I was anemic and gave me a bunch of liver shots in my butt. I didn't want to go get more shots now and have both my face and my butt sore.

Mitchell, in an effort to say something meaningful, volunteered that my face would go perfectly with the polka-dots on Harmony's ugly dress. I said at least I didn't look like a midget used car salesman, which was what Mitchell in his wedding costume looked like to me. He was short anyway and his outfit consisted of a little brown plaid coat, brown pants, a little bow tie, and a little brown hat.

The day before Valentine's Day was a Friday, but it was the day we celebrated Valentine's Day at school. Everybody had a little shoebox with our name on it that we had spent days decorating with red hearts and lacy paper doilies and little arrows and stuff. And we all brought little Valentine cards from home and put them in the shoeboxes of our friends. Some of the kids in my class got a lot of Valentines and some didn't get very many, but Miss Swanson gave everybody one. After we passed out the Valentines, we ate some Valentine shaped cookies that were decorated with little candy red hots. I only got about fifteen Valentines, mostly from the other girls in my Girl Scout troop. Of course, having that big boil on my face didn't help. I also got some from boys, but they were the guys I usually beat at tetherball. I ate four cookies though.

After we got home from school it was time for the wedding rehearsal and the rehearsal dinner, which, as far as I was concerned, couldn't hold a candle to the party I'd already been to that day. Besides, I'd already filled up on Valentine's cookies and red hots so I wasn't really hungry. Mother said I'd probably eaten too much sugar and to try not to get fussy before the night was through. I don't know why she said that. We'd all been looking forward to this wedding for a long time and now it was almost here. Why would any of us get fussy? Anyway, Mitchell and Harmony and I weren't actually in the wedding, so when we got to the church we just waited around for a long time while Mother and Dad and everybody did their rehearsing.

Uncle Rex Oliver had actually come out of the cave for the occasion. He walked through his part a couple of times and then told Dewey he had to get out of there. "Why don't you go play hide-n-seek with the kids while we finish?" Dewey told him.

"Okay," he said, and started to the back of the sanctuary where we were drawing on top of the tithing envelopes.

"I can't play," Harmony advised us, "because I have to wait here for somebody." She sounded real mysterious. So Mitchell and Rex Oliver and I went downstairs to the basement to play hide-n-seek in the Sunday School classrooms, and the choir room, and the janitor's room. It was pretty dark. I remembered once there had been a bat in one of the rooms, so I wouldn't go in that one.

When it was Rex Oliver's turn to hide we counted to one hundred real fast, but he was hid so good we couldn't find him. Uncle Rex had had a lot of practice going off to hide. We looked and looked and even turned on all the lights, but we still couldn't find him. So we went back upstairs.

Simon Vargas and Miss Georgia Verne were in the sanctuary talking to Harmony and the organist. They had come as a surprise to sing Harmony and Daffy's song "Locket" at the wedding. That was what Harmony was being so mysterious about earlier.

"Now I don't want you to feel obligated to include the song if you don't like it, Vivian," Miss Georgia kept saying.

"Well," Vivian responded, "since you've gone to so much work to write new music for it, the least Gottfried and I can do is listen. Right Gottfried?"

Uncle Gott nodded his agreement.

So Simon played the guitar, and Miss Georgia sang the new tune, and the organist played some chords as back-up. I had never heard Miss Georgia sing before and neither had Mitchell.

"What do you think, Mitchell?" I asked him.

"Well, if you don't look at Miss Georgia, the song is pretty," he said. I said I thought it was pretty too.

In fact, all the women in the rehearsal were misty-eyed, they liked it so much. "I'd be honored to have that beautiful song sung at my wedding, I mean, our wedding. Wouldn't we, Gottfried?" Uncle Gott nodded agreement again. He was being unusually quiet, even for him.

Harmony started jumping up and down like a pogo stick until Mother gave her a look that meant "stop." I guess Harmony finally had a song that was good enough for somebody to present in public and she was happy. Simon was glad too.

"After the wedding, we're gonna all get together and record that song and sell it to a big music producer," he said to Vivian. "Uh, that is, if I can talk Miss Georgia into making a demo recording with me."

"Oh yes," Miss Georgia said and got all excited. I thought she was going to be another pogo stick for a minute. "I haven't gotten many professional invitations in the last couple of years," she admitted. "This could be the beginning of my comeback."

The new song got incorporated into the rehearsal and we got to listen to it two more times. After that everybody was done and it was time to head over to the rehearsal dinner at a restaurant a few blocks away. Vivian invited Simon and Miss Georgia to dinner too, because now they would be in the wedding tomorrow. The dinner was at a downtown restaurant called The Purple Cow. It was only several blocks away and it was still warm out, so we decided to walk there from church. But first we had to find Rex Oliver.

We all spread out and looked everywhere in the church. We even opened up the office and looked under the desk, just in case Uncle Rex was hiding there. Mother sent me into the ladies' restroom and told me to look under all the stalls, even though she thought it would be strange for Rex Oliver to be in the ladies' restroom. "But do it anyway," she told me, so I did. I couldn't find him there either.

After about half an hour of looking, Dewey told everybody to go on to the restaurant and not to wait for him. "It usually don't do no good to look for Rex Oliver if he don't want to be found," Dewey said. "But the janitor wants to lock up the church for the night and go home. I can't leave Rex Oliver in there all night by himself." He stayed in the church to look some more while we walked to The Purple Cow.

Mitchell and I had never been to a fancy restaurant before because they were too expensive. Mother had warned us we had to be good and eat some of everything or she would never take us out in public again. She gave the place such a build-up I was expecting a real treat, but then the meal came, and Mitchell and I saw the peas. We both hated peas. Ordinarily I would have taken a little bite so I could tell Mother I tried everything. But I'd had so many Valentine cookies and red hots that I felt close to gagging just looking at the peas. I put my fork down and instead watched Mitchell eat around his. One by one, he very carefully hid the peas under the rim of his plate until half of them were gone. I don't think anybody would have noticed either, except some guy in a white jacket came and took all our plates after supper, leaving a perfect little green semi-circle of peas in front of Mitchell. The guy in the white jacket started smiling, then he took a napkin and brushed them all off in another napkin and winked at

Mitchell. Mother looked at Mitchell and frowned, but she didn't say anything.

Janie Bryant and Edith Kliban were chatting like they were long lost friends, which of course they weren't. Maybe it had something to do with Janie's new love life, but it seemed to me her disposition had improved slightly. She was still death on Communists and atheists though.

Uncle Gott had been acting too quiet all evening. He almost moved in slow motion he was so relaxed. That seemed pretty unusual for a confirmed bachelor who was about to get married.

"Uh, Vivian," Dad finally asked her in a low voice, "is anything the matter with Uncle Gott?"

"Janie gave him a Valium just before the rehearsal, he was so nervous," Vivian said.

"Oh," said Dad, nodding his head. None of us knew that Janie used drugs, but we all agreed she needed to.

Vivian was really the only person there who seemed completely comfortable. I just knew it was her circus training that had prepared her for life in front of the public. I don't think Vivian would have blinked an eye during the evening if a guy on a trapeze had swung down out of the ceiling and scooped her up.

Because of the Valentine's Day theme, for dessert we had slices of a heart-shaped white cake with red frosting. Each cake had those little candy hearts with sayings on them stuck in the frosting. Mine said, "Yours Truly," and Mitchell's said, "Sweet Lips."

"That's because butter wouldn't melt in your mouth," I told Mitchell. I wasn't sure what that meant and neither was Mitchell, but I'd heard Vivian use that expression several times. Mitchell wasn't sure if I was insulting him or not so he said, "Oh yeah? Big deal," which I guess he thought was a good response either way.

After dessert Dad stood up and did something they called a toast. Then Janie stood up and did one too and then the two preachers said two prayers, which was about one too many, and then it was time to go. Vivian made sure the cooks made up plates to send home for

Dewey and Uncle Rex Oliver since they'd both missed dinner.

"That meal must have cost a bundle," Dad told Mother as they were getting our coats.

"They could have saved the cost of the peas as far as I was concerned," I said. I was so full I thought I was going to burst.

We walked back to the church and discovered Dewey's truck was still there. Dad went inside and hollered for Dewey, who came to the front door.

"We still can't find him," Dewey said. "It's getting late, so go ahead and lock up the church," he told the janitor who had stayed to help him look. "If Rex Oliver needs out for a fire or something he'll have to break a window. Only please NOT A STAINED-GLASS WINDOW," he yelled real loud so his voice would carry to wherever Rex Oliver was.

About that time Uncle Gott sat down in the street. He was almost passed out he was so relaxed. He just sat in the street grinning at Vivian. He didn't look in any condition to drive himself back to the farm. The adults held a brief conference about what to do with Uncle Gott and while they were talking, Mitchell and I walked over to where he was sitting.

"Congratulations," I told him. He was getting married tomorrow and I wanted to keep it simple because of his being so relaxed.

"Thank you," he finally managed to get out. "She's a marvelous woman." Then he leaned backwards and in slow motion collapsed. Mitchell caught his head and we made him comfortable on the pavement until the adults noticed us.

"I'm afraid he can't stay at my house. It wouldn't look right, being the night before the wedding and all," Vivian said. "The only thing I can think of is to get Gottfried a room somewhere close to the church and have Dewey bring his tux in early in the morning. That way he can sleep off the Valium and won't have to wake up early."

Dewey and Dad came over to where we were guarding Uncle Gott on the pavement. They each grabbed an arm and picked him up, while Vivian opened the passenger door of her Cadillac. After Uncle

Gott was safely inside and the door closed, Vivian walked back around to the driver's side and got in. She started the engine, then rolled down the window.

"I'll get him a room at the Hotel Jayhawk," she said. "It's just a few blocks away."

"We'll follow you there and help get him inside," said Dewey, so that's what we did.

When we got to the Hotel Jayhawk, I went inside with Mother. She explained the situation to the desk clerk while Dad and Dewey got a couple of bell boys and practically dragged Uncle Gott upstairs and into a bed. Of course, everybody knew Uncle Gott from TV and they thought the whole thing was real funny. One of them said, "It looks like Gott is a bit *under the weather*," and they both laughed.

"I appreciate your help," Vivian told the clerk and the bell boys. She gave each of them a five-dollar tip because she could afford to be generous. Vivian was still in a good mood because the rehearsal had gone off more or less without a hitch and she knew Uncle Gott wouldn't be up all night at some wild bachelor party. Just as we were all getting back in our cars, she stopped and thanked us again. "When I get home and go to bed tonight, I'm saying a prayer thanking God for all my blessings. After all these years of being alone, tomorrow's going to be my wedding day."

"Amen," said Grandma Dale.

How to Upstage a Wedding

I woke up early the next morning because I had been dreaming about the bat in the church basement. I wasn't scared exactly, but it was just one more reason to avoid Sunday School. Nobody else was up yet so I put on my furry slippers and went into the living room. The cats came with me because they hoped I would feed them. But usually Mother fed them when she got up, so I told them to wait.

Outside there was just a little breeze blowing. It wasn't much of a wind but it probably meant we were going to get a rain later. I hoped it wouldn't rain until after the wedding and the reception. I also hoped the boil on my face would disappear.

The wedding wasn't until two o'clock in the afternoon, so we had all morning to play and get ready. I decided to eat some of the chocolates that were in the big red satin box on the counter. It was Valentine candy in a heart-shaped box that Dad had bought for Mother. Even though I was still pretty full from the Valentine and wedding parties yesterday, I figured that since nobody was up I could have my pick of all the nutty ones, which were my favorites.

I'd only eaten about four or five when Mitchell got up. He wanted all the caramels. We'd done a pretty good job on the box by the time we heard Mother and Dad getting up, so we ran into the other room and pretended to be watching cartoons on TV.

In the meantime, Black Mimi had jumped up on the counter and was about to lick some of the chocolates herself. Black Mimi had always loved people food. Mother was still half asleep when she saw the cat on the kitchen counter, sniffing around her Valentine candy.

"Why is the cat on my counter?" she asked us, as if we had anything to do with Black Mimi's appetite. "Get down," she told the cat while she picked up the box and studied it. "Why is the lid off? Bad cat. Bad. You're not supposed to eat chocolate. Now you're not going to get any breakfast. You've eaten enough already." She picked up Black Mimi and sat her on the floor.

Next it was our turn to be the focus of Mother's attention. "It's Uncle Gott's wedding day and we'll be at the church instead of eating lunch. So I guess I'll fix us all a big breakfast," Mother mumbled. She was still waking up and still irritated about the Valentine's candy, which after all, had been for her. Mitchell and I looked at each other as Mother started frying bacon and eggs and fixing toast and orange juice and milk. "We're gonna have to eat it, Mitchell," I whispered to him, "or Mother'll figure out about the candy and we'll be in trouble again." What I meant was that I'd be in trouble again, something I wanted to avoid.

So we took our time and tried to eat everything, but I wasn't feeling too good. "I think something from that rehearsal dinner, probably the peas, or maybe from the Valentine's Day cookies and everything from yesterday at the school party, must have upset my stomach," I said. "Bacon and eggs and Valentine's Day stuff don't always go so good together."

"Yeah," Mitchell added.

"Is that so?" Mother said and looked at us both a long time.

"Well, I think it's a wonderful breakfast, Mom," Harmony said. "You're always a wonderful cook." Harmony hadn't been awake in time to fill up on chocolates, so she could say that.

I didn't do much after breakfast because I wanted my stomach to feel better so I wouldn't throw up at the wedding. But then the phone rang. Dad went to answer it. After talking for a few minutes, he came back to the kitchen where we were doing dishes and reported his conversation to Mother.

"That was Dewey," he said. "He's at the church and they still can't find Rex Oliver. He's really hidden himself this time. Dewey's got Uncle Gott's wedding things from the farm and he's gonna drop them off at the Hotel Jayhawk in a few minutes. He said poor old Gottfried's still feeling no pain, which is probably a blessing considering all the hoopla that's gonna go on today." We nodded. Uncle Gott wasn't much for hoopla.

"Since I'm best man, I told him I'll go too, to help Uncle Gott get ready and make sure he gets to the church okay with the ring and the license and everything. We're meeting at the Hotel Jayhawk in about half an hour."

Dad got cleaned up and grabbed his tux and things that he was going to need and got everything he could think of that Uncle Gott was going to need. "I'll see you all at the church about one o'clock," he told us, giving Mother a kiss as he walked out the door.

"Tell Uncle Gott hello for me," Mother said. "He must be so excited."

By the time we had to get ready my stomach was still upset. Mother knew better than to give me Pepto-Bismol. "Is there anything that might make you feel better, Melody?" she asked me.

This was an opportunity I hadn't anticipated. I had to take advantage of Mother's sudden concern, even though it was motivated more by her wish not to spoil Uncle Gott's wedding than by worry about my stomach condition. "Maybe if I didn't have to wear that ugly old dress of Harmony's," I casually remarked.

Mother smiled. That was a good sign. "Honey, what else could you wear?"

"I don't know."

"Well," Mother said, "I have a surprise for you that might help you feel better."

She went into her room and came out with my red velvet dress. "Vivian paid a lady to make you a new one," Mother said. "Isn't it pretty? You'll have to remember to thank her. And honey, please be careful today, because velvet needs to be treated delicately."

"Oh-h," I said, like I didn't already know that. I felt a little better now that I wouldn't have to wear Harmony's old dress.

We all put on our wedding costumes. Mother was very pretty in her red bridesmaid's costume and Harmony and I in our matching red velvet dresses and white gloves looked like we should be playing croquet with Alice in Wonderland at the Queen of Hearts' party. Mitchell still looked like a midget used car salesman.

In a way, this reminded me of Halloween. We'd had candy and costumes then too. This time I hoped nobody got murdered, although Dad had said Uncle Gott was approaching marriage like a lamb to slaughter.

We got to the church real early and Mother had to go help Vivian get ready in a little room somewhere. But not before she issued us instructions.

"Okay kids, your job is to take the wedding presents people bring, say 'thank you,' and put them on those tables in the back of the room. We've even got some flowers for you to wear." She gave Harmony and me each a little white rose corsage which was pretty. Mitchell got a little white rose for his brown plaid jacket, which still made him look like a midget used car salesman. "Now don't go roaming around in the church," Mother added. "Wait right here until the guests arrive unless you need to go to the bathroom." We nodded. We could act like little angels when we needed to. Mother left to help Vivian get ready.

That left us with over half an hour with nothing to do. We shuffled through all the church pamphlets which showed a lot of pictures of Jesus looking just like Rex Oliver in his messiah costume. Then we got in a discussion of why birds always crap on cars when they could just as easily do it on the grass. Harmony said it was because people parked their cars under trees where birds lived, and I said what about all the times they weren't parked under anything and they still got bird crap on them. What was that—magic? And Mitchell said once Dad told him that you had to warsh the bird crap off as quickly as possible or it could ruin the paint on your car.

When we had exhausted that subject, Mitchell brought up Uncle Billy Glenn's toenail fungus. We had caught sight of it one day last summer when we all went swimming and it was really disgusting. Mitchell said it was even more disgusting than my boil, which made me want to tickle him. But then I remembered the delicacy of the red velvet and told him I had a big surprise for him when we got home.

Then Mitchell changed the subject again. "I wonder where Uncle Rex Oliver hid last night?" he asked. Harmony and I looked at each other and shrugged. Everybody wondered about Rex Oliver a lot, because there always seemed to be a cloud hanging over his head. Especially now with the murder inquest in a few weeks. But worrying never seemed to change anything.

"We should set out some fried chicken to trap him with because by now he's bound to be starved," Mitchell said.

The thought of fried chicken reminded me of my stomach still being upset. "I bet if we just waited awhile, we could use wedding cake instead," I told him. Wedding cake seemed easier and safer.

"Naw," Mitchell continued, "fried chicken works a lot better because you can smell fried chicken the minute you walk in the door and you never smell wedding cake."

"I don't think Uncle Gott and Vivian would appreciate having that fried chicken smell everywhere in the church while they're getting married," Harmony said.

"Well, in a few minutes Maynard and Virgil are gonna get here and they can probably find Uncle Rex real easy," I told them. "I bet he's real close. I bet he's so close he's probably watching us right now."

We all stopped talking then because we felt like we were being watched. Finally, Mitchell said, "Hey Uncle Rex, it's okay to come out now."

But no Uncle Rex emerged.

Some of the guests started to arrive and we helped them with the wedding presents like we were supposed to. All the women fussed over Harmony and me and said weren't our dresses cute because they saw my boil and they couldn't say I was cute with a straight face. Then they'd see Mitchell and say, "Oh, what a little doll. Isn't he sweet?" When they were gone, I'd come up behind him and say, "Oh you're so sweet butter wouldn't melt in your mouth," just so he wouldn't get conceited.

Maynard and Virgil came and they said hi to all of us kids. They didn't have a gift though. I guess Indians didn't believe in wedding presents. I wasn't sure if they even believed in weddings.

"Hi, Virgil. Hi, Maynard," Harmony said. "Uncle Rex Oliver is loose somewhere in the church and nobody can find him. Could you go look for him, please?" Harmony was being awfully bossy.

"I bet if we got some fried chicken as bait, he would smell it and come out," Mitchell repeated. Mitchell didn't give up easily.

Virgil looked around at all the people gathering. "Wouldn't it be better to let him be by himself until after the wedding? You know how he hates crowds."

"But Uncle Rex is supposed to be *in* the wedding," I reminded him. "It's gonna start real soon. Dewey's left Uncle Rex's tux for him in the room where the men are supposed to get ready, only none of the men have shown up yet. Just Ed somebody-or-other, Uncle Gott's weatherman friend. He's the only man in the wedding who's here and he's getting real nervous being all alone."

Virgil looked at Maynard who just raised his shoulders as if to say what next? "Well," said Virgil, "I'll go downstairs and look for your Uncle Rex, but I don't know what to tell him if I do find him. I'm not gonna drag him kicking and screaming into a tuxedo and a wedding if he doesn't feel like it."

Mother came up about then. "Have you seen your father?" she asked us. "Is he here yet?"

"No," Mitchell and Harmony and I all answered.

"What about Dewey or Uncle Gott?" Mother said.

"No," Harmony said. "Only that Ed man is here. The two preachers are looking for everybody too."

"We sent Virgil to look for Uncle Rex Oliver in the basement and Maynard's sitting in the back of the church by himself," I volunteered.

"You kids stay here and keep taking the presents," Mother said. Then she went over to Maynard and said a few words and pointed in the direction of the Hotel Jayhawk. Maynard stood up, walked out of the sanctuary and to the head of the basement stairs. He put his two fingers to his mouth and blew a real loud whistle that scared the organist in the sanctuary so bad she played a couple of wrong chords in her song, and everybody turned around and looked. The organist got mad and shot Maynard a dirty look, but he wasn't paying attention to her. We wanted to see what he was up to, but a lot of guests were coming and we were busy taking presents and shaking them to see if we could guess what was inside.

Virgil came up the stairway from the basement and Mother went over to talk to him and Maynard. She pointed to the Hotel Jayhawk again. I caught some of her conversation. "...won't answer the phone...start in ten minutes...go and check..." From where I stood, I also saw that Uncle Rex Oliver was standing at the bottom of the stairs in the shadow. It looked like he had on a choir robe, but I couldn't be sure.

Virgil and Maynard started out the door and then I saw them break into a run. Just then I heard something that sounded like firecrackers and a couple of guests came running in from the parking lot. "Somebody's firing shots a few blocks over," one of them said.

"Oh my God," Mother yelled. She grabbed the nearest guest. "Please, go call the police. There's a phone in the office. Over there." She looked at us, then she looked outside. "Stay here," she told us, then she kicked off her high heels and started running in her stocking feet in the direction Virgil and Maynard had gone. The way she kicked off her shoes and took off reminded me of Wonder Woman. I'd never seen Mother run before, much less in a hat, white gloves, and a bridesmaid's dress without her shoes. I knew something important was going on and I didn't want to miss it. It was turning out to be just like Halloween after all.

"Come on, Mitchell," I yelled at him. "Let's go!" I forgot I was wearing the delicate red velvet. As soon as I started running hard it ripped at the seam just like the other dress had done, but I just kept running. Mitchell came running too and his little brown hat flew off almost immediately. Uncle Rex Oliver ran out into the parking lot, grabbed Mitchell's hat, and ran back in the church and down the basement stairs again.

By the time we ran after Mother two blocks, we could see she had run to the Hotel Jayhawk. I was out of breath and so was Mother. Two people were lying on the sidewalk in front of the hotel, not moving, and picket signs had been dropped around the hotel entrance. As we got closer, we could see one of the people on the ground was Earl Wade and the other his plain-looking wife. The despicable Wade children were all at the scene too, kneeling by their parents trying to revive them. I saw Dewey and Dad and Uncle Gott in their tuxes standing next to three guys that looked like they were from out of town because of the way they were dressed. There was a tough looking woman with them too. A little ways behind them was the Hotel Manager and a couple of guys dressed as bellboys.

Uncle Gott tried to approach the mass of Wades on the sidewalk. "Can I help?" he asked, only he said it real funny and I saw he didn't have his false teeth in. But the oldest Wade daughter just kept screaming. "Stay away, all of you. Stay away." So Uncle Gott walked back to Dad.

The police came almost immediately with their red lights and sirens going full blast. Three cars of them. I got to thinking I'd had a lot of experience with the police this year, first at the Halloween party, then at Earl's house, and now this. Maybe it was a sign from God, only I wasn't sure if it meant I'd better straighten out my life, or if I should consider a career in law enforcement.

The police ran over to where Earl and Mrs. Wade were lying on the ground. "What happened?" the first one asked. Everybody started talking at once and pointing fingers at different people. A second policeman finally yelled above all the noise, "Was anybody actually shot? Who got shot?" and everybody looked at everybody else and finally said no, they didn't think so, nobody actually got shot. So many people were talking and yelling that we couldn't make out a thing.

Mother saw me and Mitchell then, and she motioned for us to come over to her. We did and she put an arm around each of us, drawing us up close to her. I saw she had ripped her stockings running shoeless through the streets. "Aren't your feet cold?" I asked her. I knew mine would be if I were standing on the sidewalk in the middle of February, even if it was warm.

"Shush," Mother said. She wanted to hear what they were saying.

Dad came over then and put his arm around Mother. "It looks like everybody's okay, Louise. Why don't you take the kids back to the church and we'll be along as soon as we give our statements to the police." Before Mother could indicate her agreement, Mitchell interrupted.

"Is Uncle Gott okay?"

"Well," said Dad, "his false teeth are missing and he got punched in the eye by Mrs. Wade. But other than that he's fine."

"So what were the shots?" Mitchell asked.

"Actually," said Dad, "that woman standing over by Big Aug—uh, by Mr. Messina, fired a gun up in the air a couple of times to stop the free-for-all."

I turned to look at the woman who had fired the gun and she was looking at me too. She kept looking at me and finally winked at me like we had a secret just between us two, but I couldn't remember ever seeing her before. Then the police started talking to her and she looked away.

"Hey, Dad, did you punch anybody?" Mitchell was really excited at the thought.

Dad looked at Mother before he answered. "I can't discuss it now, son," he said. "We have a wedding to attend."

Mother and the Indians and Mitchell and I all walked back to the church. Mitchell kept talking about how he bet Dad had punched a whole bunch of them despicable Wades and Mother said she hoped not. By now I could tell Mother's feet were cold and I told her I hoped she didn't catch cold. "Thank you, Melody," she said. Then she saw my dress was ripped. But she just shook her head and didn't even yell at me.

After we got back to the church Mother went to tell Vivian and the preachers what had happened. One of the preachers made an announcement that there would be a short delay, but that the wedding would take place as planned. Mother sent somebody to the store to buy her some new stockings. She looked again at my dress, then looked at

Mitchell.

"Where's your hat, young man?" she asked him.

"I saw Uncle Rex pick it up and go back to the basement," I told her.

"Oh, that's right," Mother said. "I'd forgotten about Uncle Rex. Melody, please go ask Virgil to go find him again, won't you?"

"Okay," I said. So I did. I think Virgil was getting a little irritated at being sent to run everybody's errands, but as usual he was very polite.

Dad and Dewey and Uncle Gott came in the back door then and sent somebody to tell the preachers they were ready. The preachers told the organist and she started in on the wedding march.

I have to say, all the bridesmaids looked really pretty. Mother, and Grandma Dale, and Edith Kliban were glowing. Even Janie looked especially nice. Vivian looked so beautiful that when she walked down the aisle everybody stood up out of respect. She was perfectly calm too, just like she got married every day in the middle of gangsters and shootings and picketers.

When the men had to come out it was a different story. Uncle Gott had a real shiner on his left eye, and I could tell by the way he was smiling that he still hadn't found his teeth. Dad, as best man, looked okay but worried, and he limped a little bit. I hoped he still had the ring. Dewey looked like he was miserable in a tux, but happy for Uncle Gott. Ed somebody-or-other looked like his shoes pinched him. Finally Rex Oliver came out too, only he was still wearing the black choir robe instead of his tux and he carried Mitchell's little brown hat. I bet he would have put it on, except it was too small for him. When he stood next to Ed the weatherman, Ed started sneezing.

Finally, the organist stopped playing and the congregation sat down. I don't remember all the stuff that happened, except that Uncle Gott lisped through most of his part and had a hard time giving a firm kiss to the bride. Simon and Miss Georgia performed "Locket" like they were at Carnegie Hall instead of the Methodist Church. One person in the audience even started clapping when they were done, but

I think it was Miss Georgia's elderly mother.

Then the organ played some more, Vivian and Uncle Gott and the wedding party members all walked down the aisle. The rest of us went to Fellowship Hall in the church for the reception. We had to wait a long time while people took pictures and cut the cake and shook hands with everybody and all the stuff that happens at weddings. Vivian and Uncle Gott made a point of shaking hands with everyone and there was a lot of kissing and hugging going on too.

When they came over to Mitchell and Harmony and me, Vivian threw her arms around me and Mitchell at the same time. "Thank you, kids, for all your help. You too, Harmony."

"It was a lovely wedding," Harmony told her. "A truly splendid affair. I'm glad my song was able to contribute to your happiness."

"Does your eye hurt?" Mitchell asked Uncle Gott.

"A little bit," lisped Uncle Gott.

Mother had made me promise to thank Vivian for buying me the new red velvet dress. "Thank you for the dress, Vivian," I said. I tried to stand so she couldn't see the rip.

"Just call me Aunt Vivian, Melody. We're family now." There was more kissing, then Vivian dragged Uncle Gott over to some other people and started hugging them.

I was getting bored and tired of eating wedding cake, but Vivian, who Janie said always had a good sense of timing, took Uncle Gott by the hand again and announced they were getting ready to leave. So everybody ran out to the parking lot and when Vivian and Uncle Gott came out, we got to throw rice at them. I liked that part. Somebody had decorated Vivian's Cadillac with shaving cream and tied tin cans on it. Dad as best man got to drive the happy couple away. He told Mother he was taking them to Vivian's house where they would pick up their things and leave on their honeymoon.

We all hung around until Mother and Janie made sure all the wedding presents had been collected, then Mother gathered us up too and took us home. It had been a long day. We changed out of our wedding costumes and Mother made bologna sandwiches for supper. I wasn't too hungry, so I only ate one.

After about an hour, Dad came home. He changed out of his tux and ate a bologna sandwich before we could make him tell us about the shooting at the Hotel Jayhawk. By that time, Janie Bryant and Uncle Billy Glenn had dropped by because Janie was about to die from curiosity.

Dad got a beer out of the refrigerator. "I've earned it," he said. He got one for Uncle Billy Glenn too. Then he sat down in the living room and told us the story. "It's quite remarkable," he began, "especially for Valentine's Day."

Gunshots and My Guardian Angel

"Dewey and I got to the Hotel Jayhawk about ten o'clock this morning," Dad related, "and right off the bat we discovered we were missing the groom. At least, he wasn't in the room where we'd left him the night before. We dropped our tuxes and wedding stuff off in his room and went down to the front desk to ask about him.

"The hotel manager, a guy named Orin Drake that everybody calls Cupcake behind his back because..." he shifted his eyes to us kids, "well, just because. Said he'd gotten the scoop on Uncle Gott from his night manager so he knew about the Valium and the wedding and all. He told us Uncle Gott had called the front desk about eight this morning asking why he was in a hotel room and what day it was. Cupcake said Uncle Gott didn't sound too good and it was obvious he didn't remember much from last night.

"What Cupcake didn't tell us, bless his little heart," Dad emphasized sarcastically, "was how he had decided to have some fun with Uncle Gott. Apparently, mister Cupcake Wisenheimer had told Uncle Gott some story about how he, meaning Uncle Gott, had passed out last night after a wild bachelor party on the hotel roof garden and been carried into a room to sleep it off. Uncle Gott said he couldn't remember that, but did Cupcake know where Uncle Gott's false teeth were because they seemed to be missing. Cupcake jokes around some more and says that perhaps the young lady had them. Uncle Gott asks what young lady, and Cupcake says,"—Dad lowered his voice to act like he was being real discreet—"'Why, the young lady from the party who stayed to, uh, tuck you in, sir.'

"I'll bet there was a real long silence on the phone after that," Dad nodded his head. "Finally, Uncle Gott asked again what day it was and Cupcake says, 'Why, it's Saturday, February 14th, sir. Happy Valentine's Day.' Then there's a loud groan and the phone gets hung up.

"Just to show he was a good sport, Cupcake ordered room service to take up a free breakfast to Uncle Gott, sort of a wedding present, I guess. He only ordered soft food because of Uncle Gott's missing teeth and he asked the kitchen to put some Valentine's stuff on the tray. He said he also told them to throw in a bottle of aspirin. But the waiter who tried to deliver the tray couldn't get anybody to open the door, even though he knocked," Dad made a knocking motion, "several times and yelled 'Room service' as loud as he could.

"About this time, Tiny, one of Big Augie's boys who is also staying in the hotel, comes walking back to his room after going downstairs for a newspaper. We think Tiny stopped to look at something on Uncle Gott's tray sitting in the hallway. Dewey thinks he was trying to filch the bacon, but I think he wanted to see what Valentine candy was in the little nut cup. I guess we'll never know for sure.

"Anyway, without warning the door opens and there's Uncle Gott looking real pale and weak. What Uncle Gott sees is this big bruiser standing right outside his door. In his confusion all he can think of is it must be the 'young lady's' boyfriend come to beat him up, only of course he can't remember no young lady in the first place. So he says, 'She's not here,' and then he passes out, right into Tiny's arms.

"Tiny doesn't know who Uncle Gott is or who this 'she' is he's referring to. But then he recognizes Uncle Gott from the TV weather. He doesn't want to leave any unconscious celebrities in the hall, so he picks Uncle Gott up, carries him into the room, and tosses him on the bed." Dad went through all the motions of this sequence. "Then he gets the breakfast tray from the hall and pours Uncle Gott some hot coffee and slaps his face a little to get him to come around." Dad made slapping motions.

"I don't think I'd want that guy slapping me," Dad said as an aside to Uncle Billy Glenn. "You've seen how big he is, haven't you?" Uncle Billy Glenn looked down at the rug and mumbled something. Dad kept going.

"So Uncle Gott comes around and wants to know what's going on and who Tiny is and where did the nut cup full of Valentine's candy come from. Before you know it, Uncle Gott's telling Tiny about how he's getting married today and he can't find his teeth and how his head isn't feeling too good. So Tiny gets on the phone and calls Big Augie and says," and here Dad attempted his best New England Mafia accent, "'Hey Boss, we gotta help dis poor guy,' because they'd all seen Uncle Gott quite a bit on TV. Big Augie wants to know how they can help, so they decide to retrace Uncle Gott's steps last night to see if they can find his missing teeth. Even though they're Catholic," Dad acknowledged, "you gotta respect somebody who wants to help you get married with all your teeth.

"In the meantime, *Miss* Salome Parsons—and I don't think she's missed much—is waiting downstairs in the lobby to have a meeting with Big Augie. She looked like she'd had a pretty busy night herself, if you know what I mean. Big Augie calls downstairs and asks her to go up to Uncle Gott's room and help Tiny. When she knocks on the door, Tiny goes to answer and Uncle Gott was sitting up on the bed watching. Salome says 'Hi, remember me?' to Tiny, only Uncle Gott thinks this must be the 'young lady' from last night and that she's asking him if he remembers her and of course he doesn't remember her at all. Not only that, but the gal ain't that young. But it gets worse, because when she introduces herself as Salome Parsons, he does remember that Salome in the Bible had John the Baptist's head on a platter. He thought maybe this was a sign from God that he had been very wicked last night and that God was punishing him by making his teeth disappear instead of his head.

"Uncle Gott remembers that Cupcake had told him that maybe the young lady had his teeth. So he asks Salome does she know anything about the teeth and of course she doesn't, but she says she'll be glad to help look for them. First though, she and Tiny pour about a gallon of coffee into Uncle Gott and then they help him out of the clothes he's slept in all night and get him into the shower. They also get Joey, Big Augie's other 'associate,' to loan Uncle Gott one of

Joey's clean shirts, because Tiny's shirt would have been way too big.

"So they get him cleaned up and showered and half-way alert. Tiny finishes off the breakfast tray and Big Augie and Joey come down and everybody gets introduced. Only of course Uncle Gott doesn't know who these guys are or why they're in Topeka. He just figures they're businessmen traveling through town who have also made the acquaintance of the 'young lady.' He thanks them over and over for their help. You know how polite our family is.

"By the time Dewey and I got there," continued Dad, "Uncle Gott and Big Augie and everybody was up on the roof garden looking high and low for the missing choppers. We introduce ourselves, only Dewey don't give his last name because it would have put a strain on things if Big Augie had realized Dewey's son was the one accused of murdering his daughter. Dewey says he remembers Big Augie's Lincoln sliding around in the snow and how his hired men Virgil and Maynard helped push them out. 'Well, well,' says Big Augie. 'It's a small world, isn't it?'

"We all searched that roof garden for an hour because of course none of us knew about Cupcake's little joke. Big Augie even made Tiny and Joey get down on their hands and knees and look under all the chairs. All this time Uncle Gott hasn't said anything to Salome about her 'tucking him in' because he's too embarrassed. But then he thinks, wait a minute, if it was a bachelor party maybe me and Dewey was there too. So he comes right out and asks us what time did the party end?

"I figured he meant the rehearsal dinner, so I said I left about nine-thirty. Dewey said same with him. Then Uncle Gott said what about the bachelor party here at the hotel, and Dewey and I just looked at each other, because we didn't know what the heck he was talking about.

"So we took a break and Tiny went to get Cupcake to ask him to please join us on the roof garden because we had a couple of questions about this bachelor party that nobody knew anything about except him. That's when Cupcake found out that Uncle Gott had acquired some, shall we say, friends with muscle. I think he got real worried about what Big Augie was gonna do to him when he found out about the joke, so he came upstairs accompanied by two waiters pushing a little cart with an ice bucket and champagne and Valentine's Day cookies and stuff for everybody. Maybe he was trying to be nice to Uncle Gott on his wedding day, but I also think he wanted some witnesses in case of trouble. He was right too, because Big Augie was plenty sore about him and his boys crawling around on their hands and knees for over an hour on a wild goose chase. Or maybe I should say, a wild tooth chase. Anyway, I wouldn't want to be in Cupcake's shoes when they settle that point.

"But Uncle Gott's teeth really were missing. We all went to Uncle Gott's room and searched it again. Then we searched the hotel lobby. We even checked with the janitor to see if he had encountered any spare teeth, but nobody had. I said I bet they were somewhere in Vivian's Cadillac because Uncle Gott had his teeth at the rehearsal dinner, but evidently didn't have them by the time he was carried up to his room in the hotel. I suggested why didn't we all get our tuxes on and get everything ready for the wedding and go over to the church a little early and look in Vivian's car.

"Uncle Gott invited Augie and Salome and the boys to the wedding because he felt grateful to them for coming to his rescue. Dewey wasn't too thrilled about that because he didn't want Big Augie coming face to face with Rex Oliver, but nobody knew exactly where Rex Oliver was anyhow since he hid or ran away."

Dad stopped the story for a minute because he had to belch. He put his hand over his mouth and tried to be quiet, but the beer was making him belch. He said excuse me, though. Uncle Billy Glenn had already belched a couple of times from his beer and he usually never excused himself. Mitchell and Janie and Uncle Billy Glenn were trying not to be impatient, but they wanted Dad to hurry up and get to the shooting part.

"So what was the shooting about?" asked Janie.

"Well," Dad resumed, "just as everybody was getting ready to walk over to the church a bellboy comes running in and says that Earl Wade and his group are outside picketing. Nobody knows why they picked this particular day or this particular place, because they'd never picketed the Hotel Jayhawk before. But anyway, they did. They were carrying their usual nasty signs with something to insult everybody, including one that said, 'Lunatics are only fit to kill each other.' That one got both Dewey and Big Augie pretty ticked off and they went outside before anybody could stop them. Big Augie's boys were right behind them. Cupcake and me were just coming outside too when Uncle Gott, dressed in his tux, goes charging past us and right into the middle of the picketers. He was lisping something about being a peacemaker.

"As I recall, because everything happened pretty fast just then, Big Augie got to Earl first. He grabbed Earl by the lapels and pulled him almost off the ground. I only heard part of what he said, but it was something about what happens in Rhode Island to ignorant two-bit troublemakers who went around insulting the dead. He told Earl he'd heard that Lake Shawnee out south of Topeka had catfish in it so big they could swallow something the size of a human body, especially a body that was weighted down. Of course he was talking with his funny New England accent.

"Now even though Earl couldn't see too good, he could hear the accent and he could reason just fine. He got Augie's drift loud and clear and started to back away. But before he could, Dewey, dressed in his tux, steps up to him and says, 'This is for my boy, Earl,' and slugs him hard right in the kisser. POW!" Dad made a motion of a fist slamming into something. "Earl falls down, out cold. Mrs. Wade tries to run up and Uncle Gott tries to calm her, but she doesn't want to be calmed and she pops Uncle Gott in the eye." Dad made another fist motion to indicate getting popped in the eye. "So Tiny, who's sort of adopted Uncle Gott, sorta slaps Mrs. Wade," Dad made a slapping motion, "and she falls down, out cold too. Then all the other Wades and picketers start hitting everybody with their picket signs and picket sticks. I even got punched a few times." Dad now went through the

238

motions of people all slugging each other in a big fight.

"Did you hit anybody, Dad?" Mitchell interrupted. He was so excited he was bouncing up and down in his chair.

Dad looked over at Mother, who frowned. He looked at the rug, smiled, then looked back at Mitchell. "Well..." he replied with a sly boastful smile.

"The next thing you know I heard gunshots being fired almost right next to me. I gotta tell you, it was real scary hearing a gun like that go off so close in the middle of a fight. It reminded me I was dealing with some real tough characters who made a living out of rubbing people out. I looked around to see what was happening and heard Salome Parsons say, 'Everybody just back away and stop your fighting.' She was holding a pistol pointed up in the air," he made his hand into the shape of a pistol and pointed it in the air, "and had shot it to get everybody's attention, which she certainly did. I saw the police cars coming then, and Virgil and Maynard came running over from the church, and half the hotel guests, and every wino who was downtown with time to kill seemed to be standing around when I looked. The police wanted to lock some of us up, but there was so many conflicting statements about who started what that they had to let everybody go. They couldn't even arrest Salome for disturbing the peace because one, she has a license to carry that thing, and two, she probably saved us all from killing each other.

"Earl and his wife came to and started calling the police a bunch of cowards and other things I won't repeat, for not arresting anybody. Duane Appelhans didn't appreciate that and told Earl he better shut up or he and the police would leave and Earl would be on his own with 'these fine folks here,' meaning Dewey, Big Augie and his boys, Salome and her gun, and a toothless Gott. So Earl shut up and left.

"Salome helped Uncle Gott put some ice on his eye, but it didn't do no good. Big Augie came over to Dewey, who was trying to straighten his cummerbund from where it had got pulled loose. You should've seen Dewey. He was really a mess from fighting. I think Dewey still had some fight left in him too because he didn't back down from Big Augie one bit when Augie asked him what had he meant when he hit Earl and said, 'This is for my boy.'

"Dewey looked him right in the eye and said, 'Mr. Messina, my boy is Rex Oliver Oots. He ain't dead, like your daughter, but he ain't right either and he hasn't been for years. For Earl to go around in the name of Jesus making fun of people like that is just not Christian. Now, I'm sorry about your daughter. I truly am. But Rex Oliver didn't kill her.'

"'I know,' said Big Augie. 'I'm sorry your son got blamed for it.'

"Well of course we was all speechless! That's been hanging over our heads since Halloween! But before we could say anything, Uncle Gott comes running over and says—well actually he lisps—that it's past two o'clock and he was late for his wedding. He starts pulling Dewey toward the church and we all remembered we had gone to the hotel in the first place to make sure Uncle Gott got married. I guess Big Augie and Salome and the boys decided not to come, because I didn't see them at the service or the reception. Unfortunately, by this time we was so late that we didn't have time to stop and look in Vivian's car for Uncle Gott's missing teeth. Which is too bad because that's where they were all right. Uncle Gott sat on them when I drove Vivian and him back to her house after the wedding. I wish we could've found them sooner."

"At least he has them for the hon-ey-moon," Janie purred as she smiled at Uncle Billy Glenn. Mother cleared her throat and shot a look at her that I knew meant she'd better stop it.

"So what did Big Augie mean when he said he knew Rex Oliver didn't kill his daughter?" Uncle Billy Glenn asked.

"I expect that's what Dewey's finding out right now," Dad said, looking at his watch. "He was gonna meet with Augie at seven o'clock to discuss that very topic. I didn't want him to go alone, both for his safety and because I was real curious. But he said this was his business."

"Where is the meeting?" Mother asked. "Should we be worried?"

"I don't know," said Dad. "But I think Dewey can look after himself."

"Did Uncle Rex Oliver give you back your hat, Mitchell?" Mother asked him, as if this were what we'd been discussing for an hour.

"I told him he could keep it," said Mitchell. "He liked that."

"Oh," said Dad. "Something else happened that was real strange. Salome Parsons told me I had quite a gutsy daughter. Which one of you two was she talking about and why?" Dad looked at me and at Harmony. Harmony shrugged her shoulders as if to say she didn't know anything about it. I was quiet, wondering if the same hand that had fired the gun in the air today had grabbed me from behind in Earl's front yard two weeks ago. If so, I was disappointed. Salome Parsons was not my idea of anyone's guardian angel.

Lightning Changes Everything

You would think the Valentine candy, the big extravaganza wedding, the shooting, the fighting, the police, and my possible guardian angel would have been more than enough for one day. But then something much worse happened and that part was also my fault.

By seven o'clock that evening the temperature had risen to eighty degrees, something rare for February. The rain that threatened that morning had held off, but judging how heavy and still the air was now we were going to get a storm soon.

After Dad's explanation, Janie and Uncle Billy Glenn had left to get a bite to eat. I wondered how they could eat anything after all that wedding cake, not to mention Uncle Billy Glenn's belchable beer, but Harmony said that was just an excuse for them to be alone.

I had long since taken off the heavy velvet dress and put on some shorts and a shirt. Mother had opened the windows and doors to let in some air, but nobody felt any air moving in or out. Everything seemed too still to be natural. I went to see what the cats were doing to see if they would tell me if it was going to storm. I had a lot of respect for storms and for cats too.

Little Poo had crammed her head under Mitchell's dresser and was not moving a muscle since she thought she was hidden, even though the rest of her body was a large white lump sticking out. She wouldn't tell me what she was hiding from. Black Mimi had thrown up on the rug in my room. She waited until I was in my room too, then she ran in and deposited her dinner right in front of me. I knew she was upset, but I didn't know if it was because of a storm coming, because of all the crazy things her people had been through today, or because she'd been eating the plants again. Then I remembered she'd tried to lick the chocolate Valentine candies this morning. Maybe that had given her an upset stomach. Those candies sure hadn't helped me.

I thought how Valentine's Day was supposed to be a day filled with love. That's why Vivian and Uncle Gott had gotten married today, because today was a day people loved each other even more than usual. The two of them had even tried to guarantee love by getting married in a church and asking God for His help in the deal. Both preachers had said prayers about love and happy marriages, but how did anybody know if God would really make it happen? After everything we'd been through recently, I doubted God even cared. It was obvious He just didn't love me anymore and I wasn't sure why. Not only had God ignored me during the blizzard and killed some innocent people and animals, but now my guardian angel turned out to be a person of real dubious character. None of that was very loving. I had my doubts about Valentine's Day too. Even Valentine's candy wasn't good for me. The question was, why had God turned His back on me? What was going on between me and God? Was it something I'd done? None of it made any sense. It just made me sad.

I went outside and sat on the porch so I could think. The sky was showing signs of distant lightning. I loved to watch thunderstorms, especially the early summer ones, which were huge. It would really be unusual if we got one of those in February though, even if it was strangely warm. Mitchell came out and sat next to me. We didn't say anything for a long time.

"Melody," he finally said, "do you want to know the real reason I gave Uncle Rex my hat?"

I got up and started walking away. I had reached a decision. There was something I had to get settled, even if it meant I got in trouble. Mitchell got up and followed me.

"Do you?" Mitchell repeated.

I was busy trying to remember which way I needed to go. I had to hurry before it started to storm.

"Huh?" I said.

"Do you know why I gave Uncle Rex my hat?"

"Why?" I finally said.

"Because—well—it's about a promise he made me promise. About somethin' real important."

We'd gotten to the end of our block. I turned left and Mitchell followed. "Yeah, what?" I replied without thinking. I was making this hard on him because I was in a bad mood about God and my guardian angel and I had to get this settled. It wasn't Mitchell's fault of course, but he'd started this conversation when I wanted to be left alone.

Mitchell was almost running to keep up with me.

"So what kind of a promise?"

"It's a secret," said Mitchell. "I promised not to tell."

"Well, bully for you," I said. "So why did you bring it up?"

He didn't know what to say then, so he just shrugged his shoulders and pretended to pick a scab off his arm.

I turned to the right this time, recognizing some familiar landmarks. The sky gave a low rumble.

After walking another block in silence, I finally said, "It's about the murder, isn't it?"

"No," said Mitchell too quickly. I don't know where my question had come from, my sixth sense maybe, but it had struck home. I stopped and turned to Mitchell. Now he had my full attention and now he didn't want it.

"Liar, liar, pants on fire, hangin' from a telephone wire," I sang. "It's about the murder. You and Uncle Rex made a promise about the murder, didn't you?"

"No," he said again. "And anyway, I promised I wouldn't tell."

Mitchell was incapable of keeping a secret from me for very long. Now all that remained was deciding what method to use to get it out of him. But I had something else to finish first and I had to hurry because of the storm.

"Okay," I said. "I won't ask." I resumed walking. I thought I was getting close, but I couldn't be sure. The dark clouds overhead seemed to be getting darker by the minute. After a little while Mitchell couldn't stand being ignored.

"What if there was a secret and you made a promise not to tell but it was about something bad?" he blurted out.

I made my voice real casual. "Well, it's important to keep a promise if you said you would. I'm real sure about that. But sometimes..." I paused, "if it's about something bad, it's important not to keep it inside. Because you'll start to have bad dreams." Mitchell gasped. "And you'll wonder if God is going to punish you." I let him think about that for a while. It wasn't exactly honest of me to talk about God, since I wasn't sure how much I believed in God myself.

"You know," I continued as I increased my pace, "if you really want to talk about it, maybe I could help you out." Mitchell was quiet so I added, "But if you don't, that's okay."

"Do you promise not to tell?" he asked.

"Well—okay."

But instead of rushing to tell me like he usually did, Mitchell's forehead wrinkled, and he frowned, and his eyes looked unhappy. I thought he was going to cry.

It started to lightning then and a little breeze started to pick up. I could feel the storm moving in and it made me real excited. I get that way right before a big thunderstorm. I think it has something to do with the electricity in the air, but I love to be outside watching the clouds and feeling the heavy air and waiting for the sudden rush of rain.

As I turned a corner I saw what I had come for. I thought I heard voices chanting somewhere in the distance, but maybe it was only noise from the storm. The skies were still rumbling and clouds were rolling everywhere. All at once I made out the people, walking and chanting in a circle in front of the house I'd been searching for. "Oh no," I said almost to myself. "Not twice in one day. Don't they ever give up?"

"Huh?" said Mitchell. He didn't know where I'd been going. "What are you talking about?"

"Look," I pointed. "It's the despicable Wades. They're picketing Vivian's house. Why won't they leave us alone?"

"Why are they at Vivian's house?" Mitchell asked. Then, after he thought a second continued, "Why are *we* at Vivian's house? Huh, Melody?"

"Come on," I said. "I have to talk to Uncle Gott before he and Vivian leave on their honeymoon. I hope it's not too late." I started to run toward the house, hoping to reach the safety of the front porch before the rain began. We were going to have to cross through the Wades somehow to get there.

I got as far as the curb in front of Vivian's house when I saw Earl turn silently and stare at me. The other Wades kept marching back and forth, back and forth, in front of Vivian's sidewalk. It was almost as if Earl had been waiting for me, just like before at his house. I wondered if he had the sixth sense like Grandma Dale and it told him I was coming. Even so, the fact that he was standing there waiting for me again was scary. I jerked to a stop, took a deep breath, then started forward.

"What do you want?" It was uncanny how blind Earl Wade sprang from his position on the sidewalk and shrieked before I could get any farther toward the house. He was holding a picket sign that said, "The way of the ungodly shall perish, Psalms 1:6." I kept telling myself that he couldn't see me, but my knees were beginning to get rubbery. Maybe this wasn't such a good idea.

"Well..." I began.

"I know what you want," Earl screamed. "GO HOME."

When he screamed, I almost died from fright, just like the first time he yelled at me at the fairgrounds, and the second time he yelled at me at his house. I wasn't used to anyone screaming at me, and anyway the electricity in the air had me really edgy. But I'd gotten this far and at least hadn't peed myself from fright this time. Now I had to get inside and talk to Uncle Gott. Uncle Gott would tell me why God didn't love me anymore. I just had to get by Earl Wade first.

"There aren't any lunatics here, Reverend Wade," I told him, trying to be brave. "Why are you so angry at lunatics anyway? They can't help it." I could smell the rain now, it was so close.

"I said GO HOME!" Earl yelled in a cross between a shout and a squeak. He took a another step forward. I held my ground. This time Earl wouldn't make me wet my pants, I was determined.

"No, I won't," I answered. I felt a drop of rain hit my head. It made me hurry even more. "I won't go home. Why are you picketing my aunt's house? Why do you think lunatics are from the devil? Don't you have lun—I mean, mental illness—in your own family? Wouldn't that make you of the devil then too?"

"BLASPHEMY!" roared Earl Wade. This time he stumbled three steps toward me, still holding on to his picket sign, as he reached out his other arm and pointed at me. A chilling blast of wind caught his clothes and blew his hair straight out and I saw his wild eyes looking straight at me, for all the world looking just like the mural of crazy John Brown in the Capitol. More rain drops began to fall.

"Uncle Rex didn't kill your sister," I yelled to be heard above the sudden wind. "So why are you so hateful to my family?"

"Yeah," yelled Mitchell.

I whirled to see Mitchell next to me on the curb. I'd forgotten he was there.

Earl's head jerked at the sound of a second voice. He made a half-turn and started toward Mitchell. It began to rain. He was coming directly toward Mitchell waving his sign above his head and screaming, "I will NEVER..."

As I threw my arms around Mitchell, I felt the hair on my head stand up. There wasn't time to scream.

They say lightning never strikes twice in the same place. But that's because, after the first time, that place isn't there anymore. One minute I was holding Mitchell and protecting him from Earl Wade. The next I was violently thrown off my feet as a wall of sound and light and brute force hit us like an anvil. I couldn't see or hear any of it. I could only feel a million atoms in my body vibrating, vibrating, vibrating in a strange sort of way and the pounding of rain and a terrible scorching smell somewhere in the middle of it all.

I was glowing. Little light particles were coming out of me everywhere into space. I was part of the light and it was everywhere. Why did everything feel like light, like glowing? Was I dead? I couldn't remember. Was I an angel? Was I in Heaven?

I realized I was slowly opening my eyes. Violent sheets of rain were pounding me, but I couldn't seem to move from the ground. It was cold and very wet. This didn't seem like Heaven.

I lay there sopping wet with no strength to get up, looking around at everything glowing. I saw Earl Wade, glowing, with his hair now plastered to his head, sitting up about ten feet from me. I saw his lips move but I couldn't hear anything. He put one hand in front of his face, then both hands. One hand, the one that had held the picket sign, was black and horribly burnt. Flesh was seared off of it in strips. Earl stared and stared at his burnt hand, then he dropped his hands and started looking around in a full circle like he didn't know what to look at first. It seemed like he started screaming, but I couldn't be sure. But next thing I knew the other despicable Wades were getting up from the ground and running to Earl. He started pointing to his hand, then to his eyes, but I couldn't hear a word. Mrs. Wade started saying something, then it looked like Earl screamed some more, then she dropped to her knees right there in the muddy lawn and started praying, only I still couldn't hear anything. Then all the children dropped to their knees and it looked like they were praying too. Their lips were all moving and all of them were glowing, and the house and the yard and the sidewalk were glowing, and I still wondered if maybe I was dead and watching this from someplace else.

My ear hurt. I slowly raised one hand up to my ear, but I still couldn't hear anything. It didn't seem like I could feel my ear either. I could see my hand glowing, though. Finally, I raised up on one elbow and began to remember why I was lying in the rain in front of Vivian's house. I had come to ask Uncle Gott why God didn't love me anymore. I remembered Earl had gotten mad and had started after us when I felt my hair stand up and I'd put my arms around Mitchell.

Propped up in the rain, I remembered I had a little brother who had challenged Earl Wade along with me. Where was he now? I slowly turned my head. The sidewalk where we had been standing looked as if it had been blasted apart. Chunks of glowing concrete and earth and muddy grass surrounded a hole where the sidewalk was supposed to have continued. I wondered if Mitchell had been blown away from the hole too. It was raining. I wondered why there was a hole in the sidewalk and why we were lying, glowing, in the mud and the rain. Maybe we'd been hit by lightning.

In slow motion, like there was all the time in the world, I pulled myself into a sitting position. After a while when my head quit spinning, I was able to look behind me toward the street. That's when I saw the little body that was my best friend. It was glowing too.

"Mitchell?" I whispered. At least it seemed like I whispered because I couldn't hear. Mitchell didn't move. *He's dead,* I thought. We're both dead. Right here, dead, in Vivian's front yard on her wedding day. Because of lightning. And now I'm an angel and everything's glowing and…

Why wasn't Mitchell an angel too? Why wasn't he floating around talking to me? He was always a lot nicer than I ever was. Maybe God had made another one of His mistakes at somebody's expense again, like He did during the blizzard. Maybe He'd killed Mitchell and made me an angel instead of the other way around. Why hadn't Mitchell's guardian angel been there to protect him? It wasn't even Mitchell's idea to go to Vivian's house to begin with. It was my idea. *It's all a mistake,* I thought. *A terrible, terrible mistake.* I laid back down in the mud.

After a while I looked up into the rain and tried to talk. "God," I said. "I've been to church a lot and been pretty good my whole life. But Mitchell really is a good little kid. An almost perfect little kid if you ask me. It wasn't his idea to come out in the storm, so if you want to punish somebody punish me instead. Not Mitchell. Please don't let him be dead. Please, dear God."

"Melody! Mitchell! Oh, dear God!" Somebody else was praying too, I thought, or maybe I was just imagining things. A noise that sounded like Uncle Gott's voice was coming from somewhere very far away. It wasn't lisping either. He found his teeth, I thought, and now he's going to find Mitchell dead and me an angel.

Vivian was huddled over Mitchell. Her Pentecostal hairdo, extra high for the wedding, was slowly melting in the rain as she scooped up Mitchell's lifeless form and ran toward the house. The Wades were blocking her path.

"The Lord has spoken," I could faintly hear Earl yelling through the torrents of water. "The Lord has visited his wrath on the ungodly and restoreth my sight for His glory. Praise be to God the Almighty."

"GET OUT OF MY WAY YOU CRAZY AWFUL MAN," screamed Vivian. The cords on her neck were throbbing and her face was all contorted, so I'm sure she was screaming. "You godforsaken spiteful demon. Or you'll lose more than your sight again." Vivian rammed her way through the mass of Wades like a Mack truck. Uncle Gott picked me up and followed her into the house. I didn't understand how he could pick me up if I was an angel. Maybe he didn't know it yet.

Uncle Gott was examining my face and head and arms and fingers very carefully and trying to say something to me. I think he was also reciting the Twenty-third Psalm. I still couldn't hear very well. Maybe it was the thunder.

"You're glowing," I said to him. I know it didn't make sense, but I was numb and he was glowing. At the same time, I felt incredibly sad to have been so close to the storm and the earth and the part of nature that makes things glow and to have those things that I loved so much kill Mitchell.

"How am I glowing?" Uncle Gott asked. I could barely hear him.

"You're glowing," I repeated. I really couldn't explain it.

"Oh, Melody," he said. "Oh, little Melody." He gave me a big hug ignoring all the mud, buried his face in my hair and started crying. I'd never seen Uncle Gott cry before.

People came and took me to the hospital then, only this time the ambulance ride wasn't any fun. "Am I dead?" I asked one of the attendants. "Why is everybody glowing?"

"You're very much alive," the attendant said. "Now don't say anymore. Just rest." He gave me a shot and I guess I fell asleep.

When I woke up, I was in the hospital Emergency Room again. I saw the same nurse that had given me the hot chocolate before, only I didn't feel like saying hi to her. Pretty soon Mother and Dad and Dewey and Grandma Dale were there too. Even Harmony showed up and came in to see me, so I knew I must be on death's door. I didn't care. I wanted to die and be with Mitchell.

The doctor said I had a ruptured eardrum from the concussion and force of the lightning. I couldn't hear him very well, but I think he said I would be okay after some rest. A nurse came in and said something to Dad. The glowing on everything was starting to become fainter. Dad and Mother and Dewey and Vivian and Uncle Gott got up and went somewhere, but Harmony and Grandma Dale stayed with me. After a while I asked Grandma Dale, "Where did they go?" I was very drowsy from a shot they'd given me.

"Just rest, honey," Grandma Dale said. "It'll be okay."

"They went to be with Mitchell," Harmony blurted out. "He just got here in another ambulance."

"Harmony," Grandma Dale said, "Melody needs to rest right now. We can talk to her later."

"Mitchell's not dead?" I said through a fog.

"No, honey, he's, he's still alive." Grandma Dale had something in her eye because she reached for her hankie.

Harmony started bawling. "He's hurt real bad, Melody. Don't you know better than to go outside during a thunderstorm?" she finally said. Only she didn't say it mean.

"I can't hear you," I said. I heard her a little bit, but I didn't think I could explain about going to Vivian's.

"Why do you have to be such a dummy?" Harmony offered as she ran out, still bawling.

I must have taken a nap then, because the next thing I remember I woke up and everybody was back in the room. They were all crying except Dewey, and he didn't look too good. The glowing was almost gone now.

Dad was sobbing so hard I hardly knew who he was. He was trying to explain something to Grandma Dale, only he could hardly talk for crying. I got this terrible feeling.

"...something about—" Dad sobbed, "God punishing him—" sob, "for breaking his promise—" sob, "not to tell some sort of—" sob, "a secret." Dad got his handkerchief and wiped his eyes, but his tears were coming faster than he could wipe. The terrible feeling was making me turn numb. "The last thing he said,"—sob,"was, 'I wasn't really gonna tell,'" sob. Then Dad looked at me, stopped talking, and just cried. Dewey put a hand on his shoulder.

That reminded me of Mitchell's secret that I had almost learned. Was Dad talking about Mitchell? "How's Mitchell?" I whispered. The part of me that had the terrible feeling didn't want to know, but another part of me had to find out. "Why is everybody crying?"

"Oh, Melody," Dad sobbed. He was bent over crying. Mother had to answer my question. She came and took my hand. She was crying too. She started to say something, but she could tell I couldn't hear, so she came around and yelled in my good ear. "Honey, Mitchell is hurt real bad. He went into a coma and the doctors don't think—well, he's real bad. We're all praying hard for God to spare your brother's life like He's spared yours. Pray for Mitchell, honey. Pray hard." Mother inhaled sharply and wiped her own tears away. "He didn't deserve this," she said in a quieter voice. "He's such a good little boy."

Somewhere my mind had stopped listening. How could I pray to God when God was the one who sent the lightning to strike us in the first place? What did we do? I was numb and scared and angry at God for doing this to Mitchell. I had prayed to God to save Mitchell, but God, as usual, wasn't listening to me.

"Uncle Gott," I moaned. "I need to talk to Uncle Gott." I was so sleepy I could hardly form the words.

"He and Vivian are in the hospital chapel, honey," Mother bent close to tell me. "They're praying as hard as they can, just like we all are. It's in God's hands now."

The nurse came in just then and must have suggested that everybody let me sleep. Mother tucked me in, as much as anybody can tuck anybody into a hospital bed. I think she said she would stay with me during the night while the others stayed with Mitchell.

I slept a fitful sleep, dreaming of angels who first looked like Salome Parsons, then like Harmony, and then like a woman with a beautiful Avon face. In one part of the dream they were all together talking about me. I couldn't hear what they were saying, but they were laughing and smiling. Mitchell was smiling and talking to me in the dream too. "I've got a secret to tell you, Melody," he said. "No, Mitchell. No," I told him. "It's not safe. You'll get struck by lightning if you tell me." Mitchell kept smiling at me. He was very happy. "I love you, Melody," he said.

The Hospital Again
and Augie's Explanation

I didn't wake up for twenty-four hours. I suppose it was just as well, because when I did my ear was really hurting. It took me a minute to remember where I was and why I was in the hospital dressed only in a stupid gown. At first I was going to make a big fuss and get everybody to wait on me, but then I remembered Mitchell was in a coma.

I looked around slowly. Nothing was glowing today, which was an improvement. But I still felt a little strange, as if electricity were shooting through parts of my body every once in a while. When that happened, I would twitch. Just one twitch, but enough to make me realize I wasn't back to normal yet. I'd never been a twitcher before. Now I had something in common with Rex Oliver.

Vivian was the only person in my room when I woke up. She had spent her wedding night, along with Mother, watching over me instead of going away on her honeymoon. She didn't tell me that of course.

"Vivian," I said.

"Sh-h-h," Vivian said. "You go back to sleep, honey."

"I'm not sleepy," I told her. I wasn't either. My ear hurt, though.

"Are you sure?" Vivian asked.

"Uh-huh."

"How do you feel?"

I sighed. "Awful," I told her. "I don't think I've ever been in this much trouble before in my whole entire life. I was only trying to talk to Uncle Gott before you both left. I didn't mean for this to happen and lightning to strike. Honest, Vivian. I didn't mean any of it." My thumb twitched. At some point during my long sleep, I had concluded that even though Mitchell was in a coma and I was concerned about him, I felt sure he would be okay. Wasn't Mitchell always okay, no matter what happened to him during the games I invented for us to play? He'd been okay when I accidentally stuck the rubber screwdriver in his ear playing doctor. And he'd been okay when I accidentally dislocated his shoulder playing calisthenics. He'd been okay when he'd fallen through the basement window playing hide-'n-seek, and he'd been okay when he got folded up in a folding chair playing card shark. Sometimes he had to get a couple of stitches, but he was always okay, no matter what strange accident happened to him. Hadn't this been just one more accident, only with lightning? It would just take him a little longer to get better, that was all. I wondered if he was twitching in his coma?

"I know you didn't mean it," said Vivian. "We all know you didn't mean it."

"What day is today?" It had just occurred to me I didn't know how long I'd been asleep. "How long have I been here?"

"Today is Sunday. You've been asleep for a whole day. Your folks are in the other room..." Vivian's voice trailed off, "and they're real tired. They've been up all night." She didn't have to say they were in Mitchell's room.

"I want to see Mitchell," I told her, then added, "please. I have to see him and let him know I'm sorry he got hit by lightning. It's sorta my fault." It wasn't really my fault because I didn't ask Mitchell to follow me to Vivian's house. But if God was trying to get me with lightning, I was sorry Mitchell got in the way and got hit instead. I tried to get out of bed, but there were some stupid rails that prevented it and I couldn't move too good. "Can you help me get out of here and see him? Please, Vivian?" My leg twitched.

"Honey, Mitchell's still in a coma. He won't be able to hear you and it's probably best you don't go in there right now. Anyway, he's in the Intensive Care section and I doubt they'll let you in."

"Why?" I asked.

"Because you need to get well, number one, and because— because Mitchell's been hurt pretty badly. He doesn't look very good. I'm afraid it might frighten you."

"I won't be frightened," I said. "I promise. I need to apologize to

Mitchell. Maybe if he knows I've apologized he'll get better faster."

"I wish it would work that way, honey," Vivian said. "I sure wish it would. We'd all be a lot happier."

That reminded me that Vivian had gotten married yesterday and she was supposed to be happy now. "Aren't you supposed to be on your honeymoon?" I asked her. My neck twitched just a little, throwing my head to one side.

"Oh. Well, sometimes things don't always go as planned," she sighed. "They'll be plenty of time for a honeymoon later, when everyone's well again. The important thing is that you two get better."

Vivian looked at me a little closer. "Are you twitching?" she asked.

"A little bit," I said. "I can't help it. It'll go away." I was going to add that I was tough but thought better of it. Lying there twitching in a stupid hospital gown, it would be hard for anyone to take me seriously if I claimed to be tough. "What exactly is the matter with Mitchell?" Mitchell was tough too, I thought, but still, I should know what exactly was wrong with him. I bet he was going to be up and following me around again in no time. He was probably already waking up and planning wheelchair races in the hospital hallways. I bet he was practically ready to go home. Harmony was going to be sorry she got left out of all the attention Mitchell and I were getting at the hospital.

"He's, uh, well I think you ought to ask your folks that question."

I started to ask her again because I wanted to know now, but just then Uncle Gott walked in. He looked tired and sad too. Then I felt even worse that I'd spoiled his honeymoon with Vivian. I hung my head and frowned. It was gonna be one of those days where I did nothing but apologize. My other leg twitched.

"I'm sorry, Uncle Gott," I said. "I didn't mean for anybody to get hurt and for you and Vivian to miss your honeymoon."

"Don't worry about that, Melody. Vivian and I plan to have a wonderful honeymoon when the time is right." He gave a brief weary smile to me and a wink to his new bride. I'd never seen Uncle Gott wink before. I guess he wasn't as tired as he looked when it came to Vivian.

"How are you feeling?" he asked me. "Are you okay? You look like you're—twitching."

I had to go through everything again about my ear and not twitching very much and being in big trouble and wanting to see Mitchell. "Will you help me see him? Please, Uncle Gott?"

Uncle Gott looked at Vivian. She gave him an almost indiscernible shake of her head.

"I don't think now's a good time, Melody," he said. "You need to rest and get better yourself. Twitching's not normal."

I saw I had met two immovable objects, or rather one immovable object and her adoring husband. This was a time to change tactics.

"Uncle Gott," I said, "why does God not love me anymore?" This had been the whole reason I'd been at Vivian's house in the first place, to ask Uncle Gott about God.

"God still loves you, Melody. Why do you think He doesn't?"

"Because He tries to hit me with lightning, for starters. And because my guardian angel is a creepy person. She even has a gun. How many guardian angels do you know that carry guns? And because even though I pray, God ignores me. See, first I prayed for God to bring a blizzard to prevent the piano recital and He was a day late. Then I prayed the blizzard would stop and God ignored me and a whole bunch of people and animals got killed and I felt real bad. Then I prayed for Mitchell not to die and..." I stopped.

"And what, Melody? Mitchell is still alive. We're all praying for Mitchell and for you too, of course. But even if our prayers aren't always answered the way we would like doesn't mean God doesn't love us. He loves us more than anything in the whole world. He loves you even more than your Mother and Dad do. He loves you so much He wants what's best for you. It's just that He knows what that is and we don't. Sometimes we just have to believe God knows better than we do."

"But why does God kill people and animals and strike people with lightning? Did I do something wrong?" I asked. "Have I been bad?" Killing and striking with lightning didn't seem very loving to me.

Uncle Gott sighed. "Sometimes we don't know the answer. But it isn't because you've been bad, Melody. You just need to keep praying and have faith in God."

I thought about that a minute. "Let me get this straight," I said. "I should pray even if God ignores my prayers? And strikes me with lightning? Why? What would happen to me if I *didn't* pray?" I twitched all over once on that question.

"Well," began Uncle Gott. He didn't like my twitching and was blinking furiously.

"Those are very good questions, Melody," Vivian interrupted. "I think when you get better, we should sit down and have a nice long talk about these issues. These are truly important subjects that every person needs to get settled in his mind. So we're glad you want to talk about your relationship with God. Aren't we, Gottfried?" Uncle Gott nodded his agreement. "But for now, it's best if you just rest instead of worry about these things. If you feel like praying, then please pray. If you don't, well, we all go through times when we question God. Don't we, Gottfried?" Once again Uncle Gott nodded his agreement.

"You mean everybody has these questions?" I asked. My left eye twitched. This was news to me. Maybe I should have been asking Vivian a long time ago. Maybe the Pentecostals were way ahead of the Methodists.

"Every intelligent person, kiddo. But you just rest for now."

Vivian leaned over the bed and kissed me on the forehead, then pulled the blanket up around me. Uncle Gott smiled at me, then walked over and took Vivian's hand. The look he gave her was so intense I wondered if this was what adults referred to as chemistry. Chemistry seemed a lot like electricity and that was getting a lot of people in trouble. Vivian smiled back and together they walked out of the room. *Those two had better get a honeymoon quick,* I thought, before the chemistry, or the electricity, or one of those science things gets them hurt too.

Monday morning the doctor came by and told me I was well enough to go home. He said the twitching would continue for a while until my nervous system settled down from getting all that electricity through it. He said nervous system difficulties could take some time to recover. He didn't know how long that would be. Mother had brought me some winter clothes from home since my clothes from the storm had been summery and sopping wet. As we left my room, I looked up at her. "Mother," I said, "I have to see Mitchell. I have to talk to him. He's my only brother and I have to tell him about what happened. After all, he looks up to me."

Mother gave me a funny look, then for no reason at all she put her arms around me and was on the brink of crying.

"Don't cry, Mom," I told her. I'd never called her Mom before. She didn't even notice. "It'll be all right. Mitchell's gonna be fine. He's always fine. You'll see." I was trying not to twitch.

Mother sighed. "Melody, your brother's hurt real bad. He may *not* be all right. He may even—well, honey—do you really want to see him?"

"Uh-huh," I nodded. I had to see Mitchell. I missed him.

Mother took me to the Intensive Care part of the hospital and told the nurses she was letting me look through the window to Mitchell's room. The nurse looked at me and I tried to look real sad so she would feel sorry for me and let me in. She nodded okay to Mother.

We walked around the corner and over to a room. Instead of going inside, Mother took me to a large glass window. I could see Dad and Grandma Dale sitting inside, reading different magazines. Lying in the bed was someone I didn't recognize. The little person had bandages over most of his head. Tubes were coming out of his face and hands. But what I most noticed were that this person's eyelids were dark purple, a deep black-and-blue bruise color that covered the area all around the eyes. The entire face was so swollen that it took me a minute to realize this was Mitchell.

Dad looked up and saw Mother and me through the glass. He got up and came outside to where we were standing.

"Is that really Mitchell?" I whispered. "Are you sure?"

Dad sighed. "Yes, honey, it is. He's still in a coma."

"Can I talk to him?" I asked Dad. "I really want to talk to him."

"Well..." Dad was thinking it over.

Instead of waiting for an answer, I decided I'd better act. I turned and walked into the room, being very quiet. It was hard not to think Mitchell was just asleep and I should be careful not to wake him.

I walked over to the side of the bed. "Hey, Mitchell," I said in my most encouraging voice. "You look awful. I'm sorry about the lightning." I twitched. "You've got to hurry up and get better so we can go play again." I looked to see if there was any sign of acknowledgment. Mitchell lay there in a world all his own. "I think Little Poo's forgetting her astronaut training." I tried again. "Nobody can get her in the shoebox except you. We miss you, Mitchell." Mitchell didn't move. Everybody was looking at me and I didn't know what for. I sighed. "Look," I told him. "I gotta go now because I hate hospitals. Get well right away, okay? And I'll come and visit you all the time, only not at night because I'm asleep. Bye, Mitchell. Bye."

I didn't know what else to say. Mitchell didn't say goodbye back to me, so I looked at Mother and shrugged my shoulders, which set off a shoulder twitch. "Come on, honey," she said.

Mother said I was going to miss school for the rest of the day, but that tomorrow I would have to go back. "Dewey's gone back to work because there's nothing anybody can do now except wait," she said. "I expect if this goes on much longer your father will do the same. It's hard on him to just sit there and wait. It's hard on everybody."

She told me Janie and Uncle Billy Glenn had stayed at the hospital the second night so that Mother and Dad could get some rest. Harmony had been staying at the Knotts. Mother said Harmony had been in to visit me once in the hospital, only I was asleep.

"Where's Vivian and Uncle Gott?" I asked her. "Did they go on their honeymoon?"

"They don't know what to do, poor things," Mother said. "They were supposed to go to Brazil for ten days, only now they don't want to leave because of Mitchell. Maybe they'll take a long weekend in Kansas City in the meantime."

"They need to," I said.

What do you know about the subject of honeymoons?" Mother asked. She was almost smiling, the first smile I'd seen on her face since the accident.

"Oh, stuff," I said. I shrugged. There was another twitch.

I stayed home and played with the cats for the rest of the day. Nobody said a word about practicing the piano so I didn't bring it up either. Anyway, I figured it would be hard to play if my fingers got to twitching in the middle of a piece, so maybe I could use this to my advantage. There had been no talk of punishing me for going to Vivian's house during the storm either. That had me worried. Usually, I could count on getting the punishment right away. Mother and Dad were probably just waiting until Mitchell came home, then I'd get punished real good.

I got to thinking about Mitchell and how all this had happened because he had a secret he was dying to tell me. It had something to do with the murder. That reminded me I hadn't seen Rex Oliver at the hospital. He liked Mitchell too, so I wondered why he wasn't there. Maybe he had been there to visit, like Harmony, when I was sleeping.

That night Mother and Dad came home from the hospital. Harmony was back from the Knotts, so the four of us tried to eat a normal supper. Harmony sat next to me for a change and told me not to spill my milk while I was twitching. "You're not my mother," I told her.

"Oh yeah?" said Harmony. Then she started singing "Locket" and I tried to punch her to make her stop and the next thing you know I spilled my milk. So then we had to get up and wipe it up and mop up the floor. Mother told us to behave and sit down for dinner.

When everyone was seated Dad asked us to bow our heads for grace. "Heavenly Father," he said, "thank you for this fine food we are about to eat. And thank you for this fine cook who fixed it for us. And thank you most of all for letting Melody be safe and come home to us where we can love her and care for her. Please watch out for us all, especially those we love who aren't here right now. Keep them safe in your heart. We ask it in Jesus' name. Amen."

Harmony wasn't the only one who picked at her food that night. We pretended to eat and make small talk, but all of us missed Mitchell. Every so often my arm would twitch and make it hard to control feeding myself, but I managed. Finally I asked, "Hey, Dad, why hasn't Rex Oliver been to see Mitchell in the hospital? Won't he come out of the cave for that?"

"It's a long story, honey," Dad said. I wasn't surprised. Most things involving Rex Oliver usually were. "Dewey and Grandma Dale are coming over any minute," Dad continued, "so why don't you ask them. Dewey can tell it better than I can. He already told Louise and me the night of the accident."

"What story?" I tried to entice him.

"It's a long story," Dad repeated.

After we'd cleared the table Harmony did the dishes. I was excused from dish washing because I said I couldn't be responsible if I twitched and dropped something. I hoped Dewey and Grandma Dale wouldn't take too long. I was getting restless and tired and noticed that I was twitching more.

When they did arrive, Dewey sat down in the living room. He sat in the chair closest to the front door because he didn't have a cuspidor in our house and he had to get up and go spit outside every so often. Mother had never been particularly happy with tobacco juice all over her juniper bushes in the yard, but she put up with it.

"Hi, Dewey," I went over to him. I wanted to understand about Rex Oliver.

"I guess you almost got fried the other day, kiddo," he told me. "You had us all worried for a while. I had a big bay gelding one time that got struck by lightning out in the pasture. Nice horse too," Dewey said. "I really miss him." This was Dewey's way of telling me he was sorry I got hurt. I nodded okay.

"Why hasn't Rex Oliver been to see Mitchell in the hospital?" I changed the subject and got right to the point. "Mitchell has some kind of a secret about the murder that he was about to tell me when he got hit by lightning. Something Rex Oliver made him promise not to tell."

Dewey looked at Dad and Mother, then at Grandma Dale. "Melody, Harmony, I don't know if you remember the evening of the wedding, the evening you got hit by lightning."

I nodded. How could I forget? I twitched at the thought of it.

"Well, that evening, while Melody here was out attracting lightning, I was having a meeting with Big Augie Messina. 'Cause he'd told me at the Hotel Jayhawk that day that he knew who killed his daughter."

"What'd he say to you, Dewey?" I asked. "Was he nice?"

"Well now, nice may not be the word I'd use, but yes, the man was civil. As to what he said," Dewey paused to take out his can of Skoal and fish around for a dip of tobacco, "he said Salome Parsons had uncovered some new evidence he thought I'd be interested in. I asked him what it was. 'Well, Dewey,' he says, 'you gotta understand that Brenda has always been a little strange.' I said I wasn't aware of that, but I could understand since my own boy was a little strange too.

"He said ever since she was a little girl in Rhode Island she would hurt herself just to get attention. Sometimes she'd break her arm, sometimes she'd cut her hand and need stitches, sometimes she'd even eat a whole lot of dirt and make herself sick. He said Brenda wasn't a bad girl, but she needed a lot of attention and if she didn't get it she'd hurt herself just so they had to pay attention to her.

"I thought about telling him about this dog I had once that kept biting himself," Dewey said. "But that turned out to be a real bad case of fleas and anyway, I didn't think Augie would appreciate the comparison.

"So Augie says they brought Brenda to Meadowgreen to try to get her cured of hurting herself. Only what does she do but start getting attention in a new way, which is, uh, from other women."

"Is that because she was a lesbian?" I asked. Mother had told me not to say that word, but this was a special case. This was about murder. Everybody looked at me and I saw Mother getting ready to scold me. "It's okay to say it," I said before she could get a word in. "I know all about lesbians. They're women poets. Harmony and Daffy are lesbians too." I twitched.

"I am NOT," Harmony yelled. "You take that back."

"Honey," Grandma Dale said, "let's let Dewey finish his story." She looked at Mother and rolled her eyes. Harmony stuck out her tongue at me.

"Well, let's just say she had uh, well, an un-natural attraction to uh, other women, okay, Melody? So Salome found out that Brenda and her friend Charlotte Fitch," he looked at me when he said the word friend," had been uh, close friends, uh, for several months. Brenda even started to get better. But apparently what Brenda didn't know was that Charlotte was sort of a, well, a switch hitter."

"Dewey," Grandma Dale said, "perhaps you shouldn't be quite so graphic."

"Does she play baseball?" I asked.

"No, dummy. She likes both men and women," Harmony expounded. Now everybody looked at Harmony. I wondered where she'd learned about all this because I wanted to learn it too.

"Where did you learn all this, young lady?" Mother asked. Maybe Mother wanted Harmony to explain it to her too. But before Harmony could answer she said, "Never mind. We'll talk about it later."

"That's right, Harmony," Dewey continued. "Charlotte liked men *and* women and that's all I'm gonna say about that. When Brenda found out that Charlotte was also seeing a man, she became very unhappy and jealous and needed a lot of attention again. She even started eating dirt again. Halloween night, Brenda and Charlotte went to the Meadowgreen Ball together, but Charlotte told some friends she was going to meet her, uh, boyfriend there. Apparently that was the cause of the wet dirt fight Rex Oliver and you kids got in the middle of."

"So did Charlotte meet her boyfriend?" Harmony asked. "Who was he?"

"The answer to the first question appears to be yes, and the answer to the second is, we're not sure. Salome heard from several sources that the guy is also from Meadowgreen."

"What do you mean, from Meadowgreen?" Dad asked. "A patient, an employee? A doctor? What, for pete's sake?" My arm was starting to twitch.

"Well, Big Augie and his resources are moving heaven and earth to try to find out his identity, but Meadowgreen has absolutely clamped down tight on this. Duane Appelhans has had several of his men checking the attendance lists of the Halloween party. Of course, since Meadowgreen was giving the party there were a lot of Meadowgreen-related men there that night, including your father." He turned and half-smiled at Dad.

"Well, it wasn't *me!*" Dad exclaimed, almost dropping his cup of coffee.

"Of course not, I know that. Salome believes that this man, whoever he is, found Rex Oliver's crucifix in the bathroom where Rex and the kids had been warshing off the wet dirt. Or maybe Brenda or Charlotte found it. Nobody knows for sure. Everybody's best theory is that the man met Charlotte after the wet dirt fight. The two of them went out in the alley to smoke, or get some fresh air or…*something*, and Brenda followed them."

The telephone started ringing. Mother quietly excused herself and went to answer. Dewey continued with his story.

"There was a quarrel. Brenda became jealous and angry. The mystery man hit her with the crucifix, or maybe Charlotte did. It's all speculation at this point."

"But what about Rex Oliver?" I said. "How can you be sure he didn't do it?" My arm was twitching more and more.

"That, Melody, is what Mitchell's secret is all about."

Mother came rushing back into the living room and interrupted. "It's the hospital," she said. "Mitchell's saying something. They said we should get down there right away."

Mitchell's Promise

By the time we got to the hospital the nurse was waiting for us. "Only two people can go in at a time," she said in that strict nurse's voice. Mother and Dad went in to Mitchell's room while the rest of us stayed in the waiting room.

"I bet he sat up and asked for a peanut butter sandwich," I told Harmony. "He was probably too hungry to stay in a coma any longer."

"Shut up," said Harmony. "This is serious."

"Mitchell's gonna be okay. I told you before," I said. I had told everybody that because he was my best friend and he had to be okay. I was trying hard not to twitch because I was afraid they wouldn't let me see Mitchell if I got too bad.

After a long time, Dad came out. He didn't look so good. "What is it, son?" Grandma Dale asked him. She hardly ever called him son.

"He's still not exactly talking," Dad said. "But he's singing."

"Huh?" we all said in surprise.

"One of the nurses took a radio in there to see if he would respond, and sure enough, he started singing the songs along with the radio. He doesn't know us, though. And he's opened his eyes now, but the doctor doesn't think he's seeing."

I remembered the swollen purple eyelids. I wasn't surprised Mitchell wasn't seeing. He would in time, though. I was sure.

"Well, is he going to get better?" Grandma Dale asked. "Is he going to wake up some more? What did the doctor say about his eyes getting better?"

"The doctor doesn't know. He said Mitchell suffered so much trauma and brain damage it's a miracle he's alive at all."

"He's going to be okay," I announced again to everybody.

"I hope so, honey," Dad said.

We each took a turn going in to see Mitchell singing with the radio, but Dad was right, he didn't know us at all. He didn't know anything except the songs that he heard. Maybe our years of music and junior choir training had counted for something after all. Or maybe that part of his brain hadn't been damaged. There wasn't anything we could do except watch Mitchell sing, so eventually we all went home again. The nurses said they'd call us if he woke up and started talking. I hoped it would be soon.

My twitching lasted off and on again through the rest of the week, at least when I was awake. Although it seemed to be decreasing, it came back when I got excited. I was grouchy too. I don't know if I was grouchy because of my nervous system injuries, or because everything in our family was changing, or if I just missed Mitchell a lot.

In the week after the accident, we found ourselves getting into a new routine. Instead of selling Avon, Mother stayed at the hospital almost every day while Harmony and I were in school, and Dad was at work. Harmony made supper, I had to do the dishes by myself, then Dad drove us to the hospital every evening to visit Mitchell. Then we all came home and tried to sleep. There was a constant rotation between Mother, Dad, Janie, Billy Glenn, Dewey, Grandma Dale, Vivian, and Uncle Gott to stay all night with Mitchell. They said Harmony and I were too young, or we would have taken our turn too. Everybody wanted to be sure that Mitchell wouldn't be scared when he really woke up from his coma. I soon realized I wasn't the only one getting grouchy. The lack of sleep and constant visits to the hospital were wearing everybody down.

By the following Sunday Mitchell still hadn't improved, and we had to go to church. But I wasn't in the mood and kept wondering why God had hurt Mitchell and not me when it was my idea to go to Vivian's house that day.

It was just too confusing. God was letting Mitchell stay injured too long. Dad had close calls and interventions by his guardian angel, and Mother narrowly escaped from the Wades. I'd been hospitalized twice recently. There were the awful boils, and the blizzard, and God ignoring my prayers and hitting me with lightning. God didn't make sense to me anymore. I decided I would have to go have that talk with Vivian pretty soon so I could understand all this. The way things were now, I didn't think I could ever get to liking God again.

After church we went home and changed our clothes, then drove to the farm. Grandma Dale had a big dinner waiting for us which I was looking forward to, because, between the shock of the accident and Harmony's cooking, I hadn't eaten much all week. At least now my appetite was starting to return.

Seeing Dewey reminded me of his meeting with Big Augie a week ago. After we'd gotten seated at the table and were half-way through dinner, I brought up the subject again.

"Say, Dewey," I said. "I never did find out about Mitchell's secret. You know, the one about the mur..." I stopped. Rex Oliver had appeared in the doorway, and everybody looked up and told him hi. He was studying the remaining food and didn't bother to answer for a while. I guess the food passed his inspection because he sat down at his place at the table, acting like it was perfectly normal for him to begin when the rest of us were almost done.

We passed him bowls of all the food and Mother got up and opened the window a crack because she smelled mold with her excellent nose. Dad and Dewey started talking about politics and Harmony and I sat and stared at Uncle Rex. He didn't say much. I wondered if he had been studying the art of silence from Maynard.

I was dying to know more about Mitchell's secret. Surely Dewey would finish telling me about his meeting with Big Augie. After all, he said he'd already spoken to everyone except Harmony and me about it.

But he didn't. The rest of us ate some dessert, which I do remember that day was Apple Betty. Since Uncle Rex's silence had gotten me thinking about Maynard, I finally asked, "Does anybody know why Maynard doesn't talk?"

"I do," said Uncle Rex and resumed eating. He acted like that was the end of the conversation.

"Well, why?" I persisted.

Rex Oliver looked up slowly from his plate and said, "He has rotten teeth. He's too embarrassed to open his mouth."

"Really?" I said. "How do you know, Uncle Rex?"

"One time when we were fixing the corn picker, I was feeling bad because I am so stupid. He told me we all feel embarrassed about something. That's when he told me about his teeth."

"Did you see 'em?" Harmony perked up at this thought.

"No."

"Oh," Harmony said, disappointed.

"What do you feel embarrassed about, Melody?" Uncle Rex asked.

I didn't know what to say. I felt I had to say something, because everyone was looking at me.

"Well, I guess I feel embarrassed that I get these stupid boils and that these permanents make my hair look so dumb." The boil on the side of my nose had improved slightly since the wedding, but it still looked awful. "And my twitching."

Uncle Rex looked at Harmony. "How about you?"

"Uh, well, I don't know. Lots of stuff."

"Lots of stuff? Then do you feel embarrassed most of the time?" Uncle Rex became talkative all of a sudden.

"Uh, well, I don't know." Harmony's puberty prevented her from answering a question directly.

"Say, Rex. What did you think of the wedding?" Mother came to Harmony's rescue just in time. Harmony had been turning red. She'd been doing that a lot lately.

"It was a Valentine's wedding," Uncle Rex said slowly. "It was exactly what you think of when you think of Valentine's Day. People falling in love. People getting married. Happily ever after." He sighed. Nobody said anything. I guess we were all thinking that those things would probably never happen for Uncle Rex. I wondered if he was thinking that too.

Grandma Dale got up to clear the dishes and we all helped,

thanking her for another fine meal. I felt like my eating today had made up for what I hadn't eaten for a week. I followed Dewey into the parlor where he seated himself in the maroon throne chair. I needed to know about the secret. "Tell me about Mitchell's secret, Dewey. Please," I said.

"Pull up a chair," Dewey said. I grabbed the piano stool which was nearby.

Dewey took his time. "Melody, do you remember at the Meadowgreen Ball when you were outside on the sidewalk and Earl Wade started shouting at you and at Rex Oliver?" he asked.

I thought back, remembering my costume, and Mitchell's costume, and Uncle Rex Oliver's costume, and how Earl Wade had paralyzed me with his snake eyes.

"Yes," I said. "I remember."

"And do you remember when Rex Oliver got scared and ran away?"

"Yes," I said again. "He was real scared and he screamed and ran."

"That's right," said Dewey. "Where were you then?"

"I was on the sidewalk and Mother came and whacked Mrs. Wade with her broom."

"Okay. And where was Mitchell then?"

I tried to remember back through Mother pushing me behind her black witch's skirt, and the broom, and the fight, and my gold star on my magic wand.

"I think he was fighting with us. Only, I'm not sure. I remember seeing him at the end of the fight when the police came. But..."

"Do you remember if he followed Rex Oliver into the alley?" Dewey interrupted me.

I thought and thought, trying to remember. "I don't know," I finally said.

"That's okay, Melody," Dewey said and put an after-dinner dip of Skoal in his mouth.

"So where was Mitchell? And how does Big Augie know Rex

270

Oliver didn't kill his daughter?"

"Because Brenda was already dead by the time Rex Oliver ran around the alley."

"Oh-h," I said. "But how does anybody know that? Why did the police arrest him then?"

"Because Salome Parsons just found out a week ago Friday night that someone else was present when Rex Oliver discovered Brenda's body. A witness. Someone who can clear Rex Oliver's name. That's the secret."

"Mitchell? Did Mitchell see the dead woman?" I asked.

Dewey nodded.

"Then why didn't he say so all this time?" I almost wailed. "If he knew and he let Uncle Rex go to jail and now there's going to be an inquest and everything. Why didn't he tell us?" I was furious at Mitchell for keeping a secret this important from me. How could my best friend have left me out of this part of his life? "So how did Salome find out and nobody else could?" I asked. What I meant was, how could Salome find out when I couldn't?

"The gal's got a few tricks up her sleeve all right," replied Dewey. "She waited until the rest of us was in the wedding rehearsal Friday night and she got Rex Oliver alone in the church basement. Remember when we was all hunting for him and thought he was hid?" I nodded. "Well, ole' Salome had actually taken him out for—uh—a good time. Probably the best time he's had in years. Maybe ever. I think he's still smiling from the experience. She picked his brain clean while she was at it."

"So he wasn't locked in the church all night?"

"No."

"So what were they doing? Where did Salome take him?"

"He won't tell us, so we don't know for sure. But I suspect," and here Dewey paused for quite a while and smiled to himself, "I suspect that he and Salome were doing some grown-up kinds of things. She must have done something extra special for her to get Rex to talk about the murder." Dewey nodded his head and arched his eyebrows at the thought. "Anyway, Melody, he told her he made Mitchell promise, swear-to-God, that they wouldn't tell nobody they'd seen Brenda's body, 'cause Rex got so traumatized when he seen his own Mother's body years ago that this brought those memories back. He thought—actually he was terrified—that they were going to put him in the State Hospital again. He wanted to forget he'd seen Brenda's body and wanted to make Mitchell forget he'd seen it too. So Mitchell promised. But then people started talking about a possible death penalty and hanging, and Rex Oliver got arrested, and Mitchell, poor kid, was dying to tell somebody. But he'd given his word and he kept it. You can be proud of your little brother, Melody, even if he wouldn't tell you."

"So that was why he was having bad dreams," I said. "He was afraid for Uncle Rex and afraid of God if he broke his promise to Uncle Rex."

"Yup," said Dewey and he spat.

"Do Mother and Dad know about Mitchell?" I asked.

"Yup. I told your dad last week as soon as I found out. He's so worried about Mitchell he probably forgot to talk to you about it."

"Oh," I said. "What about Harmony?"

"Well now, Harmony knows because she's been standing just outside the parlor door during this whole conversation. You might as well come on in, Harmony," he called out.

Harmony looked guilty, but she came in. "I was walking by and I heard you. I'm sorry."

"It's not polite to eavesdrop, Harmony," Dewey said. "However, no harm done this time."

I was thinking furiously, which was hard to do after one of Grandma Dale's big dinners. "But now that Mitchell's not able to talk, how's he going to confirm Uncle Rex's story to the police?"

Dewey sighed. "That's a good question, Melody. We can only hope that since Rex Oliver told all this to Salome before Mitchell got hurt, that they'll believe it. Salome says she'll take a lie detector test and everything to prove that what he told her is true. Mitchell could have confirmed it then, had anybody asked him.

"Now do you suppose one of you two fine young ladies could round me up a cup of coffee?"

Harmony bounced out for the coffee, glad to redeem herself, and I walked out on the screened-in porch. It was cold so I couldn't stay very long. I wondered how my little brother had had the strength to keep an important secret so long. A secret he'd almost been killed for. Why did God have to punish him for wanting to tell me?

March 1959

Meadowgreen's Mystery Man

It wasn't clear if God had been punishing Earl Wade or not. Dad told us some days later that Earl had to have his right hand amputated because it was so badly burned from the lightning, a sign most of us interpreted as divine chastisement. But the lightning had also somehow restored his eyesight. "A miracle," Earl proclaimed in a giant newspaper advertisement he ran in *The Topeka Daily Capital.* "God has allowed me to see again. Praise be to God." The ad was signed by the full membership of the Hosanna Baptist Church, about twenty people. Earl had never publicly admitted he'd been blind before. In the ad he explained that, not only had he previously been blind in his physical eyes, he'd also never before seen and understood God's true gift to mankind. "God has given us something back," said Earl's ad. "He restores and compensates us for our deficiencies. When He takes something away, He makes us whole in other ways so we might better serve Him." He called it God's Law of Compensation, a concept he pretended to have invented.

According to Grandma Dale, Dewey had read the ad, put down the newspaper and said, "Well, Earl may have had his eyesight restored, but there still ain't nothing between his ears. He better not go blaming his orneriness on God. That fool was mean and stubborn long before he got religion."

I had my own concern about Earl. "Is he going to get a hook on his hand like Captain Hook?" I asked Dewey the next time I saw him. I'd been worried about this since I learned of the missing hand. The thought of Earl with a hook was truly scary. I shuddered and twitched at the same time, just thinking about it.

"I don't know what the man will do," Dewey replied. "But whatever it is, it won't be normal."

"At least he won't be able to paralyze people with his eyes now he's not blind," I said. "But if he gets a hook, can I move in with you and Grandma?" I asked. "Grandma's got a shotgun." Dewey sort of smiled. "We'll wait and see, Melody."

Earl didn't get a hook. He did use his good hand to type a daily letter to *The Topeka Daily Capital* and to a list of dozens of Topekans he wanted to pester, including our family. Every day we'd get a letter from the Hosanna Baptist Church and, after reading the first two or three, every day Mother would throw them in the trash unopened. I was dying of curiosity, but Mother insisted we leave his letters alone. "There's nothing worthwhile in them, Melody," she told me. "He's a very disturbed man who has nothing better to do. Let's let him be and hope that he'll do the same for us."

I managed to retrieve one letter from the trash when Mother wasn't looking. Earl was preaching his new God of Compensation sermon. His grammar and spelling were really bad though. Dad explained that to me. "Earl's nervous system got messed up from the lightning, like yours did, Melody, and that's why his thoughts are so hard to express. But he still needs to behave, just like you need to mind your mother. No more filching letters from the trash, okay?"

"Okay," I said.

We didn't see Earl picketing around town after that, which Dewey said was a miracle in itself. I wondered if Earl was shy about appearing in public with his deformity, but Dewey had said no, unfortunately Earl was never given to shyness. Earl did stop criticizing lunatics, which was another sort of miracle. Supposedly God compensated them with some other thing when they got crazy, according to Earl's new theology. But he never said he was sorry for his previous attacks on lunatics or asked them for forgiveness.

Dad and Uncle Billy Glenn had discussed this and other developments one evening at our house after work. Janie was in the kitchen with Mother, but I found the men's talk more interesting.

"Bet he stays inside during thunderstorms," chuckled Uncle Billy Glenn.

"Yeah," Dad answered, "and Meadowgreen is sure relieved about the picketing. They've reassigned two security guards to real work now that they don't have Earl to deal with on Wednesdays." Wednesdays had been Meadowgreen's day to be picketed.

"Meadowgreen better start cooperating with the police," Billy Glenn said. "I hear how the police, Big Augie, and the District Attorney are doing everything but stand on their heads to get Meadowgreen to release information about the mystery man in Brenda Messina's murder. But they won't budge. You suppose President Eisenhower's got involved again to protect Meadowgreen? What do you hear, Alex?"

"I don't hear much," Dad said. "Oh, there's a lot of rumors, you know. Everybody's got a mystery man suspect. Some say he's a patient who's a high government official, some say a foreign prince, some even say it's Felix Kliban himself, although, personally, I think he's too old for that sort of thing. Officially the bigwigs have got a tight lid on this. I tried to talk to Dr. Knott the other day, to see if he knew Brenda and Charlotte. He got a real funny look on his face and said something about everything being confidential. So I said, 'Hey Doctor, being as how our daughters are such good friends and all, couldn't you maybe give me something that would help?' The guy got real mean and told me to mind my own damn business. I never knew he was mean like that."

The Meadowgreen mystery man's identity was a subject of intense speculation, not only by the police and our family, but by the entire community as well. Big Augie persuaded Vivian, "for the sake of justice," to run a story in *The Topeka Daily Capital* about the Meadowgreen mystery man, explaining how Mr. August Messina had increased his reward to $20,000. "There's nothing like that kind of money to bring every nut with a theory out of the woodwork," Uncle Billy Glenn said, and he was right. The police checked into more than two hundred reports, one even involving a conspiracy from alien invaders, but they couldn't prove a thing.

But the big story, and the best one from our perspective, was a follow-up article reporting that the inquest into the homicide of Brenda Messina had been dismissed due to lack of evidence, that the District

Attorney no longer considered Rex Oliver a suspect. "Salome passed the lie detector test about what Rex Oliver told her," the D.A. told Virgil, who relayed the story to the rest of us. "There's not enough of a case to go to trial." Virgil said the D.A. was sure the mystery man and Charlotte Fitch had something to do with the murder. He was trying to mount a case against *them*, but Meadowgreen wasn't cooperating.

"All right, you kids," Dad told us after we found out the good news. "I want you to keep your mouths shut about the whole thing with Rex Oliver and the murder. Poor Rex Oliver's suffered enough."

So instead of having a party to celebrate his being cleared of murder, we all went about our business without any fuss. Rex Oliver went back to being left alone, just like when we first met him. We quietly congratulated Virgil though, who we were now not quite sure how to treat. The dismissal of the charges had certainly boosted Virgil's standing in the Topeka legal community and on the Potawatomi reservation.

Edith Kliban had a major falling out with Vivian when Vivian's newspaper ran the article about the Meadowgreen mystery man. First, she called Vivian and begged her to put a stop to such stories. When that didn't work, Vivian told us she got a formal letter from Meadowgreen's attorney. "They threatened me with legal action if I printed anything untrue or libelous about Meadowgreen," Vivian said. "Imagine that. We make sure all our stories are true anyway, but coming from Edith, I'm shocked. Why is she being so protective?"

We were all wondering the same thing. Edith had been one of Vivian's bridesmaids and now Edith wouldn't invite Vivian on any more shopping trips to New York.

Janie Bryant could hardly contain her enthusiasm about their break. "It's about time," she told us. "Vivian'll skewer Meadowgreen in the press now. They've had it their way for too long in this town."

"Don't be too sure," Dad said thoughtfully. "Vivian isn't the vindictive sort and Meadowgreen is still mighty powerful."

Now with one of our two wounded family members safe again, the only thing weighing on our minds was Mitchell and how soon he would wake up from his singing coma.

April 1959

Law of Compensation and Red Roses

One day about a week after the mystery man article had appeared in the newspaper, Dad came home with some news. "Something funny's going on at Meadowgreen," he said. "Nobody's talking, but Dr. Knott has suddenly resigned from the staff. I did find out he's treated both Brenda and Charlotte for their persuasion problems. I wonder why he wouldn't tell me that when I asked him?"

"Could he be the mystery man?" Mother asked.

"I don't know," said Dad. "It sure is peculiar."

Harmony filled us in that same evening. "Daphne's parents are getting a DIVORCE," she wailed. Divorce was like leprosy as far as we were concerned. Nobody we knew had ever gotten it, but everyone knew you didn't want it. "Daphne is devastated because her mom told her that her dad's been fooling around with another woman and that's why they have to get a divorce." Mother and Dad exchanged a horrified glance. Fooling around was even worse than divorce.

"She's moving back to New York next week," Harmony continued, "and I won't ever get to see her again." She started crying in big throaty gulps. Harmony had just lost her best friend. Like I'd lost Mitchell. I knew what she was going through and actually felt sorry for her. I hated it when I felt sorry for Harmony.

Mother got up to get Harmony a hankie. "You'll make some new friends, honey," she told her. "But I'm sorry. I know you'll miss Daphne." She gave Harmony a hug, then asked, "Did Mrs. Knott happen to mention who the other woman was? The one Dr. Knott's fooling around with?"

"No," said Harmony, sniffling loudly into the hankie.

Dad asked, "Did she say if she was a patient or not?"

"No, she didn't say anything about the other woman."

I think they were wondering if Dr. Knott had been with Charlotte Fitch. I had never met Dr. Knott and only seen Charlotte once, the night she was dressed as a dandelion. She didn't look very romantic then.

A few days later Janie Bryant came running over with a packet of material from the F.B.I. "He came through, just like I told you he would," beamed Janie. "There's some real juicy stuff in here too." Mother and Janie took Janie's papers to our parents' bedroom and closed the door, so I couldn't use my heat vent spy system. When they came out, they both had that smug look adults get when they know something you don't.

"Her pal J. Edgar sent the file on Charlotte Fitch all right," Mother told us after Janie left. "But you girls can't read it so don't even ask."

"What does it say?" I wanted to know.

"Yeah, Mom," Harmony added. "What does it say?"

"Well, I'll keep it simple. It talks a lot about Charlotte's, uh, 'switch-hitting' experiences, which we already knew. But it doesn't reveal the identity of her Meadowgreen boyfriend, which is what we were hoping. That's about it."

I was disappointed. I thought the F.B.I. and J. Edgar Hoover were almost as all-knowing as God and now they'd let me down too. Still, I suspected the report contained more than Mother was telling us. I'd ask Dad after Janie let him read the report.

Meanwhile I tried one more question with Mother. "Did it say if she was a famous baseball player?"

"No, dummy," Harmony addressed me. "Women don't play baseball."

But I felt sure it was Charlotte's reputation the F.B.I. was protecting, not the mystery man's.

Dad tended to agree. "That report was really vague about Charlotte's family. It did say they had several fortunes from munitions, minerals, and frozen food. If they're that rich, they probably bought their way out of this mess, not just for Charlotte's sake, but to protect the family name. It's only little guys like us who have to answer for our transgressions." Dad sighed. "I wonder what it feels like to have that kind of money? Guess I'll never know."

I still couldn't understand how anyone who had the bad manners to throw wet dirt at somebody could come from a good family.

"So why are we little guys and they aren't?" I asked.

"Good question," said Dad. He just shook his head and walked away.

Big Augie and his boys weren't exactly little guys either, from my point of view, and they weren't used to not getting their way. Right after the announcement about Dr. Knott's departure, somebody broke into his former office at Meadowgreen and searched his records. According to Dad nothing was missing. But the violence and disrespect for others' property made us all shudder. "That's why they call it organized crime," Dad said.

"I don't see anything organized about it," Harmony said. "It's more like circumventing the system." Her intellectual symptoms had increased dramatically since Daphne's departure.

Billy Glenn, as usual, had additional information. "Chief Appelhans paid a visit to Big Augie the day after the Meadowgreen break-in, but Salome Parsons provided Augie and his boys with an alibi for that night. She said they'd all been shooting pool in her basement. Said she won twenty bucks off Tiny 'cause he can't hit the bank shots. Well, since the chief couldn't prove otherwise, even though he knew they was the ones that did it, he told Salome she'd better be careful unless she planned to spend her vacation time at the Industrial Farm for Women at Lansing. Then he told Big Augie to give up and go home. 'As much as it grieves me not to see justice served,' the chief told him, 'I think we've all run up against a brick wall.' Big Augie just started swearing something fierce, the chief told us. I think the chief was a little bit afraid right then of Big Augie getting violent. One of his boys had to talk to him to get him settled down. After all, it was his only child that got murdered. And by somebody with a crucifix no less. If you're a Catholic, like Big Augie, that's a real insult. How would you feel if the murderer couldn't be found?"

Pretty bad, we all agreed.

Big Augie did feel bad. He couldn't find anyone to claim his reward, though there were a lot of kooks who tried. Eventually he donated a year's supply of margarine to the nuns at St. Francis Hospital. He told Chief Appelhans he was going back to Rhode Island, but he wouldn't forget this hell hole of a town. After that we didn't hear from him again. We were all amazed that even the Mafia, with all its muscle, couldn't crack Meadowgreen.

Mitchell gradually started to say a few words, which was encouraging. Soon he was released to a rehabilitation nursing home where he had a lot of therapy to help him remember stuff and talk normal again. At first his thoughts would come out all wrong and sometimes he got mixed up about when to laugh and when to cry, things like that. He could still sing perfectly with the radio though.

I could tell Mother and Dad and even Harmony felt the same way about Mitchell's injuries as Big Augie did about losing Brenda. Mother cried sometimes when she thought we didn't notice. Dad got a part-time job delivering furniture so we could pay Mitchell's hospital bills. He was usually pretty tired after that.

Vivian and Uncle Gott had settled comfortably into Vivian's house following their return from their honeymoon in Rio de Janeiro. Uncle Gott resumed his popular TV weather slot, much to the delight of his fans. One Sunday at dinner Vivian showed us all the photographs they'd taken on their honeymoon trip, including one with Uncle Gott dressed up in a funny hat from South America. They even brought me a small present. It was a little wooden replica of *Christ the Redeemer*, the huge statue on top of a hill that could be seen for miles around Rio. I knew I didn't want any religious statues around to remind me of this year. Anyway, there was more than enough religion already in Kansas. I buried the thing in Vivian's front yard where the sidewalk used to be.

Janie and Billy Glenn became "engaged to be engaged," as

Mother called it, shortly after Vivian and Uncle Gott's Valentine's Day wedding. Mother said Janie got so inspired by all the gushy trappings of a big church wedding that she forgot she was picky when it came to men. "It also has something to do with losing faith in her hero, J. Edgar Hoover," Mother told us. "At first, we were all happy when he sent Janie the file on Charlotte Fitch. But then, when we really studied it, there wasn't a lot of new information there. Billy Glenn said J. Edgar was just throwing Janie a bone, that the F.B.I. could have cracked the Charlotte Fitch case if J. Edgar, or the president, or somebody high up had told them to. Janie believed him. After that, she needed another male authority figure to look up to, and there was Billy Glenn ready to step in and fill the void."

"I don't know about your brother being an authority figure," Dad said dryly, "but I wish 'em all the best. We saw what Uncle Gott went through with this wedding business. Suppose you could convince Janie to elope?"

"The way his car's over to her place every night, I think it's a safe bet something's going to happen real soon. I just hope it doesn't involve any new cousins for you kids."

That was a thought that hadn't occurred to me. Janie and Billy Glenn having kids who would be related to us. It was an awful thought.

My boil went away, and my permanent was growing out, but I still twitched when I got excited and I still missed Mitchell. Harmony got real protective of me at those times, which irritated me. "Look," I told her, "just because Mitchell's in the nursing home and Daffy moved away and you have to be a lesbian by yourself doesn't mean you get to pick on me." That's when Harmony told me what lesbian really meant.

"You better quit calling me a lesbian, or next time you're in the hospital I'll let you die before I'll come and visit you," she said.

Maybe she had a point.

When Mitchell was able to speak better and focus a little more, he got to come home. We were all really happy at that and Mom baked a big chocolate cake that said *Welcome Home Mitchell* on it. But Mitchell still wasn't completely back to normal. I spent a lot of time with him talking about our games, the cats, and astronaut training, and him playing the trombone with us, and that seemed to help a little. But just as my twitching was getting better, he developed one. That lightning business had a long reach.

By then I was ten and Mitchell had turned nine. I felt so angry at God for putting us all through those horrible experiences that year, that I swore I was never going to church again. I didn't either. Every Sunday I'd sit in my room and refuse to get dressed for Sunday School. Mother and Dad tried threatening me and shaming me and reasoning with me, but nothing worked. Once they even tried bribing me with a pony because I'd always really wanted one. But I wouldn't go ever again. It just hurt too much thinking God had allowed this terrible accident to happen to such a good little boy and to his really nice family.

But then, a funny thing happened. Uncle Rex Oliver started spending a lot of time with Mitchell, helping him find his way around, helping him remember things. Mitchell couldn't go to a regular school with his injuries, so he stayed home and Rex Oliver taught him. The two of them spent hours together listening to records and recorded books, not saying a word. It seemed to help them both. Dewey said God had sent Rex Oliver to be Mitchell's guardian angel, and vice versa. "The Lord works in mysterious ways," Dewey said. "Maybe this is what Earl's been preaching about, about God sending compensation when something goes wrong. Maybe the lightning knocked some sense into Earl after all." It was the first time I had ever heard Dewey say something nice about Earl.

I didn't know what the lightning had knocked into me. But after all that had happened, I began to notice things weren't as simple as I had believed, that what I had been taught about God and taught about people who were different than us, might not be true. Except that trying to figure it all out was really confusing. I wondered if I ever would.

As my world grew complicated, Mitchell's became simpler. Slowly, he did get better and most of his lightning scars became less noticeable, though he did still twitch from time to time. He remained friendly and trusting, with his basic sweet personality, but he was different somehow, never again quite the midget used car salesman that had been my best friend. It was the most difficult of my experiences for me to accept, especially since it had been my fault.

There was one more thing about my terrible year. It seems that Uncle Rex had waited until a warm spring day in April, then insisted Dewey drive him to a flower shop in town. When he got there, he picked out and paid for a dozen red roses and asked that they be delivered to Salome Parsons. "Just put 'Thank You' on the card," he had instructed.

"What was that all about?" Harmony had asked what we were all thinking.

"If I had to guess," said Dewey, "I'd say Rex Oliver will never again have as much fun as he did the night Salome abducted him from the church basement. She's the only date he's ever had. So I'm glad for the boy. I truly am. And I'm not surprised he sent Salome them roses. After all," he concluded, "no matter how strange any of us might be," he looked around at all of us when he said it, "we're still a polite family."

Epilogue

It's been many decades since that bizarre time when I struggled to find my way. I will tell you now some of the changes.

Since then, Forbes Air Force Base was decommissioned and the Atchison, Topeka, and Santa Fe Railroad moved its headquarters out of state, though the shops and railroad yards remain. The Prairie Band Potawatomi opened a full-service casino in Kansas. An EF5 tornado in 1966 cut diagonally through the city, killing many and causing enormous destruction. I will tell you that despite an expensive renovation on the Kansas State Capitol, that imposing mural of John Brown on the second-floor rotunda remains a furious, uneasy reminder of Kansas' "lunatic" past.

What you need to know is that Topeka is no longer the psychiatric capital of the world. The famous Meadowgreen Foundation moved to a much bigger city in another state. By then, the Kansas legislature had already closed the Topeka State Hospital, ironically on May 17, 1997, exactly forty-three years to the day from the *Brown v. Board of Education of Topeka* decision. Read into that what you will. Fortunately, when it can be delivered, treatment for mental illness today is humane, non-judgmental, and covered by health insurance. We no longer stigmatize mental illness or consider it a character deficiency. We no longer use the word "lunatics."

Also know that on a sunny day in May 2004, the fiftieth anniversary of the *Brown v. Board of Education of Topeka* Supreme Court decision, President George W. Bush inaugurated Topeka's former Monroe Elementary School as a National Historic Site. I was there watching Air Force One fly low and slow over the ceremony as it brought the President to our little town. What an honor. And a reflection of what those brave Topeka plaintiffs achieved in the fight for equal opportunity nationwide. That journey continues, but you already know that part.

I didn't grow up and marry a "Negro," a Communist, an atheist, or a lesbian, and I still don't know any nudists that I'm aware of. But I do closely monitor the weather—those big summer thunderstorms and occasional tornadoes, ice storms, blizzards, windstorms, grass fires, and floods. Weather is such an integral part of Kansas that I keep an emergency kit ready, because the brutal power behind those events—some still call them "acts of God"—never changes.

All these years later it still remains remarkable to me how in sleepy Topeka, Kansas, over the twelve months of my life spanning 1958-1959, the farmers, the hillbillies, and the mentally ill converged with the Native Americans and the Mafia, Air Force spy planes and integrationists, the railroad and the Mexicans, the firemen, the music teachers, female detectives, anti-Communist crusaders, former missionaries, radical religious protesters, a pig, severe weather, Avon, a Kansas president, and the head of the F.B.I., and left my life irrevocably changed.

I was not exactly blameless in it all. I was just young.

With Gratitude

This book has been decades in the making, so there are many wonderful friends and colleagues to whom I am deeply indebted.

Thank you to all who read the manuscript and provided critiques and/or blurbs, and who advised on cover art, (and apologies to those I may have unintentionally failed to include): The Honorable Teresa Watson, Melissa Wangemann, Thanne Rose, Jill Ohara, Annie Juarez, Kim Gronniger, Bill Stephens, Barbara Waterman-Peters, Jan Stotts, Charlie Renne, Anne Spry, Rosanna Andrews, Tracy Million Simmons, Karen Bellows, Carol Yoho, Nate Hargis, Julie Sellers, Laurie Jackson, Tim Bascom, Bill Saltman, Craig Lancaster, Linda Wood, and the late Anne Tatlock. Special thanks to Topeka Mayor Mike Padilla.

To my fabulous teacher Andy Farkas and the students of Washburn University's Advanced Fiction Writing class for your insightful comments and encouragement. To the Ada Comstock Scholars program at Smith College and my writing teachers there who started me on this path, Michael Gorra, Tracy Kidder, Richard Wilbur, and Mark Kramer.

To editors Gretchen Eick and Laura Tillem for believing in this book. To my friend and publisher Thea Rademacher of Flint Hills Publishing, for shepherding a dream into a reality!

Above all, a deep and special gratitude goes to my family for your love of all things literary and creative, and to the people of Topeka and surrounding communities for giving me such a quirky, rich, and surprisingly happy life. Thank you!

Blessings.

Book Club Questions

1. Is Melody a typical child of that period and place? In what ways does she change over the course of the year?

2. How do real-life historical events/characters such as integration, attitudes about mental health, religious fanatics, and J. Edgar Hoover, contribute to the story? Does the Midwestern mix of urban and rural lives seem credible for that time?

3. In a book with many colorful characters, who is your favorite character and why?

4. What is your favorite scene or quote from the book?

5. The author uses several literary devices in this book, such as jumping between time periods, non-standard dialect, and Melody talking directly to the reader. How did these contribute to your enjoyment of the book?

6. What surprised you most about the story?

7. Are you left with any questions about the story? If so, what are they?

8. The book begins with many comedic moments and characters but ends on a serious note. Does Melody seem happy by the end of the book? What is the biggest insight she gains?

If you or someone you know needs assistance or information about mental illness, contact:

National Alliance on Mental Health (NAMI)
www.nami.org
1-800-950-6264

For free confidential crisis assistance, 24/7, year-round, call or text the National Mental Health line at 988.

A Note About the Author

Ruth Maus, of Topeka, Kansas, has followed a love of learning around the world, with curiosity, languages, and an appreciation for all beings a constant thread.

She represented Smith College at the annual Glasscock Intercollegiate Poetry Contest where past contestants have included James Merrill, Sylvia Plath, Katha Pollitt, Mary Jo Salter, James Agee, Frederick Buechner, Kenneth Koch, Donald Hall, William Manchester, Muriel Rukeyser, and Gjertrud Schnackenberg. Her poems have appeared in a variety of literary journals and anthologies.

Her full-length poetry books *Valentine* and *Puzzled* (meadowlark-books.com), were finalists for the 2019 Birdy Poetry Prize and the 2023 High Plains Book Awards, respectively. *Lunacy and Acts of God* is her first novel.

www.ruthmaus.com

Made in the USA
Monee, IL
28 May 2025

18301170R00187